These Fragile Things

JANE DAVIS

Printed and bound in Great Britain by Clays Ltd, St Ives plc.
for Rossdale Print Productions

These Fragile Things is a work of fiction. Names, characters, places and incidents are either the product of the author's imagination or are used fictitiously.

ISBN-13: 978-0-9932776-1-0

Cover design by Andrew Candy
based on original artwork by Skoric

TO MATT

For his infinite patience.
And knowing when to make himself scarce.

PRAISE FOR THE AUTHOR

'Davis is a phenomenal writer, whose ability to create well rounded characters that are easy to relate to feels effortless.'

Compulsion Reads

'Jane Davis is an extraordinary writer, whose deft blend of polished prose and imaginative intelligence makes you feel in the safest of hands.'

J. J. Marsh, author and founder of Triskele Books

CHAPTER ONE

With growing unease, Elaine put the telephone receiver back in its cradle. Opening the front door, she stepped outside into the porch, absorbing the wail of sirens that passes for birdsong in a London suburb. It had only been a small white lie: something to put her husband's mind at rest.

"How's Judy?"

"Oh, you know. Buried in her homework."

Their daughter *had* been doing her homework - would have finished it by now - but for the small matter of the postage stamps. And stamps were one of the few things Elaine hated to run out of.

"Why don't you eat?" Graham had suggested. "I'm going to be stuck in this meeting for another hour."

She tried to put a smile in her voice. "Well, if you don't mind. Perhaps we will."

Judy should have been gone for ten minutes at the most instead of - what? A glance at her watch suggested - *surely it couldn't be ten to six?* She *knew* what time dinner would be on the table. What could be keeping the girl? The violet dusk had deepened to coal; the streetlights were encased in orange halos. Arms folded, Elaine walked to the end of the garden path, scanning the stretch of Strathdale Road. Judy wasn't allowed to use the alley after dark, not alone. Long and narrow, it was enclosed by high windowless walls on one side and playing fields on the other, the middle stretch unlit. Elaine's feet made the decision for her. They walked back into the house, infused with thyme from the Shepherd's Pie, stepped into her shoes. It only remained for her to grab her keys. She would meet her daughter coming in the opposite direction. Hurry her along.

Approaching the end of her road, Elaine tensed at the sound of raised voices in the near distance, the odd order shouted loud above the general background roar. "Come on! Over here!" *Must be the school football team practising in the playing fields*, she thought. *Keen, at this time of the evening.* The sound of crowds, even spectators like these, always made her slightly edgy.

Leaving the streetlight behind Elaine entered the alley, picking up her pace, imagining that when her feet slid it was leaf mulch rather than dog shit she was treading in. The shouts escalated: if this was football, it was no friendly match. Tension mutated to anxiety. Last summer the Brixton Riots had spilled onto nearby streets after the police had approached the Stop and Search campaign with hunger for overtime. And they'd got it: 5,000 rioters, buildings torched, looting, petrol bombs. Prior to that she had always considered that the perimeter of her home territory was encircled by a shimmering Ready Brek force-field. Perhaps it had been irresponsible to send a thirteen-year-old on an errand just as it was growing dark. But she and Graham had agreed: a gradual loosening of the reins; a little more responsibility; and then the rewards.

Through filtered streetlight, Elaine saw that her exit was blocked by haphazardly abandoned vehicles, more of a hindrance than the flimsy strip of plastic that hung limply across the alley.

"Excuse me!" she called out to a man who entered her narrow

view, and whose fluorescent jacket hinted at officialdom.

Quick to confirm her assessment, his hand jerked into a stop sign. "Do you live here?"

"No, but..." Elaine strained to look past him, between the vehicles, their headlights employed as searchlights. Columns of grey swirls were highlighted, just as sunbeams highlight golden dust motes.

"Then you can't come through, Madam. The wall's come down." The man lifted an erect index finger as his walkie-talkie crackled, inclining his head. "*Yup. Gotcha.* Afraid I'm wanted."

"Just a minute!" Elaine was on tiptoes. "I'm looking for my daughter. Which way would you have sent her if she wanted to come this way?"

She detected his slight hesitation. "Took this route, did she?"

"An hour ago. Mind you, if she's had to go via the Broadway -"

"How old is she?" As he looked at her face properly for the first time, Elaine saw that she was no longer an inconvenience.

It was her turn to pause, her response lilting questioningly. "Thirteen."

"School uniform?"

Too late: Elaine had seen his wince. "Yes."

"Back in a jiffy. Don't go anywhere." Pacing backwards, the man pointed at her before pivoting, feet tripping into a jog.

Through a veil that had the appearance of slow-moving smoke - like the Great Smog of 1952, one of her earliest memories, turning London winter into toxic night - Elaine began to make out the jagged dip of the missing section of wall. Strewn below, a pile of rubble that appeared greater in volume than the gap, wide as it was. Shadowy movement was captured in the headlights: silhouettes of human conveyor belts. She ducked beneath the inadequate cordon, brushing it from her clothing where it had clung like cobweb.

Edging between two vehicles, Elaine moved towards the source of the shouting. Solemn-faced men were captured in cross-beams: some equipped with hard hats, face-masks and boots; others dressed in shirt-sleeves and suit trousers. Some were digging bare-handed, others improvising with gardening gloves or whatever protection had come to hand. Brick by brick, debris was being quarried, new piles constructed, the effort furious and loud.

People had spilled out of terraced houses, the backdrop to the bus stop; some simply watching, their faces set in Plaster of Paris. Men removed debris from gardens, waiting to take their shift at the pit face. Waist-height children ignored limp encouragement to 'go and finish your dinner.' One woman was conducting figure-of-eight sorties, distributing mugs of tea, steam merging with dust, becoming part of the grey soup. At the end of the road blue lights rotated mutely. In the gaps between vehicles, faces flashed: ghostly, expectant. That was where Judy would be: avoiding the long walk home.

"Excuse me, coming through." Elaine felt anonymous, another shadow whose presence would go unchallenged provided she looked sufficiently purposeful.

"There! That was where she was!"

Spinning to locate the speaker, she zoned in on the half-lit face of a wretched boy with a crude gash on his forehead. He pointed towards the rubble, his hand breaching the beam of a headlight.

"Alright, son. Let him through. Everyone else: stay well back!" A policeman clapped one hand on the boy's shoulder, guiding him forwards. "There, you say?"

Acting with an intuition of their own, Elaine's feet followed before the gap had the chance to heal. They deposited her on a square foot of tarmac where she could eavesdrop.

"She was in the phone box. Like an idiot, I told her to get

out. She'd have been better off staying put."

This was someone's daughter they were talking about.

"Now, we don't know that, son."

Shaken by the ferocity of her breathing, Elaine pondered a possibility: somewhere, under the weight of the rubble...

"It would have shielded her. Even though it's gone over on its side, they're strong, those things. I mean, shit!" As a torch flashed, she feasted on the features of the boy's face. The typical look of the local estate: shaven headed; a single stud in one ear; the fingers that strayed to his mouth stained nicotine yellow.

"In your shoes, I'd have done exactly the same. Anyone would."

"I tried to grab her, but the whole thing came down so fast."

Elaine knew she must locate her voice. "Excuse me." She pressed into the narrow void between them. "You're talking about a girl."

"Sorry Gov." Flustered, another man who had elbowed his way through spectators interrupted - the man in the fluorescent jacket. "God knows where the mother went. She was over by the alley a minute ago. I specifically asked her -"

"I'm the mother." As Elaine spoke the words, she knew them to be true.

Recognising her, the man back-tracked. "N-now, we can't be sure, Madam."

"I'm sure. I sent her to the corner shop over an hour ago." The four exchanged glances: Elaine, the policeman, the boy and the man in the yellow jacket, whose gaze settled on the tips of his steel-capped boots.

There were shouts; high-pitched, urgent. The cue for them all to turn.

A mottled man with ashen hair stepped from the thick of the dust: "We've uncovered the phone box. Hardly a dent in the frame, but…" He whistled through his front teeth.

Elaine saw the skeleton of the box dissected by a metal scaffolding pole, entry wound in the safety glass. Standing astride a pile of bricks, a man in a hard hat became spokesperson for their thoughts: "Christ Almighty! It would have gone clean through her."

At this, the policeman's eyes darted towards Elaine. "I think you'd be more comfortable over by the ambulance, Madam."

But Elaine's eyes were fixed on the boy. *Clean through.* On hearing those words, the movement of his Adam's apple was as visible as his distress, and for the first time Elaine understood the phrase, 'to eat one's words'. Not something deliberately taken back, but mute shock: involuntary, uncontrolled. He folded himself in half, hands on knees, and the policeman bent over him. "Alright, son. You did the right thing, see?" And through the criss-cross of headlights, the dust and chaos, he raised his head, shouting, "Can we get some more help over here? Let's keep digging."

Men who had been on garden duty refused flimsy face-masks which hung lifelessly from a proffered wrist by their elastic straps. Jackets were pressed into wives' arms as they brushed past, grim-faced, rolling up shirt sleeves.

Turning her attention to the boy, Elaine asked, "Are you a friend of Judy's?"

"I never seen her before." The boy's arms were clamped together from wrists to elbows. "She just walked past me on her way to the phone box. She was…" He squeezed his eyes shut.

"What? She was what?"

The boy nodded, as if trying to dislodge the word. "Beautiful."

"Madam?" The yellow-jacketed man was saying firmly, one hand hovering, ready to guide.

"And you, son," the policeman said. "We'll take it from here. You should get yourself seen to."

"I can't." He shook his head.

"Stubborn so and so, aren't you? Want to see it through to the bitter end, is that it?"

Elaine didn't remember running forwards to the point where the beams converged. She was aware only of the hands that bruised her upper arms, dragging her from the place where she'd been clawing in the debris. Knees bent, she was airlifted like a child, mid-tantrum. "I'm her mother!"

"Come on, now. Get a grip."

Lowering her feet, Elaine allowed herself to be led away, understanding the need to prepare for whatever emerged from the rubble. She had seen its density, had a sense of its weight. Slump-shouldered, perched on the cold tailgate of an ambulance, she gave her name and address, Judy's date of birth. No, her daughter hadn't been taking any medication. Had no allergies she was aware of. There was no history of heart disease, fainting or fits. Religion? Elaine recited the response she always gave: Christian.

A blank-faced stranger placed a steaming mug of tea in her hands, and draped a bobbled cardigan around her shoulders. "Here, love. You must be freezing."

These were simply things that happened. Waiting for confirmation of the inevitable, Elaine felt detached from the hands that circled the mug, dirt embedded under torn fingernails. Airborne dust accumulated in her eyelashes and, like a cow persistently bothered by flies, she made no attempt to brush it aside.

Taking a five-minute break from the quarrying, a dry-coughing man thumped his chest. "S'cuse me. Gets right inside you, that stuff."

"Look at that." She allocated words to the things she saw. "Your hand's bleeding."

Voice rasping, he dismissed his injury. "Looks worse than it is."

"You don't even know us."

Observations, devoid of meaning. One more voice added to the sound of the crowd. Elaine focused on the boy, the last person to see Judy. Even reduced to a shaking wreck wrapped in a foil blanket, he refused to leave, pointing to the place where he saw a beautiful girl disappear. *Her* beautiful girl.

"You're welcome to come indoors." The tailgate dipped as the woman who had brought tea leant against the ambulance, grazing Elaine's arm with an elbow.

"No, I'm fine here." She shuffled away from the unwanted interruption. *Oh, Christ, what would Judy look like now?* One of her hands pulled at the flesh around her mouth.

"Then I'll keep you company."

Nodding - or it might have been that her whole body was rocking - Elaine realised her face was wet. "Judy should have been doing her homework. It should have been me!"

"Don't think like that." Warmth encircled a small portion of Elaine's arm. The rest of her shivered. "It doesn't do any good."

Then, the shout: "*It's a hand! We've found her!*"

Elaine heard a cry and knew it was her own. She started forwards, only to find herself bundled face-first into a solid wall of chest: captured.

"There, now. Let's allow the men to do their job, shall we?"

Realising that the purpose of the muscular arms was to comfort rather than restrain, Elaine gave up her struggle. All around were the static sounds of walkie-talkies, muffled replies muttered into collars. People who had previously slumped stood upright, striding about purposefully. The cordon at the end of the road was removed, onlookers ordered to stand well back, herded by slow-moving vehicles being made ready.

Straining her neck Elaine appealed, "Can't I at least see?"

There was hesitation before the hands were loosened. The man moved around her so that he was by her side, still gripping her, as if she couldn't be trusted. Two men jumped lightly from the back of the ambulance carrying a weightless stretcher, while a third rumbled about preparing a plastic bag for the drip. The siren was tested, several short abortive bursts. Even then, Elaine's free arm acted independently, reaching in the direction of the pile of rubble, the hand robotic and claw-like. It pulled at her body, trying to wrench her away from the soothing words, from the inviting rectangles of electric light cast from doorways.

"Almost there." His voice steady, the man repositioned his arm, wrapping it around her shoulder.

Through dark slatted figures, Elaine saw Judy prostrate on the stretcher. Segments of body, a head lolling, one shattered arm hanging limply. Slow motion: a funeral march. This time, unable to help herself, she broke free. Once loose, but for a couple of staggered steps, Elaine found she was unable to move.

"Mrs Jones." The lady paramedic who had dealt with the form-filling reached for her. "I know how it looks, but what you're seeing is dust."

Even the weight of a hand was too great. Elaine's legs buck-led. *To dust we will return.* Sitting on the lip of the pavement, staring wide-eyed at a double yellow line, a thought entered her mind: *I can't stop here.* Her feet scrambled against tarmac.

"Do you understand what I'm saying?" An anxious face loomed in front of her. "We're taking your daughter to May Day. She'll be rushed into surgery. Why don't you get yourself together and follow in the other ambulance?"

Grit grated as Elaine blinked. "She's alive?"

"Yes. And we'll do everything we can to keep her that way."

CHAPTER TWO

J udy checked her watch: 5.05pm. The last post was collected at 5.30pm. Still time, if she could invent an excuse.

"Darn it!" Hearing her mother snap, she sensed opportunity. Mum had closed the dresser drawer, one hand on her brow, the other on her hip.

"What is it?" Judy asked, sliding the pink envelope under her history textbook, pretending to be immersed in its pictureless pages.

"You didn't use the last of the stamps, did you?"

In the Jones's household, Mum was the one whose moods were so changeable she must never be upset, and that meant giving the impression of perfection.

"Not me." Her face was a picture of diligence as she met her mother's demanding eyes. "There were three left when I took one."

Her mother's neck flushed. Judy knew irritation would fester because parental allegiances prevented Elaine from naming her husband as a potential suspect. "Is it too much to expect people to tell me when we're running out?"

Now a solution presented itself: redemption and, with it, escape. "Want me to go down the road for you?"

"You're busy with your essay." The sound of irritation still present, her mother's jaw was set.

"I've hardly got started. In fact, I've got a headache coming on. Some fresh air might help."

"Well, if you really don't mind." Her mother pointed to the brown leather handbag, which lay sulking silently in the hall. "Take what you need from my purse."

Of all the sentences that would take on greater significance in time, neither Judy nor her mother could have guessed that "*Take what you need from my purse*" would top the list.

Judy stepped outside, a thief clawing back a few moments' freedom. The cheerful late-autumn debris lay underfoot, the breeze just enough to stir fresh leaf-fall into a waltz. Jangling coins in blazer pocket, she inhaled the evening, clean and dark and flinty.

After posting the card, Judy felt the magnetic pull of the telephone box at the far end of the road. She checked her watch: just long enough for a quick call. A private conversation. No parents leaning over her shoulder or, worse still, barely bothering to disguise the fact that they had rugby-tackled each other for prime position, pressed up against the brilliant white gloss of the living room door.

Judy had once been ignored while a friend's mother said to Mum, "Sometimes I only know what's going on in Lucy's life by picking up the extension in our bedroom. The minute they hit thirteen, they don't tell you anything."

As soon as the two of them were alone, Mum had feigned shock. "Well, what do you think about *that?*"

"If Lucy won't talk to them, she might not have a choice." Judy drew inspiration from the most precocious girl in her class. "Communication's really important, isn't it?"

"Well, I'm glad to hear you say that," her mother said, astonished expression suggesting the opposite. "I didn't realise I had such a mature daughter."

A convincing actress, Judy had been practising her whole

life to be someone she wasn't. Special - some would say 'unreasonable' - demands are made of only children. That she was loved was undeniable, but it never felt unconditional. From 'I only want what's best for my daughter', her mother had taken a short hop and a skip to, 'I want my daughter to be the best'.

A shout broke her reverie: "Oi! How about it?"

Obedient daughter; streetwise teenager: you had to adapt.

A dozen or so schoolboys slouched against the bus shelter, shrug-shouldered studies of boredom, bordering on aggression. Collars unbuttoned, ties worn loose or knotted around their heads in homage to Rambo. They blocked garden gates, glaring at anyone who required access or - 'Oi! What d'you think you're doing, mate?' - wanted to make use of London Transport. Judy cautioned herself: keep your pace steady. She would die before letting them detect her nerves. Looking older than her age was something Judy alternately despised and took advantage of. Rather than being hidden by the growing dusk, she felt as though she was walking onto a stage, stepping in and out of circles the streetlights had cast on the pavement. She clutched her blazer tightly around her but eyes burnt holes in the front of her jumper, that dark boyish art perfected by concentrating sunrays through a magnifying glass, setting fire to grass and scalding insects. In truth, she was no more than a welcome distraction in a string of evenings that held little promise. A game of tin-can footie. The chance to scrounge the odd fag. Little these boys did was personal: they could lob a brick through the window of a house or relieve themselves against the side of the war memorial and it wouldn't be personal.

"Oi, I *asked* you a question!" One of them stepped forwards as Judy approached, conscious of every movement of her teenage body.

"Oh, I'm sorry." She summoned as much sarcasm as she could muster. "I mustn't have heard."

"I *sa-aid*, How about it?"

As the others snorted behind their filthy hands, Judy drew on the vocabulary of the more worldly persona she had invented, raising an index finger to shoulder level. "Why don't you all go swivel?"

Monosyllabic shouts and sly laughter. Out of the corner of her eye she saw the boy shunted sideways, not standing quite as tall as before he elected himself spokesperson. Slow wolf-whistles accompanying her progress, confidence exaggerated the sway of Judy's hips. She crossed the road and, defying superstition, walked under the scaffold brace erected to support the crumbling Victorian wall. The framework had become a permanent fixture while committees formed of health and safety executives, local historians and pensioners in need of a warm cup of tea took the chicken and egg argument to new extremes as they debated the future of listed wall and the tallest London plane tree.

Last measured in the Sixties, it had then been 122 feet tall, its elephantine footprint twenty feet in circumference. As a child, Judy had imagined its gargantuan trunk being wrenched from the earth by a giant's fist. But, as well as inspiring fairy tales, it had served as her calendar. As soon as Christmas wrapping paper was displayed in W H Smiths - usually in early September - Judy began her daily enquiries: "How long is it now?"

"When all of the leaves have fallen off the big tree, you'll know it's getting close," her mother used to say.

And as soon as the Christmas baubles were packed away, she would start enquiring about her birthday.

"As soon as the big tree has its summer clothes on."

If her dad had his way, they would cut it down. Judy couldn't remember how many times he'd complained, "Something has to be done. It's been leaning against the wall this past decade!"

"It's over two hundred years old," her mother would reply. "Imagine what it's seen."

"Honestly!" He peered over the top of his newspaper, amused. "You're sentimental about the strangest things."

"It's history."

"It's a tree!"

In fact, the tree was the subject of an all-encompassing preservation order, which prevented the committee from unanimously agreeing anything other than the date of the next meeting.

The whiff of ammonia sent Judy reeling as she opened the door of the telephone box, but she wouldn't abandon her mission. She faced her newfound audience their equal, one knee bent, foot resting against the glass. Singling one of them out - a boy sitting slightly apart who had the decency to look a little less pock-marked, a little less menacing than the rest - she raised the hem of her skirt a few inches to scratch an imaginary itch. As his eyes dropped to the pavement, Judy despised herself momentarily before reminding herself: the fault was his, not hers. He hadn't insulated himself adequately against the world.

Hearing the pips, Judy dropped a warm coin into the slot. "Is Debbie there?" she asked importantly. "I'm in a box."

A man's voice bellowed, "Deb-or-ah!" There were hand-muffled noises before background shouts resumed, and she heard Debbie's breathless, "What's up?"

"Not much. What's happening your end?"

"Oh!" She sighed mysteriously. "They're slogging it out, as usual."

"Who's winning?"

"Mum - if it's about who's loudest. Where are you, anyhow?"

"Just in the box down the road." Suspended mid-way between feeling terribly grown up and very foolish, Judy giggled.

"What's the big secret?"

Hesitating, Judy curled a strand of hair around her index finger. "I was going to ask you to come to the arcade on Saturday."

"What? So I get to stand around all night again while you pluck up the courage to talk to Bingo Boy."

"He's a cashier!"

"Whatever he is, he must be eighteen!"

"Like you've never lied about your age!" Then, pleadingly: "Come with me. *Pleeease.*"

"Remind me why I'm even considering this?"

Judy encouraged the silence to stew.

"You know, fine! But we're going skating next week."

While Judy was enjoying her small victory, the Rambo boys' volume edged up several notches. Boredom to panic in two seconds. The bars of the phone box gave the impression that those orang-utans, rather than she, were caged. A couple were gawping with exaggerated expressions. "Idiots!" she scoffed.

"What's up?" Debbie asked.

Now some were pointing while others turned on their heels and ran. One boy was dancing in front of the box, arms animated, yelling, "Oi! Get out of there!" The boy who had sat slightly apart.

"He's saying I've got to -" Judy turned in time to see the collapse of the scaffolding, a slow-motion clashing and ricocheting of plank and metal. She released the receiver, leaving it swinging. "*Judy! Judy, what's happening?*"

The door of the box was opened for her, his voice close. "This way!"

Spinning blindly, Judy was an imitation of a short-sighted girl knocking back an invisible netball. The bulge in the wall tore like a gaping wound. Everything around her was falling in real time; a liquid roar. Brickwork. Suffocatingly thick air.

Doubled over, choking, Judy barely felt the blow that knocked her to her knees.

Behind debris and dust, the tree remained, standing battle-scarred but defiant, while the boy looked on, half-covering his eyes, stamping his feet, crying out, "Jesus Christ! Oh, Jesus, no!" Only moments earlier, he had watched the girl flashing her thigh, amazed by her confidence, her mocking eyes, and thought he had never seen anyone quite so beautiful. And he had looked away, knowing himself unworthy of such a vision.

CHAPTER THREE

Graham clutched his briefcase as the delayed 18.57 pulled alongside the platform at London Bridge. The day's humiliations cluttered his mind; things he wouldn't normally burden his wife with. But, having boasted about his interview for a managerial position, he would be forced to admit the promotion had gone to someone half his age.

The decision clearly already made, the interview had been a farce. "Don't worry, Jones. We have something very specific in mind for you." His managing director had offered a softener, as if the sole reason they'd passed him over was because the *specific* thing was much more up his street. But Graham knew his usefulness to the firm: he was a grafter. Another man might have walked but Graham, who had a family to support, had sportingly shaken his colleague's smug little hand, saying, "The best man won." Qualifications, manners, hard graft, a command of the Queen's English - everything he had been assured would count in the 'real world' - none of these things were valued any more. He knew what his colleagues said of him: they didn't even have the decency to do it behind his back.

"Graham Jones. Like Tom Jones, only without the *Huh!*"

And there it was: the pelvic thrust. You turned the other cheek, pretending to laugh with them. You played along, singing *What's New Pussycat?* at the Christmas bash - and still they came back at you, double-breasted and pin-striped.

Walking back into the office, head held high, he could face. It was the thought of taking his place at the dinner table that filled him with dread. And so he had phoned his wife explaining he would be late, and had nursed a lonely pint in one of the quieter pubs. That the train was delayed only added weight to his excuse.

Rattling home, stomach rumbling, Graham found himself nudging shoulders with an elderly Rastafarian, dreadlocks tucked beneath a large knitted hat. The previous evening he had watched a BBC news report: '*An orgy of burning and looting, the Brixton Riots appeared to erupt spontaneously. Now, Lord Scarman's report cites months of racial tension amidst a climate of high unemployment and social deprivation.*' Graham couldn't deny the footage of uniformed officers wearing National Front badges on their lapels. There must be a few rotten eggs, but *institutionalised* racism? Having no black friends or colleagues, he contemplated asking the man about his experiences, but his face was serene, eyes closed over as he sucked on a sizable roll-up, the smoke scrolling elegantly in Graham's direction.

Eyes smarting, Graham looked away, his eyes drawn to a newspaper headline: *I Was Deep Throat, Says FBI Chief.* The real world was encroaching on Graham's hometown too closely for his liking. Cynthia Payne and her kind had sent property prices into freefall, bringing a whole new meaning to the term, Luncheon Vouchers. There were probably a few prostitutes around him now. That sensible trench coat might well be disguising a PVC miniskirt. Dusk heralded the arrival of kerb crawlers - he glanced at male passengers hanging from the ceiling straps: bats emerging for their nightly feeding frenzy. Prostitutes and riots! You would hardly believe the area was once the favoured shopping destination of princesses.

Rather than do battle with his broadsheet, Graham rescued an abandoned copy of *Just Seventeen* from the carriage floor, shaking the cover free of ash. Resting it on top of his *Telegraph*, he was thrust hot-collared into the world of teenage girls. The content shocked, not so much by the behaviours described (which Graham had to acknowledge were universal), but by the fact that it now seemed acceptable to ask - quite openly - *What should I do if I have gone too far the night before?* Try as he might, he couldn't work out why this rankled quite so much. Shouldn't young women have access to public information? Not his daughter - thankfully she didn't read this trash. But he also knew it was unlikely that he would have ended up married to Elaine had she read similar articles. Graham had proposed as soon as she'd announced, large-eyed, fearful, that she was pregnant. Not down on one knee, as he had rehearsed. Caught off-guard, with more resignation than romance, he had said, "I suppose we should get married." She had looked so hopeful. Happy, even. But, anticipating parental recriminations, he had rounded off the sentence: "Before you begin to show."

Even now, he blinked away the painful memory of her face contorting. He had wanted his proposal to be wildly romantic, every gesture meticulously planned. Ruined by a single sentence. Secretly, he had been delighted. What boy doesn't want to know everything's in working order? But he couldn't take it back without saying something that sounded as if it was a lie. And, try as he might, he had never been able to think of a gesture big enough to make it up to Elaine.

Graham remembered Elaine's tears again after the miscarriage, the narrow hospital bed, her fierce cries: "I don't expect you want me now!" He had taken her face in his hands, insisting, "Of course I want you." He had thought, perhaps, she might not have wanted him. And although he feared it sounded as if he was reciting words as he protested that he loved her, he had meant them. How he had meant them!

When the time came to explain the reason for the hastily-arranged nuptials to parents, he was able to answer the question, "Christ, she's not pregnant, is she?" truthfully. But concerned that Elaine might translate his denial as an admission that he had never wanted the child, he gushed, "But we want to start a family as soon as possible. Don't we, darling?"

They hadn't discussed the matter. In fact, when the doctor assured Elaine that they would be able to have healthy babies - as many as they wanted - she had looked desolate. Perched uncomfortably in front of matching sets of parents, entrusted with the best sherry glasses, Graham patted Elaine's hand nervously. She had simply looked bewildered, as if they hadn't been introduced.

It was five years before Judy arrived. By that time his masculinity had been questioned at every family gathering. His mother barely allowed Elaine access to the hallway before stripping her of her coat, eyeing her disappointingly flat stomach, then looking at Graham with increasing despair.

"Well, son?" his father demanded.

Graham estimated that the stricken girl on the page in front of him with her inward-pointing toes and candy-striped socks was nearer Judy's age than 'just' seventeen. A far cry from the innocence implied. Sam Cooke's *Only Sixteen* had been too young to fall in love and, never mind the age of consent, that was exactly how it should be! Graham turned to the front cover for an indication of who the magazine was aimed at: 'Everything a girl could ask for'. Girls? The focus was sex. This was how the media wanted to mould his daughter. This and this! Flicking through the pages, he found himself face to face with a girl in minimal underwear lying on a single bed; hand on stomach, downward pointing fingers. *Every Girl Should Explore Her Erogenous Zones*. Graham glanced sideways. Thankfully his neighbour's eyes were still closed. Then he became aware of the woman opposite regarding him with undisguised disdain. Keen to straighten the record, he jabbed at the headline. "Research," he laughed, expecting sympathy. "I've got one of these at home." As the woman crossed her legs, angling them away from him, Graham added hurriedly, "What I meant is I have a teenager... I'm a father."

It dawned on Graham how woefully ill-equipped he was to deal with a thirteen-year-old daughter. His own teenage years had been dominated by the pursuit of an acne cure. Later, Graham had been the rare university student whose priority was study. Largely speaking, sex had avoided him. Opportunity only presented itself when thick-rimmed glasses - his out of necessity - became temporarily fashionable. Elaine was the first girl whose openness eliminated the need for embarrassing guesswork. She had found the way he checked behind him for a deserving recipient of her glances, his suggestion of coffee - and actually meaning it - charming.

Graham's immediate reaction to whatever his daughter asked for was a firm 'no'. To impose unreasonably strict bedtimes. To ban everything he wasn't familiar with. And perhaps, more importantly, everything that he was. Elaine, he knew, naturally occupied the middle ground, allowing herself to be manipulated, convinced of the harmlessness, the need to let their daughter 'find herself'. The latest request from Judy? A lock for her bedroom door, would you believe? He'd put a stop to that. There would be no secrets in his house!

A boy would have been easier: he would have felt less protective. It often crossed Graham's mind that it might be fun to have a son to do battle with. One who shared his love of cricket, who took an interest in *Tomorrow's World*. Why did girls' magazines have to be so... grubby? Wanting to distance himself from it, Graham leaned across his knitted-hatted neighbour with a humble, "Excuse me," and deposited the magazine on the aisle seat, its grey patch of gum deterring potential occupants.

Rules would rescue Judy. He must sit down with Elaine and devise a set covering everything from… what was it girls did? Skirt lengths to… his mind wandered back to the image of the girl lying on her bed. Parents who aren't unified in their thinking can't be relied on for proper guidance. (What, he wondered with growing agitation, had Elaine already told Judy about contraception?) And, once the rules were established, they mustn't be persuaded to waiver.

His eyes came to rest on a woman's silver crucifix worn low on her breasts over a tight-fitting polo-necked sweater. Blind to the way that the woman shifted uncomfortably, pulling the collar of her sheepskin jacket around her, the image remained in Graham's mind as he hurried from the station, through the obstacle course of puddles, raised paving stones and the mess that dogs had left behind. It gave him a calming sense of unreality as he slammed the front door, shouting his habitual statement of the obvious: "I'm home!" Famished, Graham hoped that Elaine had kept his dinner warm. It was Tuesday, and Tuesdays meant Shepherd's Pie made with leftovers from Sunday's roast. "Sorry I'm late. Blasted meeting!"

Strange, the absence of sound. Not even canned laughter from the radio.

His coat hung on its allocated hook, his newspaper deposited on the telephone table, Graham approached the kitchen, optimism that he might be confronted with a vision of domestic activity fading. The worktop was backlit by his neighbour's security light. Where were they? More importantly, where was his dinner? He opened the oven - cold - and extracted an oblong Pyrex dish, its contents untouched. Graham tapped the overcooked potato topping as a builder might tap suspect brickwork. Tea and toast, then. He hooked the handle of the electric kettle over the tap. Only when returning the kettle to its rightful place did Graham discover the note, hastily scribbled on a sheet torn from a ring-bound pad, weighed down with the lightest bronze weight from the kitchen scales. *Judy has had an accident. Your wife says to go to May Day as soon as you can.*

He had just passed the car, parked outside in the road. They must have gone by bus. Cheaper than paying for the car park, he concluded: probably only needed his taxi service. If he knew the workings of A & E as well as he thought he did, Judy wouldn't have been seen yet. Graham had once waited six hours to have a broken toe taped to its neighbour: he could have done a better job himself! Plenty of time for a cup of tea. No need for panic.

Clapping one hand to his chest as the toaster jolted loudly, Graham felt as if his heart was trying to break free from his ribcage. His churning thoughts had camouflaged its palpitations. Now, there was pounding in his ears. Pressure at his temples. Leaning against the worktop for support, he examined his neighbour's unfamiliar scrawl: *Judy has had an accident.* He stuffed the note into one of his jacket pockets, dropped the two-ounce weight into the other. After slamming the front door, while searching for his car keys, he realised he was still holding the mug. Stooping, he abandoned it in a flowerbed.

CHAPTER FOUR

Elaine woke on an intake of a breath that splintered through her lungs. Images came back to her; a disconnected dream sequence, ending with the sight of her daughter, limp and alabaster-pale. Finding herself shivering on a metal-framed cot in a curtained-off cubicle, she knew that she couldn't dispute them. Below the drop of curtain she could see the to-ing and fro-ing of sensible-soled shoes, the swivelling wheels of gurneys. She allowed herself a moment to blink at the ceiling. *A telephone box? Why a telephone box?* What did it matter? Except that Graham would expect her to supply answers. Elaine wondered what else she didn't know about her daughter's life. She recalled her own teenage secrets, blending protectiveness with embarrassment. The dog-eared copy of *Lady Chatterley's Lover* that lived in her pillowcase. The explicit Valentine's card she'd received, too personal to dispose of in the normal manner...

This wouldn't do. Elaine had seen plenty of televised examples of how mothers should behave in hospitals, from news reports to *Dr Kildare*. None simply surrendered to exhaustion. But this sleep was exceptionally hard to shrug off. It was almost as if she were... hung over. Locating the shoes that someone had removed, she ground grit into lino. As she pulled the curtain aside, a passing nurse doubled back and enquired cheerfully, "Everything alright there?"

The prompt collapse of the young woman's bright expression confirmed to Elaine that she looked a fright. Smoothing her hair, she felt its post-beach coating. "I need to find my daughter. Judy. I-I was told she would be taken into surgery."

"And you are?"

Her skin itched. "Elaine. Elaine Jones." The taste in her mouth was brick dust. Even the coating she could feel on the hairs in her nostrils was brick dust.

"Wait here. I'll have someone come and take you up."

A glance at her watch: she envied Graham his last hour of oblivion. He would be reading about other people's misfortunes, never imagining... Breath caught in her throat. Then, as she visualised the shock altering his features on his arrival home, she wished she could be there for him.

Elaine bent over a drinking fountain, sipping from her cupped hand. Then, splashing cool water over her eyelids, ignoring the water's sting, she willed herself, *wake up!* She rotated her skirt to what, in her disorientation, she thought was the right way round; attempted to button an unfamiliar cardigan.

A jolt. Another gap in her memory. She was sitting on a waiting-room chair, no recollection of how she came to arrive here. She supposed she must have walked, perhaps been led here. To begin with Elaine raised her face to every orderly who hurried past. When there was time to reflect on the next hour spent alone, she would remember it as the longest of her life. So much so that Elaine condensed into it all the years of her married life, journeying the long white corridors of her mind. She paused at the loss of her first child; at the bittersweet joy of Judy's birth. (*Now you're here and everything will be better; make it better.*) And what stung like a slap was this: she had never allowed herself to appreciate her daughter, all the time knowing this day would come when Judy would be taken away by ambulance and she wouldn't be able to bear the agony.

"I said, can I get you a coffee?"

Elaine startled: a nurse was standing in front of her, kindly, concerned. She found that she was chewing on the rough edge of her thumbnail. "I was, I was -"

The nurse perched next to her. "It's not surprising you feel a little disorientated. The tranquiliser probably hasn't quite worn off yet."

"Tranquiliser?" she found herself repeating stupidly.

"You were given something. For the shock."

To Elaine, who liked to feel in control, this news was humiliating. Had she embarrassed herself? She heard a scream-like echo: *Judy!* Her mind reached out to her daughter. "Is there any...?"

"No. News, that is. I'm afraid it could be a very long wait."

Elaine exhaled. "And my...?" She seemed incapable of finishing a sentence.

"I'm sure your husband's on his way. Why don't I get you that coffee?"

After the nurse's back had turned Elaine wanted to call after her and ask for water, but her mouth seemed unwilling to cooperate. Close to tears, she thanked the nurse, even though the bitter smell rising from the flimsy plastic cup added to her feeling of nausea.

After pacing for a while - it felt wrong to be doing nothing - sensing the futility of it, she sat. Nothing could distract her from the unpalatable home-truth: the accident was her fault, and now her daughter was going to die without ever knowing she was loved. Even their last family meal - because that was how Elaine was already thinking of it - had been comprised of moments that paralysed her with remorse; words she would give anything to retract. But worse than words, the things she had thought!

Graham had been telling one of his stories, one of three that received frequent airings, the lines so familiar it was as though Elaine were a ventriloquist. "I was in my digs studying one evening when Hornby came racing down the corridor, yelling his head off like a bloody lunatic!"

Elaine had pretended to be absorbed by the relentless winding of a spool of spaghetti, silently fuming as she rehearsed her complaint: *How can I criticise Judy's language if you insist on...* The spool unravelled the moment she raised it towards her lips.

"There was blind panic until we worked out the building wasn't on fire. And what was the cause of this hysteria?"

"Music," Judy mumbled through a mouthful.

"*Pop* music, I ask you! 'Come on. You've got to hear this new band on the radio.' When I realised it was only the Beatles, I turned my record player back up and carried on listening to Schubert. Did you know, they couldn't even *read* music?"

Amused by the Frisbee Judy mimed whizzing over the top of her head, Elaine had been tempted to mention that their daughter had been named in honour of a Beatles' track. (*Judy, Judy, Judy, Judy!*) A smug thought. The type of one-upmanship she criticised in friends' relationships. Graham had never made the connection, simply insisting that 'Judith' appeared on their daughter's birth certificate. It didn't matter. She had been Judy from the day they brought her home - from this very same hospital. A white worsted-weight parcel intent on stamping her identity on the world. Instead, Elaine remembered blinking at the empty chair to her right, as she so often found herself doing. Graham had insisted they bought the expandable table that catered for six, the spare panel still slotted neatly underneath. Elaine had never planned for more than two children - one of each - but she didn't create scenes. Not in the middle of the Budget Furniture Emporium. Laying the table, leaving the same space vacant, she'd never imagined that a woven placemat and a high-backed chair would take on such significance. Once, Elaine had sat Judy to her right, but it had seemed disrespectful to the child who had been lost before it had the chance to become a he or a she (although, quite vividly, she imagined a boy). Her first pregnancy: her sad song...

Even now, with Judy in the operating theatre, it seemed that empty place-setting could command more of her attention than her beautiful daughter! Elaine bit down on a white knuckle, blinking away another image: two empty placemats, two empty chairs. She shivered at what felt like a cold breath on her neck; more likely a burst of air conditioning. *No!* an internal voice scolded: *you need to be stronger than this!*

Where was Graham? Elaine glanced down the corridor. He should be here by now. She recoiled, recalling her silent accusation that he barely noticed Judy was no longer a child. She had opinions, wit, and breasts two cup-sizes larger than Elaine's own. And yet when there had been the opportunity to draw Judy into the conversation, Elaine had stalled. Her daughter's glorious Technicolor remained concealed beneath a veneer of pouting lip and bored expression.

And then of course there had been Graham's red rag to any self-respecting teenager: "I hope you're not going to leave your mother with the washing up." And Elaine hadn't even tried to conceal her irritation at finding herself shoehorned into the role of peacemaker.

She had located Judy standing at the sink, the boiler kicking into gear - *clunk-whoosh* - while the glasses lay drowning on their sides in the washing-up bowl. Wondering if she was to be given the silent treatment, the cheerfulness of her, "Shall I dry?" was exaggerated. Judy's response had been to hand her a glass studded with white peaks, which Elaine had rejected: "Rinse that under the tap, will you?"

But Judy had retaliated. "I offer you rainbows, and *that's* the thanks I get?"

And although Elaine had paused to marvel at the oil slick of colours, she hadn't marvelled at the daughter who saw rainbows in washing-up bowls. She'd rinsed Judy's wonder down the plughole.

Why couldn't she let the slightest thing go? It always had to be her way or not at all. Even the least important things.

Silence had resumed until she ventured, "You seemed quiet at dinner. Everything alright?" And for some reason - perhaps release from the formality of mealtimes, a hangover from Elaine's own childhood when conversation had been all but taboo - she had found herself stifling laughter.

Seeming unsure how she was supposed to react, the corners of Judy's mouth twitched until they were both vibrating on the wood-effect vinyl flooring, wiping tears from the corners of their eyes, her daughter forcing words between what sounded like hiccups. "If I... have to... listen to Dad telling that story one... more time."

"Shhhhh!" But Elaine didn't heed her own warning. "It was Vivaldi yesterday. I bet Beethoven puts in an appearance tomorrow."

Of course, it was unfair, this 'ganging up', but in a family of three, two against one was the natural equation. Only Elaine knew that Graham wasn't nearly as much of a stick-in-the-mud as he made himself out to be. There were stories Judy had never heard. Private stories. Like the time they saw Led Zeppelin play and, noticing the effect Robert Plant's lean torso had on her, Graham had ripped open the buttons of his shirt. Later, parading round their bedroom, with Judy asleep in the nursery next door, the shirt was tossed aside. But Graham had a picture of himself as a father lodged in his mind, which bore an uncanny resemblance to his own father in middle age. And he would not - *could* not - let it go. At the age of thirty-five he had shed the skin Elaine recognised, discarding it as easily as he had the torn shirt. It was knowing what lay beneath the surface that made her want to shake a little life back into him.

"And to think we were going to change the world when we met!" Sacred memories. Surprising herself with this small betrayal, Elaine had knocked a tumbler off the work surface.

An image of falling bricks now tried to force itself to the front of Elaine's mind. Crashing, thundering down, a dust cloud rising in their wake. Her breath came in jagged bursts. No! She wouldn't give it air-time, supplementing the image with Judy's stocking feet on tiptoes, one sock inside out. There! That was what she would focus on.

"I thought you met Dad at drama club? Wasn't he an Ugly Sister?"

That was the story Elaine had always told Judy. But she had brushed her daughter's certainty into a dustpan along with the glass shards. "No, we met at the Wholly Communion."

"At *church*?"

"No, the Albert Hall! It was poetry!" Elaine now found herself toying with the cotton of her skirt, just as she had woven the tea towel through her fingers. "The Beat Generation, they were called. If I'm honest, I was just curious. Four-letter words spoil poetry. They embarrassed me, said out loud in that echoey space." She remembered blinking at one corner of the ceiling, mourning the loss of her freedom and how utterly mundane her life had become. How she would settle for mundane now!

"I found myself behind a long-haired girl who was smoking pot." It had amused Elaine to discover it was still possible to shock her daughter. What did it say about her that she had *enjoyed* Judy's discomfort? "All of a sudden, the girl started dancing, as if there was music in the rhythm of the words." Her own hands trailing with the tea towel in symmetrical

30

patterns, Elaine had felt liberated. Dancing in public always made her slightly uncomfortable. It wasn't that she didn't enjoy it but, without a partner, her arms swung like ungainly pendulums. And Graham didn't dance. Only then, in the kitchen, had it occurred to Elaine that she should allow her hands to lead. And they had danced, she and Judy, to a song on the radio. Each holding a corner of a tea towel raised high above their heads, all thought of washing up abandoned.

It was Judy who had broken off, asking breathlessly, "Where did Dad come into it?"

The word took a few moments to enter Elaine's orbit. "I looked around for someone who was as lost as me. He was sitting a few seats to my right. Open-mouthed with disbelief."

As Elaine's lower jaw dropped into a zombie-like stance - the betrayal having already taken place, it was only one small step further to turn it into a joke.

Judy had laughed, demanding, "And?"

"I'd found my ally. That was all it took." That, and the dozens of doe-eyed glances she had cast in his direction during what remained of the performance. She had recounted for Judy how he had invited her for coffee afterwards "To talk about it." How they never felt they'd got their money's worth until they'd squeezed every last drop of blood out of it. But they hadn't needed to talk. They had just sat and listened to everyone else, saying, "Like... wow, man." The only people who weren't pretending they'd enjoyed it. And she'd sighed, "No, poetry didn't change my life."

"It was music!" Judy had clearly thought she was adding the full stop to her sentence.

"You see, everyone assumes music was this huge vehicle for change, but that's not how I remember the Sixties. As far as I was concerned, the real change came later."

"So, what was it?"

Exhausted, Elaine allowed herself to sob, quite openly.

What did it matter who saw her tears? She wanted Graham. She wanted his arms, his quiet reassurance. But all she had were the words that came back to her. Four words that spelled redemption.

"Actually," she had smiled at the young woman she had by some miracle created. Her very own living, breathing doll. "It was you."

CHAPTER FIVE

In 1982, despite eight million testimonies, the fledgling International Association for Near-Death Studies was struggling to secure funding for medical research. But with advances in resuscitation techniques, testimonies once dismissed as deluded, confabulating and self-dramatising, would soon gain the respect of the scientific community.

Judy, who would have sided with the sceptics, crunched her way through grit to watch the paramedics load the stretchered body into the back of the ambulance. Her head filled with the white noise of other people's thoughts. '*Is she dead?*' '*Oh, my God, do you see that? She's not moving.*' '*Look: she's no more than a child!*' '*Why didn't they do something about the wall? It was an accident waiting to happen.*' She was about to cover her ears, when she heard: '*Where's the mother? Can you see her? I hope to God she's not watching this.*'

Was Mum here? Judy was going to have to come up with one hell of an excuse for having missed dinner. She found it possible to block out the clutter so she could hear the few who spoke when others - horrified - didn't trust that they could articulate. Among the voices, she located the paramedic's: "Mrs Jones. I know how it looks, but what you're seeing is dust."

She spun towards it. "Mum!"

But Mum was sitting in the gutter, her feet scrambling against tarmac as if she were trying to escape some inevitable truth.

"Do you understand what I'm saying?" The paramedic, who was trying to get her mother to look her in the eye, spoke in the type of voice normally reserved for infants or foreigners. "We're taking your daughter to May Day. She'll be rushed into surgery. Why don't you get yourself together and follow in the other ambulance?"

Judy was torn: should she go with the prostrate girl or remain with her near-hysterical mother? Behind her, the doors of the first ambulance slammed. The siren started up, drowning the calls for people to mind out of the way. Only her mother's cries were loud enough to be heard above the solemn wail: *"Judy! Judy!"* Never before had she heard her name used with such desperation.

"OK, it's alright." The paramedic was enveloping her mother in her arms, an attempt to contain disguised as an embrace. As she cast her eyes about - '*I need help over here. I'm going to need some drugs*' - Judy stepped forwards.

"I'm here, Mum. I'm sorry I got held up."

"*Judy!*" The voice had lost none of its need.

She joined her mother on the lip of the pavement. "Right next to you."

"Judy!" Her mother sobbed, defeated, smaller than she had ever seen her, so small and dishevelled, not even caring that her mouth was open, distorting the shape of her face.

She thought of what Grandma would say: *The wind will change and you'll be stuck like that.* Rocking back and forth, Mum's violent movements carried the paramedic with her.

"I'm fine," Judy reassured her. And as she spoke the words of comfort, she acknowledged a remarkable sense of well-being. Heightened awareness. To think she'd been intimidated by those boys! Freed from the body that had been giving

34

her so much trouble recently, she had a distinct feeling that everything was exactly as it should be.

But her mother turned to the paramedic, wide-eyed and stricken. "You won't let her die, will you? You won't... I can't..."

Swelling with compassion Judy reached out, but her mother lurched sideways across the paramedic's lap. They had tranquilised her. Judy could see the need for it. And, with Mum whimpering softly beside her in the second ambulance, she felt strangely disconnected. Dying had been mentioned, yet here she was. Still 'conscious', but on some level that didn't depend on a connection with her body. The flesh and bone casing was no more 'her' than school uniform was! The rush of grief for the body she had lived in for so long translated into a feeling of being pulled into a vortex, a little like the moment when a plane accelerates before take-off, and she passed through the metal of the ambulance, leaving her unconscious mother in safe hands. Travelling, a sensation recognisable from dreams, soaring, sometimes-swimming; this unfamiliar God's-eye view of a familiar landscape.

She descended into the hospital, passing along corridors, through solid walls and closed doors until she located the correct room, recognising splashes of nail varnish pilfered from her mother's dressing table on otherwise pale feet. Unsurprised, unafraid, she gazed down fondly. The body on the bed was covered by a sheet save for a cutaway square, face obscured by a mask. The room was busy. Thoughts darted and swooped.

'This is one ugly mess. Where the hell do I start?' The surgeon.

Interested in these observations, Judy made no attempt to block them.

The nurse with the checked laces in her otherwise sensible shoes: *'Crush injuries are never pretty, but this... I think I'd rather not wake up.'*

The junior nurse, there to observe as part of her training: '*I think I'm going to throw up. No, really.*'

All of this undignified prodding! Taking her place by the junior nurse, head angled to one side, Judy admitted, "I've looked better."

The nurse: '*Any minute now. Oh shit, the saw. Not the saw.*'

A high-pitched whine started up. "Alright?" The surgeon asked, looking up as he positioned his feet; slightly apart.

Judy began, "Is that really necess-?"

"Uh-huh," said the nurse next to her.

Judy was about to protest, 'Er, hello! Am I invisible?' but, seeing how pale the girl was, she apologised. "Sorry. I thought he was talking to me."

'*Why must these people apply if they're so squeamish? The last thing I need is to be distracted.*' "Because if you're not up to this, I'd rather you just -"

Covering her mouth, the young nurse ran towards a sink.

'*Great. Will someone -? Are you just going to stand there?*' "Get her out of here!"

"I'm onto it." Judy tried to put one hand on the girl's shoulder. It went right through. *Huh?* She tried again. Same thing. Looking at where her hand should be, she saw only a vague outline. She could barely contemplate the logical question: Am I a *ghost?* Is *that* what this is? She had never believed in the paranormal, dismissing those who did as weirdos. In her distress, Judy backed towards the door but, as she did so, the level of light in the room increased, bleaching everything - even the green of the nurses' tunics - white. She turned and saw a pure shimmering form enter.

"*Everything is as it should be.*"

The brightness almost blinding, Judy shielded her eyes, squinting through the gaps between her fingers. "Have you come for me?" she asked, her voice sounding - remarkably - as if she had been expecting something like this.

"I have a message for you."

After listening to people's thoughts, the fact that she couldn't see a mouth that moved wasn't particularly disconcerting. "A message?"

"You must go back. There are still things you must do."

"What things?"

There was no reply.

However changed she was, a remnant of argumentative teenager remained. "How do I know if I *want* to go back if you won't tell me?"

"It's not for you to decide." The light flowed towards the body lying on the gurney. Not an arm, but pointing nonetheless.

"Let's just say I agree." Judy swallowed, nodding towards the train crash they were making of her empty shell. "Will that thing even work?"

Without moving, she was projected into a waiting room where her mother was pacing the floor, biting down on her white knuckles, tormenting herself: *'If only I'd... I never once told her... Why do I always?'* She felt a pang, that only child's pull of guilt. With her mind still on her mother, Judy said, "This is a hospital. There must be other bodies I can use."

"Don't worry. It's like diving into a pool of water."

It seemed what she had to do was unavoidable. There was little point arguing. But *dive?* With no other advice, she shut out everything else and visualised.

It was like putting on wet and misshapen clothes after taking a warm bath, except the shock was so great that, if she could have done, Judy would have screamed. There had been no pain when she had left her body. In reverse, the process felt as if she were pulling herself apart rather than putting herself back together. Something was clearly very wrong.

CHAPTER SIX

Arriving breathlessly at May Day's Accident and Emergency Unit, Graham scanned the waiting room, hopeful of finding his daughter. His wife, at least. But it was another woman who glared up from her *Reader's Digest*, satisfying herself that he posed no threat to her position in the queue. He stood anxiously in line. The man at the counter was holding an eye pad in place, noisy shallow breathing suggesting his pain was considerable, while compulsory form-filling took priority. *Come on!* Graham shifted his weight onto the balls of his feet, trying to make eye contact with someone - anyone - uncertain precisely how much fuss he was entitled to create.

"Excuse me." He accosted a passing nurse whose flat-soled sense of purpose suggested efficiency.

"Just one minute, Sir!" She breezed towards the entrance, where an anonymous blanketed form was being stretchered in.

Minutes multiplied. When his turn arrived, Graham smoothed his neighbour's hand-written note out on the wide counter: evidence of his claim to a moment of their hard-pressed time.

"Name?" The receptionist raised her eyebrows with barely concealed impatience.

"Graham Jones. Father of Judith."

What she found in her notes caused her mouth to twitch. It was as though, after his appearance suggested he might require a small beer with a meal, he had ordered the most expensive wine on the restaurant's menu. "I'll have someone come and take you through." She lifted the telephone receiver to her ear, announcing, "Mr Jones has just arrived."

"Through?" Graham's hand closed around the cold bronze weight in his jacket pocket. Rotating it, he tightened his fist, allowing the hard flat edges to press into his soft flesh as he attempted to interpret her efficient gestures. Only a fool could miss how her eyes pitied.

"I'm afraid I'm not permitted to discuss patient treatment. Grab a seat and I'll hurry them along for you."

Elbows on the counter, leaning forwards, Graham lowered his voice. "I don't want to 'grab' anything: I want to know what's happened to my daughter!"

A nurse entered the stage-like reception, stamping a document and depositing it in a tray.

"Here we are! That didn't take too long, now, did it?" the woman patronised, then averted her eyes, whispering the things, no doubt, that he needed to hear.

The nurse placed a hand on Graham's arm. He was led away, blinking back words, "Emergency surgery," "Rushed her in," and, "lucky," that seemed to impede his vision.

"But she's alright?" Graham asked, as if he were the kitchen scales and each new piece of information another bronze weight. Four ounces, eight...

"Take a seat, Mr Jones."

Something in her matronly tone demanded obedience. Despite his instinct that he should be doing something, he perched on the moulded orange seat. Galloping her own chair opposite his, the nurse stopped just short of taking his hand. Graham looked down at her fingers, dangerously close to his knees. She was about to add the heaviest bronze weight, the hole in its uppermost section large enough to hook two fingers through. "Your daughter has been seriously injured. A wall collapsed, burying her underneath. Luckily, witnesses managed to get help. There are broken bones, but hopefully they'll mend. It's the internal bleeding that worries us."

"Where?" Graham fought the facts as if, by catching the nurse out, he might be able to balance the scales.

She angled her head. "To begin with there's her spleen and her pancreas."

Try as he might, Graham couldn't stop babbling. "I bet it was the wall round the corner from us. I've been saying that tree's unsafe for years."

The nurse's extended blink, an instinctive shutting out of a seemingly unrelated concern, was enough to still Graham's tongue. "I'm going to take you to your wife now."

Fingernails grazed his trouser leg as the nurse levered herself to standing. Graham seemed incapable of movement.

"Mr Jones?" Her stance was impatient.

This was why he had not wanted to sit: the fear that, with all those bronze weights, standing again might prove impossible. "Judy's going to be alright, isn't she?"

"We're doing everything we possibly can."

Not that! He buried his hands in his hair. His precious little girl! He had delayed going home. Been annoyed about his lack of dinner. Queued uncomplainingly as if waiting for a sodding bus.

"Mr Jones!"

"Yes." Graham swallowed, stood. Act like a man. One foot in front of the other: a show of dignity on the walk to the gallows.

In the white corridor, he saw a discreet sign for a chapel and his mind filled with the image of the swinging crucifix. More than anything, Graham wanted to step inside its womb-like embrace, hold a flame to a candle, string ancient words into sentences. But he continued, one foot in front of the other. *Our Father, who art in Heaven; Hallowed be thy name.*

"Graham!" A small room had opened up unexpectedly, and a woman who looked like an older version of his wife was there in front of him: small, grey and surprisingly dishevelled. *Thy Kingdom come, Thy will be done.* She gripped the sides of his face violently, and sank her head against his chest. There was a smell about her: dust, like the dust of his DIY projects. "Oh, Graham! You're here!" *Here as it is in Heaven.*

"Judy was so still." The woman, who sounded so very much like Elaine that there could be no room for doubt, shook. "So still and quiet." Her hands dropped from his face, finding their own watery level lapping at the knit of his jumper.

The severity of the situation struck him anew. Stroking the back of his wife's shivering head Graham felt the unusual coarseness of her hair. Seeing the need to take charge, he pressed his lips to her forehead. *Give us this day our daily bread.* "How long has it been?"

"What time is it?" Elaine sniffed and stepped away from him, her eyes searching the walls. "I've no idea what time I…"

Locating a clock, Graham remembered his father's complaints that the NHS operated on a different time system. Minutes and hours ceased to have any relevance, except that they had to be endured. *And forgive us our trespasses.* "Did they tell you anything else?"

"They told me it would be a long wait." Elaine steepled her conjoined hands to her lips as if in silent prayer.

The trembling words reminded Graham of his own helplessness as he had watched her in labour. *As we forgive those who trespass against us.* "You look exhausted. Why don't you sit down?"

Graham steered his wife towards a group of low-backed chairs in alternating olive and beige, applying pressure to her shoulders in encouragement. He had only been in this place a quarter of an hour, and already he was stressing the importance of sitting. *And deliver us from evil.* Without prompting, Elaine lay across three seats, making a headrest with her hands, drawing her knees to her chest. It was a position she might have fallen asleep in, but her red-rimmed eyes were staring. Graham wasn't sure where to place himself in the scene. Newly married, he might have massaged his wife's feet. These days, when they had the opportunity to spend the evening alone - a rediscovered treat now Judy was old enough to go out with friends - they occupied separate sofas, claiming to enjoy the luxury of space. Already, the picture of the living room without Judy was taking on new meaning.

"Graham?" Seeming to have unearthed a new source of strength, Elaine had propped herself up on one elbow. "Judy's going to be alright, isn't she?"

And deliver us from evil. What was it that came next? *And deliver us from evil...*

"You'd tell me if you knew, wouldn't you?" He felt his wife's soft and fragile hand touching his. "I'd rather hear it from you."

Elaine's eyes searched his, desperate for clues. Normally, she wouldn't have looked old enough to be a mother, let alone the mother of a teenage daughter. What was it the nurse had said? *We're doing everything we possibly can.* Elaine didn't need uncertainty: what she needed was a clear, confident voice. "She's going to be fine. Stay right here. I'll go and see if there's an update."

Turning away, making a fist around the bronze weight, Graham's flesh offered no resistance to its solidity. His short nails pressed into the palm of his other hand.

"Graham?"

He composed himself. "Yes?"

"When you called...?" Elaine's face contorted. "I thought she'd only be gone a few minutes."

"It's not important." He cursed the hour he had wasted in the pub.

After walking back down the corridor, he turned into the small chapel. Save for the dim glow of a few wilting candles, the only illumination was an exterior light, which cast an inverted shadow of the plain wooden cross, stretched out at an angle down the aisle. It was melded with distorted shapes thrown from the modern stained glass. He wasn't tempted to reach for the light switch. Graham hadn't troubled God for some time. It pleased him to be a shadow, perching uncomfortably at the back. Forehead on his clasped hands, Graham began carefully punctuating his silent plea: 'Dear God, please save my daughter, Judy. I don't want to hear that the doctors and nurses are doing their best when I've no idea if that's good enough. I'm not interested in their medical jargon. So I'm asking: save her, I beg of you.' Finding his hands clamped tightly together, he opened his eyes and saw the sheen of a laminated card on the shelf below. An illustration of a blonde-haired Jesus tending a flock, something he would have dismissed as sentimental at any other time. Reading the title, *The Lord is my Shepherd,* the words flooded back: *There is nothing I shall want.* Apparently there all along; waiting for his hour of need. The green pastures calmed him. They made breathing possible.

It was while Graham was mouthing rediscovered words, aware of every movement of his chest, that someone flicked on the light, but, finding they weren't alone, reversed the action. He felt a hand on his shoulder; heard a soft female voice: "Peace be with you."

Seeing that he had been joined by a nun, Graham was reminded that he had offered nothing in return for this enormous service he was asking. Clearing his throat, his cough sounded unnaturally loud, resonating in the silent place.

The nun crossed herself, sat and half-turned her head

in his direction. The quiet rasp of her voice had suggested someone who had earned her place in the world - certainly of having earned her front pew position. Graham imagined her as a Mother Teresa figure, someone small and unassuming, whose lined face spoke of compassion. Feeling the distance between them as something physical, Graham took a seat on the end of the row opposite her.

"I hope I didn't disturb your prayers," she said. "Just in case, I added one of my own for you."

Graham bowed his head. "It's my daughter."

"Yes," she said, apparently in need of no further explanation.

He cleared his throat again, quieter this time, pondering how best to articulate his concern. "I was wondering... should I promise something in return when asking God for something?"

She didn't laugh or seem to think his question odd. "If that's what you want to do, by all means. But a prayer isn't a bargain. Don't make it conditional on receiving the answer you want."

"You're a Catholic?" He could see her features now in the half-darkness and, whilst they didn't mirror his imaginings, she had that quality of otherness he had observed in photographs of the Dalai Lama. He had the sense that she, too, had unlocked the secret of how to exist in the world without compromising her principles.

"Yes." The nun looked down at her clothes and then back at him with a hint of humour.

"Have you always been...?" Tailing off, he waved one hand.

"Actually, no: I'm a convert."

"Can I ask? Obviously, if it's personal..."

"Not at all. I believe Catholicism is the most complete form of Christianity there is. In my mind, there was no point in a girl from a long tradition of atheists taking on anything

44

less. Believe it or not, I was the cause of a great scandal in my family. My mother and father were considered terrible failures. A shame really, because I'd always thought they were wonderful parents." Her serene expression reflected the esteem she clearly held them in. "Always teaching me about the natural world. Telling me the names of wild flowers and butterflies." She paused to sigh. "But you can't ignore something when you know it's true, can you?"

"Was there anything in particular...?"

"An epiphany?" The nun laughed as Graham looked at her hopefully. "No, nothing so dramatic. When I was fifteen I had all the answers. By the time I was eighteen I wasn't so confident. By the time I reached my majority, I was completely lost. It became obvious - not overnight, of course - that the reason was because I was intent on ignoring the evidence around me."

"And did religion help you find the answers?"

"No, just an awful lot more questions." She smiled kindly, which Graham translated as a subject change. "Tell me your daughter's name."

"Judy. After my mother's favourite: Judy Garland."

"Ah! Such a beautiful voice!" The nun hugged herself. There was something about her smile that made Graham feel as though she was conferring a favour on him. "I remember her in *Meet Me in St Louis*. Of course, I don't get out to the cinema very often these days. It's probably the thing I miss the most." Having seen Graham rotating the weight in his hand, the nun nodded towards it. "What's that you have there?"

"This?" He opened his fist, feeling foolish. "It's a weight, from my wife's kitchen scales. I have no idea why I brought it with me."

"But how interesting! Scales are a symbol of matters being held in the balance. You're holding one of the most potent symbols of hope we have. I wonder..." Leaning across the narrow aisle, the nun folded Graham's hand around the weight, letting hers rest on top. "Would you like me to pray with you?"

"Very much." Graham knelt again. "I don't know why, but I'm struggling with the words."

"Then let me take care of them. Just close your eyes and focus on your daughter."

This was what Graham most wanted to hear: the voice of someone else taking charge. Already, with little further encouragement, words were taking form inside his head: "If you do this one thing for me…"

CHAPTER SEVEN

Elaine opened her eyes to violent fluorescent light. There, opposite her, was Graham: upright, eyes closed, lips moving. He often spoke in his sleep, reeling off peculiar shopping lists of unrelated words. But these sentences were lengthy, purposeful. He looked different. Not something she could put a name to, but altered nonetheless. How strange that someone could be so comfortingly familiar and yet barely recognisable at the same time.

Suddenly self-conscious that she had allowed herself to lie uncovered in front of strangers, Elaine let her legs drop to the floor. The momentum deposited her in a sitting position and, without being aware of her own movement, she found herself on the vinyl seat next to her husband's.

Surprised by incoming pressure on his thigh, Graham heard himself inhale sharply. Meeting the incoming hand, he identified the diamond of his wife's engagement ring. His mouth twitched into what was almost a smile. So often, he was upset by the sight of the ring, abandoned in a small saucer by the kitchen sink amid a mountain of used teabags destined for the compost. He would hook it onto the first joint of his little finger and seek out his wife to propose to her all over again. "A month's wages," his father had advised.

"The best investment you'll ever make." Graham had spent two months' wages and considered the look in Elaine's eyes return enough. He was struck again by how extraordinary it was that this beautiful woman should have singled him out. Looking as she did now - a vision of how she might age - he felt marginally more deserving of her. His love for his family had never been in doubt but, beyond providing for them, he had done little to protect them. He saw that now. Something had to change.

"Is there any news?" she asked, her hair, always tousled, mussed up from when she had thrown herself at him. The force of his wife had surprised him: anger mingled with relief and something akin to submission. Now Graham saw his wife's exhausted hopefulness and was able to respond with the news he had been waiting to deliver: "Judy's been taken to the recovery room."

"Oh!" There was audible relief at the word 'recovery' and all it implied. "You should have woken me!"

He put a restraining hand on hers. "We can't see her yet."

"Did they say how the surgery went?"

Graham was selective in his choice of words. "She's stable." 'Critical but stable' was what they had told him, but the surgeon didn't realise God had answered his prayers.

Elaine rested her head against Graham's shoulder, then recoiled. She sniffed his clothing before pulling the underarm of her own cardigan upwards, concluding miserably, "I stink."

Encircling his wife's shoulder, Graham inhaled her familiar earthy, salty-sweet scent and the now-damp DIY smell. "That's your morning smell."

"Oh God, is it?" She wrinkled her nose, then appeared to remember something. "What were you saying to yourself back then?"

"When?"

"I was watching you talking to yourself."

Not quite ready to speak about his experience yet, Graham said, "Nothing." Save for private moments shared with Elaine, it had been the most intense hour of his life.

"It was a very long nothing!"

"I was reciting *The Lord is my Shepherd*." Graham toyed with the ring on Elaine's finger. "I had no idea I still knew the words, but I only needed to be reminded of the first line." He smiled, marvelling at how the brain works; wondering what else might be locked away in there. And infused with the nun's serenity, Graham now felt capable of coping with whatever had to be faced.

"Really?" Twisted sideways, an elbow on one knee, Elaine was looking at him intently.

"Why are you so surprised?"

"It's just that…" Graham saw his wife's eyes darken. "Not once, in all the confusion, did it cross my mind to pray."

They were silent, each absorbed with private thoughts until, both finding a need to share them, there was a collision of words.

"You go first," Graham volunteered.

"I was just thinking of that barge holiday on the Norfolk Broads when Judy was three. I only turned my back for an instant and she fell overboard. I went into panic-mode, but you - you just jumped straight in and dragged her out before she knew what had happened."

"I was terrified!"

"I never would have known. You were amazing." Elaine nuzzled into his bulk.

"I was thinking of the time she was stung by a wasp just above her left eye. Except that we didn't know what had happened because she wouldn't let us near her. She just kept on screaming and flapping her hands."

"She was terrified for weeks that it was coming back to get her."

"I don't think we've ever had to take her to hospital before, have we?"

"Never."

Crashing, ricocheting, a liquid roar... Panic rose in Judy's throat. Reaching for her mouth with the one hand that responded to her direction, she encountered stoppers and tubes blocking its path. In her narrow flickering view, an image came into focus: the back of a man wearing a white coat. When he turned, Judy saw his black wiry hair, the dark brows shrouding mocking eyes (they were usually pictured in shadow), the moustache dropping away at right angles from the corners of his mouth, the patch of hair that met his lower lip, the area on either side where hair refused to grow: that distinctive outline of dark on white. She clamped her eyes shut. In her short life there had been many things that had frightened Judy, but only one that terrified her.

For the past few years, the evening news had carried frequent reports about mutilated women. The media had dubbed the perpetrator The Yorkshire Ripper. Unlike his namesake, their man had not passed into legend. His trail wasn't celebrated with guided walks on inky November evenings. Very real and very dangerous, he felled girls as young as sixteen with hammers and knives; writing teasing notes in child-like scrawl; dropping clues; threatening future kills. The message clear: he would never stop. Since his mission was ridding the world of prostitutes, Judy had always known he would find his way to her hometown. Then she had seen the face of Peter Sutcliffe and it was not the horned image of evil she'd pictured. All the more shocking for the fact that he appeared in court well-dressed. (Her father reserved greater disgust for his choice of an open-collared shirt than he did for the man's crimes.) Good-looking, albeit in a slightly foreign, creepy kind of way. Her memory took her back to the last thing she could remember: raising a finger at the gang of schoolboys by the bus stop. Now - here, in this room - she was to be punished. Still woozy with anaesthetic, it didn't occur to her that the man who was the cause of such terror - to whom, in reality, the doctor bore only a passing resemblance - had been sentenced to life imprisonment.

"Anything?" Judy heard a woman's voice enquire.

"I thought I saw a flicker."

"Then it's time."

They were operating as a pair: it was often the way. A woman deflected attention from the man. Etta lent Butch Cassidy and the Sundance Kid the appearance of respectability. Clyde had his Bonnie. Ian Bradley his Myra Hindley. Judy resolved to lie very, very still.

Despite exhaustion, the young recovery nurse executed a skip as she journeyed through early-morning corridors, silent but for the mechanical whir of floor polishers, grazing greedily. The part she dreaded over, there had been no need to act evasively while she waited for the doctor to recite the all too-familiar, 'I'm so sorry, we did everything we could.'

Stopping short of the group of low chairs, the nurse registered surprise at the transformation that had taken place. The two very separate people who had arrived, first the woman then, hours later, the man (not at all what she had imagined, and she was usually so good at couples), had emerged from the long night: a team. On hearing her approach, the woman jerked her head from her husband's shoulder. A hand shot up to her mouth, stifling an involuntary mew.

"Mr and Mrs Jones? I know you've had a dreadful wait, but it's over now."

The man looked up, his expression balanced but hopeful. "Is she...?" Hands on thighs, he levered himself to standing.

"You can see your daughter now." Smiling, the nurse allowed her words to oxygenate the air.

"Do you hear that?" The man turned to support his wife, her legs as determined and unrehearsed as a newborn lamb's. Then he puffed out his cheeks, exhaled loudly, and laughed; a joyous and unrestrained sound that had the nurse nodding and smiling. "Thank God! Thank God! And thank you!" She thought he might kiss her - people reacted to good news in all sorts of different ways - but he stopped short.

Now for the not-so-good news: the nurse aimed her next comments specifically at the man. "I have to warn you. She's not a pretty sight. Some people are upset by all the tubes and machinery."

His expression suggesting he recognised the seriousness of her tone, he focused his entire attention on his wife, who seemed to shrink tearfully beneath his shoulder: "She's alive. That's all that matters."

CHAPTER EIGHT

Driving home, Graham knew he should feel tired, but he was unnaturally wide-eyed in a jet-lag of sorts. With hazy sunlight bathing rooftops in an otherworldly glow, he struggled with the question of how to tell his wife about his experience in the hospital chapel. It was important to tackle it while he retained that feeling of having been submerged in the River Jordan.

Elaine was hunkered down beside him in the passenger seat, occupying a glazed state of semi-consciousness. Their needs were unlikely to coincide.

"Your wife needs rest," the nurse had advised. "She's in shock."

Rocking to a halt at the traffic lights, it was the tree that captured Graham's attention first. Magnificent in the morning light, taller than he remembered, its trunk was fully displayed. Far more impressive than the ancient mulberry he had been forbidden from climbing as a boy because it was said to have belonged to Dr Samuel Johnson. No clues were provided as to Dr Johnson's identity in response to his enquiry, simply an exasperated, "Oh, you know: *the* Samuel Johnson." Their own family doctor was a friendly man who, Graham felt sure, would have let him climb the tree if it were his, but it didn't appear to be something that came with the job.

It had been many years since Graham had looked at the world with wonder. As a boy he had paused to examine jewelled spiders' webs, monitored transformation of tadpole to frog, nursed sunflowers from seedlings to beanstalks, coaxed stag beetles into matchboxes. His own small scale lent itself to an appreciation of the potency of life contained in a simple back garden. As an adult, the patch of dry grass optimistically described as 'lawn' was nothing short of a nuisance, its weekly back and sides keeping him from his beloved *Grandstand*. Elaine tackled plenty of unpleasant tasks other women wouldn't dream of, but for some unfathomable reason she refused to master the lawnmower. "I don't want you to feel redundant," was the reason she gave.

Slowly, only slowly, Graham lowered his eyes from the tree's lofty branches, realising that its naked trunk shouldn't be on public display, the view reserved for those who lived on the far side of the wall... the wall - or what little remained of it! His face putty, he re-moulded it from the cheeks downwards. It took time before his eyes identified other details: the end of the road cordoned off with a yellow strip, hung like cheerful bunting; metal and wood and shattered brickwork strewn across pavement and road; the phone box upended, its glass shattered; the bus shelter, still standing, but its roof dented - presumably by falling masonry; the road sign anonymously face down; a streetlight now diagonal, lifting a clump of tarmac from the pavement like a shallow-rooted storm-slain tree; large black footprints in the heavy dust where the bulk of the debris lay; lighter footprints trailing onto the pavement of the main road. Two policemen stood like sentries, hands behind backs, rocking on their heels.

Behind him, a car horn honked: once, twice, then an extended blast of exasperation. The driver's window was laboriously wound down. Graham registered that the traffic lights had turned green, but couldn't find it in himself to put the car into first gear and accelerate. Unbuckling his seatbelt, he opened the car door; gaze level, movements slow and deliberate.

"Oi! What the hell d'you think you're up to?" The man leaned out of the car, elbow first, his head appearing at an obtuse angle. "Some of us have work to get to!"

Graham acknowledged him absently. "Won't be a minute." He walked across the junction, halting traffic like a dishevelled Moses parting the Red Sea.

"Sir, we'll have to ask…"

"Now, hang on! You can't just - "

"Graham!" Face looming close, voice distant, Graham registered Elaine's panic-stricken expression, but couldn't absorb the images his eyes were receiving.

As a child, constantly reminded that he had missed the end of the war by a year, Graham had felt his punctuality was being called into question. But he had seen reels of footage, played in bomb craters, remembering the end of sweet rationing as his personal V-day. What now lay before him was the set of a gritty British wartime drama. As though he were subconsciously directing it, he placed Judy next to the wall; saw her disappear beneath the rubble. Surely - surely no one could have emerged alive?

"Graham?" Elaine had hooked her hand into the bend of his elbow.

Graham opened his mouth but no words came out.

"It'll be a bloody miracle if my wages aren't docked!" The driver arrived panting at his other side. "Fuck me!" His jaw dropped, anger evaporating. "What's happened here?"

They stood in front of the police cordon, shoulder to shoulder: Stewart Granger, Margaret Lockwood and James Mason. Behind them, other drivers were sounding their horns, opening doors, stepping out. The man turned back and yelled, "Keep your hair on! Are you lot blind or something?"

He turned to a man with a professional-looking camera, who had taken an interest in him. "And you can get that sodding thing out of my face!"

The policemen (more Jack Warner than Jack Hawkins), slow to spring into action, were now ready with their, "Come along, Sir. You're causing an obstruction."

Graham pointed. "My daughter," was all he could manage.

Glances that said 'You poor devil' were exchanged. They obviously thought the worst. Who wouldn't? Crossing the junction, one of the officers began to direct traffic around the two abandoned vehicles.

He heard Elaine explaining: "Our daughter was buried, but they got her out - God knows how. She's alive. Barely - but she's alive."

At the sound of his wife's voice - while the man with the camera asked, "And you are?" - Graham saw the cine film rewind. Each brick resumed its rightful place; the scaffolding reassembled; the phone box righted itself; Judy emerged and walked backwards in the direction of home.

"Lucky bitch." The man whistled through his front teeth. "No offence." He seemed in no hurry, all thought of work and wages forgotten.

"It's a miracle," Graham said to the photographer. "A miracle, that's what it is."

Trying to contain her shaking, Elaine thought of Judy entrapped in wire and tubes and framework. She had looked less vulnerable as a tiny baby, naked and sightless, but already fighting, very much her own person. Better to be blind but utterly sure of yourself than the open-eyed terror begging for something that wasn't Elaine's to give. She hadn't wanted to leave her daughter in that room with its bleeping machines. There was no Richard Chamberlain with orange skin and fluoride-white teeth, timing pulses to perfection with a fob watch. In his place, a sinister-looking doctor whose attentiveness bordered on possessiveness.

"It's a miracle," Graham was repeating, appearing to need her endorsement.

But it was men who had saved her daughter. Strangers who came together, working under the beams of car headlights. One boy who had cared enough to stay. There had been no supernatural intervention: no angry Old Testament God reaping vengeance on a South London suburb; no New Testament God had appeared, white-robed, to pull Judy to her feet, illuminating her way with rays of light. It had been dusty and bloody, sweaty and loud. Elaine remembered being dragged away from where she had clawed at the debris. She had allowed herself to weep. Thrown herself against a chest that didn't belong to her husband. It had happened like this, here in this place. Elaine let the cordon slip through her hands, looking towards the front doors that had opened, spilling families out onto the pavement; the workers and the huddled witnesses who had stood vigil. She must find them, thank them - just as soon as she'd had a few hours' sleep.

Turning back, Elaine saw that her husband was being asked to move to the left so the photographer could frame his shot: Graham, posing against the chaotic backdrop, proclaiming his absolute certainty. Even though she knew he'd come back down to earth, Elaine felt an uneasiness she couldn't account for. *How could you possibly know? You weren't here.*

CHAPTER NINE

The grate of cutlery against china and an announcement: "Breakfast in bed!"

Soft sunlight, filtered through the net curtains, played on Elaine's face. "What time is it?" she asked in panic.

"Don't you worry about that. The hospital promised to ring if there was any change." Graham stood at the ready while she propped herself up on a nest of pillows and glanced nervously at the bedlinen, finding it already reddened with brick dust. "Eat!" he ordered, presenting her with the tray.

If her husband's calm was exasperating, it provided the counterbalance she needed. Elaine was determined to look grateful. She wouldn't complain that the scrambled eggs were the consistency of rubber. There had been thought and effort.

"I've made the first round of telephone calls." Graham reeled off a list. "Judy's school. Work, of course. My mother. Your dad..."

Elaine's cutlery froze mid-air. "Oh, God." Bullish was a generous description of her difficult-to-handle father. She could almost imagine his demands of whys and wherefores: *Who's at the hospital with Judy now? After Gloria's operation I sat with her twenty-four hours a day!* And Graham's attempts to pacify him: *Brian, I know how concerned you must be...*

"Your parents are going to drive down first thing

tomorrow." Graham smiled nervously. "I have to admit, I would have preferred we had a little time to ourselves first."

"Sorry." Elaine winced. "I doubt you could have stopped them." She resigned herself to the thought of her parents using the spare room - the room that should have belonged to that other child. "I'll make up the bed."

"I'll do it while you're having a bath. I've already ironed the sheets."

Trying to control her eyebrows, Elaine sipped her tea: *you've ironed sheets?* Then her coltish thoughts turned to her sister. "What about Liz? Did you call her?"

"No -"

"Oh, God, I'd better do it now!"

"Slow down. By all means ring her later, but there's no need just now. Your father said he'd take care of it."

She allowed herself a moment to breathe before asking, "How did your mother take the news?"

Graham frowned. "Not much to say for herself."

Joyce, who veered towards Unhealthy on the Scale of Hypochondriacs, had an unusual thirst for medical details, and rarely let an opportunity to offer inappropriate advice pass by. Still, it was a lot to take in, especially if you had no one to halve it with. "I expect she was shocked." It wasn't as if Graham had announced that Judy had a childhood bout of the measles.

"I felt awful. She asked me to repeat myself. I pictured her sinking back into the chair by the phone." He was shaking his head. "I should have told her face-to-face."

"Perhaps you'd better go and see her."

"Next week. Right now, Judy's our priority."

Elaine saw this as her cue to deposit the tray on the bedside table. "We should get going."

Her husband silenced her with a hand on her arm. "Not so fast. I want you to finish eating, then I want you to have a bath, and then we'll go to the hospital. In that order."

Elaine did as she was told. There was comfort in it, and it gave Graham the illusion that he had his small corner of the world under control. Because now she knew: an illusion of control was all she'd ever had.

"I'm glad I saw the wall." His voice came from a distant place.

Elaine glanced up. "Without doing Monty Python a disservice, technically, I think it's an ex-wall."

He was back with her, smiling. "I don't think I would have appreciated what happened otherwise."

"No," Elaine said, knowing that her husband would never really appreciate what had happened. "Graham." Her white lie had magnified, assuming disproportionate significance. "It was my fault. You see, I sent Judy out for stamps..."

"Don't be daft." Graham shifted towards her, clamping her head to his chest and sending the plate sliding across the tray. "How could you have known?"

Elaine didn't want her shame to be brushed aside. Guilt had to be acknowledged if it was to be assuaged. "It should have been me instead of Judy."

"Shhhh! Please don't even think that."

Overreaction had caused the accident. Elaine could never admit to Graham that she'd been annoyed he had used the last of the stamps. One lapse, and all of the times she'd been there counted for nothing. She had failed.

Released, Elaine heard her husband ask, "Better now?" His expectation was that one word from him had the power to make everything alright!

She nodded out of habit, catching sight of herself in the mirrored door of the wardrobe, sweeping tears from the corner of her eye.

"I wanted to talk to you about something."

Elaine registered the tone of her husband's voice, his choice of 'wanted' instead of 'want'. As Graham stood, the headboard knocked against the wall taking her head with it. He began pacing in the manner of someone who is about to make an announcement. "There won't be an opportunity once your parents arrive. Just listen." His sharp about-turn brought them into eye contact. "Don't feel you have to say anything."

Oh, God, Elaine thought, sitting very still. She didn't like the tremor of this particular drum roll. *As if they didn't have enough to cope with!* "Go ahead," she said, trying to sound encouraging.

"I've been thinking for a while now that we need to do more to help Judy through the next few years. She's growing up so quickly."

Elaine relaxed a little. She was too hard on him: he'd noticed his daughter was a teenager, after all.

"Only yesterday, I was looking at a girls' magazine and it was all sex, sex and more sex. The message was that if you aren't at it by the age of seventeen, there's something wrong with you. We have to counter that attitude. Judy needs boundaries, and we need to agree where they should be set."

Elaine opened her mouth to protest - *boundaries?* - but Graham continued: "I don't want her to be able to play one of us off against the other. We're not talking guinea pigs and ice-skating parties anymore."

This time when she positioned the tray on the bedside table he didn't resist. "Right this minute, our daughter's lying in hospital." All the time that she tried to sound reasonable, her internal voice screamed, *broken and battered and bruised!* "We'll have to take every day as it comes. We may have to face up to the fact that Judy may not be able to do the things normal teenagers do." At that moment Elaine wished for Valentine cards for her daughter; for secrets and short skirts, parties and late nights, and all the delights that would lead to her discovering her sexuality while she still had hormones

61

coursing round her body. Her beautiful, crushed body.

Graham, beside her again, was prising Elaine's hand away from her mouth: "She's going to be fine."

The urge to yell was so overwhelming that, to Elaine, her voice sounded peculiarly small and quiet. "How can you be so sure?" He gave her a pitying smile, as if there was something she hadn't the capacity to grasp. "What did the doctors tell you that they didn't tell me? Please! I've had my moment. I'm going to be able to cope, whatever happens."

"I don't doubt it." Graham had adopted a pained look. His expressions were like clues to a cryptic crossword. Pacing resumed. "Elaine, I know this is going to sound strange but, while you were asleep, I prayed. For the first time in years. All the times I went to church as a child, I never actually thought - perhaps 'felt' is a better word - that anyone was listening. But this was different."

Another turn: too late to smooth over her misgivings, Elaine exaggerated her frown as if to imply she was taking what he said seriously. "You've never had anything this important to pray for."

"It wasn't just that." He appeared to be stalling.

"What then?"

"I prayed in the hospital chapel. With a nun."

Elaine didn't have the energy for theological debate. She knew that wars had been fought about the differences between the Christian faiths, new punishments devised for those who didn't toe the line, a great many people tortured and killed, all as a result of a flawed translation: not 'kill the non-believers' but, as Erasmus had pointed out, *ignore* them. It was the same God with man-made frills as far as she was concerned. "You don't really believe in all that stuff," she said.

Elaine's own beliefs were indistinct, consisting mainly of a fondness for traditions she associated with Englishness. She threw open her windows on Sunday mornings to hear the sound of bell-ringing; stood shivering on her doorstep listening to carol singers. Declaring herself Christian on official documents was a question of superstition. Somehow, stating that she didn't believe in anything would make her feel less of a person - although, the majority of the time, incomplete was precisely how she felt. It was the same superstition that had persuaded her to have Judy baptised. Although unspoken, she had always presumed Graham held similar views.

"I think I can decide to believe and it will happen."

"Faith isn't like that, Graham!"

"I think it is. It's a bit like love. I decided that I was going to love you -"

"You *decided* to love me?" Aghast, Elaine blinked slowly in protest. She harboured memories of long days and sleepless nights. When they had taken ridiculous risks, pushing all thought of consequences aside. "Don't you remember?"

"How could I forget? But love and lust aren't the same thing. We'd only known each other a couple of months when we decided to get married. We couldn't have known that we truly loved each other, but we made a commitment. It just took a little practice."

Listening to her husband, all of the gestures, the suggestions of closeness and understanding of the past day, melted away. Perhaps it really had just been about the sex as far as he was concerned. Perhaps he thought she'd been that free with everybody! Casting the duvet aside, Elaine launched her legs over the side of the bed.

Graham's expression as she pummelled the pillows was one of bafflement. "I haven't finished…"

"Oh, I think you have." Elaine repositioned them, a fist in the centre of each.

"What are you doing?"

"I've eaten my breakfast, so now I'm going to have a bath. Just like you told me." Brushing past, Elaine caught her husband abruptly with an elbow and snatched her dressing gown from its hook. "And then you're going to take me to the hospital to see our daughter. Remember?"

She bolted the bathroom door, saw that the seat of the toilet had been left up and slammed it down. After a violent shedding of clothes, Elaine sat and stared trance-like at the heavy flow of water, the rising steam. As the pores of her face opened, her heartbeat returned to normal. She heard Graham's timid knock, his voice drowning in the tides she summoned like Amphitrite with a trailing hand. "Elaine? Have I said something that's upset you?"

Her reply was as cold as the side of the enamel bath on which she perched. "Go away Graham! I've *decided* to hold my tongue. It's just that it's going to take a little *practice*."

CHAPTER TEN

Once the anaesthetic had worn off, Judy was consumed by outrage. Encased in plaster shell, she shared none of the elation that she was alive. Assurances of how 'lucky' she was left her screaming inside, until what was seen by others as ingratitude erupted with venom and spit, in a strangled voice she barely recognised: disagreeable, frightening - "Lucky is winning the lottery. *This* isn't lucky!" - crumbling her mother's features, causing her to excuse herself.

"If only you could have seen -" Her father wore a new expression, but with none of the pity she saw in other people's eyes. "I know!" Rushing from the room, he turned. "Back soon!"

Which left her under the surveillance of grandparents: her grandmother forcing an uncomfortable smile, obliged to comment on the latest bouquet, the inappropriate 'Get Well Soon' cards, when her aunt might visit; her grandfather critical of anyone who would abandon his or her post. Neither of them of more use than a baby bird; blind, open-mouthed and waiting to be fed.

A little over an hour later, after ushering them out and insisting that he could be trusted with the care of his daughter, Dad showered Judy's hospital bed with a confetti of newspaper clippings. Apparently delighted by his ingenuity, he held them up for her to see, one by one. A hand uncovered; the stillness of the body trapped under the pile of rubble; a corpse being stretchered away; the telephone box dissected by the scaffolding pole.

The bulge of the wall, tearing like a gaping wound...

She recoiled: "This is me?" then forced herself to look closer. Like the aftermath of an earthquake except that, for any other victim, Judy wouldn't have had any difficulty in moving on to the next shot. And yet, on some level, there was a sense that she was simply blinking at images that were already imprinted on her retina, had she chosen to look. "Mum would never have shown me these!"

"She'd agree that you need to appreciate what you've been through. Look how strong you are!"

Strong? Her heavily medicated body was held together with pins and plaster. Like a papier mache covered balloon, the original outline intact, but with no substance inside. Nothing, that is, except pulp and pain.

Nodding, Dad presented her with further proof: a picture of her mother collapsed in a gutter like a drunk, legs splayed. Something tried to exert itself - a dream-like memory, so vague and unformed that it might have been from a former life, or from the womb. And suddenly Judy's anger found its focus.

A nurse poked her head around the door. "Just thought I'd come to see how you're doing."

"We're fine, thanks to you," her father said, greeting the young woman like an old friend. "And you've had a well-deserved rest, I hope?"

"Three days off doing nothing." The nurse hugged herself. "Bliss! What's that you're looking at?"

"Just a few newspaper clippings."

As she walked into the room, something - the slight squeak of her soles, perhaps - drew Judy's eyes downwards.

Something was curiously familiar.

"You made quite a few headlines, didn't you?" They stood shoulder to shoulder, looking down on her. "Miraculous Escape for Streatham Schoolgirl."

"It sounds as if I was hosed down and set back on my feet." Judy almost choked on the word. *Feet*: checked laces in otherwise sensible white shoes.

"Soon enough, soon enough." Her father's confident laughter took no account of her reality.

Without thinking, Judy opened her mouth and spoke to the nurse: "Why did you bother? You said it yourself. In my place, you'd rather they had let you die."

Dad gave his disappointed look - as if she were all of five - and then turned to the nurse apologetically.

Her look falling between astonishment and embarrassment at having been caught out, the young woman asked, "When?" She took a couple of timid steps towards the bed.

"In the operating theatre!"

"I was there but -" A nervous twitch, hesitation. An unconvincing laugh. "You were unconscious."

"You were wearing those same shoes," Judy insisted. "I recognise the laces."

The nurse looked down at her footwear, unspeaking, blinking, until Dad volunteered, "I expect they're the fashion. They probably sell them everywhere."

But Judy could tell from the nurse's pale gaze that the shoelaces were important. Her small rebellion against uniform. Something that, perhaps, others failed to notice.

"Sorry to interrupt." The voice from the door was businesslike, abrupt. "Sal, you're needed."

Judy had rarely seen someone so relieved at being granted an opportunity for escape, but she also saw the nurse look at her with troubled eyes through the wired glass pane, neck straining even as she hurried away. What was she so afraid of? Did *thinking* qualify as a breach of those oaths to preserve life? Besides, it wasn't as if Judy had criticised her. Given the choice, she wouldn't have come back.

It was then that Judy experienced a distinct memory of looking down from ceiling height at the body on the operating theatre: *impossible*.

"Are you alright, love?" her father was asking.

This couldn't have happened. But it *felt* so real. "Yes. Fine." She wanted to distance herself from the image. Push it away.

"I think I should call someone. You look very pale."

"I *said* I'm fine."

"Perhaps this wasn't such a good idea." He started to gather the clippings up. "I'll put these in a scrapbook. We can take another look when you're ready."

It was beyond the same wired glass some weeks later that Judy's prognosis was played out, a silent movie, the doctor assuming the role of villain. She watched her mother's hands shoot up to stifle a gasp; downcast eyes, lashes flickering; her father's strong arm providing a crutch. Lips moving to a heavily-chorded piano accompaniment. The helping hand that cupped her mother's stricken face. Close up. Cut to text:

**"Don't let her see you like this.
Chin up, now."**

Brave words followed. The breezy, "Let's get you home," and the welcome banner strung from her parents' bedroom window; extravagant red letters painted on Egyptian cotton. A neighbour standing on the pavement, holding a helium balloon, as Judy was carried from the ambulance. Thank God it was only Mrs Webber and not her son, Tommy. That really would have been the ultimate humiliation.

Running ahead on the staircase, her mother babbled, apparently unable to contain herself. "We had a long debate whether to have you upstairs or down. But, in the end, we thought up. That way you can have a bit more privacy."

Only Dad's cheerfulness seemed genuine. Not the Ugly Sister's crudely painted smile, but his own self. If anything, hanging stiffly in white armour from her father's neck as he negotiated the halfway landing, Judy detected a quiet confidence: something that didn't need to seek refuge behind a waterfall of words.

She saw the marks on the doorframe where she had stood, arms tightly by her sides, chin thrust as high as it would go, while her mother measured her. Every one of them a lie.

"Stand up straight, Judy!"

"I *am* straight," she'd insisted, head pressed uncomfortably against the door frame.

Two lines appeared between Mummy's brows as the parenting manual was consulted again. "Never mind." Her smile quivered. "We'll feed you up and try again next week."

Standing on tiptoes had become routine: the pretence of perfection. Now, there could be no more pretence. Delivered to the room that had been hers for as long as she could remember, Judy's initial view was of her dressing table, her rite of passage on becoming a teenager. She had stuck postcards and photographs in the frame of the mirror, decorated it with the long strand of plastic beads and the pink feather boa she had worn to a fancy dress party. A collage of items she had thought described someone on the brink of a dazzling future, never imagining...

Equipment shouted *'Invalid!'* at Judy. Clinical-looking, height adjustable, wheeled. "What's that?" she protested in horror as Dad manoeuvred alongside the hospital bed. Another one of those awful thin mattresses.

"Something to make you more comfortable," he said,

fitting the fretwork frame over her torso and making a tent of the sheets. "It's only temporary. Don't worry. We haven't got rid of your old one." All this was to him was a family camping expedition!

Soon, a ring at the doorbell; footsteps thundering upstairs in the way hers used to.

"Sur-pri-ise!" Debbie clung to the doorframe, her excited expression cracking. Her approach was timid, wide eyes straying from the plumped-up pillows, surveying Judy's exaggerated form. Judy foresaw a lifetime of people peering down at her. *Just call me Quasimodo and have done with it,* she thought, making an equally careful study of her friend. Although Debbie inscribed promises of eternal friendship on plaster casts, her eyes pleaded for rescue. When the opportunity arose - the 'Please can I get down from the table' moment that took the form of Mum's offer of tea - Judy let her off the hook.

"Another time. I'm tired."

"You should have said!" Jumping from the bed, Debbie executed a landing Nadia Comaneci would have been proud of. "I'll see you soon, yeah?"

"Does it look like I'm going anywhere?" Carefully controlled, the words were no more scornful or scathing than the average teenage girl's.

"You have wheels," Debbie said in a strangled sing-song voice. "I could always kidnap you."

"Next time, bring some of the girls." Judy overheard her mother ushering Debbie out. "We'll have a little homecoming party."

Moments later, Mum perched nervously on the side of the mattress. "Wasn't it nice of Debbie to welcome you home?"

"Nice?" she snapped. "You should have seen how she looked at me! I thought she might be able to see through all..." It was all that Judy could do to nod her chin at the expanse of sheeting. "This!"

Her mother patted the metal framework in the approximate place she might have been expected to find a knee. "Give her a chance, love. We all have to adapt."

"It's not as if I have any choice!"

"None of us do." Her mother stood up and crossed her arms, her voice having toughened. "We're all in this together." Then she turned and left the room.

"That's not true!" Judy yelled after her, voice splintering. "You have the option of walking away!"

The footsteps paused. The reply was flat. "Only as far as the kitchen."

Events were evidently relayed to her father, who held Judy's hand recommending patience.

"Stop trying to be nice! I saw the doctor telling you I'm not going to walk again!"

His slow nod confirmed what, so far, no one had actually had the guts to say.

"When were you and Mum going to tell me, exactly?" she demanded.

"We weren't trying to hide anything. We wanted to get you away from that sort of negative attitude. Now" - he locked eyes with her - "you're going to prove them wrong."

Judy turned away from his certainty to face the wall.

"I mean it, Judy. Think of your plaster cast as a chrysalis. Every day you're getting stronger. Soon, it will be time for the butterfly to emerge."

He would have sat there all night if she hadn't promised to try.

"You won't just try. I know you: you'll do it."

Stoppers and tubes blocking its path... a crushing weight on her chest... her flickering eyelashes providing an image coming into focus...

"Shhhh, shhhh, darling." Judy gasped at the cool touch of

her mother's hand on her forehead.

Her heart was thumping wildly. "I saw…"

"It's all over now. It was only a dream."

She might have been awake, but the nightmarish fear still gripped her, the sense that something nameless - nothing as specific as the Yorkshire Ripper or Fuseli's goblin - had been interrupted. The essence of evil. And she was trapped under her metal fretwork, encased in plaster, with no prospect of escape. "Can you turn on the light?" But the dusky halo of half-light from the bedside table threw demon-shaped shadows into corners. "The main light," Judy pleaded.

"Do you want me to check under the bed for monsters?"

Not monsters: the devil. *But you can't believe in the devil unless you believe in God, can you?*

Mum was down on her knees, her head low. "You know, I haven't done this for you since you were five. Nothing but an odd sock down here. Oh, and look at this! My nail varnish. I wondered where that had got to."

The clock merciless, what Judy came to think of as 'time-lapses' weren't immediately apparent. She lost chunks of time. Sometimes minutes. Sometimes hours. Staring, fixated on some small object. 'Meditating', Dad called it. "And she's back with us," he'd declare. What disturbed Judy the most was that it was possible to be awake and for her mind to be completely blank. When she complained, the doctors blamed the drugs and reduced her dose until the pain soared to a level where she agreed that blankness was preferable.

Never entirely comfortable in London, her grandparents announced their return to Berkshire. ("Be patient with yourself," Grandma had said, irritatingly well-meaning. "The dogs will be glad to see me," her grandfather had said.) Judy thought it would be a relief not to have to make an effort anymore, but found she was anxious to be on her own, even in a familiar room with her mother crashing about downstairs in the kitchen. Comings and goings of neighbours and friends frittered until homework became the only regular arrival. Judy had never taken a great interest in learning for its own sake. School was the place she gossiped, pouted and preened, learning the complex rules of being a teenager. Education was a side-effect (often faked, albeit so convincingly that Judy scraped an occasional 'A'). Now there were chapters to be read and essays to be written with none of the compensatory carrots. Nothing came easily. She had to wait for shapes to take recognisable forms. Sometimes they cooperated, sometimes they were stubborn. She read the foreign-looking combinations of letters she'd managed to write out loud, wondering if she had created new words. Mum's slight sigh as she returned exercise books betrayed her systematic checking of grades. Unaccustomed to disappointment, her learning curve was going to have to be steep.

"Really, what's the point? I'm never going to be the next Stephen Hawking."

For the girl who had wanted a lock on her bedroom door, Judy lost her hour of privacy in the bathroom where she used to retreat underwater, enjoying the soft sensation of hair floating around her face. Blowing iridescent bubbles through the 'O' of her index finger and thumb. Learning to love the emerging contours of her slick seal-like body. The rise of her subtly freckled breasts. The inside-out knot of her belly button that seemed to still be connected to something deep within her. The flatness of her stomach. The pleasing coarseness of her pubic hair. The indentations of each rib where her skeleton, dangerously close to the surface, left no scope for conjecture that she was constructed of anything but skin and bone. Judy had always known herself to be fragile.

And then came the day for the plaster to be prised away. Before leaving for work, Dad whispered secretively, "I'll look forward to seeing my butterfly this evening." Even at the hospital, some cheerful soul remarked, "It'll be a relief to get this off." Assured the oscillating saw wouldn't touch her, she experienced a memory of the sound as the doctor smiled and said, "The moment of truth." Hair ripped out by the roots, an intake of breath later and, as dark glances were exchanged, Judy watched her mother step backwards. Her core was utterly exposed, no longer slick and seal-like, but shivering, naked, marked. She didn't need to look: the horror she provoked was palpable.

"Cover me up. I don't want anyone else to see," Judy said with her only child's fear of imperfection. "Not even Dad."

"Whatever you think is best."

"Promise!"

And, smile quivering, Mum had seemed only too happy to comply, replacing plaster casts with overlapping white cotton: baby clothes in adult sizes.

Her winter limbs were massaged, legs straightened, wrists flexed, ankles revolved, as if she were a working model; a prototype that would ultimately be rejected. "Good," they told her, and, "Excellent progress." But there was never any pretence that their intention was to get her back on her feet. And because there was no pretence, Judy had no expectations of what they called Passive Joint Mobilisations. They tried to engage her with talk of ball and socket joints; pivot joints. Phrases like Muscle Atrophy and Decreased Muscle Torque seemed to have been designed to float in the air above her. It was better she didn't understand what she'd lost.

But worse was to come.

"I don't want it," she said of the wheelchair they presented her with.

"It's not for you. It's for your parents."

"How is it for them, exactly?"

"We need to plan for the longer term. They can't be

expected to lift you. And if you're to stay up here, we'll need to install a stair lift."

Total humiliation. Her mother even knew when she was having her period before she did. Judy would be frowned at for spoiling another good pair of knickers - as if she'd had any choice. And, if that wasn't undignified enough, there were the questions. Hadn't she finished yet? Didn't she think she ought to have a fresh sanitary towel? Did her bot-bot need wiping?

"For Christ's sake, Mum!" Judy exploded with frustration. "Enough of the fucking baby language! Can't you just call an arse an arse?"

Covering her face, as if she'd already been on the brink of tears, her mother ran from the bathroom.

"Mum!" Judy yelled after her, impatiently at first, then, realising how utterly dependant she was, calling, "Can you come and help me? I'm getting cold." And finally, stranded and in desperation, "I'm sorry I swore. It's just that I hate… feeling so useless."

Sniffing, brisk and unrepentant, Mum reappeared. "You know something? Given the choice, I wouldn't have to do this either. I thought I was done with it years ago. But we're -" and she scrunched her lips together, her disgust only too apparent "- stuck with each other."

"And whose fault is that?" Judy retaliated. "I was more than happy to go. It was you who begged me not to!"

"Calm down, darling," her mother said, her eyes suddenly quite dry. "What do you mean?"

But Judy couldn't explain her outburst. She had a sense of something just out of her grasp. Images that made no sense. A diving board? A pool?

Before the wall came down, Judy had felt closer to her mother than her father, but enforced captivity, this burden of secrecy, had driven a wedge between them. Daughter became aware she was occupying her mother's sacred space. The house - the so-called family home - was essentially Mum's private retreat. Judy was using up too much oxygen, leaving her mother gasping at the windows and the back door, like a fish at the water's surface.

The front door slammed.

"That's your father. Let's get you back to bed. He'll be up to see you soon."

Elaine found Judy particularly passive as she manoeuvred her between bathroom and bedroom, allowing herself to be tucked in, the sheets smoothed, her arms folded across her chest. Preoccupied, she acknowledged the coldness of her daughter's skin; wondered if she'd acted irresponsibly. On reaching the door, she turned back to Judy, feeling something more ought to be said: "We'll talk. Later."

Graham turned while Elaine's hands were sliding down the banister: "How did today go?" No longer the, "Have I got time to watch the news before dinner?"

She tolerated what had become daily enquiries, reporting how Judy had tried some homemade celery soup, leaving out the telephone call with her sister, Liz - who, by the way, Elaine felt she was entitled to slightly more in the way of support from and who had sympathetically listed all of the things that they could no longer do as a family - *as if she needed them to be pointed out* - which had been followed by the horrible exchange in the bathroom.

"And how about you?"

"Me?" There was no logical reason why his question should fuel Elaine's slow-bubbling fury, but something inside her snapped. "Do you really want to know how I am?" Not even her tightly-folded arms could contain the truth. "I feel trapped. Trapped!"

Instead of leaping in with words of comfort, Graham nodded, frowning in agreement.

"This is no life, Graham. And I know it's not Judy's fault,

but I'm beginning to hold it against her! I'm scared that, if I carry on like this much longer, I'll start to hate her." Ashamed of her outburst, she lowered her eyes. Three solid months of nursing was all it had taken for Elaine to go from blaming herself to blaming Judy for what her life had become. Still more shocking was the realisation that she didn't want to retract the words. If Graham had said, 'You don't mean that,' Elaine would have wept. But she would also have replied, 'I do. I really do.'

"Come here." In spite of the accumulation of stale cigarette smoke from office and train, Elaine allowed Graham to gather her to his shoulder, her forehead to rest against the padding of his suit. "You're exhausted."

She closed her eyes, hoping to ease the pain behind them, but experienced the uncanny feeling that they remained open, staring. She felt so exhausted it was as if she were being turned inside out, like a pair of socks. Never had she felt less maternal: her well of unconditional love was dry.

Graham was speaking over her shoulder. "I'll ask for a couple of days off. Why don't you get away? Visit your sister."

For an instant, the proposition sounded viable. Then - *Cover me up. I don't want anyone else to see* - it shrivelled like a crisp packet in the flames. "I can't," Elaine said, her tone flat.

"I don't see why not. We're a team."

She pushed away from him. "It's not just the cooking and the cleaning, Graham! What about bath time, and dressing? And who's going to take Judy to the toilet?"

"I…"

"She's not a child anymore! Think about it."

Graham closed his mouth, breathed out through his nose. "You're right. I can't think who'd be more embarrassed."

"You haven't seen your daughter naked since she was a baby."

"She was three!" he said, smiling. "We bought a paddling

pool, remember? Judy was so excited she came running out of the back door completely starkers…"

Recalling several shrieking circuits of the garden while the two adults gave slow-motion chase, despite herself, Elaine managed a pained laugh. "Even when I caught up with her, I couldn't persuade her to put her swimming costume on."

They held onto each other again, Graham with his chin on the top of her head. She could feel the movement of his jaw as he spoke. "We could always invite Liz to stay with us."

"What, with her two little ones and the dog? We couldn't cope. Where would they all sleep?" But Elaine was glad: glad there was an excuse that made an extended invitation point-less. Besides, if Liz had wanted to visit, she would have invited herself. She would have found a way.

"Well, it must be possible for you to escape for a few hours. I know it wouldn't be much, but you could at least go to the library… Take a walk in the park… Buy yourself a new dress."

"When would *I* wear a dress?"

"It doesn't have to be shopping. The point is that you have some time to yourself. Alright?"

Elaine nodded, hoping that the offer of a dress hadn't been retracted.

Of course, the time off didn't materialise. Graham was sheepish as he relayed his manager's response. Graham's colleagues had cancelled their holidays to cover his compassionate leave. Now it was their turn.

"I'll find a way to do more," he said.

And Elaine understood - her husband's firm had been surprisingly generous. But the idea of escape - of time to be herself - began to germinate. Elaine fantasised about what she might do with a couple of hours' freedom. And returning library books was not what sprang to mind.

CHAPTER ELEVEN

"How's my Miracle Girl?" Judy's father now paid her a visit soon after he arrived home from work, launching into his daily commentary. Strange that Dad, whom she had always considered slightly out of step with reality, became her window to the outside world. The Falklands War. The Queen waking to find a stranger perched on the end of her bed, asking for a cigarette, "as if it was completely normal." He described roadworks clogging up the High Street, advertising boards with misplaced apostrophes, and bright slithers of waxing crescent moon. Best of all, after she told him he had given her more ink cartridges and chewing gum than she could use in a lifetime, began the strange and wonderful offerings. First, a brick. It seemed to fascinate him as he used the sleeve of his jacket to sweep imaginary house dust from Judy's bedside table, and then position it carefully (where it soon accumulated a halo of brick dust), announcing, "Rescued from your wall! Look: the graffiti artist even wrote a 'J' for Judy."

Seeing it, Mum gasped. "What's that doing there?"

"It's being a brick."

"Very funny, young lady. I meant what's it doing in the house?"

"Don't look at me!" But when Elaine's hand inched closer

as if she was about to remove it, Judy begged, "Leave it. Please."

It was a brick like any other but, gradually, it revealed particular characteristics: its ridges; constellations of pock-marks; crumbling corners. An object is always more than the thing itself. Just as fragments of the Berlin Wall would come to represent freedom, the brick became symbolic of her father's faith in her.

Judy was not aware that it was also the first building block in the wall between her parents. Had she been awake later that night, she might have heard her mother hiss behind the closed bedroom door. "How could you have brought that thing into the house?"

"It's part of Judy's history."

"Part of the wall that crushed her!" Elaine needed distance from the memory, firmly believing that Judy's needs mirrored her own.

"And I thought she might be able to face a small part of it."

"First those newspaper articles and now this! You know she's been having night terrors, don't you?"

"I…"

"The difference between us is that you didn't see what I saw. You weren't there!" Neither had Graham seen her poor baby bird emerge from the plaster casts, but telling him now would mean breaking her promise.

"Judy remembers things," her husband was saying. "Things I'm not sure she should be able to remember."

"What do you mean?"

"Things that happened while she was unconscious."

"What kind of things?"

"The shoelaces a nurse was wearing during surgery. The layout of the waiting room."

Elaine experienced a sudden chill. *I was happy to go.* "She's confused," she said to convince herself, as if that might some-how make it true. "The doctors said we could expect it."

Then there was a tiny bottle of Holy Water. "I had to go straight to the top for this," Dad beamed. "Blessed by the Pope, no less."

"You've been to Rome?" Judy looked at it dubiously, as if it were a urine sample and, as she did so, she saw that the plastic was embossed with an image of the Virgin Mary.

"Not quite: Canterbury. I heard about John Paul's visit on the news but I'm still not entirely sure how I ended up there. We crowded into the narrow maze of streets waiting for his helicopter. And to hear him speak! I'm not sure I've ever been in the presence of holiness before."

"Why the Pope? We're not Catholics."

"It's funny you should mention that." And Judy listened open-mouthed as her father spoke about the hour he spent in the hospital chapel, understanding that *this was the reason for his newfound certainty.* When he described his calm as the nun prayed with him, she was spooked by several overlapping thoughts: What if her father broke his promise? Would she be trapped forever *like this?* What if she could improve?

"But you haven't kept your side of the bargain!"

His voice was low with the sound of defeat as he said, "I've been trying to convince your mother. If I'm honest, it's something I hoped we'd do as a family."

Why didn't he appreciate the need for urgency? "You should do it. If that's what you believe happened."

"You'd support me?"

"Definitely." Judy twisted the blue lid of the small bottle. "What am I supposed to do with this?"

"Whatever feels right." He ruffled her hair, sounding light-headed.

She would ration it, she decided: one drop, three times a day - until her father kept his promise.

"That'll keep your monsters at bay," Mum said sceptically when she came to make her routine checks under the bed and in the wardrobe. But when she'd gone, using her finger as a stopper, Judy upended the bottle and brought a drop of liquid to her tongue.

Graham smuggled contraband from McDonalds underneath his overcoat: "Don't tell your mother."

He brought gossip pages salvaged from trains, papers that had travelled further than Judy could hope to. Images of a large eyed and platinum-blonde Paula Yates, and a figure in dreadlocks and heavily made-up eyes under plucked brows.

"What's *that*?" Graham asked.

"*He's* Boy George."

"It's wearing a dress."

"Dad, you're such a hypocrite!"

"I am not!"

"No? What about that album by David Bowie you have?"

"Must be your mother's," he said, winking at her.

English strawberries, sweet-smelling, dimpled and stalked. "The first of the season are always the best. Oh, now don't..." Dad had always hated the sight of tears. "What is it?"

"Nothing. Except that it's summer. I've spent six months of my life in bed!"

"Come on," he said decisively.

"What are you doing?" she squealed, as he scooped her up.

"We're going downstairs. Not much of an adventure. Just a break from the same four walls."

As Graham deposited her on the sofa, he silenced her mother's protests, saying, "And a bit of..." He squinted in the direction of the television set to see a fat balding man and a thin man with folded arms facing each other across a table. "Whatever this nonsense is?"

"*Alas Smith and Jones.*"

Forehead duly kissed, Judy was briefly human again, sitting next to her father who laughed a little too loudly, feet on the coffee table. Mum said nothing other than, "Up," as she wedged the *Radio Times* underneath and tucked Judy's tracksuit bottoms safely inside her socks with a, "Don't want you getting cold." Then, retreating, she sulked from the safety of the two-seater, furious to have been overruled on What was Best for her Daughter. *Her* chosen *Mastermind* subject: not Graham's.

"We've got to get her back to school," Judy heard her father say from the landing. These days, her bedroom door was only closed when something was being said that they didn't want her to hear, the lowering of voices a clear indication that it was time to tune in.

"They won't take her unless she can walk. And you heard what the doctors said, Graham!"

"I don't understand why you're so willing to accept it."

"I'd like you to meet Yvonne," her father announced, standing back and holding Judy's bedroom door open. "She's going to get you back on your feet."

"Hello, Judy."

There had been no warning. Judy scowled, unimpressed. Where Dad had dug this dwarf-like woman with her small crooked smile up from, she didn't know!

"Well." He turned from one of them to the other, rubbing his palms together. "I'll leave you two to get acquainted."

"OK." The door closed, Yvonne dispensed with the small-talk. "First things first: we work on your breathing. The best way to make sure you're breathing properly is to sing. Try singing while you're holding your breath: it won't work."

There was no pity, no interest in Judy or her medical history; no promises. "I thought you were here to teach me to walk!"

Yvonne narrowed her eyes. "Sarcasm's good. I can work with that. Now, give me your best Julie Andrews."

"Listen, you can forget it -"

"No! You listen to me! Your recovery won't be a miracle, Judy. It's going to hurt. More than you can ever remember hurting before. In fact, if you think you already know about pain, you're wrong. You'll want to give up, but I'm not going to let you."

Judy opened her mouth to speak.

"'Why?' you ask. Because I know you can take it. I had to."

She closed her mouth, her eyes falling on Yvonne's curved spine.

"But before you can learn to walk, you need to learn how to breathe properly."

"I *know* how to breathe."

"You only think you do." And Yvonne had started her rendition of *My Favourite Things* from *The Sound of Music*, so loudly and out of tune that Judy hadn't been afraid to risk damaging her vocal chords - if only to drown the racket out.

"Good! Tomorrow we start the real work. My place. Be on time."

"Smiling makes you stronger," Yvonne said, drawing on one of the mantras she would demand Judy chanted over the coming weeks. "Say after me," she insisted as Judy stood between the parallel bars, weight supported on her wasted arms, waiting for her blood to settle. "My name is Judy and I can walk."

"I can't," she wailed, legs weak with the effort of simply holding herself upright.

"Yes you can! Remember what we said about breathing?"

"We breathe through the pain." Somehow these words seemed to have a power of their own. She breathed. Forced herself to sing a single line. The pain became slightly more bearable.

"Now, say it with me: *My name is Judy and I can walk.* Come on!"

"My name is Judy and I can walk," Judy said feebly.

"Like you mean it!"

"This feels stupid!" The newspaper her father was pretending to read shook. Yvonne simply looked at her as if she was having a childish tahtrum. "OK, OK! My name is Judy and I can walk."

"Better! Now do it: I want one step on the 'name' and another on the 'I'"

Judy saw that her father's hands were fists as they clutched the pages. It was the closest he'd ever come to cheering on a son on the lines of a football field.

"My *name* -"

"Good!"

"- is Judy and *I* -"

When Judy fell heavily and shouted in frustration, "Fucking wall!" her father's protest was vocal, but Yvonne shouted, "Excellent! Let's use that energy," grabbing her elbow, stirring the air with her spare hand. "*Fuck* the wall. *Fuck* the wall…"

"I won't go to see her again!" Judy shouted in frustration as Graham deposited her on her bed. "I hate her!"

"Hate's a strong word for someone you've only met twice," he said. "But love her or hate her, that woman is going to get you walking. And, by the way, I won't have you using the F-word in this house."

Graham hadn't felt so drained since Judy was a tiny baby, but then the tiredness had been cause for celebration. Turning over in bed to find his tiny daughter suckling at Elaine's breast had filled him with a joy he'd never known before. He remembered revelling: 'This is why we're here. This is what it's all about.' Take care of them both he would, his resolve strengthened. But, closing the door, he felt every inch as mean as when he removed the stabilisers from Judy's first bike and stood by as she fell, time and time again. Let her take it out on him. After everything she'd been through, a punchbag was the least he could offer.

"I hate you! I hate you!"

Standing outside the closed bedroom door, one hand on the frame, Graham absorbed each cry of frustration, each blow. "And I love you." He had anticipated tears. Expected anger. Now there were both, by the bucketful.

"Go away! I'm not talking to you!"

"I won't give up on you, Judy. You're going to walk again. And, one day, you'll thank me." There was silence, which he interpreted as an invitation. "You walk and I'll take dancing lessons, is that a deal?"

"I said I'm not *talking* to you!"

No wonder Elaine was at her wits' end. It was hard not to react. In a distant room, *Memories* was playing on a radio. That was when Graham had the idea about the record player. What could be a better use of his rainy-day savings? Placed just out of reach, Judy would have to get out of bed if she wanted to use it. With outstretched arms, he swung on the banisters, bypassing the lower run of the stairs to land with a heavy thud.

"Everything alright up there?" Elaine called out.

Graham put his head round the door to the breakfast room. His wife was behind the ironing board, her hair frizzy from the steam. "Fine."

"I heard shouting."

"Shouting's progress." Graham clapped his hands and rubbed the palms together. "Where's the *Yellow Pages*?"

Elaine frowned. "Cupboard under the telephone. Where it always is."

He returned to the breakfast room, already flicking through its pages. "You know more about chart music than I do. If I was going to buy a record player for my favourite girl, and was thinking of getting a couple of albums, what would you suggest?"

"Well, I suppose something romantic…" Elaine positioned herself behind him as he seated himself at the table. He felt her warm breath on his neck as she folded her arms around his shoulders, while he traced one finger down the listings for 'Hi-fi'. "Some Barbara Streisand, perhaps. Oh, and something to dance to."

"Good thinking!" Graham pressed one of his wife's hands to his lips. Elaine was obviously feeling far more positive about Judy's prospects. "Anything in particular?"

"Mmmm. If I had to choose one, it would be Michael Jackson."

"You think she'd like that?"

"Oh." Elaine nuzzled his collar. "Very much so."

Judy's father staggered through her bedroom door, hunched around and over a large cardboard box containing - as it turned out - not more physio equipment, but a record player: the most generous present she'd ever received.

"And there's more," he announced, leaving the room.

Her mother tutted, always angry with something these days. "You'd have been better off with a radio. I haven't got time to run up the stairs every time you want the record turned over."

"Here we are!" He handed her two LPs her mother might have chosen for herself: *Memories* by Barbara Streisand; Michael Jackson's *Thriller*. Judy would have preferred Yazoo and Tears for Fears. "Wow," she feigned enthusiasm. But, studying the playlist on *Thriller*, Judy realised that, as with all her father's presents, this one had a purpose. He didn't only expect her to walk again: he expected her to dance.

From the confines of her bedroom, Judy heard things that teenagers with more to occupy their time might not have noticed so keenly. Feet that walked away from slammed doors. The occasional squeaking of her parents' bed. *Christ, they were Doing It in the room next door.* Sometimes, the sound of weeping. For the first time, she appreciated the tensions that existed in the house - and her role as their cause.

There was no choice: the level of the holy water dangerously low, if her father was going to delay keeping his side of the bargain Judy would have to fight back. She placed both hands against the brick, her precious talisman, summoning all the strength it possessed, then swung her wasted legs over the side of the bed. Despite eye-watering pain, despite all of the medical opinions - and perhaps in spite of them - Judy hoisted herself to her feet. There were no parallel bars here. No handles to hold on to.

"Come along, Miracle Girl," she said. "If you're who they say you are."

Taking her hand from the bedpost, Judy fixed her eyes on her record player and shuffled, one foot in front of the other, before she fell. She laughed out loud as she heard footsteps come pounding up the stairs: there was no risk of dancing quite yet, but it was a start.

The physio sessions continued; demanding, relentless, but Judy had found her motivation. Yvonne chanted with every shuffling step Judy managed, "My name is Judy and I can walk," until Judy couldn't take a single step without the words forcing themselves inside her head. Until she managed to fit four steps into the phrase and Yvonne was finally satisfied.

They parted, not as friends, but as two people who knew things about each other that they would otherwise go to great lengths to keep hidden: Judy had been crushed by a wall; Yvonne, born with a twisted spine. Both were strong, beating the odds with nothing more than bloody-mindedness, a little encouragement and - as it turned out - singing loudly and out of tune.

CHAPTER TWELVE

Graham had never been a decisive man but today he woke with resolve. Having stalled for over a year, he would stall no more. And, unexpectedly, he had gained an ally. Back on her feet, Judy had offered, "I'll come with you."

Bidding his daughter to stay in the hall, he entered the kitchen to find Elaine trying to hide what could only be his birthday cake. He hated to say it: "We need to talk, love."

She turned and, eyes drifting to his buttoned overcoat, with a laboured movement disproportionate to the task, put the spatula she was holding down: "It looks as if you've made your decision."

Throughout the past year, Graham had battled against his wife's prejudices - opinions his past self had voiced, never anticipating he would enter the debate from a different angle. He had heard echoes of 'old' Graham as Elaine reminded him how the Catholic Church flaunted its wealth whilst those it represented lived in poverty. Who could respect a church that had backed the Inquisition and the Crusades? And what about the Pope's denial of the holocaust? She had ended one tirade, hands on hips. "And what will your mum say?"

Graham had been unable to contain a schoolboy snigger. Elaine looked on open-mouthed, then her former sparkle asserted itself as she lifted her chin and laughed. "It's almost worth considering! Oh God, Graham, you're serious aren't you? You do know you'll have to smear yourself with ashes, don't you?"

"I think that's only once a year."

So far, words had failed to translate into action. Now, Graham simply took his wife's hands in his and studied them. How to explain that he had applied logic all his life and it had failed him? He had to admit that what he was asking her to believe sounded incredible, but miracles were, by their nature, incredible.

Elaine leaned her forehead against his - was it a sign that she was weakening? But she grabbed his arms near the elbows. "I thought you were being brave for my sake!" He took the limp role of the rag-doll while her frustration became a jolting current. "But you thought you knew, right from the beginning!"

The shock therapy proved ineffective. "And I thought you understood: God answered me."

Although this was old ground, again she challenged, "How do you know it wasn't your subconscious telling you what you wanted to hear?"

"Because there was a *change*." He reached out, intending to embrace Elaine. "I know you feel it."

His wife stepped backwards. "Neither of us are the same people we were," she said quietly. "You've found something that makes sense to you and... well, I don't feel as safe in the world as I did before."

Graham looked at his wife, her arms wrapped around her small frame, eyes turned away from him. "We've faced this as a family and come through it. Doesn't that make you feel stronger?"

Elaine pinned her chin to her chest. "No. I've learned things about myself I'd prefer not to know, and it makes me feel very small."

"You're being too hard on yourself. But if that's really how you feel, come with us," Graham appealed, waiting for her to pick up on the plural.

"You know I can't. Go. I won't stop you."

Elaine lifted her eyes to look out of the window, willing her husband to leave so that she could give way to tears. Gulls were lit in bright white against a backdrop of charcoal clouds. She knew that she would only ever see unusual light conditions where Graham saw God, and the thought made her unbearably sad. Did it matter where a husband and wife directed their innermost thoughts? Was a difference of faith enough to rock a steady but unexceptional marriage? One that had seen its share of good times, but mostly the minutiae of intertwined lives and its vicious cycles: meals that took hours to cook and minutes to demolish; the reappearance of the same shirt in the laundry basket that she had ironed only the day before; the dandelion pulled from the path only to be replaced by three of its taller friends. Life was punctuated by the arrival of a dozen roses on Valentine's Day, a homemade card on Mothers' Day, an increasing number of birthday candles, and the annual ritual of unwrapping the Christmas baubles, each with its distinct memory. This was her life. It had been enough. Now she felt it unravelling.

But Graham was still there, battling with his conscience, no doubt. And now Judy was swinging in the doorway. "Dad, are we -?"

"Just a minute, love." Graham's voice was impatient but his eyes didn't stray from her face. "Judy's coming with me."

Though she held herself tall, something inside Elaine's chest plummeted. For an extended moment, all she could do was blink. Then she felt her lips peel apart, astonished breath leave her mouth.

"I haven't…" he backtracked. "She's expressed an interest, that's all."

What teenager *expresses an interest* in going to church?

"Go." She spoke very quietly. Graham reached for the side of her face, just below the cheekbone. She flinched from his touch. "Please. Just…"

Closing her eyes, Elaine experienced a vision of the three of them freewheeling downhill on bicycles: her in front; Judy in the middle; Graham bringing up the rear. With one knee bent, a light touch of the brake, she glanced over her shoulder in time to see Graham overtaking Judy. "Slow down, Graham!" she shouted into the breeze. Thrusting out her right arm in best cycling-proficiency fashion, Elaine angled the handlebars to turn, as the route demanded. But Graham didn't slow down. Instead he took the left fork, forcing Judy to follow one of them or the other.

"Mum?" Judy asked from the kitchen doorway, a single syllable spoken in a small voice, pleading for permission.

What choice did she have but to consent? Judy had been through enough. *Take what you need from my purse.* More than any teenager should have to. *It looks as if we're stuck with each other.* As the one who lacked religious convictions, Elaine decided not to offer counsel or criticism.

"I'm fine," she replied, surprised that her voice didn't quaver with the force of the hot, resentful tears she knew would follow once the door had slammed. "You go with your father."

In the past, having always considered faith to be a private matter, Graham would have been embarrassed to be seen entering a church in broad daylight. Now, with his daughter by his side, he pushed open the heavy oak doors of St Joseph's.

Once inside, the urgency that had carried him there was intimidated by the height of the vaulted stone ceiling and gothic arches. There was nothing of the womb-like quality of the small white chapel where there had been no barriers between God and man. Brasso, wax and incense, damp, ancient and cold, invaded his senses.

He watched Judy shiver slightly as she conducted a similar survey, eyes wandering to the short, guilty queue kneeling outside the confessional, its traffic light system looking as displaced as McDonald's golden arches within medieval city walls. He tucked one of his hands under her elbow. "Good practice, this." He began humming *Here Comes the Bride* as they walked slowly forwards.

She slapped his hand playfully - "Dad!" - and then said more contemplatively, "I don't think I'll ever get married."

"What? And deny me my proudest moment?"

"Don't tell me: you've already written your speech."

"I'm saving up a few stories."

She hated to think. "You do know I'm fourteen?" As she rolled her eyes, they found the crucifix, suspended over the altar by metal chains. Judy felt her skin flush as she continued forwards, taking in the crown of thorns, the raised nails on hands and feet, the ribcage with its weeping gash, the loin-cloth a scant rag. The image was disturbing: not only the depiction of suffering, but the... nakedness. In church. The downcast face with its sorrowful eyes engaged hers. The King of the Jews stripped bare, as fragile as she was; and as human. It's *supposed* to be horrific, Judy told herself - and yet people went about their business in its shadow without an upwards glance.

"I think he's our man." Her father was nodding towards the altar, where a priest was dispersing wisps of fragrant white smoke as he snuffed candles. God had waited a year for Dad to keep his promise but now, having only just arrived, he was pulling back his sleeve to reveal the roman numerals of his watch.

"Worried you're going to miss *Grandstand*?" She intended to surprise as she went to grab his wrist. The macro shock jerked her hand upwards, muscles contracting. Having pulled away sharply, her father was cradling his wrist protectively.

Judy shook her hand as if trying to rid it of something, checked her palm for damage. They found themselves under the glare of a middle-aged woman who, a minute earlier, had been cheerfully replenishing a floral display with lilies. Judy thought it likely that she had sworn.

"Was that your watch?" she hissed disbelievingly, reaching out tentatively to test its strap again.

"Don't!" Graham cautioned, twisting away and then moving his other hand very slowly, making the lightest and briefest contact possible with the metallic wrist band. "Huh! Look at that!" He repeated the action. "Nothing."

Father Patrick rehearsed Sunday's sermon as he prepared for the afternoon's wedding. A poor wedding it would be in Lent. He had always been drawn to the story of Lazarus being raised from the dead, evidence of Jesus's humanity. Lazarus's sisters appeal to Him: "Lord, behold, he whom Thou lovest is sick." But, arriving too late, on seeing his friend - one of the few Jesus is reported to have loved - He weeps openly. A fan of simple language, Father Patrick remembered being taught that 'Jesus wept' is the most perfect sentence in the English language.

Here too, a miracle is performed in front of witnesses: evidence of Jesus's power. He cries with a loud voice, "Lazarus, come forth!" *And he that was dead came forth.*

What Father Patrick likes about the Church calendar is that it brings the New Testament into the present, allowing him to use modern language to tell the story in a way his congregation will understand. Last year's focus was the relationship between Jesus and Lazarus, but talk of love between two men made several members of the congregation uncomfortable. The same people who watched *Morecambe and Wise* tucked up in bed together without a second thought. This year's focus will be 'celebrity'. Lazarus's role as a crowd-pleaser, drawing the hoards to welcome Jesus to His final destination.

Distracted by a voice calling, "Father," he turned to encounter a man, impatient with eagerness, a girl in his shadow. Father Patrick smiled: "What can I do for you?"

"I'm here to become a Catholic."

A slight raise of his eyebrows was the outward sign that Father Patrick was suppressing his tendency towards sarcasm. *Right you are! I'll just grab my magic wand.* "I don't believe I've seen you in church before," was what he said.

His hands occupied, the priest found his wrist being squeezed. "Graham Jones. And this is my daughter. It's our first visit."

Father Patrick smiled vaguely in the girl's direction, adding little to his initial impression of her. "You're very welcome, but I recommend people come to Mass for several Sundays before they take the next step. That usually means joining one of our courses. You'll find leaflets in the porch with the times." Already turning towards the sacristy, his halo slipped in irritation as he heard footsteps echoing in the gaps between his own.

"Actually, I'm keeping a promise." The man was there, alongside him. "One that's long overdue."

Pausing, Father Patrick focused on maintaining a bland and steady smile.

"My daughter had an accident last year. The doctors said she wouldn't make it, but God had other plans."

The silent girl, the priest noted, watched everything in a way he found unsettling. "Plans, you say?" Scratching his chin, he made a mental note to shave before the afternoon's service.

"I sat up all night praying in the hospital chapel and He answered my prayers."

"I'm not disputing what you're telling me, but…" Father Patrick slid his upper lip through his teeth, selecting his words carefully. "Hospital chapels aren't affiliated to any particular religion."

"Perhaps I should explain." The man appeared to be warming to his subject. "A nun told me the story of her own conversion and then prayed with me."

He might have guessed a nun would be at the bottom of this!

"I've always found that prayer was empty before. You see, I was brought up C of E. But this was, I don't know..."

"Different?" Father Patrick suggested as sympathetically as he could while feeling a kind of defeat. He'd always struggled with private prayer, understanding only too well the feeling of futility many of his parishioners described.

"Yes!" The man's countenance was as puppy-like as the pet Labrador, whose demise under the hooves of the rag and bone man's horse had been declared an 'accident' by his father, the self-appointed coroner. The last living and breathing thing the priest had allowed himself to care for.

"It must have been a very emotional experience."

"It was life-changing."

Father Patrick nodded. "Still, I'm going to recommend for you what I recommend for anyone considering questions of faith. Becoming a Catholic is a huge commitment. Think of it as you would marriage."

"Come on, Dad."

"Give me a minute."

Graham felt rejected. He had read that the service of the Easter Vigil was when adults were received into the Church. Having entered a small and surprisingly untidy room ahead, the priest was pulling his white vestments over his head. If a *priest* was reluctant to believe in Judy's miracle, who could he turn to? He silenced his anger with prayer: 'I know the priest is not You.' Then he said loudly enough to be heard: "Lazarus, come forth," and turned from the door towards the main body of the church.

There was a sharp intake of breath behind him, a voice

of genuine wonder. "What made you choose that particular quote?" The priest's hands were still caught up in the garment, his thinning hair dishevelled, a grey shirt and dog-collar revealed.

It was Graham's turn to look at the priest in pity. He was clearly just a man - and not one blessed with a great deal of charisma. "My daughter was brought back from the dead. The local journalists had no trouble understanding that. I thought miracles would be your line of work, but you..."

"Mr... er..."

"Jones. Graham Jones."

Father Patrick was ready to accept that now, in these sophisticated times, perhaps more than ever, people needed a miracle. He could do with one himself. "Mr Jones, I don't mean to sound dismissive. Understandably, the Church approaches these matters with caution. Can I ask what your wife - assuming you have a wife - thinks about all this?"

"My wife believes that doctors saved our daughter. She thinks they prepared us for the worst so that we'd be equipped to deal with whatever happened." The man's expression softened as he smiled at his daughter indulgently. "She believes stubbornness and determination got Judy back on her feet."

The penny dropped: now the priest knew who he had standing in front of him! Both she and her father had been splashed all over the local headlines. This unremarkable teenager was Streatham's very own Miracle Girl. "And you, young lady? You're father's done all the talking so far."

She shrugged. "Why can't it be all of those things?"

Clever answer, he thought: *avoid siding with either parent.* "Well, I'm a firm believer in giving the Almighty a helping hand."

As the girl stepped forward, Father Patrick observed how awkwardly she moved, her back foot trailing. "I have a question, if you don't mind," she said.

"Go ahead, go ahead." The tea brewing for his elevenses would be cold by now in any event.

She turned and looked pointedly at her father, who seemed to grasp something and backed out of the room apologetically. Father Patrick put his own awkwardness down to finding himself alone with someone of the opposite sex who wasn't wearing a habit.

"I want to know what happens when we die."

It was a question that a child of four of five might ask, but clearly this girl wasn't expecting the sort of answer a child of that age would fall for. And if she'd wanted a medical explanation she'd be asking a doctor. Giving the Last Rites, Father Patrick had been close enough - too close in some cases - to the medical side of things to understand that, within ten seconds of the heart stopping, brain activity ceases.

"You were resuscitated, I take it?" he asked.

In the flicker of her eyes he saw the haunted look of those who have known extreme pain, but when the girl spoke it was with typical teenage flippancy. "Brought back from the dead."

"And you had an experience?" he prompted. "A memory of the time in between perhaps?"

She nodded. "Flashes come back to me. Not all at once. I'll be looking at something I know I shouldn't be able to remember. But I can."

"Nothing unpleasant, I hope."

"If anything it was waking up again that was unpleasant. Does that sound mad?"

"Not at all. You're far from being alone. Several parishioners of mine have reported similar experiences."

"And you believed them?"

There was no scientific justification to support their claims and yet, in Father Patrick's line of business, it would be wrong to deny the possibility. "Of course! I know these people. They aren't attention-seekers. Just people who - perhaps like you - fear no one else will."

"You see, I wouldn't. I don't believe in the paranormal."

"Neither do they, I suspect. Most felt that it was a religious experience. Is that how you'd describe it?"

"A light spoke to me." Again the sarcasm, but perhaps it was self-mocking. "Is that religious?"

"Some would say so."

"What would you say?"

He took a moment, chin in hand, as was his habit. Answers that come too easily don't carry the weight of those that appear to have been deliberated. "Let me try to answer your original question with what I believe happens when we die. I believe in the immortal rational soul and that it's this part of us, and this alone, that God created in his image. The soul never loses consciousness because it isn't subject to the weaknesses of the body. And, as the soul never loses consciousness, it would know what is taking place when it is separated from the body. Even after death."

"Sounds about right." She sighed, giving no indication that his answer offered comfort. If anything, it appeared to have presented another problem. "There's no proof for the existence of the soul, is there?"

"Ah! If you're looking for proof, you've come to the wrong place. Here, we take things on faith."

"It seems that's all I can do. Well." He felt as if, having inconvenienced her, he was the one being dismissed. "Thanks. I guess."

"You're very welcome."

CHAPTER THIRTEEN

Judy eyed the netball trophies in the glass-fronted cabinets as they passed through the entrance hall.

"Do you play?" The headmistress enquired.

Athletics. That had been her thing before her boobs arrived. Netball had been the compromise. "I used to," she replied, surprised that, with the sound of her shuffle on the polished lino, she had needed to say this much.

They hadn't examined each other in any detail by that time. Judy had formed a general impression of grey. Now she was aware of the headmistress's eyes creeping down, settling on her feet. "Yes," was all that was said: her assessment a single word.

"You'll play again, soldier." Dad used his best Rallying the Troops voice. The downturn of her mother's eyes suggested strong disagreement.

Seated in the headmistress's office, Judy felt the full impact of Sister Euphemia's stony gaze, exaggerated through bi-focals. "Normally we have a waiting list, but you're in luck: a vacancy has just arisen." She had the appearance of what Judy had come to recognise as a plain-clothes nun (confirmed by a meek secretary who peered through a crack in the door, addressing her as 'Sister'). Her father might have assembled her from his manual for how a headmistress should look: total lack of regard for vanity; hair cropped unflatteringly short; face devoid of make-up; clothes colourless; default expression, a frown. The only adornment she permitted herself was a silver cross of the size Judy had received as a christening gift, a gift she hadn't been allowed to wear 'in case she lost it' and had only been allowed to examine on its stamp-sized cotton wool bedding under careful supervision.

"Well, that's fantastic news, isn't it?" Her father smiled at their good fortune, turning to her mother who sat, apparently paralysed.

"Of course, you've missed a substantial chunk of curriculum." Judy detected blame, as if it had been her choice to lie listlessly in bed for months on end. "I propose we hold you back a year."

Her nostrils prickled. Although it made sense - although she suspected it would be very necessary - it was a further blow to her already scarred confidence. If Judy had been returning to her old school, this would have meant being battery-farmed with girls she and Debbie had looked down their noses at from a vertigo-inducing height: those who wore blue-framed National Health glasses; ankle socks instead of knee-highs shrugged down to look like leg-warmers. At least it was better this way: a new start.

"You'll soon be showing them how it's done," her father told her.

"We'd like you to take the whole of the year you missed," the headmistress clarified, and Judy was aware that she was being addressed directly, as if only she had the capacity to grasp what was being proposed. "The O-Level syllabus is complicated enough. You won't want to be sitting exams without adequate preparation."

Dad shaped his mouth into an objection, suggesting this was not what he had expected. Hands folded in her lap, her mother was passive, just as she'd been since Judy had announced her decision to become a Catholic. The Joneses used to describe themselves as regular church-goers, by which they'd meant Christmases (although Mum stayed behind if the turkey wasn't bound, gagged and under control). And, they had all sat mesmerised by Robert Powell in *Jesus of Nazareth*, Mum commenting that she hadn't seen such blue eyes since Peter O'Toole in *Lawrence of Arabia*. But nothing as simple as religion was the cause of her mother's powerful silence. Sides had been taken and she was making it known that she felt slighted, outnumbered. The more Judy tried to compensate by deferring to her on other mother-daughter matters, the more she felt Mum was shutting her out.

"It's alright, Dad, I'm going to be rusty." Judy summoned a smile, aiming it at the headmistress. "I expect you know what you're talking about."

Instead of reciprocating, she pushed her glasses back up her nose with a deliberate prod, steel-grey irises magnified through the lower portion of her bi-focals. Judy found that she was holding her breath: *All the better for seeing you with.* "I like to think so. We've been doing this for a long time. Still, it's good that we see eye to eye."

There was no feeling of triumph when Judy learned that the place was hers.

On the way back to the car, her mother marched ahead, handbag tight in the crook of her arm, muttering, "Eye to eye! That woman could kill with a single look."

Her father circled Judy with an arm that suggested, *Give her space.* None of them spoke on the drive home, but her mother's silence was by far the loudest.

CHAPTER FOURTEEN

Sister Euphemia walked in shadow towards the sacristy but, on seeing Father Patrick's rotund shape illuminated in the room ahead, she hesitated. Both headmistress and priest had endured a particularly trying encounter with the Parish Council, and she had an early start to look forward to: a breakfast meeting with the working mother of one of her least favourite pupils. She would confirm the accuracy of a considerably less-than-average report and absorb the vitriol that follows when a parent refuses to accept her offspring is anything less than a genius. When Sister Euphemia answered her calling more than forty years ago she had not expected it to transport her from closeted rural Kent back into the world. Sometimes she wondered if she was suited to the life that had been chosen for her. Executing a neat about-turn, the headmistress's rubber-soled shoes betrayed her, shrieking her presence on the polished wooden floor.

"Making your escape, Sister?" Father Patrick was obviously unable to resist this small opportunity to show he had the upper hand, if only temporarily. He often jested that baiting her was his main form of exercise.

"It's been a long evening," she admitted, turning. "I was just..." The circular gesture of her hand trailed (her pupils called it her 'royal wave'), finding only air.

"I understand. You think a few more minutes of my company might push you over the edge."

She sighed, refusing to rise to his provocation.

"What we need is a new chairman: one who's capable of controlling that dreadful Didsbury woman. When she took the argument back to square one, I don't mind admitting I was ready to invent an emergency just to extract myself."

"We all have our own agendas, Father."

"That we do. I just thought we might manage to get to item number two before Mr Mellows returned to the great *Life of Brian* debate. I blame Malcolm Muggeridge. Now he's seen fit to join our team, we can't get off the subject."

"You can quote the parable of the Prodigal Son all you like, Father. You'll never convince Mrs Didsbury that those who turn over a new leaf late in life are entitled to the same reward as those of us who were christened as babies."

"She talks about 'rights!'" He shook his head. "I'm telling you, when I arrive at the Pearly Gates, I won't be at all surprised to find her chanting, 'Muggeridge out!'"

Sister Euphemia didn't share Father Patrick's sense of humour. She looked at him straight-faced, wishing that the priest was less worldly. How could he command the respect of his parishioners if he drank with them? I mean, the man illustrates his sermons with quotations from *Coronation Street*. He was no doubt wondering the opposite of her. How could she expect her pupils to relate to her when she locks herself away behind the convent walls with no interest in the outside world?

"So!" Father Patrick clasped and unclasped his hands. "How's your end holding up?"

She tried to control the flashing of her eyes, mentally flinching from his verbal pinch on the backside.

"What I meant was, has the whole Julie Thompson episode settled down?"

This is a girl's life we're talking about! When the headmistress opened her mouth the words were meek. "There's a good deal of anger. Understandably so. But the decision was made by the Disciplinary Committee, and I must act as if it was mine alone."

"It's a lonely place, the top of the tree."

"All we can do is offer it up."

"Indeed." His demeanour was slightly disappointed, as if he had hoped her to bite at the apple. "Well, I must be getting along myself. I've arranged to meet Mr McCrae in the Three Bells for a swift half. Oh, but wait."

"Father?" She lifted her chin.

"I hear you're to have the pleasure of the Miracle Girl's company in the new term."

Sister Euphemia felt suffocated by her own intake of breath. "I beg your pardon, Father?"

"It's what the local rag has been calling Judy Jones."

Hardly her chosen reading material, but the girl's name... It rang a distant bell. "Perhaps you'll be so good as to expand. I don't have time for gossip."

"Gossip? It made the local news! She survived a wall falling on her. Terrible, it was. The quacks said she wouldn't make it but she proved them wrong. Then they said she wouldn't walk, but she defied them yet again. Her father called it a miracle and the name stuck."

I wish someone would tell me these things! "What does the girl have to say about it?"

"Judy struggles to get a word in edgeways when her father's there. Too enthusiastic for my liking - you know the sort?"

Sister Euphemia gave Father Patrick what she hoped was a thoroughly blank look.

"Anyway," he sighed. "I don't doubt his heart's in the right place, but I worry that she's caught in a tug-of-war."

"In what way?"

"Mrs Jones is more, shall we say, practical than her husband. She was there when Judy was pulled from the rubble." Rather than hand her a copy of the latest press offering, he perched it on a cluttered surface where the headmistress couldn't avoid it. *Miracle Girl's Mother Breaks Silence: Normally press-shy, the mother of Streatham's Miracle Girl broke her refusal to comment to praise the NHS hospital where her daughter was treated. Defending the family's decision not to seek legal re-dress, Elaine Jones, 40, said, "I have nothing but thanks for the doctors and nurses of May Day. Without them I have no doubt that Judy wouldn't be with us today." But, in a separate statement, Mr Jones appeared to disagree, telling of how he felt negative attitudes might have hampered his daughter's recovery had he not removed her from that detrimental environment. Asked to confirm who, in his opinion, was responsible for getting Judy back on her feet, he recommended, "Never underestimate the power of prayer." Meanwhile, Judy (pictured above) prepares for her return to school, telling our reporter, "I can't wait."*

Sister Euphemia prodded her spectacles back up her nose. "Tricky."

"Take Judy under your wing, will you, Sister? She's been through an awful lot."

"She's obviously tough. That should stand her in good stead."

"Hah! Don't be fooled. Underneath she's vulnerable. Who wouldn't struggle to live up to the picture her father paints? She doesn't need to be labelled the Miracle Girl any more than you'll want that sort of association at the convent."

"We'll stamp it out, Father."

"I'm surprised you haven't had that poisonous little weasel of a journalist snooping around. Could I confirm it was a miracle? he wanted to know!"

"Well, Father. Could you?"

As the priest glanced at her, then performed a double-take, Sister Euphemia allowed her mouth to take on the slightest of upward curves.

"Don't joke with me, Sister! It makes me nervous. Mind you, we could have done with a miracle this evening, eh? I thought the meeting would never come to an end." He glanced at his watch. Estimating if he could still make last orders if she left in the next couple of minutes, no doubt! And his yawn wasn't in the least convincing. "Oh, excuse me!"

"It's late, Father and we're both tired."

It was twenty past ten and their working day was over. Father Patrick opened the side door, inclining one hand to usher her out, cheerfully patting the contents of his pockets: jangling; rectangular. After turning the key in the ancient lock, he glanced upwards.

"Not a cloud in the sky. Do you see that, Sister?" He pointed to a line of three bright stars. "The belt of Orion. And just smell that fresh air!"

Sister Euphemia made a reciprocal noise, but inhaled only diesel fumes and a faintly hoppy aroma. Beside her, Father Patrick sang the closing lines from Taps - "From my scouting days" - as he walked among his ex-parishioners, positively patriarchal: "All is well, safely rest." His voice was accompanied by the distant wail of a police siren. "God is nigh."

CHAPTER FIFTEEN

Wistfully, Elaine watched as her daughter studied her new school uniform critically in the hall mirror. There had been countless occasions over the past year when she'd craved solitude, longing for freedoms of old - although, prior to Judy's accident, Elaine would never have referred to her daily routine in such affectionate terms.

Once a fervent women's libber, after Judy had started primary school, a six-month attempt at juggling a job at the local library with doctors' appointments and parents' evenings put paid to that. With renewed enthusiasm for homemaking, she joined the ranks of those who insisted being a mother was The Most Important Job in the World. Rather than storm the stage at the Miss World Contest, Elaine had turned being a housewife into a profession. Her family would enjoy the benefits of home-made bread - although perhaps 'enjoy' was too strong a word.

"What's this?" Judy had asked after Elaine had finally managed to saw through the crust.

"It's lovely home-made bread. Try some."

Her daughter turned up her nose, bottom lip firmly in the 'out' position.

Accustomed to the battle of wills that was teatime, Elaine took up her knife. "Don't be silly. Here, let me cut it into soldiers for you."

But later, Elaine had caught Graham tapping an upended slice against the worktop. "One of your experiments?" he asked.

She stamped her foot on the pedal of the bin and thrust out a hand, yelling, 'Give it here! *What did you do with your day, darling?*" "*I wasted six pigging hours of it cooking for my ungrateful family. What did you do?*"' she'd followed the recipe so precisely, looking forward to that special praise reserved for those who don't feed their families shop-bought plastic. The offending loaf seemed intent on proving her husband right by landing with the force of a brick.

"If it's any consolation, my presentation didn't go down too well either. Let's just write today off and start again tomorrow. Deal?"

So easing up on herself, Elaine wrung small pleasures out of everyday tasks: detouring through the park to monitor the progress of cherry blossom and daffodils on her way to the Co-op; a cup of tea on the patio to admire her handiwork in the garden; singing along to *Steve Wright in the Afternoon* as she steam-ironed cuffs and collars. But now that the house would be hers again, the days ahead looked cavernously empty. The lists of things Elaine had planned to do when she had the time - the thoughts of longed-for escape - were completely forgotten.

Judy was still staring at her reflection as if she might be able to alter some element of it.

"Don't you look smart?" Standing behind Judy, Elaine scanned her daughter's reflected image in the full-length mirror checking that her scars were hidden. Satisfied that Judy was leaving the house looking pristine, Elaine smoothed the shoulders of her blazer.

Judy jumped: one of her time-lapse moments. Then she cringed. "I'll be the only girl with a hemline three inches below her knees."

Elaine knew better than to comment, understanding that, although that was precisely what her daughter had requested, no teenage girl would actually *want* to be seen in something so screamingly unfashionable. "Perhaps I could ask if they'd allow you to wear trousers," she suggested as she handed over Judy's packed lunch.

"Unlikely!" Her daughter scoffed at this. "We have to wear uniform knickers!"

Elaine knew it was the last possible opportunity to voice concern. "Are you sure you're OK with this, love? It's not too late to change your mind."

"Like we agreed." Judy shrugged. "There won't be so much pressure this way."

"Oh, I don't mean being set back a year!" Elaine barked in frustration. Her daughter had never simply repeated lines; had always held opinions of her own. Elaine was concerned that this change was as a result of Judy's church attendance; the repetition of prayers and responses. She now understood the cause of her gut reaction to Graham's *I can choose to believe and it will happen.* What if he chose to believe in something that was flawed? But Elaine had resolved not to pass comment and so she restricted herself to a motherly response, turning her focus to the headmistress. Elaine, who could never be accused of vanity, couldn't believe there was a God who would want to see a woman shorn like a sheep. But more important than outward signs of femininity, she had been keenly aware that the headmistress lacked maternal qualities. Elaine didn't feel optimistic that her daughter would be treated as an individual when such rigid attitudes had been expressed. *Ask not what your school can do for you.* Despite Graham's assertions, Elaine felt that rules should be viewed as a benchmark for good behaviour, flaunted or broken as the need arose. She steam-ironed her voice. "What I mean is that the convent is going to be very different from what you've been used to. Think about it."

"No boys," Judy pretended to lament, although that was the least of her worries. Quite apart from her horror of the scars that covered her legs and torso, the idea that her accident had been a punishment had taken root.

"Not just that. I'm serious, Judy. Daily assemblies, weekly Mass..."

Dismissing her mother's concerns with a simple shrug, Judy talked to her reflection strictly. "It's a better school than Garthside. I think this will be good. And seeing as we're all becoming Catholics -"

"What on *earth* gave you *that* idea?"

She blinked at her horrified mother. "But, I thought you said..." Judy tried to recall the precise words Mum had used: *"I won't try to influence you. Whatever you choose, I'll support you."*

"No, Judy. I deliberately didn't say. Now that you've made your mind up, I'm asking you to respect *my* views. Stop trying to talk me round. Can you do that?"

"Isn't it going to be awkward?"

"I don't see why. You two can go to church while I put the roast on." Judy noticed the return of her mother's mask, the static smile. "Anyway, never mind that now. Today's your special day."

They both recognised that the moment had arrived. As she compressed her packed lunch into a corner of her already full bag, Judy felt a twinge of anxiety. At the same moment, Elaine was remembering the first time she'd delivered her daughter to a new school. Other children had clung to their mother's legs. Howls of "I don't want to!" and "Why do I have to?" as snotty fingers were prised away one by one. Judy had caught a glimpse of a girl hanging upside down from the climbing frame, long hair vertical, grey knickers on display; another crouching to throw a stone onto the hopscotch grid; whirring lengths of skipping ropes. She had trotted off towards them on what Graham referred to as her 'cowboy legs'.

"Don't call them that, Graham!"

"Why not? I love her bandy little legs."

"Haven't you forgotten something?" Elaine called out, following close behind. Judy's warning glare decreed that the playground was not to be invaded by parents. Elaine held up her white flag: the backpack containing the lovingly-made sandwiches, crusts cut off. Judy thrust her arms out as if it was a huge imposition and shrugged the straps onto her shoulders.

"I'll miss you." Elaine trapped her small daughter in rope-like arms, feeling her strong-willed struggle.

Judy had rolled her eyes dramatically, repeating what she, herself, had told her the day before: "It's only a few hours, Mummy!"

Empty-armed and crouching, Elaine blinked unrestrained coal-dust tears. She was barely able to nod when another mum asked laughingly, "Are you alright, love?"

Elaine had wanted so much to say, 'Fine, thank you.' But she'd surrendered with a shake of her head, aware that her tears were not for Judy (who, like the fictional Belinda, would have happily chased lions) but for that other nameless child, who would have been clingy and meant it when he said, 'Thank you, Mummy.'

"Tell you what." The stranger had hooked one hand into the crook of Elaine's arm, and she had allowed herself to be led like a blind person. "You look as if you could do with a cuppa."

Reminded of the kindness of strangers, Elaine realised that a year had passed and she had yet to track down the boy from the estate and return the dusky bobbled cardigan to its owner. An unscheduled snapshot of wall, rubble and dust reinforced her knowledge that the world wasn't a safe place. She grabbed her car keys decisively: "Why don't I give you a lift?"

"I can walk." For Judy, this was a statement of considerable importance.

"I know you can. But let me drive you. Just this once."

Why couldn't her mother see that she needed this? That morning, holding her trophy brick - her lucky charm - Judy had challenged herself to walk in the shadow of what was known locally as the 'new' wall. It was such a small thing to want but, in Judy's mind, it would mark her recovery. And now - on top of everything else that had been stripped away, little by little - Mum wanted to steal her triumph.

Their relationship had become claustrophobic. She'd become an extension of her mother, a spare limb. The time for amputation had arrived, and only one of them was prepared. "You have to let me out on my own sometime," Judy said, negotiating the terms of the compromise as her goal slipped from sight.

"I know I do." Her mother's head dropped to one side. "Just not today."

Judy sighed purposefully. This was blackmail, plain and simple.

"I don't want you to be hounded by reporters on your first day."

"You don't think -?" She was suddenly anxious.

"I don't know, darling. I hope not. I really do." The car keys dangled.

"Fine." Judy caved, seeing the sense in it. Given the possibility. She gave her reflection a final glance. "You can drop me at the end of the road."

Elaine felt weightless. Here was an opportunity to protect her daughter: a gift. This time she wouldn't fail.

CHAPTER SIXTEEN

Miranda Potipher flattened her back against the brick wall, inhaling her first and final cigarette of the morning, hidden from prying eyes in the palm of her hand. Twice now she had scorched her favourite pair of black fingerless gloves. The first day of the new term, she savoured the last few moments of freedom. Using one finger as a bookmark, Miranda reserved her place in *Tess of the D'Urbervilles*, watching the rush spill from the late bus. The huddles of twos and threes embroiled in conspiracy or shrieking greetings in the way that gives teenage girls a bad name: evolution in its worst form. Personally, Miranda rarely felt that level of enthusiasm about seeing anyone. She didn't need anything except her books, her Sony Walkman and the voice of Robert Smith affirming there was one other person on the planet who felt the same way she did. Calculating the latest possible moment before she needed to walk towards the gates, she let the smoking stub of cigarette fall casually to the pavement and folded a stick of gum with geometric precision.

From her vantage point, Miranda watched a car pull up by the kerb and a girl emerge: knees first, a slight stumble. New. The length of her skirt suggested either the religious type or someone who gave fashion the two-fingered salute. Either might be entertaining. The girl turned to retrieve a bag held at arm's length by her slightly desperate-looking mother. (Miranda knew that expression only too well.) There was a disagreement of sorts, negotiation, the handing over of money. Then the girl slammed the car door and hooked the bag over one shoulder. Miranda sympathised. She'd had a run-in with her own mother that morning.

"Wipe that stuff off your face. You're going to school, not one of your *rock* concerts."

"Fine!" Slamming the bathroom door behind her, she spoke to her reflection in the mirror. "But it's *not* rock." Then she'd scrubbed her face until it was featureless.

There was a determination about the girl, but a vulnerability too: the combination irresistible. She glared after the departing vehicle then, using the lamp post for balance, lifted one foot and then the other to shrug her knee-highs down, giving the false impression of sturdy ankles jutting out beneath the hem of her calf-length skirt. Even her new pair of shoes had to be punished, scuffed against the kerb. Eyeing the wall suspiciously, to a degree Miranda approved of, she began her pronounced uphill shuffle.

Miranda gained on her easily. Hands in pockets, overtaking, she deliberately grazed her with an elbow.

"Oi! Watch it, will you!" Having recovered her balance, Judy clocked the dyed black hair, the neat row of studs along the top of the girl's ear, the Dr Martins. Reading danger signs, she attempted to exude confidence. Running wasn't an option.

"I haven't seen you around before." The black-haired girl walked uphill backwards. "You must be new."

Judy narrowed her eyes. "First day."

"Know where you're going?"

An apology was out of the question but Judy hadn't expected friendliness. "2B," she said.

"So!" There was much in the way of slow nodding. "You're the replacement Julie."

"It's Judy, actually."

"Even better. You'll only have to change a few letters."

Struggling to keep up, Judy found herself increasing pace. "I won't be changing my name for anyone."

"You will. Once you hear about her."

Pretending not to be intrigued, Judy shrugged. "What about her?"

"Only that she got kicked out last term because she was pregnant."

At thirteen or fourteen! Perhaps the rumours about convent girls were true.

"Didn't 'reflect well' on the school. And then the bloody hypocrites expect you to believe in the virgin birth! The girls here are angry. They plan to carry on as if you're her."

Judy was still playing catch-up. On the one hand, she resented being used. But perhaps this would be a way to fit in. And maybe this Julie was like the other Judy, the one who was streetwise and more confident than she was.

"Anyway, what's with the limp?"

Distracted by possibilities, Judy looked at her shoes dismissively. "It's nothing. Well, almost nothing. I had an accident. I've been off school for the best part of a year."

"Please!" The black-haired girl shook her clasped hands. "Tell me what kind of accident gets you a whole year off."

Plank and metal. Brickwork. Suffocatingly thick air...

Heart pounding, Judy's breath formed the letter 'h'. "The kind where a wall falls on you," she managed.

The girl laughed.

"Think it's funny?"

"What? You were joking, right?"

The fury that Judy thought she had suppressed returned. "Let me show you just how hysterical it was." Looking the black-haired girl straight in the eye she hitched her skirt up fold by fold, like a Roman blind.

Click, wind.

The girl's eyes dropped, drawn to the marks above Judy's right knee where staples and pins had been removed.

Click, wind.

Judy saw reflected there what she'd seen in the mirror when she had persuaded herself to face the truth: a child's crude drawing of fictional scars, half-remembered images of Frankenstein's monster.

"Shit." The word wasn't spoken with disgust. There was no pity. If anything, the emotion Judy detected was envy. "I guess I'm not going to be able to impress you with my BCG scar."

Click, wind.

Judy released her skirt, self-conscious.

"Are there more like that?" the girl was asking.

She squinted at the spaces between the cars where she could have sworn she'd seen movement. "Put it this way: you won't catch me wearing a bikini."

Appearing to regain control of her eyes, the girl raised them to Judy's face. "You're the Miracle Girl I've read about!"

"That's what my dad insists on telling everyone."

"Unlucky."

Judy couldn't help laughing, but made sure her voice was heavily seasoned with sarcasm. "Most people tell me how lucky I was."

"Let me guess: people who haven't had a wall fall on them."

They had reached the ominous spikes of the iron gates that Judy had only seen in silhouette on the evening of her interview. Someone had run a knitted red hat straight through one.

"Behold, a warning to our enemies! All boys will be beheaded." Extracting a grey ball of gum from her mouth, the girl squashed it deliberately on top of a concrete post which, by its clam-covered appearance, might have been designed exclusively for this purpose. She appeared momentarily distracted by something over Judy's shoulder. "Don't turn around."

"Why?"

Her lips barely moved. "There's a man pointing a camera at you."

Her mother had been right! It dawned on Judy as she cowered that she'd just put on quite a show.

"Let's get you inside."

Stepping within the redbrick embrace of a courtyard, Judy was confronted by a statue of Our Lady standing high above an unenthusiastic fountain, unfortunate in that the trickle appeared to originate from underneath her skirts.

"So here we are. Welcome to Hell." The black-haired girl, who had reached one arm around her shoulder withdrew with a jerk. "Shit!"

"What?"

"Don't tell me you didn't feel that?" She shook her hand as if trying to detach it from her wrist, eyeing Judy disbelievingly. "You just gave me a massive electric shock!"

Thinking back six months to her first visit to St Joseph's, Judy instinctively looked at her palm. "Did I?"

"Good morning, ladies!" A voice said sharply, and Judy tucked her hand away guiltily as if it were something she needed to hide. She twisted round in time to see the headmistress striding towards them, extending one arm to expose her wrist then bending it sharply, bringing her watch into view. "Sailing close to the wind, I see, Miranda. I thought we might have turned over a new leaf for the start of term."

So Miranda was the girl's name. Judy noticed how she automatically straightened her back at the sight of the headmistress. "Just giving our new recruit the grand tour, Sister."

There was history between these two. Perhaps even respect.

"So I see. Socks up, please, Judith." A curt nod of dismissal was aimed in her general direction; eyes appeared to look through her as she blushed furiously. "And Miranda, mind you don't make our new lady late for registration. Excuse me one moment." Raising one hand, the Sister strode out of the gates and sidled between two parked cars. "Young man! Yes, you with the camera! I'm talking to you!"

Having persuaded the journalist to hand over his film, Sister Euphemia curved her mouth into a discreet smile. To be honest, their 'miracle' couldn't have fallen into better hands. Although loath to admit it, she had missed her exchanges with Miranda over the school holidays. This was the girl who stopped after the first line of the Creed. While the rest of those assembled mumbled in unison, this girl made no attempt to move her lips, adopting the stance of an athlete on the podium, listening to the National Anthem. It was impossible to accuse her of lack of respect. Nonetheless the headmistress had pulled Miranda to one side. "A word, if you don't mind. Surely you know the prayer that sets out your belief?"

"Yes, Sister. I know the Creed that sets out the Catholic faith."

"Then I trust we can rely on your participation in future."

"I participate. It's just that I stop after the part I'm comfortable with."

"And what is that?"

"*We believe in one God.*"

"We'll have to build on that. Come to my office after school."

Sister Euphemia wasn't accustomed to debate, but she appreciated rare signs of intelligence.

"Some of our ladies turn away from God during their teens. I see it as my job to steer them back in the right direction."

"Yes, Sister," the girl had replied. "But surely that depends what you mean by 'God'?"

Sister Euphemia found that her hand had reached for the silver cross that nestled in the warm hollow of her neck. "I'm sorry?"

"If you're talking about a white-bearded bloke perched on

a cloud, then I can save you a lot of time by telling you that I rejected him shortly after Father Christmas. But if you're asking me if I accept there's a force in the universe that all other life stemmed from, and you want to call that life-force 'God', only an idiot would reject that."

"That sounds like St Anselm: in order to prove the existence of God, it is firstly necessary to agree on a definition of God."

"I was thinking of Descartes. Either way, it's stating the obvious really."

Sister Euphemia stalled for time, prodding her glasses back up her nose. She had a reader on her hands, one who performed that rare miracle among teenagers of turning thoughts into cohesive sentences.

"It's not that I don't like the words." Miranda had shrugged. "*All things seen and unseen* is pretty powerful as statements go."

Where did that confidence come from? At her age, Sister Euphemia reflected, she'd been afraid to open her mouth, except to agree - strictly on cue. "It's an admission that there are mysteries in the universe we may never understand."

"It's a bit more than that."

"Oh?"

"It's an acknowledgement that there are things out there that are invisible!"

As the girl spoke, the headmistress's childhood fears rose up to choke her: the feeling of being under constant observation; the fear that the presence she sensed was not her guardian angel, but something essentially malicious sent to lure her into temptation.

"You wouldn't read Edgar Allen Poe to a child, but these are the words you'd have them recite."

"Tell me, Miranda. What do you believe in?"

"The power of nature, I suppose. I think nature and God

are the same when it boils down to it. That way, there's no conflict between science and Christianity."

Something rang a bell with the Sister. She recovered her firm voice sufficiently to say, "Your father's the scientist, is he not?"

"That doesn't mean I think like he does, Sister. He has no problem with the whole of the Creed."

They had begged to differ, with the understanding that Miranda would be permitted to express her opinions in R.E. lessons - provided she backed them up with research. And that had been the start. No pupil studied obscure religious texts as fervently as Miranda. But it wasn't a question of competition or keeping score. The girl was on her own truth-seeking mission.

Miranda saluted the grey knitted back of the woman. "You heard what Die Gut Schwester said. We wouldn't want to be late for registration, would we?" Pulling open one of a pair of double doors, she stood back so that Judy had a view of the clinical corridor with its identical cell-like doors. "After you, Julie."

Judy swallowed. "It's Julie Thompson, right?"

"Correct. And that means you'll have to pretend to be my best friend. I explained that, didn't I?"

"No -"

"Stick with me. You'll be fine."

But the girls' attempts to upstage their teacher bounced back on Judy almost immediately. Her idea of arriving with the minimum of fuss and knuckling down to some serious catching up flew straight out of the window.

"Right now, girls. My name is Miss Stubbs."

"Fresh out of teacher training college," Miranda observed, leaning close. "See how she's perched on the corner of her desk? She's listened to all their mumbo-jumbo about not erecting barriers."

"First…" And here Miss Stubbs made an unnecessary rabbit-eared gesture. "The Register."

Miranda cringed: "Mistake number two."

Miss Stubbs's expression suggested she thought it was going swimmingly. Around her, girls sat up straight. Only an insider (or an informed outsider like Judy) would have known their play at attentiveness was a pressure cooker on the boil.

"She won't last the day. See how she does her ticks?"

"No. Someone's head's in the way."

"A short down stroke, then a curve. Like a child. A reminder she's only a few years older than us."

"Judith Jones?"

On automatic pilot, Judy had been about to respond but Miranda put a warning finger on her lips.

Miss Stubbs glanced around the room. "Do we have a Judith in class?"

Judy's heart beat fast. Outwardly, she adopted a poker face, appreciative of being in on the 'in joke'.

Amid a volley of false coughs, an unseen girl volunteered, "It's Julie, Miss."

"We have you down as Judith. Just let me change that for you." Balancing the good book on her knee, she turned to locate a wooden rule, which she used to strike through the supposed error with not one but two heavy lines.

"Not me, Miss. That's Julie over there. But it's not Julie Jones: it's Julie Thompson."

Miss Stubbs turned to Judy and smiled. "Is that right?"

Judy's mouth twitched, reluctant to co-operate. She glanced sideways, away from Miranda's promised protection, to find narrowed eyes hinting at what they might be capable of. Her neck flushed, she nodded compliantly.

The class erupted, an explosion of banging desks and stomping feet.

Talk about reflecting badly. Hauled in front of the

amply-proportioned secretary, Judy was told to explain herself.

"They asked me to play along," she uttered miserably. "It was supposed to be some sort of joke."

To be fair to Miss Stubbs, she attempted to alleviate her agony: "To be fair, it was another girl…"

The register confiscated, Tippex was applied liberally, followed by a noisy stream of hot air. Miss Stubbs made fists as Judy's name was etched crookedly before the liquid had time to set. "You're both new: you don't know the background. It's extremely delicate."

Miss Stubbs held her head up and spoke. "Then, perhaps an," her index and middle fingers formed angry rabbit-ears. "*Explanation* wouldn't have gone amiss. I'm not *psychic*."

Judy recalled Sister Euphemia saying, "Normally we have a waiting list…" Now that she knew why the vacancy had arisen it seemed more like taking advantage of someone else's misfortune than her own good luck. And that couldn't be right.

Having coerced her into humiliating Miss Stubbs, 2B turned their particular brand of venom on Judy, as if she had been personally responsible for Julie's expulsion.

Miranda faced the mob after the bell had rung for first break. "Have you lot got a problem or something?"

"This isn't about her," one of them replied, while the others formed a semicircular wall of heaving hormones. "This is about Julie."

"You could have fooled me," Miranda said. "Because it *looks* as if you've decided to take it out on Judy. And, by the way, while we're at it, do you even know who this is? Tell them, Judy."

Surprised to hear her name spoken - her first victory of the day - Judy decided that she preferred it to her alias. "Judy Jones."

Miranda looked momentarily exasperated, then impressed. She bared her fangs. "Perhaps you've forgotten who the enemy is."

"You should be on our side. Julie was *your* friend."

"She still is," said Miranda, snatching up her bag and grabbing Judy's arm.

"For God's sake!" Judy complained after a few stiff-shuffling paces. "Slow down, will you?"

"Sorry." Miranda let go and Judy saw from her tight-lipped fire-breathing that she was fuming. "That lot didn't even like her. Not one of them's been to see her over the holidays. This is just the latest bandwagon." She paused. "You know what happens when you stick a bunch of girls together, don't you?"

"No." Judy winced her arm back into its socket, something she had learned from those passive manipulations coming in useful at last.

"The question was rhetorical." Looking away, Miranda said, "If you must know, they all end up with PMT at the same time. Something to do with the moon."

"This is the first all-girls school I've been to."

"Yeah?" she scoffed. "I dumped you right in it, didn't I? It seems I didn't quite understand the whole plan. Pack of bitches!"

They had arrived at a small patch of grass behind a wooden annexe. Judy could see a clutter of unvarnished clay pots through the window. "I suppose you're going to tell me they're really nice when you get to know them."

Having thrown herself down on the ground with enviable ease, Miranda picked a fat blade of grass, then split it expertly down the middle. "You've got to be kidding! Give them half a chance and most of them would stab you in the back."

Judy noticed for the first time that, for all her confidence, Miranda looked very much alone. "You stood up to them. Thank you."

"More fool me!" She made her hand gun-shaped, held it to the side of her head and fired.

Knowing sitting was going to hurt, but not how much, Judy took several deep breaths. She dropped her bag, then, flattening her skirt to her sides, slumped down self-consciously.

"Want a fag?" Miranda offered, oblivious to the pain she was in.

"I don't smoke."

"Ever tried?"

"Never wanted to." Judy inhaled the same faint traces of the nicotine stench that permeated her father's work suit. "They stink."

"Fair enough, you don't smoke." Miranda thrust a packet of Wrigley's Doublemint in her direction. "Have something, for God's sake."

The offer of gum could be translated as an offer of friendship between two teenage girls. Amused at the thought of how her dad would react if she asked if she could bring Miranda home for tea, Judy imagined announcing, "She's a goth." Watching the dials of his mind re-tuning, his face taking on the stance of a question mark: *The ancient Teutonic people who overthrew Athens?*

Her mother intervening: "Honestly, Graham, you barely know your Madness from your Motorhead! They're the ones who dress in black."

"As long as she's not one of those punks, I don't care what music she likes."

Would her father be able to tell the difference between punks and goths? Judy wasn't sure she understood it herself.

Laughing, she pulled a stick of gum from the pack.

"What's so funny?"

"I don't know. This! Us!"

Miranda joined her, a single mirthless syllable. "Did you ever play that game where you knelt in a circle, and said in the worst accent you could come up with, 'This is a sad and solemn occasion Sister Mary Immaculate Conception, this is a sad and solemn occasion,' and if you laughed you were out?"

"No," admitted Judy, demoted to outsider quicker than she had hoped.

"I could have won with a Sister Euphemia. Don't look at me like I'm mad! You change the nun's name, you know?"

"Actually," Judy confessed. "This is the first Catholic school I've been to."

"Whoa!" Miranda laughed, then stopped abruptly. "You're joking, right?"

Raising her eyebrows, Judy shook her head slowly.

"How come?"

"We're converts."

"When?"

"Last Easter."

"Now you really are kidding me!"

Again, the slow shake of denial.

"So -" Miranda let out a slow whistle. "You're a believer!"

"Aren't you?" Judy had thought that within the convent walls she might find a few. She lay back, layered hands cupping her head, squinting as she tracked the progress of an aeroplane. Strange how, from down on the ground, something travelling at 500 miles per hour appeared to move so slowly.

"Don't ever get me started on religion." Miranda pressed her thumbs together and, blowing through the blade of grass, produced a note that wouldn't have sounded out of place in any mediocre school orchestra.

"Why not?" The vapour trail from the plane dissected Judy's blue field of vision diagonally, disintegrating gradually until it became woolly-edged.

"It will probably be my downfall. Ultimately, I'm doomed."

"Ultimately, we're all doomed." The trail tailed off in a series of fine cotton wool balls. *And that's how clouds are made*, her father had once told her. At the time it had sounded probable. "Know anything about aeroplanes?"

"Big things with wings?"

"It's weird." Judy nodded. "The fact it's full of people. That's an awful lot of faith to put in one pilot and a machine."

"How that thing stays in the sky is the least of your worries. You're down here on a little planet, gently rotating on its axis, revolving around this big fiery thing called the sun."

The ground beneath Judy's back felt trustworthy, solid. "Still…" But a moment later her brow furrowed. "So what keeps the earth in place?"

"The pull of the sun's gravity. But before gravity was invented, it was all down to that God of yours."

CHAPTER SEVENTEEN

Nursing a cup of Café Hag (could freeze-drying actually make coffee taste like that?), Elaine was struck by the realisation that she was utterly alone. But for the buzz of the fridge, the distant ticking of a clock, the house was silent. The dinner plates were washed and put away, the pile of laundry reduced from leaning tower to manageable height. Graham who, up to this point in their marriage, could have predictably been located snoring in front of the *Nine O'clock News*, was attending one of his church meetings. Judy was up to her neck in an English essay, having rejected Elaine's offer of counsel. *To Kill a Mocking Bird* had been one of her favourites; she knew the background to the civil rights issues her daughter seemed completely ignorant of. Both had outgrown a need for her. Even a request for tea would have been welcome. Elaine remembered Graham's, "When you're making one, I'll have a cuppa," shortly after she entered any room, with surprising nostalgia.

Left with a bewildering choice of four television channels, there was nothing Elaine wanted to watch. Even the adverts were a source of irritation. Those Caledonian girls looked so smug. About to jet off somewhere exotic, with their pristine hair and manicured nails, it was inconceivable that they would understand how it felt to be an abandoned housewife.

Every cell of her being wanted to scream, *What about me?* But the words would echo and reverberate, unheard.

Grateful for the distraction of a small task, Elaine made a glass glove, placing a finger inside the necks of four clinking milk bottles, and stepped outside the front door. She paused at the memory of a pint-sized Judy methodically applying a Hula Hoop to each finger, beaming as she wriggled them aloft for inspection and then biting down on them in strict order. Those had been simple days when everyone knew their roles, Mum bringing up the rear guard in the natural order of priorities.

Elaine had been good at being the mother of a three-year-old, well-versed in the rules of potty-training, mealtimes, naps, bedtime routines. She was an expert at kissing grazed knees better and making fairy tale castles out of the innards of toilet rolls, rendering them with tin foil. Artefacts remained: small bottles of food colouring, icing sugar and silver balls, remnants of rainy afternoons when she and Judy decorated fairy cakes.

"Daddy one." Judy would distribute the fruits of their labours with stained fingertips.

Graham grimaced at the hundreds and thousands in the lurid green icing. "It looks like a Petri dish."

Make-believe had never been Graham's forte. There was something stubborn in him that refused to deny himself, even to please his daughter.

Elaine couldn't bear to throw the contents of her cupboards away, confident that the day would arrive when Judy would hang from the frame of the kitchen door complaining, "I'm bored. Can we make cakes like we used to?"

Her reputation for being able to do everything better than anyone else had remained unblemished until she failed to bring a dead sparrow back to life. Judy had discovered it when retrieving Dolly (who had spent the night camping, dressed

129

only in white knee-length boots and, by rights, should have been suffering from hypothermia) from a flowerbed at the bottom of the garden. Elaine was alerted to impending disaster by Judy's increasingly frustrated demands that it should, "Wake up, birdy, wake up!"

The poor thing was upside down, claws curled inwards in defeat, eyes eaten away (although Judy supposed them closed).

"Wake it up, Mummy." Judy was crouching over the bird, seeming confused that there were things in the universe that didn't jump to her bidding, no matter how much of a hullabaloo she created.

Elaine was nervous about using the word 'dead', but here was an opportunity to explain that all things come to an end. She held out her arms to her daughter. "Leave it alone, darling. The birdy's not going to wake up. He had a nasty accident, but he's not hurting anymore."

"Fix it, Mummy, fix it!" Judy's eyes had taken on that wide-eyed expression with potential to dissolve into panic.

She had no option but to dispel her daughter's unshakable belief in her ability to perform miracles: "I'm sorry, darling, but there are some things Mummy can't fix."

There was no solace when Elaine draped a daisy-chain garland around the bird's neck, wrapped it in tissue, and placed it in a Clarks shoebox. She buried it in a hole in the damp earth, a ceremony that involved respectful whispers. Half an hour later, Elaine found her daughter clawing at the soil, sobs so violent they resembled hiccups. Was that the first time that Judy had felt betrayed by her?

Elaine sighed. What good were memories when she suspected Judy had been too young to remember the long hours spent? Would her daughter have remembered if Elaine had stuck her in a playpen and invited friends over for coffee? It wasn't that she regretted a single moment invested. She had loved their intimacy, thinking the bond they forged unbreakable. Now she doubted her efforts had made the slightest difference.

Elaine stepped forwards onto the garden path, its black and white tiles cold and smooth under her bare feet. She glanced up to see the almost-full moon suspended above the uppermost branches of the unrepentant plane tree - the tree responsible for the demise of the wall that had crushed her daughter's bones. The sight heightened Elaine's sense of yearning: here she was, her life just beginning if the embossed words of birthday cards were to be believed. And yet she felt desolate. She remembered being told how Yuri Gagarin had flown all the way to outer space, only to find God wasn't there after all: just an awful lot of blue. *Let them have their faith*, Elaine thought. *It's one hell of a lot easier than endless emptiness.*

'Little' Tommy Webber startled her as he bounced next door's garden gate off its fixings. "Night, Mrs J." He shuffled to a slack-laced halt in front of the pillars of the adjoining porch.

Elaine wrapped her arms around herself. Remembering him as a seven-year-old knocking on the door to ask for his ball back, she'd made a secret ally by loosening a fence panel that he could push aside whenever he wanted to creep through. Elaine had always hated the "Haven't you grown?" of spinster aunts, but was shocked to find Tommy towering over her, an attractive young man. Swallowing, she located her right hand at the base of her throat, absorbing heat from the surface of her skin. Oh God! Wasn't this what she used to do when flirting? "Tommy!" She lowered her hand, placing it on her hip. "I didn't see you there. How's things?"

"Oh, you know." He threw his head back to rid his eyes of fringe, a source of irritation tolerated, she presumed, for the sake of fashion. "How's Judy getting on?"

Never, 'How are you, Mrs J?' Was she really so insignificant?

She forced a maternal smile, one that took more credit than she felt she deserved. "Really, really well. In fact, she's back at school."

"I saw. It was in the paper, wasn't it?"

She sighed: would they never be left alone? "I suppose it makes a change from all the bad news."

"Page seven. She's slipping."

"Hopefully that'll be the end of it as far as they're concerned."

"Anyway, tell her I said hi." Tommy turned his head in the direction of Elaine's upturned gaze, while fumbling for his front door key. "Full moon?"

Aware she was vulnerable to self-pity, Elaine was glad of the subject change. "Tomorrow, I think."

He grinned. "Did you see *An American Werewolf in London*?"

Elaine feigned shock. "Wasn't that a horror film?"

Hunching his shoulders, Tommy tried to shrug his embarrassment aside. "More of a comedy. It won an Oscar, you know."

Teasing: "All the same, I'm surprised your mother allowed you..."

"I saw it on video at a mate's, OK? Point is, you should stay inside and lock the door."

She was halfway up the path, looking backwards into the Webber's porch, wondering what she could say to prolong the moment. The tone she trusted was strict and functional: "Thank you, Tommy. I'll bear that in mind." But escape rather than safety was what appealed.

Key poised, he grinned over his shoulder, nodding as if his head were spring-loaded: a parcel-shelf dog. "You won't tell on me, will you?"

"Have I ever?" She shook her head. Their laughing exchange had brought an unfamiliar ache to her jaw.

Inside, leaning against the closed front door, facing the stairs, Elaine made her decision. With one hand on the banister, she shouted, "Judy!" From the small halfway landing with its stand for a potted fern (she had seen something similar in *Home and Garden*, but it turned out it was just a bloody nuisance to vacuum round), she shouted again. "Judy!"

No reply - perhaps she'd dozed off - Elaine rapped on her daughter's bedroom door, turned the handle. "Judy, I'm…"

Bedcovers were rearranged in a blur of movement. "Mum!" Her daughter was red-faced, angry.

Immediately defensive, Elaine went on the attack. "Well, I'm sorry, but you didn't reply."

"I didn't hear you. I had headphones on."

"What headphones?" Elaine knew that the question was wrong. Judy was clearly wearing a set round her neck, her hands only too obviously itching to put them back over her ears.

"The ones from the Walkman I borrowed off of Miranda."

Elaine winced, wanting to say, *From*. But she would only make things worse by correcting her daughter. "I didn't realise you'd finished your essay."

"Hours ago!"

"Want me to give it a proofread?"

"Nah. It's fine."

Elaine felt her face drop. She wished she had corrected Judy's English. Then she recalled the blurred movement. "Are you sure that's all you were doing?"

"What do you mean?" Judy asked defiantly.

Elaine closed her eyes and breathed. So what if Judy had been masturbating? It wasn't as if Elaine disapproved. She shook her head, hating the moment, willing it to end. "It doesn't matter. I came to say I'm going for a walk. Will you be alright?"

"Why wouldn't I be?"

"It was a figure of speech," Elaine said, sensing that whatever she said was bound to be wrong. "I won't be long."

"Where are you going?" Judy called her back, appearing smaller and more vulnerable once the bedclothes were pulled up.

"To get some air," Elaine said as she retreated onto the landing. Remembering, she pushed the door open again, noticing that the duvet had been cast aside, the hem of her daughter's skirt hitched up. The eyes that met hers were accusatory. She deliberately ignored them, smiling. "I forgot to tell you, Tommy said hi."

"Tommy?"

"Tommy from next door."

"What did he want?"

Elaine snapped: "He was just being nice! Perhaps you should try it."

Was everything going to be a battle from now on? Elaine asked herself. How was it that she was capable of bruising so easily? She tried to remember similar conversations with her own mother, supposing she must have caused equal levels of hurt in her own war of independence. But there were two daughters - herself and Liz - less opportunity for hand-to-hand combat. Elaine bit her lip and remembered that other child. The one who should have been in the spare room with his music blaring and his football posters. She touched the door on the opposite side of the landing, letting her forehead rest briefly against the paintwork. Her hand lingered on the brass of the door handle, but she knew she couldn't face the disappointment of finding the room empty.

Already, Elaine felt less like going out. Should she apologise? But that would involve intruding again - and the confrontation that would follow. Instead she resolved to do something that was long-overdue. She found the dusky pink cardigan at the bottom of the laundry pile, shook it out, and stepped into her shoes.

Rebelliously, she used the alley at night, alone, the clicking of her heels and their contact with an empty can betraying her presence. She encountered only a ghostly dog-walker, detected by the red glow of a cigarette that moved from hand to mouth level and back again, and whose hound was a damp snuffling around her ankles. Elaine gave the tall thin shadow as wide a berth as the narrow path permitted.

The scene beyond was sterile; the new brick wall straight but for a semicircular portion built to accommodate the bulk of the unforgiven tree. Hesitating outside the pale blue gate of one of the gardens opposite, Elaine couldn't be sure she had the correct house. She had a vivid memory of a red gate.

A woman appeared at the downstairs window, drawing the curtains. She paused, frowned, then disappeared. The front door opened, spilling an elongated rectangle of light onto the path. The woman, her face in shadow, asked nervously, "Anything I can help you with?"

"I was looking…" Feeling rather foolish, Elaine turned to point at the wall.

"We all remember that night, love." The woman stepped forwards, slippers and quilted dressing gown coming into view.

"I think this is yours." Elaine held the dusky pink cardigan at arm's length. "I'm sorry I kept it so long. I've no idea where the last year's gone."

"I always wondered what had happened to you!" Elaine wasn't sure if it was she who was being addressed or the cardigan. It was only after hugging the garment to her chest like an old friend that the woman seemed to look at her. "Come inside."

Elaine's feet were already fighting to retreat. "It's late. I just wanted to say thank you, that's all."

"Say it where I can see you properly." The woman turned, leaving Elaine with little option but to follow. "Kettle's just boiled."

Elaine stepped through the doorway, finding a living room instead of the anticipated hall: a television; a two-seater; an armchair containing abandoned knitting; framed wedding photographs on the mantelpiece; a gas fire. She thought it delightful, this life in miniature, as she might find a dolls' house delightful - although she fretted about the lack of space for bookshelves, and where on earth you would put a Christmas tree?

"Through here, love!"

Elaine closed the front door behind her, took two steps forwards and found herself outside a kitchen.

"Look who it isn't." The woman turned to her husband, who sat polishing his shoes at a small table that was covered with the black and white of yesterday's newspaper.

Elaine thought of all the people she wasn't and would have liked to be.

"Page seven!" The man seemed to take up more than his fair share of available space, leaving his wife pressed against a worktop. "It was your girl, Judy!" he said, tapping a photograph smeared with shoe polish, and looking up at her. "We've kept up to date with her story."

Elaine smiled: strange that these people knew so much about her, when she knew nothing about them. "Please. Call me Elaine."

"I'm John. And you've already met the wife, Paula."

"I wanted to say how grateful I am. I'm just embarrassed it's taken me so long."

"You've had more important things on your mind. Go on, love, take the weight off."

Paula deposited a cup and saucer on the table in front of a spare seat, opposite her husband's. "Milk?"

Alice-like, Elaine edged herself onto the chair. John made no concession to the size of his environment. His arms sawed back and forth with the brush, pausing only while he clouded the sheen with his breath. Reminded of his strength, Elaine realised it was those same arms that had held her back, providing the human contact she needed: physical but not remotely personal. Longing for that same comfort again (there was no attraction, other than to his physicality), Elaine forced herself to say something. "You were so kind," and in case her words might be misconstrued, she directed the accompanying smile at Paula. "Both of you."

"How is she, then?" John asked, pulling Elaine's gaze back to his rolled-up sleeves and the cluttered ginger hair of his forearms. As Elaine hesitated, he zigzagged his head from side to side. "Your Judy."

"I won't say it hasn't been hard this last year, but touch wood." Remembering there was something she should do, Elaine reached underneath the newspaper. Her eyes navigated the width of the table before they found Paula's dressing gown, climbing to safety button by button.

"Formica." Paula was smiling.

"Oh well. We're not in need of so much luck now."

John prompted gently, "So, she's walking, is she?"

"Walking, talking, answering back." Elaine struggled to control her quivering mouth and shape it into something resembling words. She felt a strong desire to look at John, but couldn't trust herself. "Typical teenager, really."

"It's amazing what they can do these days." Paula joined them at the table, slipping quite naturally into her seat. "I don't mind telling you, when I saw them pull her out of the rubble…"

Biting her lip, Elaine let her head drop.

Paula placed a hand on Elaine's forearm, laughing slightly. "Look at that! I've found your pulse. B-boom, b-boom, b-boom."

The moment that followed felt intensely personal, as if they shared a single heartbeat. "Do you have children?" she asked, desperate for distraction.

"Two boys." Paula beamed. "We're grandparents, aren't we, John?"

He laughed his agreement, as if the idea was still a little ridiculous.

Where did you find the space for them? "You don't look nearly old enough."

"Well, if you ladies don't mind, I'll take my tea next door and catch the weather."

As John gathered up the shoe-polishing paraphernalia in a newspaper parcel and deposited the whole thing in a heap by the back door, Paula rolled her eyes as if to say what a terrible inconvenience husbands were, what with their shoes and everything. Over Michael Fish's prophecy of grey skies and drizzle, Paula insisted, "But I want to hear how *you* are."

"Me?" Resisting the temptation to follow John, Elaine forced her focus on Paula with every ounce of concentration she possessed. "I'm fighting fit." The phrase sounded wrong coming from her own mouth; she had so little fight remaining.

"You know, I nursed my mother at home after she'd had her stroke." Paula's frown hinted at painful memories. "I coped with everything she threw at me. Worse than a teenager, she was. I was fine - until the day she went back home. It was only then that I fell apart. I remember staring into the freezers in Bejams, thinking, 'There's nothing here I want to buy.' Next thing I knew I was in a heap on the floor, bawling my eyes out. They asked me to leave - said I was upsetting the other customers!"

"I'm tired, that's all."

Paula looked doubtful. "Don't ignore the warnings. The body finds ways to keep going while it has to, then one day it just shuts down. I don't know how I'd have managed without

John. Is your husband... you know?"

Elaine didn't, so she sipped her tea, waiting.

"Supportive?"

"Actually, my husband's found God." Better to have the conversation with someone they didn't know. That way, there was no question of disloyalty. Besides, Graham hadn't suffered any qualms before appointing himself family spokesperson, without a thought for how she would field the questions the reporters fired at her when she let the man in to read the gas meter: *Mrs Jones, your husband says God answered his prayers. Is that how you see it?*

As if reading her thoughts, Paula said, "I can understand why he thinks it was a miracle. I don't mind admitting I said a few prayers myself that night."

"You see, I didn't. Do you think that's unnatural?" The opinion of a stranger seemed to matter desperately.

"You want the truth?" Paula sat back a little. "I'm fifty-two years old and I have no idea what I believe in. I keep God in reserve for emergencies. Now my mother, she's High Church. Never swore in her life until she had her stroke, but the language that came out of her mouth when she couldn't be held accountable. How she knew half of those words - I had to look a few of them up!"

Suddenly, Elaine remembered: "I don't suppose you know where the boy lives? I'd like to thank him."

Paula looked confused. "What boy?"

"The one who told Judy to get out of the phone box."

"Sorry, love." She shook her head.

"He showed the men where to dig. I think he was from the estate."

"There was no shortage of boys from the estate. They scarpered the moment the police arrived. Now the policeman who took charge, he was the real hero. I don't expect you'd have any trouble tracking him down."

Elaine knew what she had seen. "It's my fault for leaving it so long." Her eyes followed Paula's arm, and the face of her wristwatch came into view. "Look at the time! My husband will be wondering where I've escaped to."

"He's not all bad, then."

"Oh, I hope I didn't make it sound as if…"

"But he didn't see what we did, did he?" Paula pushed back her chair until it collided with the skirting board. "I'll see you out."

John sat forwards as they passed through. "Night, love."

Elaine felt as if she were intruding. "Goodnight, John. Don't get up." Too late.

As Paula held open the door, John nuzzled his wife's neck, one arm circling her waist, the other lifted in salute. Embarrassed to witness their intimacy, Elaine hesitated before asking, "*You* don't remember a boy, do you?"

"What boy?" John said.

"The one who was helping the police. I think he was from the estate."

"Not likely. Not if he was from the estate."

"Never mind." There was a brief moment when Elaine's eyes locked with Paula's and she found understanding.

"Don't be a stranger."

When she closed the garden gate, they were still standing there watching, Paula half-heartedly protesting that her husband was scratching her; John noisily planting kisses on her cheek, undeterred.

Elaine closed her own front door quietly behind her. The cold evening air had done nothing to quash the feeling that she had made an awful fool of herself, and she felt guilty without quite understanding why. She'd deserted her post long enough to appreciate that she too had needs, however vague and unformed they might be. She looked in at Judy sitting alone on the sofa, legs stuck straight out in front on the coffee table. Not quite ready to face her daughter's wrath again, Elaine considered creeping past, but her feet found the loose floorboard.

"Is that you, Mum?" Judy called out, eyes on the television.

Seamlessly slipping into the role of mother, Elaine perched on the edge of the table and cupped one of her daughter's knees in the palm of her hand. "Isn't your dad home?"

"Don't think so." Judy stifled a yawn. "I fell asleep."

"You should be in bed."

"I wanted to wait up." Judy stared intently at the hand on her knee and gushed: "To say sorry if I was rude... earlier on."

Taken aback, Elaine wondered if this unprompted apology was a truce. "Never mind. I probably should have waited for you to reply before I came in."

"Still, I wasn't very nice." Judy smiled sheepishly. "Want to see what I was doing?"

Elaine raised her eyebrows, trying to disguise her alarm. "Only if you want to show me."

She held her breath as Judy rolled up her pyjama bottoms to reveal the blue biro marks hiding the red grooves. Elaine remembered her initial shock after the casts had been peeled away. The size of the scars. Their rawness. How she had avoided looking at them as she administered showers, while her daughter sat shivering in the bath. Now, rather than battle scars, they resembled tattoos. To Elaine, they also represented the price of having Judy back in one piece. But, once concealed, they had become unmentionable. Now, it was too late to give those unspoken words a voice.

Decisively, Elaine delved into her handbag and took out a laundry marker - indelible ink. She sat beside her daughter, planting a rebellious foot on the coffee table. One leg of her trousers rolled up, she drew herself a matching scar. Admiring her handiwork, Elaine wondered how she would have felt undressing in front of Graham for the first time if her thighs and torso were covered in similar-sized scars. Then, seeing Judy grinning, thought, *Are you worried how you'll feel, undressing in front of your boyfriend?*

"Here! Let me have a go!"

Elaine allowed her daughter to draw another scar on the side of her calf. She had a sense that this was exactly what needed to be said - while there was still no boyfriend on the scene. Graham, she knew, would object, but with Judy's fifteenth birthday approaching it might not be too long.

He chose that moment to appear, framed in the doorway. His eyes tracked the blur of downward movement settling on their freshly-ironed faces. "What are you two up to?"

"Nothing," two voices replied in unison, wide mouths and matching eyes repressing laughter.

As he unbuttoned his overcoat, an amused expression formed on his face. "Anyone for hot chocolate?" he asked.

For some reason, this made them both laugh out loud.

"Keep your secret. I'm just happy to see my two favourite ladies having a good time."

CHAPTER EIGHTEEN

Slowly undressing, Elaine studied her reflection in the mirror on the front of the bathroom cabinet. Her naked body was the blueprint by which she judged other women's figures. Her top half - neck to belly button - was still presentable, she decided, turning for a sideways view. Her collar bone stood a little proud; her breasts, reasonably flat until Judy's arrival, remained firm. She could still account for the majority of her ribs, but her shape flared nearer her waist. Although she could be trimmer, she detested the concept of totting up the calories in every chocolate digestive. How strange that her daughter's body was so unlike hers. Over the past year, Elaine had come to know it almost as well as her own. She had made a study of Judy's narrow back marked with its mysterious Nazca lines, the full breasts that obscured much of her ribcage. It was a body type that, unscarred, Elaine might have envied: the type men admired.

With nowhere to see her entire reflection in one snapshot, Elaine balanced precariously, knees bent, feet gripping the rim of the bath. Like a child's picture book with movable sections for head, body and legs, her middle portion appeared to have been borrowed. She felt detached from the swollen stomach, the narrow hips, the lumpy thighs. But here was her wedding ring; there, her watch. Even though she'd watched her husband's shape progressively change over two decades, Elaine had somehow imagined herself immune to the march of time. Who was it other people saw when they looked at her? A confident mature woman? No, the answer stared back at her: a middle-aged housewife.

It was foolish to be vain at her age. Elaine stepped down carefully. What did a few lumps and bumps matter? Who would see her naked anyhow?

"There you are." Graham, propped up in bed, was reading a book. "I was about to mount a search party."

"I want you to do something, Graham."

"Mmm?" His eyes remained on the page. No more detective novels, everything he read these days seemed to have an embossed cross on the cover.

Elaine found it off-putting to have her bedroom invaded by religion. She had already rehearsed arguments for the day Graham proposed they nail a crucifix above their bed. "Do you think you could put your book down?"

Looking up, Graham noticed how his wife leaned back against the bedroom door, eliciting a soft click. She was holding her dressing gown by its collar. Alarm bells ringing, he snapped the book shut, took off his reading glasses and folded back their arms. "You have my undivided attention."

"I want you to look at me."

"I'm looking."

"*Really* look."

As Elaine let her dressing gown fall to the floor, Graham raised his reading glasses to eye level and, squinting through them, decided he was better off without. Thrusting his arm in the direction of the bedside table, he couldn't find solid anchor: abandoned, they too fell.

"What do you see?"

The moment felt strangely charged. This wasn't a come on (if it was, it was something new and unfamiliar). Whatever his reply, it would be analysed, shoe-horned into future con-versations. That said, Graham couldn't help feeling aroused. He had never stopped being attracted to his wife. If anything, he liked Elaine's figure even more since she'd gained a little weight. He cleared his throat and settled on, "I see my beauti-ful wife." *Argue with that.*

"Huh!" A noise of denial escaped Elaine.

Graham closed his eyes momentarily. His inclination had been to ask what this nonsense was all about, but his gut now told him that was precisely the wrong thing to do. He had to focus.

"You see!" Elaine's hands had wandered self-consciously to her stomach. "You don't *want* to look."

"That's not true. I'm looking right now." Elaine had turned away and, after retrieving her towelling dressing gown, was draping it round her shoulders. It was Elaine's eyes Graham strained to see in the mirrored door of the wardrobe, hoping they would offer a clue to her thoughts, but they remained downcast. As she lifted her hair clear of the collar, securing it with the fabric band she had been wearing as a bracelet, he was reminded of something. "In fact, I'm looking at the spot on the back of your neck where I first kissed you."

Elaine froze, breath suspended. Graham had never pre-viously mentioned that he remembered *that*. She assumed it was only her who had found the simple brush of his lips profoundly moving.

"Just below your hairline, on the left." As she opened her mouth to protest, Graham corrected himself: "My left: your right." Her hand automatically found the spot and she was smiling. "Stop! Just there. I remember saying how smooth your skin was, and you said it was only Johnson's baby lotion."

"It's only Johnson's baby lotion." Elaine would never admit it, but he had memorised something she hadn't. She let the dress-ing gown drop to the floor to learn what else he remembered.

"Now, that view reminds me of you sunbathing naked the summer before Judy was born. I said, 'What about the neighbours?' and, if I remember correctly, your reply was, Sod them. You wouldn't have another opportunity until she'd left home."

Glowing with pleasure, Elaine pivoted.

"Now I can see the spot where I liked to rest my head, before it was replaced by Judy's. Not that I minded making way for her. I used to come home from work and find you both sleeping, and I'd climb into bed beside you and doze away the early evening. Remember?

'I see the mole just to the left of your belly button, and the place on your stomach that your hand always finds when you're nervous.

'And I can't look at your thighs without remembering that pair of boots you had. You used to call them your kinky boots. Whatever happened to them?"

Elaine dropped her head forwards and grinned, one hand resting on her collar bone. "I think I gave them to Oxfam."

"You *gave* them away?" Graham feigned horror. "Pity. I was about to suggest they had another outing." Opening his mouth as if to continue, he sat up frowning. "What's that you've got all over your legs?"

The moment was over and, with this knowledge, Elaine answered, "Ink," as straightforwardly as she could.

"I can see that! What's it doing there?"

"It's being…" She sighed deeply. "Scar-shaped."

"Why would you deliberately do that to yourself?" Graham began, then brought one hand to his forehead. "What an idiotic question! That's what this is all about: you wanted to know if it was you I saw first, or the ink marks."

Appalled at herself - that Graham should have thought of this and she hadn't - Elaine slipped her nightdress over her head and climbed into bed. "It is interesting, though. That you saw me."

Graham winced. "The scars must have been hidden by the foot of the bed."

"Oh." Elaine blinked at his honesty.

"Darling?" Pushing the duvet down, he stroked her leg slowly, knee to thigh.

She turned to him, not ignoring his seductive tone, but setting it aside. "Do you think you would have been put off if I'd been covered with scars?"

Graham's hand continued its lazy exploration. "That's hard to say."

"Is it?" Elaine placed one hand on top of his, as she might place an upturned glass over a spider. For Judy's sake, if not her own, she now hoped for a firm denial.

"When you love the whole person, it's hard to think of them just as a body." Graham sat back against the headboard, setting the bedside tables rattling.

Elaine looked at her awkward husband and remembered why she loved him. She rested her head against his shoulder. "It's going to be difficult for Judy to form relationships with this hanging over her."

"You're making a huge assumption there."

"Am I?"

"Yes! A relationship doesn't necessarily need to be physical before it's formed. It might be unrealistic to expect our daughter to remain a virgin until her wedding night, but it would be nice to think the person she decides to sleep with loves her enough not to be put off by a few scars."

"That's just it." After months of concealing the truth, it rushed out of Elaine. "They're not just a few scars. They're big and they're jagged and..." She jostled with her conscience. To call them ugly would be an even worse betrayal - although that was the fact of it: her daughter's beautiful young body was covered in great ugly scars.

"They can't be nearly as bad as these." Graham traced the outlines of the ink tattoos with an index finger, then slid down the bed to kiss them.

Elaine reined in her heels, linking her hands together in front of her knees. Graham needed to understand. "That's just it: they are." Her eyes pooled. "Why do you think she keeps herself covered up?"

One elbow serving as a buttress for his head, Graham looked up at her, his expression pained. "You're upset." Shuffling upwards, he offered her his shoulder again, patting it. "Talk to me."

"Seriously, Graham. I think we've made a mistake - no, *I've* made a mistake by avoiding the subject."

"I don't understand."

"Judy didn't want you to see. I've hated lying to you but she asked me to promise."

"I see."

"Teenage girls are very body-conscious. If she isn't comfortable with herself... if she doesn't... love herself... there's a risk she could..." Turning her head away, Elaine's thoughts involuntarily returned to her neighbour's boy, Tommy - although he could have been any modern-day Dustin Hoffman, hands in pocket and barefoot. She knew that, in the place of Ann Bancroft, she wouldn't be able to laugh his rejection aside. Then she saw Judy in her place, cowering, shoulders shuddering. And it was a far, far worse picture.

Beside her, Graham's thoughts had turned to his teenage acne, his self-loathing. It wasn't just girls who need to find out if they are attractive to the opposite sex, or if it matters all that much if they aren't. He understood the justification for his wife's concern. There was danger looming: danger that rules, however comprehensive, however rigid, might not be able to cage.

CHAPTER NINETEEN

"**C**ome on, Judy! In the shower with the rest of the class!" Forced to reject the idea of being an inspiration, Miss Stubbs had settled on an alternative strategy: no mercy. An ex-convent girl herself, aware how fake - how unrealistic - the life of nuns appeared to teenagers, she had hoped to inject a little balance. But, ever since the incident with the register on the first day of term, Miss Stubbs had realised this was a simple case of self-preservation. Through tears of frustration in the privacy of her rented room, Miss Stubbs found new determination: she would show them. Ladies? They were animals! No more sitting on the fronts of desks. No more fluffy rabbit ears - what had she been thinking of? She could only teach once she had control - and she *would* have control. The Jones girl still appeared to be staring ahead, gazing intently at nothing. Tempted to use her whistle, Miss Stubbs restricted herself to use of her best referee's voice; her pointing arm. "Judy! Shower! Now!" Behave like dogs, she would treat them like dogs.

"But..."

There could be no exceptions. "When I want 'buts' I'll ask for them."

An audience of damp-haired girls, standing around in knickers and bras, drying between toes, turned and smirked.

"I didn't go on the cross-country run."

Miss Stubbs realised her stupidity immediately - this was Judy Jones: the girl who came equipped with an excuse note for every occasion. It was too late to back down. "What part of 'in the shower' didn't you understand?"

"But Miss!"

Folding her arms over the red of her tracksuit (a colour she had given much thought to), Miss Stubbs stood her ground. "Come on. Off with them."

A slow *"Off! Off! Off!"* started in one corner, quickly joined by voices belonging to others who hurried from the showers, keen not to miss an opportunity to humiliate. Miss Stubbs did nothing to discourage them, watching the girl's throat move as she swallowed.

"Off! Off! Off!" Each word accompanied by a stamp.

"Fine," Judy said in a voice that spoke of defiance. Then, exactly where she stood, she began shedding clothes.

"Off! Off!"

A strange little striptease. Her shoes. Her socks. Her pullover. Her skirt. Her blouse.

"Off..."

To be fair, Judy offered her several chances between layers: the pause in a game of pass the parcel. Opportunities to show a little humanity slipped by as Miss Stubbs hesitated: too long, too long! As the scars were revealed one by one - as Miss Stubbs heard the chant peter out - she knew she had made no ordinary mistake. Technically speaking, this was a total fuck up. She had been a fool to ignore staffroom gossip about the headlines: Miraculous Escape. Standing on the coarsely tiled floor, Judy peeled away the final layer. The girl's glassy eyes locked hers as she stood: naked. Even the hush had its own accusing echo. Then Judy bit her quivering lip, hung her head and hugged her damaged body as she walked slowly towards the showers: the victim.

But Miss Stubbs's torment was not quite complete. It wasn't enough that she had made the new girl expose her scarred body to her classmates. Not enough that she had felt their venom as they rapidly changed allegiance. My God, those girls could turn! After thirty seconds under the lukewarm jet, the girl was back in front of her, juddering, wet, goose bumps raised. Folded arms providing inadequate support for her breasts.

"When you've finished making a spectacle of yourself," Miss Stubbs said, her voice low.

Tight-lipped, teeth chattering: "I don't have a towel."

"Why don't you have a towel? There should be one in your P.E. kit!"

"I haven't got a P.E. kit. My mother didn't think I'd be needing one."

Miss Stubbs sighed and then raised her voice, "Will *somebody* please lend Judy a towel?" intimating that blame for the girl's nakedness lay elsewhere.

Miranda Potipher loped over. Normally someone who covered herself at the earliest opportunity, in a gesture of solidarity Miss Stubbs had to admire, Miranda unwrapped her own body and draped the drab yellow towel damply around Judy's shoulders. The contrasts between the two girls - their goosepimpled body shapes, the damaged and the healthy - and the added contrast between the colour of Miranda's dyed black hair and her pubic hair did not escape Miss Stubbs's attention, even though she pretended to angle her gaze away. Control, or the appearance of such a thing, was crucial. "Thank you, Miranda. Now, perhaps we can all get dressed!"

Miss Stubbs turned her back and closed her eyes. She had lost the game: she would not lose the match. Behind her, she was aware of Judy and Miranda being welcomed into the fold. The class had found their inspiration. And it was not her.

CHAPTER TWENTY

The first time Judy Jones had ever been accepted for being herself, she had not only been exposed, she had been naked. In revealing her vulnerability she'd become powerful. No longer the girl who had stepped into Julie Thompson's last season's shoes, every corner would soon be buzzing with tall tales about the Miracle Girl, but the first sign that news had spread was the arrival of a pink-inked summons, delivered by a panting minion. "Join us for lunch," Judy read, turned it over and shrugged. No clues, no signatures: she was simply expected to know.

Miranda groaned. "My sister and her cronies!" Not people to make enemies of, she politely invented an excuse, something that had the advantage of sounding true. "Judy's upset. I'm just going to sit with her. Somewhere quiet."

Accustomed to being an outsider, Miranda didn't court approval from those who decided the unwritten rules of school politics. Still new to this self-imposed regime, Judy understood full well what it was to decide who was in and who was out; who might be allowed to rise through the ranks to self-appointed leader; who would take the role of scapegoat. In her past life (before the wall came tumbling down), she had craved attention, done what was required to get it. With girls who had previously ignored her or sniggered behind her back now swarming, pawing and fawning, she no longer needed it. There was only one person whose opinion mattered.

Alone later (Judy sprawled on her back on a slight slope of grass chewing gum, her friend hunched over with her chin on her knees, hiding a cigarette), Miranda said, "Seriously. You should complain."

"You think anyone would listen?"

"Sister Euphemia might. You'd be surprised."

Judy rejected that idea. "When you're new, everyone's waiting for you to screw up."

"True. But Stubbs was bang out of order."

"She was only trying to show people who's boss. Anyway, she might have done me a favour."

"Your method, Sherlock?"

Judy turned away slightly. "Apart from the quacks and my mother, you're the only person who's ever seen my scars before."

"Seriously?"

She winced. "I've sort of kept them hidden. Now, I've got it all out of the way in one go. Hey." Judy kicked Miranda playfully with the toe of her shoe. "Thanks for coming to my rescue. Again."

"Yeah, I'm a hero." Miranda smirked, but Judy saw that this was a mask for her embarrassment. "Still, I can't believe you're so relaxed about it."

"I actually feel pretty good."

"You shouldn't hide your scars, you know. You've got to start thinking of them as a feature."

"A feature?" She sat up on her elbows.

"Yes."

"A *feature*?"

As Judy turned to swat Miranda with a rolled exercise book, she felt the sun being blocked by what she took to be a cloud. And, in a way, it was the cloud to her unexpected silver lining.

"Forgive the intrusion, ladies. A word, please, Judith."

Finding the headmistress's distinctive shadow stretching larger than Nosferatu's when creeping downstairs, Judy scrambled awkwardly to her feet. Sister Euphemia looked the other way discreetly but said, "My office, if you don't mind. I won't take up too much of your time."

Behind the headmistress, Judy raised a pair of questioning eyebrows to Miranda's w-shaped shrug.

"And, Miranda, I wasn't born yesterday. Put that cigarette out. I'll see you in detention on Friday."

Sister Euphemia held her hand out behind her for the packet. Miranda complied, having obviously - or so Judy thought - upended the remainder of its contents into the depths of her bag. "I look forward to it, Sister," she muttered. Detention was Miranda's afterschool club.

They walked silently across the quad, the long walk, with Sister Euphemia leading, circumnavigating the statue of Our Lady in pride of place above her insipid fountain, her smiling eyes drowning them in pity. The headmistress's hands were tucked into the sleeves of her jumper as if she yearned for the anonymity of a habit. Learning that Sister Euphemia would have chosen the name herself, Judy had consulted an encyclopaedia of saints. After surviving torture at the hands of the Romans, St Euphemia was thrown to wild animals in the arena. Fitting for a woman who ruled over 300 hormonal teenagers, each ready to rip you apart with her teeth. Both were aware of eyes, greedy and curious, flickering; staring down from high windows. Of Chinese whispers and wagers. *Fifty pence says Miss Stubbs is for the high jump. You've got to be kidding. My money says Judy Jones needs another miracle.* Through the swinging double doors and along the corridor to Die Gut Schwester's lair, with its lingering smell of liver and onions.

The older woman took her place behind her desk, the

symbol of authority a wall between them. "The door please, Judith."

"Yes Sister." Judy silenced the scrape of plates and clatter of cutlery that heralded the end of lunch service.

Not invited to take a seat, she watched Sister Euphemia edge her chair under the desk with three distinct gallops. "Miss Stubbs has been to see me. I hear that we have got off to..." She proceeded to clear her throat. "Something of a bad start."

Judy imagined the situation being reported in such a way that she was blamed. "Sister?"

"It is not the ethos of this school to humiliate pupils in front of their classmates."

Relieved to hear what might be interpreted as an apology, Judy felt obliged to speak. "I don't know what Miss Stubbs has told you, but I wasn't humiliated, Sister. I was only asked to take a shower."

"Oh?" The word was a challenge. "I understood there was more to it than that."

Judy refused to react to the head held on one side, the chin resting on hands that looked as if they were clasped in prayer. "It was a misunderstanding, that's all."

"A misunderstanding?"

"It must happen in a class of thirty. Miss Stubbs thought I'd been on the cross-country run."

"But surely you were dressed in your uniform?"

"She thought I'd changed without showering."

"Judith, we have the slightly difficult situation in that the - let's call it an incident for want of a better word - was witnessed by an entire class. Is that not correct?"

"But I wasn't singled out."

Sister Euphemia clicked her biro impatiently, the nib reappearing and then disappearing in rapid fire. "For the sake of argument, perhaps you'd talk me through what happened."

Judy listed the facts with a military lack of emotion: "Miss Stubbs asked me to shower. I tried to explain that I hadn't been running. She didn't think it was relevant. And I didn't want to create a scene."

"So, you were trying to *avoid* a scene?" The headmistress's expression was one of surprise.

Judy's resolve was unwavering. "Yes, Sister. I thought that would be best."

"You didn't think to explain that you're excused from P.E.?"

"I didn't think I should argue with a teacher. I'm excused from P.E., not from taking showers."

"Quite so."

There was an extended pause while Sister Euphemia rearranged files on her desk. Judy knew that the headmistress couldn't risk mentioning her scars, as though they were something to be ashamed of. And if the incident had taught her one thing, it was that she would *not* be ashamed. Perhaps they were, as Miranda had suggested, a feature. "Can I go, please, Sister? I'm late for double maths."

The headmistress looked up, apparently surprised to find her still standing there, and rattled the end of her pen between her teeth, a frustrated round of applause. "Yes, Judith, you may."

CHAPTER TWENTY-ONE

Judy's decision was hers alone. Furtive sorties to the kitchen and bathroom resulted in an accumulation of necessary contraband, deposited on her dressing table, now doused liberally in Dettol: a bowl of ice cubes; a thimble; rubber gloves; cotton wool balls; supermarket vodka, circa Christmas 1979. She experimented with a stray bead to get the positioning correct. (After going to all this trouble, she didn't want it to look like a spot.) Painstakingly, she filed down the pillar of a plain gold stud. Then, after scrubbing her face raw, she made one final trip to the kitchen, satisfied by the muffled news report filtering through the living room door, and held the sharp tip over the blue flame of the gas cooker. Her excuse if discovered? A science project.

Judy sat, her face reflected in the mirror: disappointing in its ordinariness. Hands encased in yellow Marigolds pressed ice against one side of her nose, the cold penetrating, burning. Waiting for flesh to numb, she looked up the meaning of 'perpendicular' one final time. Featuring prominently in the instructions for home-piercing, it appeared to be key. Judy was not afraid of pain. The self-inflicted variety, like the pain of teaching herself to walk again, she already knew she could breathe through.

The neck of the vodka bottle between her lips, Judy threw

back her head and let the forbidden liquid flow into her mouth. *Jesus!* To think adults drank this out of choice. She closed her eyes tightly, swallowing hard. Then she spoke mockingly to her reflection: "OK, Miracle Girl. Do your worst."

Miranda had warned against piercing the top of her ear. That had been stupidly painful - although, as Judy pointed out, Miranda had repeated the experience four times.

"Like I said: stupid."

The skin of her nose was softer, but more padded. Thumb inserted, index finger on top, Judy calculated its width at half a centimetre. It was important to know what you were up against. She exhaled slowly through her mouth, as if controlling an extended note on the recorder. Then, applying the filed-down point to the side of her nose, the angle strictly perpendicular, she took several deep breaths and began chanting her personal mantra. "Nothing is ever as bad as you think it's going to be." Other people would have chosen to bite down on something solid. Judy sang.

She leapt up at the sound of a knock on her bedroom door. "Shit!" The point of the pillar had come through the other side of her nose and pierced the tender pad of her thumb. Shaking away the pain proving ineffective, she sucked it.

"Judy?" Her mother's voice was timid. "Almost time for Kenny Everett!" Another knock. "Judy, did you hear me?"

She removed her thumb from her mouth - "I *said* I'll be down in a minute!" and turned back to the mirror. The gold stud was in, the skin around it hot to the touch despite the pain of thawing flesh. It didn't look quite as different as she'd imagined. This was the unspoken part of her mantra, the yin to the yang: 'Nothing is ever quite as good as you think it's going to be.' The reek of Dettol, associated with sickness and sawdust, suddenly overpowering, Judy reached over her dressing table to push the window open. Now, the next challenge: how to hide a nose piercing. Choosing a circular plaster, cutting it down to size with a pair of nail scissors, she made the earring an imperfect tent. It would have to do.

Graham glanced up as his daughter entered the living room. Her hair curtained her face as she bypassed him to claim a place on the sofa - not her usual position, but to his left. "Change of scenery?" He shuffled sideways to make room.

To Judy's nonchalant shrug, Graham sighed, belt straining as he leaned forwards to swap their mugs of tea around: Big Daddy for him; the Royal Wedding for her. Already, Judy looked far older than the girl who had been besotted by the shy princess: all puffed sleeves, ruffles and bows; train trailing down the red carpet on the steps of St Paul's. Charles, in heavily-decorated uniform and immaculate white gloves. Judy had worn the tape thin, rewinding to the kiss on the balcony: the happily ever after of fairy tales.

"Remember that?" Graham turned to Judy nostalgically, offering her the souvenir mug, its fading image victim to Elaine's enthusiastic scouring.

There was the sound of tinny laughter from the television set, an irritated, "Da-ad! You made me miss the punchline."

Remembering how Judy had said to him, "I don't think I'll ever get married," Graham returned his attention to the screen where a blonde-wigged and heavily made-up (but still bearded) Everett in a low-cut dress reversed the position of his crossed legs by launching them into the air. *Cupid Stunt! How does he get away with it?* "I don't understand why you think he's so funny."

Elaine glared in his direction. "My dad used to say the same thing about Monty Python."

"Mine too!"

"Didn't you find it annoying?"

Later, standing slightly behind his wife as she washed the dishes, Graham listened to the boiler's temperamental furnace. "It needs servicing," he frowned.

A view of the soft skin behind Elaine's ear as she released hair from her collar. "That's what I've been telling you."

"I'll phone someone at the weekend." He dried a Pyrex bowl thoughtfully. As soon as he deposited it on the worktop, Elaine sighed and interrupted what she was doing to brush past and remove the offending item. After twenty years of being ignored, the mysteries of kitchen storage were reluctant to reveal themselves to Graham. Defying his logic, nothing was where he expected, and yet - according to his wife - there was a 'right' place for everything. Had he picked a cupboard, it would have been the wrong one. But, a latecomer to the pleasures the kitchen offered, Graham relished its intimacy: stolen moments in close quarters with his wife; warmth from the oven dispensing with the need for outer layers; whispered confidences. Elaine wanted to knock through the wall to the breakfast room and, since she asked for so little, he was inclined to let her have her way. But Judy's private physio had drained his rainy-day fund and his managing director's promise of the something 'up his street' had yet to materialise.

"You really shouldn't talk all the way through Judy's favourite programme," Elaine chided.

"I barely spoke!" The implied, 'Besides, it was a load of rubbish,' was silent. "I thought she seemed very stiff tonight." Graham sketched a circle in the air in front of his face. "Her neck and shoulders."

Elaine smiled, handing him a plate, apparently capable of ignoring the suds she was dripping onto the floor. She beckoned conspiratorially and whispered a warm-breathed secret. "It wasn't her neck. I think she's got a spot."

Graham mouthed a silent, 'Oh.'

Delight lit his wife's eyes. "She's put a plaster on it. One of the little round ones."

"I wondered why she sat on my left."

"What are you two joking about?"

Guilty faces twisted to see their slipper-footed daughter in the doorway. "Nothing," they said in unison.

Unconvinced, Judy challenged, "Mum?"

"Something about your father's day at work. Silly really."

Graham was surprised when Judy accepted this obvious lie, or perhaps Elaine's answer, even her shy display of embarrassment, had been perfectly weighted. Something designed to draw teenage scorn.

"Can I get a glass of water?"

"I'll get it," he offered.

His daughter's eyebrows twitched in impatience or irritation, her hand reaching for the Elastoplast self-consciously. The plumbing glugging objections, Graham filled a hi-ball tumbler (one of the freebies from the garage) and turned. As Judy took the tumbler, he felt his ribcage expand. He knew all there was to know about acne. This bump was too distinct: evidence of something solid.

With a ballerina's turn of her head, Judy announced, "I'm going to my room."

Waiting for his daughter's retreat upstairs, Graham breathed out, lowering his voice. "That's no spot," he said to his wife.

Elaine pivoted in the direction of his nod, and performed a double-take at the space their daughter had vacated. "Oh, you don't think...? She wouldn't."

Graham bunched the drying-up cloth in his fist. "I'll deal with this!"

"I'd rather you didn't." Elaine grabbed his arm. "Not like this."

"Like what?" he asked, knowing full well what she meant. *Aren't I entitled to be angry?*

"It's..." A flap of Elaine's arms might have been intended to show how hopelessly inadequate the available words were to

161

describe these uncharted territories. "Delicate."

"Did she ask for your permission?" Graham demanded.

Elaine stammered, as if he had accused her of being responsible for the fact that Judy no longer confided in her. "N-no, she didn't."

"Then it's not delicate: it's disobedience. *Judy!*" He stormed from the kitchen, aware that Elaine was still trying to plead with him. She would have them all sit down and discuss things. 'Like adults'. But only just turned fifteen, Judy was not an adult, despite what she'd been through. And perhaps it was his wife's attitude that had her thinking that she no longer needed their permission. He allowed his march upstairs to thunder loudly enough to serve as a warning, reminding himself: choose your words *carefully*. It couldn't be disobedience unless permission had been denied - or could it? Was Judy's failure to ask permission disobedience in itself? Shouldering his way into his daughter's domain - it wouldn't have crossed Graham's mind to knock - he was assaulted by the sickly smell of disinfectant masking something less familiar. Was that bottle on his daughter's dressing table *vodka?* This was the reason Graham would never agree to her request for a lock. "Have you been drinking?" he demanded.

Despite incriminating evidence, Judy, open-mouthed, managed to look outraged at his intrusion. "Hardly." She pointed to the level of the liquid, which was only just shy of the neck.

Graham cleared his throat and folded his arms. It was clearly not the drink that had brought him here. "Well?" He nodded towards her, stopping shy of saying, 'young lady.' "I'm waiting."

Cornered, Judy's first instinct was to resort to lying, but she had come so far in the last year that she didn't want to. Her view was that her father should make it possible for her to tell the truth. But she thought of the explanations why she had made a secret of her plan, each one sounding ever so slightly ridiculous: *it's my body; it's none of your business.* Lifting her chin, Judy peeled back the plaster and allowed her face to be inspected.

The small gold stud didn't look 'punk' as Graham had feared. On the other hand, it wasn't particularly attractive. It was just a small stud at the side of his daughter's nose. Why, then, did it make Graham bristle? Because she'd chosen to harm herself? Because piercing was an initiation rite and Graham wasn't ready to accept that Judy's childhood was at an end? He cautioned himself with the words of St Paul, the subject of last Sunday's sermon: 'Fathers, do not provoke your children to anger.' Finding that he was shaking, Graham asked in what he felt was a rational tone, "You did that to yourself?"

"Yes."

"Here? In this house?"

Judy gave him a look that said, '*Objection! Irrelevant, your Honour.*'

"Without permission?" he continued.

"You wouldn't have let me if I had -"

"No!" Graham dismissed the notion that his refusal would have been anything other than completely reasonable. "I don't understand why you'd choose to disfigure yourself like that."

"*Disfigure* myself?" Judy twisted his words into a question, the implications of which made him doubly nervous.

"Is this your friend Miranda's doing?"

A small hiccup of a laugh escaped Judy. "You have no idea, do you?"

"Now, hang on. I was a teenager myself."

"Let me show you, Dad." His daughter turned and looked over her shoulder. Was it pity he saw? Graham could do nothing but watch as Judy lifted the hem of her sweatshirt, saying, "This is me."

Nothing his wife had told him had prepared him for sight

of Judy's pale underside glowing with raggedy scars. Not even the little bedroom scene (played back in his mind with alternating endings) when he had somehow thought his comparison with teenage acne appropriate. Here was the reality: what had emerged from the chrysalis. *My little butterfly, look at your wings.* Then as she pulled up her track-suit bottoms, pushed down her socks, Graham saw her poor legs. *Look at your markings.* He took his glasses off, blindly lowering himself onto the edge of Judy's bed, knowing that he shouldn't allow her to see him weep. But it was shocking: wasn't it right to acknowledge that?

"Are you alright, Dad?" Judy was asking.

"Give me a minute." For the first time he understood how close they had come to losing her.

"It's my fault," she was saying. "I wanted to stay covered up. I made Mum promise. But I'm not going to hide anymore."

He dabbed at his unfocused eyes. "You know that you won't be allowed to wear it at school. Your headmistress was very specific about jewellery."

"Sister Euphemia is very 'specific' about everything."

Graham felt a slight bounce on the mattress beside him and looked around, damp-lashed, to see his daughter's face looming outside the range of his long-sighted vision. He managed a tortured smile. "I had no idea. I mean, I had *some* idea. But obviously…" It was coming out wrong. He should be saying, 'It's not so bad,' instead of conjuring shapes out of thin air with his hands. Having witnessed the marks left by the rough stitches, the staples that had held her flesh together, Graham's wonder at his daughter was renewed. "I would never have pushed you so hard if I'd known…" He understood, now, Elaine's reluctance.

"And I'd still be lying in bed!"

He marvelled at Judy's strength, the sheer effort it must have taken her to get this far. The pain. He remembered how she had yelled when he told her he wouldn't let her give up.

"I don't mind the scars." She sat on her hands. "Really, Dad. They're part of who I am. They remind me I can do anything if I want it badly enough."

"That's just it, Judy." Graham turned bodily to his daughter, his mind on the Sixties. "You can't just do anything you want to. There are rules -"

"You and your bloody rules!" Judy made a grab for his hands. "Why do you *always* have to think of the bad stuff when I'm trying really hard to turn this into something positive?"

Conceding that she was right, Graham offered a conciliatory smile. "I'm your father. It's my job to think of the worst-case scenario."

"And the wall? I suppose you saw that coming?"

Graham had always said the tree was dangerous. But it stood two roads away: he had never imagined it would harm his family. "No."

"So you have to accept you can't protect me from everything."

Graham felt less than confident as he insisted, "Judy, I've been around longer than you. Give me a little credit for understanding how the world works."

"You both want to keep me wrapped up in cotton wool! But I don't want to be afraid every time I step outside the front door."

"And your answer is what? Piercing your nose?"

Judy hung her head. "It wasn't supposed to be a big deal."

"So what *was* it supposed to be?"

She opened her mouth to speak, sighed and closed it, throwing him one of her *you-wouldn't-understand* looks. He remembered a feeling: sitting in his bedroom; fearful and yet impatient. It sounded melodramatic all these years later to say that he had been waiting for his life to begin. But, yes, that is what the feeling was.

"Well." He mirrored his daughter's stubborn stance. "What are we going to do? Your mother's very upset. And before we know it, we'll have Sister What's-her-face breathing fire down our necks."

Judy shrugged.

Graham's eyes lingered on the stud. His voice wasn't lacking in admiration when he asked, "You actually stuck that thing through your nose?"

He heard his daughter's sigh. "It didn't hurt half as much as I thought it would. The ice was worse."

As Judy started at the sound of his dry laughter, he applied one hand to his forehead. "I'm not cut out for this, am I? Come here."

Wrapping a weighted arm around his daughter, his thoughts fixed on his role as father to a teenager. One who wasn't going to behave predictably. Who wouldn't necessarily seek his approval. He had thought a framework of rules would do the job: he had been wrong. "How long before that thing heals?" he sighed. "Worst-case scenario."

"I dunno." She blinked.

"You're not telling me you did all this," Graham's arm circumnavigated the room, "...and you didn't bother to find out?"

She cringed. "Maybe eight weeks?"

"Eight weeks! How were you planning to keep it hidden all that time? Why didn't you wait until the summer holidays when it wouldn't have mattered so much?"

"I suppose I just needed something... to happen?"

Surprised to find that his instincts had been correct, Graham remained silent long enough to unnerve his daughter: it was the only punishment he intended, so it was right she should suffer. "I'll tell you what we're going to do. Provided you can show that you know when it's appropriate to wear that thing, you can keep it."

"I can?"

The mattress bounced again as arms garlanded Graham's neck. "And that means not at school. And not at church. And it also means keeping it hidden from Sister Euphemia while it heals."

Judy withdrew her embrace. "And how am I supposed to do that?" Her shoulders slumped.

Wearily, Graham stood, confronted by a look of dismay. This was the start of a new relationship with his daughter. It required a different approach. He repeated a phrase he often heard used in the office, "Not my problem," relishing the irresponsible feeling he was left with.

CHAPTER TWENTY-TWO

The girls of 2B scraped back their chairs in clumsy unison as Sister Euphemia swept into the classroom.

"Good morning, ladies. Please be seated." At her most deadly, the headmistress smiled. "I've decided to join you. Ah! I see there's a spare desk at the back." She deferred to Miss Clark. "May I?"

Miss Clark swallowed, hoping her hesitation would be interpreted as politeness. "By all means." Authority in the classroom hung in fine balance. If the girls detected her nerves, she would lose their confidence and, with it, all control. Could it be that the Sister had heard Miss Clark was embarking on her most controversial lesson, daring to mention that the Good Book addressed issues of sexuality? Perhaps the only subject that prompted enthusiasm - other than from Miranda Potipher, that is. Miranda could always be relied on to shake things up.

Forcing a smile she didn't feel inclined towards, Miss Clark extended one arm. "Be my guest, Sister." She felt slightly ridiculous, like an airhostess demonstrating the location of the emergency exits: *here, here and here.* Was it too late to change track? But Miss Clark's eyes settled on the title she'd chalked on the blackboard. Not her customary sprawl of unruly capitals resulting from the rapid clash of chalk. These were joined-up letters, neater than her ordinary handwriting, indicative of what was to follow. Miss Clark found herself drawing on vocabulary her mother reserved for unwanted guests. "This is an unexpected pleasure!"

"Pretend I'm not here." Dismissing her insincere flattery, Sister Euphemia closed an imaginary zip over her mouth - a gesture playful enough to fool those around her into thinking she was one of 'the girls'.

"So." Struck by stage-fright, Miss Clark cleared her throat. "As I was saying." *Here goes*: she used an extended blink as a springboard. "We think of Eve's disobedience as the first sin, but the concept of Original Sin wasn't introduced until eight hundred years after the Garden of Eden was written about; the same as us imposing modern standards on something written by - oh, I don't know - the Normans!" Miss Clark had intended to talk about how St Augustine, tormented by desire, labelled sex as evil. And how, for women, he reserved his harshest words. 'St Augustine painted a picture of God condemning man to eternal damnation because of Eve's actions. He said that Adam's offspring, created during acts of passion - when all thought of God was forgotten - would be burdened with Original Sin, which would drag them down to that final and never-ending torment with the rebel angels. In other words?"

"Hell?" One not-so bright spark responded dramatically from the periphery of Miss Clark's radar.

"Hell!" Hallelujah: someone was listening.

A stony glance from Sister Euphemia demanded moderation. In need of a lifeline, Miss Clark's gaze fell on Miranda, bored to the point of chewing on her nails. She would have to throw the girl some bait if the lesson was to be salvaged. "Miranda?" Miss Clark's voice adopted a mantle of concern.

"Yes, Miss."

"You look troubled. Would you care to expand?"

Miranda's humourless smirk suggested she knew when she was being set up. Miss Clark half-expected her to resort to sarcasm ('No, Miss, I always look like this') or employ a delaying tactic ('If you don't mind, I'd like to hear what else you have to say'). But, after a single rise and fall of her chest, she said, "I find the whole Original Sin thing very wrong." And during the shuffling that followed, despite her obvious discomfort, Miranda tagged on the words, "If I'm honest, I think it's obscene."

The resultant silence had an expectant quality.

"Go on." Miss Clark frowned encouragement.

"Think about it: from the minute we're born, we're told not to behave in ways that come naturally. But the Christian Church goes one step further. It writes the whole population off as sinners before they even learn to talk."

A mature voice protested: "No one is 'written off'. God sent His only Son to give us hope for redemption."

"What about all the people who don't get it? 'Your honour, I was born a sinner and it all went downhill from there.'" Miranda made it clear that she hadn't intended laughter as a response. "I'm serious! Remember *Tess of The D'Urbervilles*? You know the scene where Tess baptizes her dying child because she can't find a parson. How she's refused a Christian burial for the baby. We thought something like that could *never* happen today. Well, it happened right here. Under our noses."

Miss Clark realised what was happening: they were being held collectively responsible for having failed to prevent Julie Thompson's expulsion. She hesitated: how would the headmistress expect her to react? Allowing the debate risked criticism of the school, but how could she steer Miranda back to her original commentary on Eve?

Sister Euphemia's voice cut through uncertain murmurs. "Miranda, your problem is that you're confusing fact with fiction."

"So that's my problem, is it?" A hush: Miranda pushed back her chair, having apparently lost the appetite for argument. "And you. You never confuse the two. You always know the difference, I suppose."

Miss Clark recognised the headmistress's speechless display of shock for the Oscar-winning performance it was. Thirty wide-eyed girls froze, breath suspended; doubt as to whose side they should be on. Miss Clark glanced between headmistress and girl, expecting another ball to be propelled over the net. Instead, the girl slung her bag over her shoulder and walked off Centre Court.

"Miranda!"

One hand on the door, the girl turned. "You know something? I'm done here."

Helpless, Miss Clark wondered if, as umpire, she could be held responsible.

Outwardly, the headmistress appeared unconcerned. Dismissive, almost. "Go ahead, Miss Clark. We can manage without any further contributions like that." But behind the façade Miss Clark detected a heart pounding wildly.

"Yes, Sister." Swallowing, she located her mental bookmark. "I was about to explain that Original Sin is a Western concept, opposed by the Jews and the Greek Orthodox Church and, later, by the Muslims." Seeing that the majority of eyes remained on the open door, Miss Clark made the decision to stride across the room to shut it as firmly as was necessary to close thirty gaping mouths. If the Bible had taught her anything, it was the importance of symbols. *There! That'll rattle them.* "For Christians, woman's image was permanently damaged by the revisions to the Creation story." Licking the tip of an index finger, she opened a heavyweight volume at a place she had earmarked, and read aloud. "Do you not know that you are each an Eve? You are the devil's gateway; you are the unsealer of that forbidden tree; you are the first deserter of the divine law; you are she who persuaded him whom the devil was not valiant enough to attack. You so carelessly destroyed man, God's image. On account of your desert, even the Son of God had to die." She snapped the book shut. *How do you like that, turncoats of 2B?* Miss Clark expected protest when she quoted Jerome, but what never failed to shock was that, in any class of thirty, some of the girls - the sullen, apathetic, eyeliner girls - hung their heads and squirmed. Those who had already tasted the forbidden fruit, she presumed. "Instead of blaming Eve, Genesis finds fault with the serpent. Interestingly, the Bible doesn't make the connection between the serpent and the devil. We do that. At the time, the snake was a symbol of -"

"Fascinating." Miss Clark found she was interrupted mid-flow, just as she was regaining momentum. Sister Euphemia stood, twenty-nine girls on autopilot following suit. "Sadly I can't stay for the whole lesson. Ladies." The headmistress nodded in a generalised direction, and then swept out of the room.

It was Miss Clark's turn to stand open-mouthed, looking from the gaping door to the girls. "Elizabeth." She frowned in the direction of the exit, as if her cue shouldn't have been necessary. "If you wouldn't mind." Recognising the need for swift recovery, Miss Clark then picked up her notes. Slowly, carefully, she ripped them down the middle, letting the pieces flutter where they would like autumn leaves.

Judy Jones raised her hand. *Why not?* she thought in irritation. "Yes, Judy?"

"About IVF, Miss?"

"I beg your pardon, Judy. *What* about IVF?"

"A baby born after IVF hasn't been conceived in an act of passion, so would it be born without Original Sin?"

The thought of her own failed attempts to conceive knotted her throat. The thermometer; the relentless counting of days; the *Let's get it over with*; the humiliating doctors' appointments: passion a memory so distant she wondered if it had ever existed. "That's a very interesting thought." Miss Clark found herself nodding. Against the odds she had discovered another thinker in her midst. "Let's throw it out for discussion."

Sister Euphemia marched along the corridor in bull-like fashion, cursing the insolence of the girl. "*Unmitigated disaster!*" She cast words this way and that, as if she'd developed Tourette's. "*Truculent! Bold! Facetious!*" The headmistress was oblivious to students who leaped aside, wondering what they'd done to offend. "*In front of an entire class. How many times have I told her, 'There is room for all sorts of opinions at this school, provided they're appropriately expressed?'* Yes?" she barked on seeing her secretary suspending a cardboard wallet at arm's length, like a particularly nervous relay runner.

"The letter that needs to go out tonight, Sister. If you could just sign -"

Sister Euphemia snatched the folder while still on the move, responding with an impatient sigh. Seeing Miranda seated on one of the two intentionally uncomfortable chairs positioned outside her office, the headmistress slowed her approach to a dignified speed.

Looking up, the girl pushed herself to standing. "Sister."

She nodded, a conciliatory gesture. "The fact that you've come to apologise does you credit."

"I'm not here to apologise: I just thought I'd save you the trouble of sending someone to find me."

"I see." Sister Euphemia craned herself into position behind the desk as a judge would behind a bench, her Royal Coat of Arms replaced by a crucifix. "Then I have to ask myself, Miranda: have we reached the end of the road?" She waited for her words to take effect. Unblinking, the girl held her gaze, the apples of her cheeks colouring slightly. "Don't you have anything to say for yourself?"

"I'm afraid that, once I get started, I'll say too much." The girl's body language reflected her self-restraint, everything taut but, at the same time, restless.

"You'll have to give me more than that to go on." Detecting unforeseen levels of anger, the headmistress softened her voice. "Miranda, we may not see eye to eye, but we've always been honest with each other."

"You want me to be *honest?*" This, said with a re-shuffling of arms.

"Of course." Sister Euphemia invited.

"You see." Miranda shook her head, stepped backwards. "People always say that…"

"Try me." Both a command and a challenge.

"Alright." Miranda rearranged her mouth; licked her lips. "What you did was hypocritical."

She was direct, you had to give her that. "Explain."

"Jesus spoke about forgiveness, but you expelled a girl - for one, single mistake - because you were more concerned about the reputation of your precious convent than the future of a fourteen-year-old and her baby son!" The words were out, and Miranda wore an expression that could almost be described as shock.

"I see." Sister Euphemia cautioned herself to maintain control. She would do exactly as she had promised the Disciplinary Committee, taking full responsibility for the decision to expel Julie Thompson. "You'll understand, I hope, when I say I can't agree with you."

Miranda shifted her weight onto the other foot. "So, how do you think you would have reacted if Mary had told you she was pregnant? Would *you* have believed she was a virgin?"

The headmistress allowed herself to scoff, "I hardly think we're talking about the Immaculate Conception here."

"You're mixing up your doctrines." The girl almost tutted. "But I'm glad you've brought up the convenient explanation of how Mary managed to avoid Original Sin."

Sister Euphemia's mouth curved upwards only very slightly.

"Oh, I see what you've done. I took the bait - again."

"Very good, Miranda. Not many students would have picked me up on that. Still, that 'convenient explanation' you refer to was the result of much theological debate."

"Are you avoiding my question, Sister?"

"Not avoiding, no. But I don't really think you've come here for discussion. You've already made up your mind about how I reacted and I imagine it goes something like this: if Mary had been your daughter, you would have kicked her out; if Mary had knocked on your door, you would have told her there was no room at the inn; but seeing as Mary was your *pupil* - and came to you for advice - you expelled her. Am I right?"

"Close enough."

The good sister risked a betrayal of trust. "You do know it wasn't my decision alone? The Disciplinary Committee, composed of parents, teachers - and Julie's peers, I might add - voted."

"Didn't Pilate give the crowd a vote when he didn't want to have to make a decision?"

The headmistress's nostrils flared. "Be careful, Miranda. A good argument can be spoiled by too many metaphors."

"You could have overruled the Committee."

"Ye-s." Sister Euphemia dragged the syllable out in a curved line. "It wouldn't have been very democratic - but I *suppose* I could have. There are previous rulings that set a precedent, however. You must realise that your friend broke the law: she was underage."

Miranda's eyes had wandered to the crucifix behind the

headmistress's head. "Don't you think Jesus's teachings should take precedence in a Catholic school?"

Sister Euphemia silently applauded. At the same time she hadn't thought that she would have to explain the real world to a fourteen-year-old. "I took the job of headmistress, Miranda. And, with it, I accepted certain responsibilities."

"When Emma Harman shaved her head, you suspended her for as long as it took for her hair to grow back." Miranda's lower lip began to tremble. She bit down in an attempt to compose herself, the headmistress presumed.

Finally: solid ground. "We don't allow skinheads. The dress code makes that very clear."

"Julie Thompson had her baby yesterday. Did you know that?"

"Actually, I didn't…" At least, now, the anger made sense. Knowing Miranda as she did, the headmistress understood that the girl felt she owed a debt to her friend, one that would be paid instalment by instalment. And Sister Euphemia herself was not so far removed from the world that she couldn't remember a swelling of wonder as she held her newborn niece for the first time; that exquisite hot little body: quite perfect.

"So, she could come back to school now she's no longer pregnant. Because that was the issue, wasn't it? I mean, I'm assuming it wasn't that you don't allow sinners, otherwise this place would be empty." Miranda's agitation evident, she stepped from side to side: the agonised dance of first dates.

Sister Euphemia remembered a time when everything had been black and white, but not even then had she fought a friend's corner so valiantly. "How are they both?"

Miranda levelled her head and raised her eyes to the corner of the room. "They're fine."

The *No thanks to you!* was silent. The headmistress conceded that, from the girl's perspective, she deserved no more. It would have been nice to know if the child was a boy or a girl, its weight, a name: nice, but - as far as this discussion was concerned - irrelevant. Facts would only cloud the issue.

"I'm glad." Sister Euphemia leaned forwards. "I'm also glad that you have such a developed sense of right and wrong. I hope things are always as clear-cut for you as they are today." She paused to remove the bi-focals from her nose and sat back stiffly in her chair. "We both know you overstepped the mark. It's a shame you chose to walk out of the lesson when, with your verbal skills, you might have recovered the situation. It saddens me to say this -" She paused, not for dramatic effect, but to reflect: *you will never know how deeply.* "You leave me with no option but to refer your case to the Disciplinary Committee - over which I will not be presiding. Perhaps, when you see the way the process works, you'll understand how your friend came to be expelled."

It was apparent, from the misshapen appearance of Miranda's face, that the point at which standing up for her beliefs was reward enough came to a sudden end. Even then, she forced words through stringy saliva: "And Julie Thompson, Sister? Will you recommend she's reinstated?"

Oh, to have so loyal a friend! "I like you, Miranda. I've always liked you." Straightening her back, the headmistress replaced her spectacles. "You are suspended until the hearing. I'll be writing to your parents."

CHAPTER TWENTY-THREE

When at first it happened, Judy told no one. Not of the scent of freshly-cut grass and incense that increased her need to swallow, nor of the sound in her ears, faint at first, then swelling; a continuously-ascending tone that never seemed to get any higher; the objects in focus moving closer, enlarging; the sense that time was slowing down; and, all the time, a delicious build-up of tension in her muscles. No one heard about her strong sense of *déjà vu*; the sensation of crossing a line, as if the world was somehow divided. And then the moment's release when Judy's soul left her body, that heightening of awareness, of floating, of *everything being exactly as it should be*.

Somewhere in this calm perfection, she encountered a woman who spoke in a language she didn't understand but who seemed intent on communicating a message of some importance. Without understanding the words, Judy grasped that there was something only she could do. Perhaps the one thing she'd been sent back for. But before matters became clearer, she heard the tail of a throaty noise and woke in a quiet corner of the convent grounds - if waking was the right term for it. Her neck twisted at an uncomfortable angle, she was looking up and into the small wooden face of Jesus as he hung from the cross: one of twelve Stations used by the school during Holy Week services, but where nuns might often be found in private meditation. A crumpled heap of a girl, Judy's disappointment - her simple longing to return to the state of ecstasy - was exceeded only by the need to pee, but her limbs were heavy and unresponsive. And then warmth spread rapidly in her navy blue uniform knickers.

Seeing that the other girls were still on the hockey field - their true personalities revealed with the clashing of wooden sticks - she moved secretively, peeling off wet underwear. Repulsed by what she held in her hand, and finding no suitable place to hide it in her bag, she abandoned it in the shrubbery. Gathering her body about her as if it were a cloak, Judy rotated her skirt until the dark patch was in the least conspicuous place. When was the last time she had wet herself? Not in all of the year she had spent in bed. Not since her first year at primary school. After the shame of putting her hand up to ask permission, the humiliation of being told she must wait for first break. Perhaps her body hadn't healed as well as she had thought, or perhaps her body had healed but something had happened to her mind.

Was there an alternative? Could her immortal rational soul have worked out how to detach itself from her body and travel between this world and the next?

Judy craved friendly reassurance, but Miranda had said, "Don't talk to me about religion." And, besides, Miranda had her own problems. Both suspended and grounded, she wasn't even supposed to use the phone.

Dad would welcome this, publicise it.

Her mother, who had always said, "You can tell me anything," would give her that all-too-familiar look of disappointment.

Judy contemplated confiding in Father Patrick: "Do you still think I'm sane?" She imagined telling him - a priest! - about her hastily abandoned knickers. A *religious* experience?

She didn't want to be chosen. It was ridiculous. Who, in their right mind, would choose her? A pure soul she was not. The knickers-incident was just one example. She'd abandoned them safe in the knowledge that no blame would be attached to her.

Another thought struck. Was it possible she had triggered this herself? How many other people had consumed an entire bottle of Holy water, drop by drop?

No: she would tell no one.

After glancing over one shoulder, Judy's shameful route to the toilet block took her across the enclosed courtyard with its central statue and, as she passed, she looked upon Our Lady's face, a face she seemed to have known all of her life.

CHAPTER TWENTY-FOUR

Elaine's next supermarket experience was not at all like the one Paula had described. After discovering a variety of new products she wanted to buy (wasn't it *amazing* that pasta now came in all sorts of shapes and sizes?) Elaine stood in a gradually shuffling queue at the checkout.

A pleasurable sensation of touch drew her attention to the fruit in the basket at the end of the conveyor. Strange that the hand holding it was wearing a wedding band not dissimilar to her own, that she wasn't the only person who left her engagement ring by the kitchen sink. Coincidental that the sleeve of the jumper above the hand was identical to hers, down to the snagged pale, blue wool, caught on a nail in the under-stairs cupboard. Dimpled like an orange, bright green in colour, the skin of the fruit was cool, its flesh firm. Only with its smooth shape - not unlike a pebble that demanded to be skimmed - sitting comfortably in her palm did Elaine make the connection: her wedding band; the snagged sleeve of her jumper.

Another hand, larger than hers, circled the basket, hovering above the neat fold of the newspaper, finding nothing to halt its progress. Elaine heard a voice that could be described in the same terms as a full-bodied red saying, "I'm afraid I'm going to have to ask you to unhand my avocado."

Elaine found herself being grinned at by a good-natured face above a collar and tie. "Is that what it is?" she asked.

"You haven't tried one?"

"Never." Elaine weighed the situation, judging it safe: the man, she estimated, was older than her by a good ten years and Elaine didn't consider the possibility that she might be attracted to older men. "What does it taste like?"

"It tastes of... avocado." Holding up a palm, he raised his eyebrows as if reprimanding a dog or a small child.

"You're teasing." She released her grip reluctantly.

"I am not!" He held the forbidden fruit between thumb and middle finger as easily as Elaine might an egg. "You've put me on the spot."

The checkout lady scanned her price list with customary disapproval. "It says here it's a fruit. Blimey, love, you've got expensive taste!"

"It might be a fruit, technically." When he turned to Elaine she was surprised that, unlike most people she encountered, he didn't look straight through her. She also saw that he was younger than her initial estimate. The grey hair must have arrived prematurely, providing the perfect match for his soft grey eyes. "But it's not sweet. Just clean-tasting."

"Like cucumber?"

"Creamier than that. I like mine filled with prawn cocktail." They had become the focus of gawpers. The man's discomfort apparent, he leaned towards Elaine, confiding, "To be honest, I'm hardly an authority. I had my first avocado last week at a business lunch."

"My husband doesn't eat shellfish." Elaine said, feeling a dip of disappointment.

As she was about to enquire about the price, the checkout lady gave a knowing look: "I've got one at home with a weak stomach."

"It's not that they don't agree with him." Elaine shook her

head. "I don't think he's ever tried prawns."

"Never tried prawns? I'd sack him if I were you," the man recommended.

Compelled to defend Graham, Elaine replied, "Being cautious is hardly a crime." But cautious was not how she would describe the new Graham. Now might be the time to plant a few in his egg salad.

"I'm afraid I have to disagree." The grey-eyed man counted the coins in his palm with small dips of his head and tipped an avalanche of silver into the cupped hand of the cashier.

"They do get set in their ways if you don't give them the occasional boot up the you-know-what."

"Hang on!" the man protested. "Who's this 'they' you're talking about?"

"Husbands," the cashier said, with a disparaging wrinkle of her nose.

It was obvious that his laughter drew more attention than he had bargained for. "How do you know I won't be offended by that sweeping generalisation?"

"You're not a husband!" the checkout lady proclaimed. "You wouldn't be doing your own shopping for starters. And I'm guessing from this little lot that you live alone." The self-declared expert on men stretched her mouth into the shape of a smile and then, just as quickly, retracted it, dropping change into his hand from a safe height.

"I have been married, you know." His flinch suggested he regretted his choice of words, as he packed a carrier bag with the ingredients for his lonely dinner under the predatory gaze of middle-aged women. Elaine resented the fact that they appeared to judge, some turning their backs, resuming weather and child-related chit-chat, others watching his every move as if he was someone to be wary of. When it came to the avocado, the grey-eyed man launched it into the air and caught it, firm-gripped, like a cricket ball. "Here." He turned towards her applause and, executing an extravagant gesture, said, "A present."

"I couldn't." Elaine's hand reached for her mouth and brushed the lips that had remained unkissed recently - except when Graham anticipated sex was on the cards.

"Live a little." He threw the words over his shoulder, as though, having tried both, he'd found that living alone was infinitely more attractive than married life.

It was the following week when Elaine next heard the sound of claret: "Well? How did you enjoy the avocado?"

She glanced up from her indecisive scrutiny of almost identical cuts of topside, glad she'd made the effort to wash her hair and put on some lipstick; sorry she'd retrieved yesterday's t-shirt and jeans from the bedroom floor. "Oh! Hello."

"So? How was it for you?"

"Very good." Aware she was being flirted with, Elaine didn't find the concept entirely objectionable.

Actually, it transpired that Elaine's longing for avocado had been satisfied by possession alone. It had reminded her of how, as a teenager, she wouldn't be able to get a certain song out of her head. She squirreled away pocket money to buy the record but, as soon as she got it home, Elaine only needed one listen before the stuck needle in her mind moved on.

"You didn't like it."

She hated to see the man's disappointment. "I can see why they call it a pear. I waited and waited, and then it was just…" Elaine cowered behind one hand. When she had tried to cut into the flesh of the avocado it was too hard, so she'd left it a couple of days, only to find that the pale flesh had adopted the colour and texture of overripe banana. What little she ate had been putrid.

"Too late?" As she laughed, the man performed a double-take. "Let me take you to a place where they serve it properly."

"Now?" Here, at last, was the offer of escape Elaine had been promised.

If she had been aware of the journalist who was devouring every word of this exchange, Elaine might have responded less enthusiastically, or at least exercised greater discretion. But, only a few feet to her left, Edwin Kay clapped his hand over his mouth, excitement flaring in the pit of his stomach. While his colleague on the news desk had been stalking the Jones girl, Edwin had only nipped out for a sandwich when, on a hunch, he had trailed the mother, and now found her accepting a proposition. His was an industry where careers were made on the basis of a single story and he was in dire need of a break. He had talked himself up from selling advertising space to the position of junior reporter, but had yet to deliver. Was it possible he had stumbled on the real story?

The grey-haired man, whose wire basket contained a single egg and cress sandwich and a newspaper, seemed surprised to have been taken up on his offer. Perhaps he had expected Mrs Jones to protest that she couldn't possibly, dressed as casually as she was, but she had already set hers down in the aisle. To Edwin, it almost appeared as if she was inviting the man rather than the other way around.

"Alright." The man agreed.

Only now, looking down at his egg and cress sandwich, did Mrs Jones hesitate. "You did mean 'now'?"

"Of course, I did!" Bending his knees, the man released the handle of his basket, only feet from hers.

To Elaine, his act had an enviably end-of-term feeling about it: unmistakably reckless. Recalling an explosion of flour bombs and eggs, she imagined autographing his shirt with lipstick. He grinned back at her, an explosion of crows' feet at the corners of his eyes, and they bypassed the tills, giggling like amateur shoplifters.

Outside the supermarket they were scowled at by a

pedestrian who felt her double pushchair entitled her to take up the entire pavement, while an ugly brown dog tied them in a reef knot with a battered leather lead. But instead of letting it put her off, Elaine succumbed to an irresistible urge to laugh out loud.

"I like that," the grey-eyed man said.

"What?"

"Your first reaction when you don't know what else to do is to smile."

It wasn't a quality Elaine recognised in herself, but she made a decision to be the person he described, if only for a few short hours. "Well." She began her teasing prelude, surprised at the fluttering of butterflies in her stomach - surely she'd outgrown such teenage reactions? "Are you going to tell me your name?"

He narrowed his eyes, as though giving the matter serious deliberation, and said, "That depends on whether you're going to tell me yours."

Elaine hoped that, when she spoke, her words had the sound of spontaneity: "Perhaps I won't."

"Anonymous: I like that too."

She watched him fall victim to a flat-capped man rattling a yellow charity box, who insisted on pressing a sticker onto his lapel as if awarding a prize rosette. She waved the box aside as she would when with Graham, suggesting that his contribution was from them both. "What if I bump into someone I know, and they expect me to introduce you?"

"You'll be able to tell the truth: 'Hello, Mrs Ledbetter. I have absolutely no idea who this man I'm having lunch with is.'"

"She won't believe me." Finding that she was holding her hands behind her back and walking from her hips, as if swinging the skirts of a wonderful dress, Elaine cast aside any thought that she might look ridiculous. Today Judy was not here to complain she was embarrassing her.

"Does it matter?"

"I suppose not." Exercising her smiling muscles was already causing an unfamiliar ache in her jaw. "I have no idea who Mrs Ledbetter is either!"

"Shall we?"

"Why not?" It was a decision and, untangled, they were free to walk.

There followed an obstacle-course of transactions, negotiated as if everything had been agreed in advance.

"Table for two?" the waiter asked.

Their inclination towards frivolity lingering, her companion conducted an unnecessary head-count. "Yes, two please."

"Wine?" The offer of wine on a Wednesday lunchtime. How could they object?

In fact, only one thing had been agreed on: they were to have avocado, and he ordered for her, snapping the menu shut.

The first glass of Chablis had already been poured, their glasses clinked, when the waiter returned with sorrowful eyes designed to overcome any objection. "Very sorry, Chef say avocado no ripe." He added a w-shaped shrug to the equation. "Garlic mushroom very good."

The grey-eyed man stood, took the waiter by the elbow and, steering him a metre away, lowered his voice. "I promised the lady avocado and I don't want to disappoint her. There are ripe avocados in the supermarket along the road."

"But, Sir…"

Elaine, embarrassed by public confrontations, no matter how small, pretended to look elsewhere. The only other customer was a young man dressed in a shiny jacket, alone in a discreet and half-lit corner. After studying the menu, he glanced around him looking somewhat embarrassed and checked the contents of his thin brown wallet. Elaine felt a maternal pang. Perhaps he had chosen an expensive restaurant in the hope of impressing a new girlfriend.

The grey-eyed man was pressing a note into the waiter's palm. "Please. It's not as if you're busy. You won't be gone a few minutes."

She sipped her wine, pretending not to notice when the waiter knowingly tapped the side of his nose and murmured, "Aphrodisiac."

Doubt arrived like an uninvited guest. Looking down at her lap, wondering what she was doing in a place like this wearing jeans, Elaine scratched at what looked like dried-on toothpaste. But already the grey-eyed man was drawing back his seat, and she found his look of relief strangely touching as he said, "I'm ninety-nine per cent sure I've talked him round."

"However did you manage that?"

"Bribery." He raised his eyebrows. "Don't tell me you missed anything?"

She leaned one shoulder towards him. "I could have sworn I just heard that avocados are renowned as an aphrodisiac."

"News to me." The grey-eyed man's voice grew croaky and he apologised before turning his head and coughing into his fist. "There was me thinking they were just an excellent companion for prawns."

The decision was hers. She set her glass down, quite deliberately. "Maybe we didn't need the wine."

Afterwards Elaine faced the wall as she dressed, conscious that her every move was being watched. Behind her, the grey-eyed man, propped up on one elbow, was covered by a sheet worn almost to transparency. Already, the moment she had straddled him seemed less and less likely to have been something that had happened a quarter of an hour earlier. But stripped of his suit, Elaine had sensed a vulnerability and a loneliness she felt entirely in tune with. Something she could respond to. She replayed the memory: the flush of his cheeks; the movement of his Adam's apple as his eyes scaled her torso; the salt and pepper hair of his chest; the occasional sight of her own breasts and the curve of her stomach; their contrasting skin tones. Her breathing was changing, and just as she was telling herself, *This shouldn't have happened*, he said in a voice laden with regret: "I'm not going to see you again, am I?"

"What makes you say that?" Tucking the t-shirt that had been untucked when she arrived into her jeans, Elaine glanced over her shoulder, catching sight of his long and elegant feet. "Just because I didn't tell you my name."

"No." He hesitated. "It's the fact that you weren't interested in mine. Somehow, I can't imagine you asking for my number."

Elaine now wanted to ask his name - wanted, quite urgently, for him to know hers. But she had to be strict with herself. *If you have his name it won't stop there*. She sat down on the mattress, facing the wall. Simulating a smile, her emerging voice sounded unnaturally cheerful: "I expect we'll bump into each other soon enough. We use the same supermarket." The image of respectability!

She shivered as he trailed one finger down the dry river-bed of her spine. "Something tells me you'll change the place you shop."

Even as he said the words, Elaine knew he was right. She was surprised how quickly her inner stillness had subsided. This had not been the answer, she knew that. But it had opened up a whole host of questions, some of which had yet to take the form of anything as tangible as words. She turned, placing one hand on his chest. "This isn't me, you know. I don't do things like this."

"I suppose I should be flattered." His eyes were rainclouds as he looked at her wedding band. "I should have known from the way you put your basket down."

"Whatever do you mean?"

"Oh, I sense you're someone who can put things to one side, but you'll always return to your responsibilities." Elaine's throat was in knots. "Right now, I imagine you'll go back to the supermarket and fill another basket with identical items."

She tried - and failed - to return to the lightness of the pre-lunch atmosphere. "Someone else will have had my joint of beef!" It was surprising to learn she'd been the cause of regret. It had been a long time since Elaine had felt anything other than utterly insignificant. She fought the urge to ask what he'd thought of her when he first saw her. It wasn't a question someone who was about to walk away had any right to ask. Needing to know the answer, she compromised: "Would you have still asked me to lunch? If you'd realised?"

"Almost certainly. But it would have been… different."

"How?"

"Well, I would have known that today was going to be the whole of something, for a start." He placed his hand on hers, covering it completely. Taken aback, Elaine was transported to the temple at Luxor where she had once seen the ruin of a statue, a fragment of the original: just a small foot resting on a large foot, and nothing else. "Does he know how lucky he is?" the man was saying.

"Lucky!" Elaine dismissed the notion, glancing away. When she had judged him safe, it was because she'd had in mind her twenty-year-old self. That the forty-year-old Elaine could be moved by so small a gesture was a dangerous thing to learn.

"Lucky," he assured her. "Go home to your husband - who isn't prepared to try shellfish - before he misses you. I hope you won't mind if I think of you sometimes in the fruit and veg aisle."

By then, kissing him on the lips would have seemed too

forward. And yet, not nearly personal enough. Elaine bent her head and pressed her lips to the place on his chest where his hand had overlapped hers.

Before leaving she paused in the doorway. The dishevelment before her looked like the scene of a burglary, and yet it was just the damage two lonely people can do to a room in less than an hour. "It was the whole of something," she said, the idea having put down roots. "For me."

He was sitting on the bed folding the stiff collar of his shirt over his tie, before noosing the knot upwards. His head dropped before he replied, "Yes, I can see that."

She wondered if he felt used, but had nothing else to offer. Stark realisation struck: this is how the man usually feels. *Leave, just leave.* Elaine opened the front door tentatively and, having reassured herself that there was no reporter waiting to pounce - just a man waiting at the bus stop with his back turned - broke into the outside world in the disguise of a middle-aged woman with errands to run.

Elaine excused the humble offering of beans on toast. "I can't believe how much the Co-op's gone downhill." She rotated the plate until the pattern was the right way up, as if presenting something from an *a la carte* menu. "I think I'll have to try shopping elsewhere."

She glanced at her daughter, who remained silent about the fact that she'd arrived home to find there was no dinner cooking, and that she'd been sent to the corner shop for bread, milk and two tins of beans. It struck Elaine now: she hadn't given the slightest thought to sending her daughter on an errand, whilst there had been a time in the not too distant past when she would have nervously paced the hall until she heard Judy's key in the lock. Elaine knew this revision of priorities would be interpreted as something meaningful.

Her own mother had turned into an emotional wreck in her mid-forties, until her GP had prescribed high-dose HRT. Was it possible...?

Picking up his knife and fork, Graham smiled. "Thank you, darling. Did you hear about the bush fires in Australia? The worst they've ever had, apparently."

She studied her husband. Graham was a meat-and-two-veg man. In his frequently expressed opinion, a meal without meat was no meal at all. Then she bristled. "What's that you've got on your forehead?" Elaine's matronly frown prepared to dampen a tissue with spittle to scrub the offending area raw.

"It's only ashes."

As he spoke, Elaine saw that the smudge was in the shape of a distorted cross.

Graham had turned to Judy. "I assume you had Mass at school today."

Her daughter stilled the movement of her knife and fork long enough to brush her fringe aside, revealing that she had been similarly stamped.

It was Ash Wednesday. Elaine had almost forgotten Pancake Day yesterday, resulting in a last minute dash to buy a new tin of golden syrup after discovering that the lid of the old was welded into position quite spectacularly. But she'd failed to make the connection between what had become a boon for Tate & Lyle and the subsequent day of fasting and abstinence. Graham thought she had *planned* the menu!

"I didn't realise you'd found time to go to church already," she said.

"Eight o'clock this morning." Graham was evidently pleased with himself. "I arranged to go in late and skip lunch."

"So you went to work." Horrified, Elaine nodded unblinkingly in her husband's direction. "Like that?"

"Ye-es?" Graham's voice contained amusement, as though it were perfectly normal to use public transport smeared with a blend of oil and ashes.

"But didn't you have the Bryant presentation this afternoon?"

"I did." Elaine watched her husband wave his fork excitedly. "Turns out, Mr Bryant's a Catholic. Of course, I'd completely forgotten about the ashes by then, but I'd say they won me the deal. He said it's high time we stopped being embarrassed about being Christians in a Christian country. I'd suggest we celebrate if it wasn't -"

"For Lent. Yes I know." Irritation rising, Elaine abandoned her loaded fork: she had never particularly liked baked beans. It landed with a louder clatter than she had intended.

"Listen to me!" her husband said. "I've done nothing but talk about my day. What did you get up to, love?"

"Oh, this and that." She replied too quickly, then, after touching a napkin to one side of her mouth, excused herself. Hurrying to the kitchen, Elaine opened the back door and fanned herself until the racing in her chest subsided. The irony of how she had spent her Ash Wednesday didn't escape her. There had been no fasting or abstinence - in fact, it occurred to Elaine that her headache might be a hangover. Her eyes made the short journey to the water jug and glasses that she had laid out on a tray earlier, validating her hasty exit.

"Look what I forgot!" Depositing the tray on the table, Elaine smiled - chiefly for Judy's benefit - amazed at how comfortably the lie sat with her.

"I was just thinking that a coffee would go down nicely." Graham cautioned himself with a self-deprecating slap of his own wrist. "Only when you've finished, of course."

"I'm not hungry. Don't you want any afters?"

"Not unless you've made something that will go off." Elaine detected hope in Graham's voice.

"I was just going to open a tin of pineapple rings. What about you, Judy? More toast?"

But her daughter was staring at the cross her knife and fork had made, her cheeks flushed.

"Judy?" she asked.

Graham snapped his fingers in front of their daughter's eyes. "Penny for them?"

Judy emitted a sharp little gasp. She looked at them both as if in panic.

Elaine smiled. "I was only asking if you wanted anything else."

"No. Thank you."

"Pass me your plate, then." She held out her hand.

Judy sat, her eyes glazed.

"Your plate," Graham prompted. He sighed, made a pantomime of reaching across, lifting it from her placemat and handing it to Elaine. Judy's eyes trailed the journey of the plate and then continued, climbing Elaine's arm, her neck, until mother and daughter met each other's gaze. Mother quickly found that she had to look away, unnerved by the feeling that her daughter could see into the very core of her.

Later in bed, leaning on her husband's shoulder as she kissed his forehead, Elaine felt the warmth of his hand staying hers. Hope rose: perhaps past intimacies were not altogether outgrown. She settled against him contentedly, recalling a tangle of limbs within the four walls of a small rented room: refracted sunlight dancing on the wall. It had almost been... heavenly. But, with the smile still forming on her lips, Graham withdrew his hand. The tidal image, so vivid, receded beyond arm's reach. It seemed to belong to another CV. Not that of Elaine Jones, wife and mother.

Had the collision of hands been accidental? Perhaps it meant as little as the brief descent of a bluebottle on a window-sill as it goes in search of escape or sustenance. Elaine turned to face the wall with a brisk "Goodnight," aware that she left

Graham hanging onto the duvet. Her unseeing eyes open, it struck Elaine: the fact that this was capable of wounding her was a chasm as wide as the cold column of sheet that separated them. She was his wife. It was something she should have been capable of crossing. Instead Elaine apologised when she brushed against him as she moulded herself in the shape she would pretend to sleep in, until the ringing of the alarm clock dictated she need pretend no more. That Graham patted her as if she were a child irritated Elaine further. He thought that Judy's accident had strengthened their relationship, but how much easier it had been to find intimacy with a man whose name she didn't know! How much easier to give what she instinctively knew was needed and to receive in return.

Elaine indulged her anger. How could Graham fail to notice the change in her? Should she have to recount the touch of another man's hands on her breasts for her husband to realise *it had happened*? Shouldn't he be able to detect their passage, like the fingerprints of oil and ash that left their marks. As surely as Graham's kiss had left its imprint on the private place on her neck, labelling her as his far more clearly than any diamond ring. Unlike Judy's scars, it wasn't something that should be capable of being blocked from view by bedposts. But she knew where to direct the real blame. At the greedy God who had stolen her husband and, still dissatisfied, had demanded her daughter, leaving her excluded. Alone.

The next time it happened, and the next, Elaine would not reveal her name. It was neater that way. She had no need for a mechanism by which to recall numbers and locations; afternoons when she allowed herself to forget her family momentarily. It was not Elaine's fault that she was forced to behave like this. All she longed for was evidence that she wasn't invisible, acknowledged as someone other than hotel receptionist, secretary, taxi driver, cleaner and laundry assistant combined.

She wouldn't feel accountable. And if, sometimes, lingering in another supermarket aisle, Elaine paused to weigh an avocado in her hand - hoping that the man with grey eyes would instinctively know to come in search of her - it didn't have to mean anything. She was just another middle-aged woman shopping for groceries.

CHAPTER TWENTY-FIVE

S ome things, teenagers know instinctively. That they feel
things more deeply than adults is one of them. There are
things adults know instinctively too: that their teenage
children are incapable of understanding their own feelings,
for example.

Graham was not surprised to learn from a Radio 4 broadcast that teenagers are not uncommunicative and sulky for the
sake of it: scientific research has revealed how the adolescent
brain undergoes metamorphic re-development.

"That explains it!" he said to his wife. She was staring
out of the window, bending her knees to look at something
beyond his horizon.

Listening intently, Graham marvelled at the scope of God's
carefully preordained plan: "*More research is needed, but we
wouldn't be surprised to find that the way in which the brain
processes information completely changes during the teenage
years, and that the adult brain is not completely formed until
the mid-twenties.*"

"We've still got the upper hand for a few years." Graham
made a second attempt at conversation. Of late, Elaine seemed
as unresponsive as his daughter. Strange that his colleagues
felt the need to escape to the pub for an hour's peace before
going home to face 'the Missus', when his two examples of

womanhood, lovely though they were, needed to be drawn out like splinters. Increasingly, embarking on a conversation felt like navigating shark-infested waters at the tiller of a small boat. "Darling? Remember this: '*I would there were no age between sixteen and three-and-twenty, or that youth would sleep out the rest…*'"

"'*- for there is nothing in the between but getting wenches with child.' A Winter's Tale*: you were the shepherd." Elaine's voice was flat, but at least it was conversation. "It's starting to spit," she said. "I'm going to bring the washing in."

"Do you want any help?"

"No, you stay. There's no point in both of us getting wet."

Elaine surfaced from the house like a diver, gasping. The restlessness of the trees as they stirred and trembled spoke to her of longing - of yearning - defying the fact that she didn't believe in the soul. She reached upwards, blindly grasping, distributing wooden pegs here and there, piling socks and t-shirts onto her left shoulder. Yearning: a word she'd internalised but found hard to define. Present in the fluttering of leaves; in the aching in her breast; in her longing for the child she didn't know; for something constantly out of reach; echoed in music on the radio. She recalled the illusion of simplicity in a song the DJ had announced as *Nightporter*. Just an old-fashioned waltz, a tumbling of piano notes, before the cello steals in from a side entrance; its appearance so subtle that she detected it only in the slowing of her breathing. This, even before the voice, deep and rich - before the strains of the clarinet wrenched her heart from her chest - and, suddenly, it wasn't someone else's life the man was singing about: it was hers. What right does anyone have to peer inside her and sing about these things only she feels? To cause her to abandon her tower of ironing and press her back flat, seeking the coolness of the wall? It was only an old-fashioned waltz. How could it possibly mean so much?

Elaine's feet began to move in time with the lilting music inside her head. She held the sheet from the top of the pile on her shoulder, as she would the skirts of an evening dress, if she had such a thing. Wondering if she was alone in being sane while the rest of the world had gone quite mad, this perception became a possibility - *what if I am the only thing that exists.* An absence, not just of God, but of fellow man. And Elaine looked up, up through fat droplets of rain, wishing: *wash me clean again.*

At the same moment, perching on her windowsill, Judy was secretly consuming the non-curriculum copy of *The Life of St Bernadette* with Aztec Camera's *Oblivious* playing on the stereo as a cover. She could no longer find the answers she needed in *Just Seventeen*. Miranda would say she'd taken to the whole guilt thing like a duck to water, even when there was nothing to feel guilty about. She clasped the book to her chest after reading the passage in which Father Peyramale has asked Bernadeta to prove that the lady was real by asking her to perform a miracle. Something in the periphery of her vision caught Judy's eye. Against a churning backdrop of dark clouds, she saw her mother dancing slowly with a heavy white sheet, hair plastered to the side of her face. She laughed out loud at the spectacle, horrified by the possibility that Tommy Webber (only a metre away on the other side of this brick and plaster wall) might be sharing the same vision. She would never live it down, never! Judy lifted the needle, silencing the scrambling guitar; the arm slipping out of her hand to etch a matt black scratch across shiny vinyl grooves. Through the wall, she could hear Tommy singing, his voice loud and unashamed: *"Fifteen minutes with you..."*

In the midst of exchanging school uniform for drainpipe jeans adorned with unnecessary zips, Tommy paused at his bedroom window, hands still toying with his fringe. "Go for it, Mrs J!" he whispered as he watched her: a whirlwind, lifted face revealing closed lids, oblivious to the rain. He saw a woman who, unlike his own mother, was not constrained by being a housewife. Comfortable enough in her own skin to dance alone in her garden without caring what the world thinks. Tonight he would dance, but not without alcohol, not with the abandon he was witnessing. The recognition that he wasn't as free as Mrs J made him melancholic, a word employed by the NME journalist to describe The Smiths' music. Tommy would like to be a music journalist, a job that would lend itself neatly to his current lifestyle. His older brother does something called Credit Control, a 'proper job' according to his father (who thinks that only occupations requiring a suit and tie are worthy of contemplation). But his brother sets the alarm for six o'clock every morning, the time that Tommy intends to stagger home, so Dad will have to settle for disappointment.

For a moment, Tommy was tempted to run downstairs and seek out the loose fence panel, still hidden behind the overgrown border. Taking a wide stance, thumbs hooked inside pockets, he propositioned his reflection: "You look lonely dancing by yourself. Mind if I join you?" But that was the thing: Mrs J didn't look lonely. Tommy could see the irony. Not needing anyone was what made other people want to be with you. He practised looking self-contained then stole another glance outside. Where was Mr Jones? Any man in his right mind would be out there holding a woman like that.

Graham looked on with the expression he described as 'fly-catching' when someone else's jaw was hanging open. Half-tempted to rap on the window - a few short raps should do it - he was deterred by the possibility that this might be another challenge. The evening when his wife's dressing gown had fallen to the floor remained fresh in his mind. Wasn't there something that he - as the husband - should automatically know how to do? But Graham didn't dance, despite his promise to Judy that he would take lessons. And although slow dancing *looked* easy, the circular shuffling made him feel clownish. The truth was, Graham loved to watch his wife move. He had even learned to enjoy the moment of her return from temporary partners when, flushed and breathless, she reclaimed him. The trouble was, *this* Elaine didn't resemble his wife, flushed or otherwise: this Halloween-sheeted ghost was someone to be nervous of.

"Dad!" Graham turned to find Judy standing behind him, her face contorted. "Why are you just standing there? Make Mum come inside!"

"It's only a little rain." But there had been a sports' teacher who had once decreed it 'only rain', insisting they played on ankle-deep in mud, bruised by hailstones the size of conkers. Graham positioned himself directly behind the kitchen door, poised to act the moment decisiveness arrived.

"Only rain? You think this behaviour's normal? Anyone could be watching!"

"Oh... sod it!" Graham twisted the door handle.

"No." Judy was disbelieving, following her father as he stepped outside, each of his hops a silent apology in response to the sickening crunch of snails. She saw him throw the sodden sheet over his own shoulder and bow stiffly: his idea of how a man asks a woman to dance. Was there a male equivalent of the menopause? Because she couldn't cope with the two of them losing it at the same time. Not with everything else she had on her plate. Pillow cases and underpants were strewn around the wet grass. Judy covered her eyes with a hand to block out the view. "This can't be happening."

The doorbell rang. It would be Miranda, here to celebrate her release from what she called 'house arrest'. *Come in. Witness the madness.* Judy limped back inside and along the hallway using the top of the radiator as a handrail. Opening the door, she found Tommy Webber peering out from under his fringe. He seemed to be looking past her, see-sawing his weight from left to right.

"Something I can do for you?" Judy employed as much sarcasm as she could muster.

"I heard you were up and about. I was just wondering…" His gaze came to rest on her in a frown. "If you wanted to come to the club. You know…" He offered a strange little shoulder shimmy. "Practise your moves."

Was he asking her *out*?

She shrank under his blue gaze as he conducted a top to toe survey before his trainers backed away. "Only asking."

Found lacking, the invitation had been retracted before she'd had the opportunity to refuse. "Why the fuck is everyone obsessed with *dancing* all of a sudden?" Judy erupted, using all of her energy to slam the door.

CHAPTER TWENTY-SIX

Chosen or not, Judy's yearning to return to the state of ecstasy she had experienced - of freedom from her damaged body - became a physical ache. She returned to the Station of the Cross in the convent grounds, hoping for answers. Let people think she was one of those pious girls who attended early morning Mass or volunteered to read in church. This was a need, pure and simple. Like Miranda's nicotine cravings that had caused her to creep out to 'Smokers' Alley' through what, with frequent use, became a bald patch in the hedge. Judy scrunched her eyes closed and pleaded, her wishes more fervent than all those she had wasted on birthday candles; more desperate than when her mother had refused to bring a dead bird back to life; more concentrated than when she'd imagined she possessed the ability to make Tommy Webber notice her using the power of her own thoughts.

Nothing.

She opened her eyes, scowling at the now-familiar sight of Christ crucified, not just disappointed but slighted. You *made* me come back because you said there was something I needed to do. Well, here I am. You could at least give me a clue!

Nothing.

Judy slumped down to the ground, her inelegant way of

sitting that avoided painful kneeling, and looked up. The tops of the trees rippled in a liquid motion. She watched as part of a wispy cloud broke away and floated off. *If I can teach myself to walk again, I can teach myself to do this. I just have to remember how I did it before.*

She deliberately blurred her vision until treetops and cloud became indistinct, and the overall colour became grey but, try as she might, Judy couldn't work out how to achieve the same distortion with her hearing. And then she remembered that sound had not simply been distorted: there had been music. Strange, scale-like music, that rose and rose but never seemed to get any higher.

"There's a name for it?" Judy said, stunned to find there was a textbook answer. She had thought her question would sound so foolish that she'd waited until the last of her classmates had left the music room.

"Absolutely. It's called Shepard Tone." Mr Conway, the only male member of staff at the convent, wore a beard and shoulder-length hair a decade after they'd been fashion accessories, giving the impression that he'd come disguised as one of his ancestors and earning him the rather obvious nick-name of 'Jesus'.

"As in sheep?"

"No." She made a note as he spelt it for her. "It's an auditory illusion referred to as the sonic barber's pole."

She looked around the room, hoping for a keyboard with an organ effect, but found herself nodding towards the battered upright piano. "Can you play it for me?"

"Me?" Mr Conway took a step back. "No! But I do know where you can find a very good example."

Judy found the Qs in the music section in Woolworths and ran a fingertip along the shelf until she located a cellophane-wrapped cassette with a heraldic design on its cover. The track wasn't listed on *A Day at the Races,* but Mr Conway had assured her it was there, both at the beginning and the end, describing Brian May's guitar-playing as 'sublime'. With the justification that she was on a genuine mission, she slipped it inside her blazer, excusing herself politely as she bypassed those queuing with their bags of pick and mix.

Back in the safety of her bedroom, she tore at the wrapper with her teeth, slid the cassette into Miranda's Walkman and pressed play. A hiss, and the track began: two reverberating gongs, followed by what sounded like the soundtrack of an oriental film; something made in Hollywood without access to authentic instruments. Perhaps Mr Conway had misunderstood. To be honest, Judy had been surprised when he appeared to grasp what she thought she had described only vaguely. But then, just as she was about to fast-forward, the tone changed and - yes! - immediately, she felt her chest rise, her breathing slow. The soaring guitar climbed Escher's staircase in sets of three notes. It lasted just over thirty seconds before a dramatic gear-change - the equivalent of clicking fingers - just as she was slipping into a hypnotic state. With that feeling of being thrown back into the real world - cold, wet and angry - she re-wound the tape and pressed play. The same effect. Judy was excited by the potential, but just as she began to relax, in came that raw intro of competing guitars. Thirty seconds wasn't nearly enough. Ten minutes might do it, perhaps five at a push. Judy punched eject, turned the tape over and fast-forwarded to the end. After several impatient attempts, bypassing piano chords and children's voices, there it was again: sublime, not a word she'd normally use, but just as Mr Conway had said; rising, rising. Just over a minute before the sequence faded to a silence that felt particularly lonely.

She sat still for a while before she thought, *Perhaps*, and roused herself. Judy spent the evening experimenting with blank cassettes and her mother's tape-to-tape recorder but, with tears of frustration - she had thought she was *this* close - she dismissed her endeavours as pathetic: the joins sounded like a shotgun when played through headphones.

"Judy!"

She stopped and turned, seeing Mr Conway jogging up the corridor leading to the library. When he caught up with her his voice was breathless. "Well? Did you find what you needed?"

His look was one of pity. No longer deemed newsworthy, Judy was the school loner, a weirdo. She dismissed it, managing a wan smile. "Thanks. That was spot on."

He raised his eyebrows. "Don't tell me you didn't like it?"

"I did -"

"Believe me, I know a look of disappointment when I see one."

She sighed. "I was hoping for more. I spent the evening trying to tape a longer sequence but -" Tailing off and feeling her nostrils prickle, Judy looked away to shake her head.

He nodded. "Too clunky."

Embarrassed to find herself crying in front of a teacher, and a male one at that, Judy could only bite her bottom lip by way of response. She longed for the refuge of the library, where she could hide between the shelves.

He looked distracted for a moment, but perhaps he was pretending out of kindness. "Leave it with me. I have a friend who works at a recording studio and it just so happens that he owes me a favour."

"You think he could -?"

"I have no idea, but it's got to be worth a try."

CHAPTER TWENTY-SEVEN

Miranda and Judy waved to Julie, who was framed in the doorway rocking her small son. His face contorted in preparation to exercise his lungs as soon as he could remember the mechanics of screaming. Julie's eyes trailed the two girls enviously then, looking down at the bundle in her arms, she let out a sigh of resignation.

"Who'd have thought I'd miss the convent, eh? Stupid, hypocritical place! If it was down to me, there'd be a special corner of Hell reserved for every last one of them. Apart from Miranda... and the new girl, maybe." She crash-landed in the armchair she'd taken ownership of, previously designated her dad's special chair. Propping herself up with cushions, Julie reached for the fastenings of her nursing bra. "Right then, mister. You hungry? Let's give it another try."

"Jesus Christ!" Her brother passed through the room en route to the kitchen. "Can't you put them away?"

"It's this or he screams the place down. Take your pick. Anyway, I thought you were off out."

"I can hardly ask my mates round when you get them out every ten minutes."

"Lucky you. What I wouldn't give for that option."

"Perhaps you should have kept your knickers on."

There was a space in Hell with her brother's name on it as

well. "If your mates were gentlemen, I wouldn't have had to." She rotated her son's face towards him. "Who do you think he looks like?"

"You -!" He turned on his heels, his expression teetering between horror and disbelief. "You're... you're sick!"

The door slammed and Julie beamed down at her small son who was eyeing her judiciously. "Oh, give me a break!"

"So," said Miranda. "What did you think of Julie?"

Judy hesitated. It was a measure of their friendship that Miranda had introduced her to her best friend, and a leap of faith on Julie's part to invite her in. But when Miranda phoned, she'd thought the day was going to be about *them*. Time to put the world to rights. "The trouble with you is that you make it impossible to lie."

"You didn't like Jools!"

"It isn't that. It was more the -" Judy dragged her feet, unable to relate to the baby grows and muslins and squeaky toys strewn across what must have, until recently, been a perfectly civilised family living room "- Feed, wind, lift child to smell nappy routine. The last bit's gross, by the way." And the idea that some people, her own mother included, would do this out of choice. "I wouldn't swap with her."

"Perhaps they should let Julie run sex education lessons," Miranda said. "Instead of the whole thing with the condom and the cucumber." Over the months, Judy had noticed how Miranda had reduced her pace, often using a mechanism to slow herself down: in this case, an improvised game of hop-scotch. "We've been best friends since we were five."

Judy attempted to banish any feeling of jealousy. "That long?"

"Except for six months." She jumped onto both feet and executed a turn. "When she dumped me for Sarah Carling. Then I paired up with this girl from Paris called Michele

Duvray who taught me to swear in French. *Merde! Ce fils de salope me fait chier.*"

"That son of a bitch… makes me…"

"…Pisses me off." Crouching, Miranda used a penny in the place of a stone, then hopped after it. "I thought it would come in more useful than it has."

"My first best friend was Elsie Blunt. Strictly no swearing. But we always won the three-legged race."

Hop, hop, jump. "Egg and spoon?"

"Nah." Judy shook her head. "No sense of balance. Elsie had to have twenty stitches after she fell off the horse in gym class and cracked her head open."

"Ouch!"

A motor bike zoomed past, perilously close, causing Judy to leap away from the kerb, stumbling on a raised paving stone. Its passenger turned her helmet; a flare of recognition through the raised visor as the bike leaned violently into the corner.

"Nutter! Watch where you're going!" Even though her wrist was throbbing, it amused Judy to see Miranda running after the bike to brandish a fist before turning. "Christ, look at you!" She helped her up. "Are you OK?"

"Not really." Judy gave an involuntary wince as she inspected a grazed elbow. But it wasn't the possibility of injury that had shocked. She considered herself immune, like a person who has been bitten by a dog and all other dogs now leave well alone. No: the first time she'd seen Debbie since she'd been back on her feet, and not so much as a wave. What's more, Judy suspected that the leathered biker had been the cashier from the gaming arcade, the one Debbie had christened Bingo Boy.

"Probably another bloody journo."

"I wouldn't mind if it was." Judy cradled her sore arm. "I know her."

"What have you done to make enemies like that?"

"Believe it or not - that was my last best friend. Pre-wall."

Miranda laughed mirthlessly, walking backwards. "And I thought I was unpopular!"

Judy saw that the only fake things about Miranda were her make-up and the colour of her hair. Time to stop skirting around the issue. Still, it wasn't the easiest thing to say out loud. Putting it off, she ventured, "Do you know when the Disciplinary Committee meets?"

Miranda withdrew, shrugging her shoulders. "Doesn't make any difference. It's a foregone."

"Don't say that." It was true Miss Clark had already said she missed Miranda - in the past tense - and when Judy had pointed out she'd only been suspended, Miss Clark had let out a small 'huhf' as if to say, 'Oh, come on!'

"You were there. It was fine while Sister Euphemia was on my side, but I blew it." Triangular bulges in Miranda's pockets betrayed fists. "I always blow it."

"You were set up!"

"I saw it coming in slow motion, and I still had to open my big mouth."

Judy provided a small laugh with an escape route. "You were quite something. Nobody knew where to put them-selves."

"Yeah? Well, I'm glad to have provided your afternoon's entertainment."

"They can't expel you for saying what you think."

"Bullshit!"

Judy looked away and let her feet drag. "Who's going to teach me to swear in French?"

"So, this is about you, is it? I thought, for one minute, it was my future you were worried about."

It hadn't struck Judy until then that Miranda's future was in jeopardy. She wasn't the only person with things on her mind. Perhaps it was unfair to off-load. But the urgency she felt was a growing pressure at her temples, a buzzing in her ears. They turned the corner. "If it comes down to it..."

"Huh!"

"*If!* You won't have any trouble getting into another school." Suddenly shy, Judy elbow-barged Miranda. "You're the most intelligent person I know."

"Do you know what it means to have the word 'expelled' stamped on the front of your file in big fat letters? No one's going to listen to the facts and say, 'They pushed her too far.' They'll say, 'This is the girl who talks back to headmistresses.' End of. No, it's going to be home-schooling for me. Whoopee." Miranda recalled the heated discussion with her parents. Her mother had called it a bloody inconvenience. Mrs Potipher, who hated the second-class citizenship implied by *Dr* and *Mrs*, felt she was being demoted further: 'I'll be shackled to the house.' There had been talk of misplaced trust. Of reins being shortened (when Miranda wasn't aware they had been lengthened). The fact that her bitch-from-hell sister never caused them a moment's worry. Blame was placed on Miranda's choice of reading material, her taste in music and the way she dressed. Even Julie didn't escape mention. Somehow, it made sense to her parents - normally rational people - to blame someone who hadn't even been there at the time.

"You're the ones who taught me to say what I think!"

"*No, no, no!*" Grabbing his hair by the roots and pulling, her father appeared to have lost all concept of figurative speech. "We taught you to question what you're told."

"I thought that's what I was doing!"

"You didn't stick to the facts. If you believed the school was wrong about Julie, you could have talked to us. You could have discussed it with your headmistress in private. But you had to go and make it personal!"

"You think the decision to expel Julie was right," Miranda

said with realisation.

"*Of course* it was right. *There wasn't any bloody choice!*"

Her thoughts interrupted, Miranda heard Judy say something that sounded very much like, "I think I'm having visions." Although it couldn't have been. Obviously. Expecting to be annoyed that the conversation had taken an unscheduled detour, Miranda found she was grateful for a diversion. Judy was attempting to cheer her up, that was it. Trying to show appreciation, Miranda's reaction was suitably dry: "Oh, yeah? What kind would that be?"

Judy's gaze was firmly focused on the toes of her scuffed shoes. "I don't know exactly. The kind involving the Virgin Mary, I think."

"Bog standard, then." Run with the theme, why not? "Hey! You'll have to have a message. Something along the lines of 'say the rosary for the souls of poor sinners and build a small chapel in my honour.'"

"The hardest part is the sign. People will expect something big. What do you think I should ask for? An eclipse…?"

"Whoa there, Miracle Girl! Not even *you* can manage blinding lights." But as her friend dropped her schoolbag and slumped sideways against the wall, it dawned on Miranda. "You're serious?"

"…It's still unclear what I'm supposed to do."

Not detecting the full extent of Judy's distress, Miranda said, "Jesus, Mary and Joseph, you're as mad as the rest of them!"

This provoked a reaction Miranda hadn't anticipated. "Am I?" It appeared from the way Judy turned on her that her seriousness was deadly. "I survive a wall falling on me when they say I'll be a vegetable at the very least. But my dad claims he's received a message from God telling him everything will be OK as long as he converts. And, apparently, he's not mad. So he takes his story to Father Patrick and is all but laughed out of Streatham because - apparently - miracles only happen in the past. But Dad says, 'It's alright, I'll throw my daughter into the deal. Let's splash her face all over the newspapers and see if we can't convince a few non-believers.' And apparently that's not mad either. And then we have the convent - which is like stepping back into the past, let's face it. I get to queue up to be told I'm going to return to dust and have my forehead smeared with ashes, which feels pretty insane to me. And the thing is, everything I've read tells me Jesus was as anti-establishment as you get. But Julie gets thrown out for... well, being human, basically. And you're about to be slung out for sticking up for her..." Disturbingly, beads of sweat stood out on Judy's forehead.

"Don't upset yourself on my account. I'll be fine."

"And, meanwhile, my family sits round the dinner table being polite to each other, and my mother spends her evenings dancing in the back garden in the middle of the pouring rain. So tell me - because I really don't know the answer anymore: am I any madder than the rest of them?"

There was no answer to a question like that. With her friend close to hysterics, Miranda chose instead to administer a verbal slap round the face: "You can't do it."

"You make it sound as if I have a choice!"

"The local papers will have a field day: Read all about it - Miracle Girl in new Miracle. Can You Keep Up With The Joneses Because I Sure As Hell Can't?"

"Perfect. Free publicity."

It crossed Miranda's mind as she cupped her hand around what felt like a much-needed cigarette that this might still be some protest Judy was thinking of staging to prevent her expulsion. The sort of thing that she should have done for Julie, rather than just crossing her fingers. "If this is a plan to get thrown out of the convent, there are easier ways I can think of." The cigarette in Miranda's mouth moved in and out of her eye line as she spoke. She clicked her lighter until the spark became a flame, and narrowed her eyes as she inhaled. They set off again slowly. "Oh, no!" With two exaggerated footsteps, Miranda's Dr Martins came to a halt.

"What?"

She made a drama of grabbing Judy's good arm. "You don't think you're on some kind of mission, do you?"

Judy was silent.

My God, she did! Miranda tried another tack. "If it's an experiment in faith, forget it. God tried that 2,000 years ago and it didn't end well." The idea tickled her. *An experiment in faith.* "I'd always said the nuns would be the last people to believe in a miracle if it happened in their back yard."

"I thought you said Sister Euphemia was open-minded."

"Open-minded, yes. Not stark raving bonkers! Hey, there's no need for you to sacrifice yourself. I could do it, now I've got nothing to lose!"

Judy looked reproachful. "I thought you of all people might believe me."

Miranda felt distinctly uncomfortable, but protested, "Now, hang about!"

"You're treating it like a joke!"

"I'm trying - but it's quite hard to take in!"

"Well, don't bother." Judy limped on ahead. "You're not the Miracle Girl: I am."

CHAPTER TWENTY-EIGHT

Sister Euphemia occasionally invited a guest student to join the Disciplinary Committee. Sometimes, a close friend of the girl being disciplined. It was not for her own amusement, or even to cause a rift in a relationship (although that might be an unfortunate consequence). The primary reason was so that the friend would understand the outcome from the school's perspective. She would see that the decision, whichever way it went, was not made by one person alone. Certainly not by the headmistress, who didn't even think it was her place to chair proceedings (although she had been known to intervene if a committee member confided that a final decision wasn't within reach). The outcome wasn't always predictable. Sometimes, when the headmistress thought things would go in one direction, an emotional character reference was enough to tip the scales. Tapping a pen against her front teeth, Sister Euphemia had toyed long and hard with the idea of inviting the so-called 'Miracle Girl' to join the Committee. Their encounters thus far had not been particularly revealing. Judy was guarded, saying only what she thought was required. The headmistress had decided against it. Now she wondered if she'd been wrong. Judy would have spoken highly of Miranda, arguing that the school was full of girls who were willing to say 'yes' when they meant 'no'; that they would be left without someone to stimulate intelligent debate. Sister Euphemia signed the letter addressed to Dr and Mrs Potipher with misgivings. It was with considerable sadness that she stamped it Private and Confidential.

The headmistress asked for reports on the close friends of girls who had been excluded (the new terminology for 'expelled') from school. It was important to control the fallout. On the one hand she was genuinely concerned for the welfare of her pupils. (She might call them 'ladies' in public, but they were still girls.) It was hard to lose a friend. On the other hand, a single teenage girl with an appetite for vengeance could crop-spray significant areas with poison. Sometimes, all that was required was a quiet reminder that she should keep her thoughts to herself if she saw her future at the school. Counselling was an option if that didn't do the trick. It was a shame the school therapist was such a wishy-washy individual, the butt of many a staffroom joke. One could only imagine how the girls referred to her. It was unrealistic to expect them to approach the process with any degree of seriousness. Sister Euphemia's firm opinion was that the English do not do counselling well, either in terms of giving or receiving.

Judy's teachers all said the same: she conformed but was withdrawn; she made no attempt to form new friendships; she sat alone at lunch break, moving away if anyone so much as attempted to sit beside her. Frankly, it was rare to see a girl so determined to remain a loner. Having made a reasonable recovery academically-speaking - more so than the head-mistress had anticipated - Judy had turned into something of a daydreamer, frequently caught staring straight ahead or distractedly out of windows. The dark semicircles under her eyes were becoming impossible to ignore.

"Do you think it could be drugs?" Sister Euphemia asked Judy's form teacher in confidence.

"No!" Miss Stubbs replied, then, more reflectively: "No."

"I'm sorry, but we do have to ask ourselves these difficult questions."

"Not her." Miss Stubbs was surer this time. "She's not the type."

"And therein lies the problem. There never is a 'type'. Only someone who is tempted when they're vulnerable. Just last week I had a visit from a community police officer telling me he had removed some dealers from the alleyway. We were lucky. These things weren't nearly so accessible when we were teenagers."

Miss Stubbs rolled her eyes. "They were where I lived. Although you had to know where to look." Back-tracking from the implications of this remark, she raised her hand as if she were in class. "I didn't mean…"

"Really," said the headmistress dismissively. She was beginning to suspect that her latest recruit was not the right person for the job, but they were stuck with her for the remainder of the academic year.

Only the Religious Education teacher and the librarian had anything complimentary to say about Judy. It was a different girl they described.

"She's always very verbal in her contribution." Miss Clark was adamant. "Very lively, I'd say."

Sister Euphemia raised her eyebrows. "Oh?"

"An active and enquiring mind. As a convert, everything must seem very new to her."

"I'm pleased to hear it, I must say."

"And perhaps a little strange, even." Under Sister Euphemia's steely gaze, Miss Clark appeared nervous. "Ignore me, I'm rambling."

"She's ever so interested in the lives of the saints," the librarian piped up. "Especially the contemporary ones."

"Contemporary?"

The mousy woman mouthed the word silently, apparently

counting syllables and reviewing her last sentence mentally. She settled on a clarification. "By that, I mean the nineteenth and twentieth century saints."

"Yes, yes, I'm familiar. What I meant is that it's an unusual preoccupation for a fifteen-year-old."

"She's also terribly interested in the planets. She was researching comets -" Another rambler who needed to be put out of her misery.

"Well, we must encourage Judy to come out of her shell. That's what we're here for, after all."

"Yes, Sister." The librarian's relief was audible.

Pushing open her office window, Sister Euphemia heard the desolate cry of a gull, as if it had been blown off-course. Just then, Judy was navigating the courtyard. Sister Euphemia stopped what she'd been doing to observe. Keeping her distance behind the last group of her classmates, Judy paused in front of the statue of Our Lady, shifting her overladen bag from one shoulder to the other as if she were carrying the weight of the world. Two laughing girls loping in the opposite direction parted to negotiate the fountain with symmetry suggestive of rehearsed choreography. One, on finding Judy in her path, elbowed her sideways. When this mean little action failed to prompt the expected response, Laughing Girl turned to goad Judy.

"Oi! Miracle Girl! Whachoo looking at?"

Aware that she shouldn't have overheard the exchange, the grey cheerleader pounded one palm with a clenched fist. *Come on, Judy! Stand up for yourself.*

But the girl was silent. It was as if the exchange simply escaped her notice. No hunching of shoulders indicating fear or defeat. Judy's gaze appeared to be fixed on some small detail of the statue. Sister Euphemia had never liked the centrepiece. Where was it written that Mary was beautiful? She was fairly sure from her experience of life that beauty did not equate to holiness. The artistic challenge was to convey purity and, somehow, the male mind - as most artists possessed - confused the two.

Laughing Girl came back for another jibe, this time a hand applied forcibly to Judy's shoulder. She rocked, her bag slipping to the ground, its contents cascading onto the paving slabs - an unfortunate addition of nineteen-seventies' concrete - and still the girl didn't react. Another shove. Judy stood her ground. A slap to her face that Sister Euphemia experienced as a sharp intake of breath. It was unsettling watching violence from a girl. Boys settled their differences with fists and moved swiftly on. Girls, on the other hand, usually had an infinite capacity for spite. *Come on, Judy!* But perhaps Judy Jones had judged the situation correctly. React to a bully and you have a fight on your hands.

Laughing Girl's friend was looking anxious, eyes darting. Then they shot upwards - perhaps Sister Euphemia had betrayed herself. The headmistress recovered herself, pointed to the girl, then to Laughing Girl's back, then to her own feet: *The two of you! Here! Now!* Two faces looked up at her, then the pair huddled together in a jostling quick-march. As they passed under the veranda, thinking she was out of view, the girl who had not administered the blows grabbed a fistful of her cohort's hair, jerking her head sideways. By the time they were finished with each other, devising a suitable punishment would be almost unnecessary. And yet a few early morning Masses would be good for the pair. Sister Euphemia would have them both read. Matthew 5:39: *If someone strikes you on the right cheek, turn to him the other also.* Proverbs 24:29: *Do not say, "I'll do to him as he has done to me; I'll pay that man back for what he did."*

When at last she moved, Judy's hand went to her shoulder in search of the strap of her bag. The jagged movement of her head suggested surprise that it was missing. She squatted awkwardly, crab-like, leaning on one hand while she retrieved what was scattered around her feet.

"*Your fountain pen!*" Sister Euphemia would like to have shouted, seeing it lying in a gutter. No matter: she would retrieve it later.

Judy's limp was noticeable in a way that wasn't apparent at close quarters. There was a slight shuffle, a dragging of one foot. Had she been any of the other girls, the headmistress would have put it down to ill-fitting fashion shoes. *She'll never quite lose that,* thought Sister Euphemia.

"I must get round to inviting her up for a chat," she mused out loud. "Perhaps she'd be better off with girls her own age."

"Yes, Sister. Shall I make an appointment for you?" The secretary's response from the office next door served as a stark reminder that the headmistress was surrounded by people who only said what they thought she wanted to hear - even if they didn't have a clue what she was on about.

"No need. But I'm expecting a couple of girls very shortly." I can't move her now. She'll never catch up with the syllabus.

"Shall I send them in?"

"We'll let them stew for five minutes."

Yes, she should have asked Judy to stand up for Miranda: Miranda would have known exactly how to handle those despicable bullies. Far better than she ever could.

CHAPTER TWENTY-NINE

Before answering the ringing phone, Elaine checked her lipstick in the hallway mirror. The long morning and its tedious chores were over; the afternoon's freedoms beckoned.

"Mrs Jones?" the voice demanded before she'd even announced herself.

"Yes?"

"I'm glad I caught you. It's Sister Euphemia. I wonder if you wouldn't mind coming up to the school. As soon as you can."

"Isn't it something we could discuss over the phone? It's just that I'm -"

"There's been a small incident, I'm afraid."

Elaine's heart filled with an almost-forgotten chill. "Have you called an ambulance?" The hand that held the receiver now shaking, she tried to keep the terror from her voice. "The consultant said Judy should be taken straight to May Day if she was ever…"

"It's not a medical emergency, so to speak."

Elaine's relief was such that all she could do for a moment was breathe.

"Mrs Jones?"

"Yes. I'm here. I'm afraid that, what with everything our family has been through, my imagination tends to…"

"I should have realised. I apologise."

The problem with the convent is that there are so many rules it's difficult not to fall out of line. "Is it Judy's school work, then?"

Elaine heard the headmistress exhale and sensed discomfort. "I'd be more comfortable having this conversation face to face."

A summons to the headmistress's office. Nerve-inducing for a pupil; more so for the mother of the Miracle Girl. "Give me fifteen minutes," she said.

Added to everything else, Elaine experienced the distinct feeling of being watched as she parked her car and walked to the gates. Looking about her and finding no evidence Elaine wondered, *Is it possible I'm suffering from paranoia?*

"Mrs Jones, take a seat, won't you?" Sister Euphemia invited. An almost too-pleasant tone.

Now that they were seated opposite each other, neither woman looked remotely comfortable. Elaine was the more outwardly anxious of the two. With only the headmistress's assurances that Judy was safe, her memory was inclined to stray to the night when the torchlight rescue party had moved rubble, brick by brick.

"You're well, I trust?"

Disobeying her instruction to smile, Elaine's mouth twitched. She gripped the straps of her handbag, which offered the only available support. A clock on the wall dispensed seconds noisily, first a strong beat and then an aside. Like a metronome, it seemed to demand she kept strict time. Her mind crying out, *Tell me why I'm here!* she failed to join the conversation at her first attempt. Like a small girl with pigtails, she waited for the skipping rope to be turned again so that she could jump in. "Sister, would you mind getting to the point?"

"I wonder, Mrs Jones..." Sister Euphemia gave Elaine the

appearance of needing to check Judy's surname on the file in front of her and to apply it with unnatural frequency. "Would you mind telling me how things have been at home recently?"

"At home?" Elaine's thoughts turned not to domesticity, but to her weekday afternoons. Perhaps the summons had nothing to do with Judy. Had she been spotted somewhere she ought not to have been? Accompanied by someone she had no business being with? Shaking her head and looking down, unbidden, Elaine saw the pale skin of her parted thighs contrasting with a tanned torso lying beneath them. Even here she was not immune. Clamping her knees together, she decided against volunteering personal details without first being told what this was all about.

Sister Euphemia was smiling. "Have you noticed any - oh, I don't know - changes?"

Elaine's mind fast-forwarded to her husband's frequent absences; of the hours Judy spent alone in her bedroom, headphones on. And the pretence of normality that was played out around the dining room table: the 'how-was-your-day-darling?' that was supposed to make everything alright. "Changes?"

"Has Judy had any upsets, perhaps?"

So, it *was* her daughter's welfare that was under discussion, but what was the headmistress looking for, exactly? "Not since Miranda Potipher was expelled." Elaine allowed herself a small, carefully aimed dig. "But she seems to have got over that well enough." Nerves ignited in her the same claustrophobic anxiety that might be caused by an invading wasp dive-bombing around her kitchen. "Sister, can you tell me what this is all about?"

"In good time. Tell me first, did Judy, perhaps, receive any counselling after her accident?"

"No!" Recoiling internally from the thought, Elaine suddenly found herself on the back foot. She knew how much she

- as Judy's mother - had needed to talk, and there had been no one to listen; at least no one capable of listening without offering an opinion. Except perhaps Paula, there at the scene of the accident, whose practicality and kindness she'd all but rejected. "Once Judy was well enough, the priority was getting her home. Giving her a bit of normality. Her father arranged for a physiotherapist, but not a counsellor, no."

"And then Judy made the decision to join the Church?"

Suddenly, the chronology seemed terribly important. "That came later, after my husband..."

"But you didn't feel the same way." It wasn't a question.

"No, I didn't." Elaine moistened her lips and said curtly. "Still don't, in fact."

"If it's not too personal, can I ask why?"

"I can't believe you've called me here to discuss my personal beliefs!"

"Don't think for one moment I'm judging you, Mrs Jones. Your objectivity is the reason I invited you here today. It's the facts I'm after, nothing more."

Elaine fully intended that her stubborn sigh should imply that the endless questions - for which the headmistress was willing to hold up whatever was to follow - were not only unnecessary but pointless. "I was brought up C. of E., Sister. Graham and I both were. The night of Judy's accident, after the doctors told us she wouldn't pull through, my husband's first impulse was to pray. He believes the only reason his prayers were answered was because there was a nun in the hospital chapel. And because he made a promise. That whether or not Judy lived, he would become a Catholic. The fact that she lived... well, that was a miracle in his eyes."

"And in yours?"

"I was *there*, Sister. It was men who saved Judy. Paramedics. Surgeons." In the searchlights of Elaine's mind, the all-but-forgotten boy lingered and she was troubled that his heroic role remained unacknowledged. "But even if Graham's prayers *were* answered, I still don't understand. He was praying to the same God he's always prayed to."

"Yes, I see." It was an infuriatingly inadequate response as far as Elaine was concerned. "And before Judy's accident, did she show much interest in religion?"

"None."

"But you had her baptized? You took her to church, I presume?"

"Very occasionally."

"Understand that I'm not criticising you, Mrs Jones. I'm just trying to build a clear picture. Judy had this terrible accident. She spent, what, a year in recovery?"

"Eleven months."

"A long time for a girl of her age. And much of it on her own, I dare say. Cut off from her friends. A painful process of learning to walk again. And, with her father claiming it was a miracle, the local papers jumped on board."

Elaine heard her own sharp intake of breath, nodded, but said nothing. As Graham liked to point out, she didn't have to read the local rag. But, as long as he answered their questions - proudly and at length - as long as other people's eyes lingered, believing they knew her personally, she continued to do so. Sometimes it was comforting to read about her own tireless efforts, her pride in her daughter, God's personal interest in their lives (which Elaine doubted more than she doubted His existence). But, in the main, she checked the columns to assure herself that she hadn't been caught out. She had no fear that an angry deity would strike her down with bolts of lightning when the flash of a camera would be a far more destructive force.

"- but Judy has it in the back of her mind that when she recovers, things will go back to normal. Except that they don't. She has to take on board a new faith, a new school."

"She made her own choice when it came to religion."

"Presented with two options, it doesn't always feel as if we have freedom of choice. Sometimes - especially in smaller families -" Elaine bristled at Sister Euphemia's words, sounding so very like criticism "- I'm afraid the child can feel as if they're the referee. It can be agonising to have to take the side of one parent over the other."

"You see, I was determined not to put Judy in that position. Is she afraid to say that she thinks she's made the wrong decision?" *That was it!* Elaine felt an overwhelming sense of relief, and her fingers found the buttons of her coat as she readied herself to leave. "Her father *will* understand."

"No, Mrs Jones, I'm afraid that's not it."

And Elaine saw that the headmistress was afraid. *Actually* afraid. "What then?"

Sister Euphemia reminded herself to give the appearance of being in charge, never having anticipated the need for this particular conversation, despite her line of business. Not in 1984. Certainly not in Streatham. She had believed the convent walls to be impenetrable: she was wrong. "Judy believes she's had a vision."

"A vision?" Mrs Jones blinked rapidly.

"Here. In the grounds of the convent."

It was clearly not the anticipated response. "A vision of *what*?"

"Of the Virgin Mary, I suspect." Sister Euphemia felt her upper lip twitch. "Although she's reluctant to say as much. She's afraid to tell you because she doesn't think you'll believe her."

"And you do?"

Sister Euphemia heard the challenge in Mrs Jones's voice. "I have to be very cautious. On the one hand, I don't want to destroy a young girl's faith. On the other, I'm keen to avoid the hysteria that can accompany a claim like this."

"You *don't* believe her! You're more than happy to feed them mumbo-jumbo day in, day out… you see, to me, this typifies the Catholic Church. You ask rational-minded people to accept the impossible but, when something comes your way that appears to be a miracle, you reject it outright!" Mrs Jones had buried her fists in her mop of blonde hair, apparently having run out of steam, but her expression remained untethered.

"Mrs Jones, if I could stop you there." Holding her pen by the middle of the barrel, with a small adjustment of forefinger and thumb, the headmistress let the movement of the pen blur. "There may be another explanation: given Judy's medical history, I wonder if she's experienced a mild fit."

"But you said she was fine!" Mrs Jones's hands returned to the straps of her handbag, her knuckles white.

"And so she is. Some fits are no more than a disturbance in the activity of the brain. They can be brought on by stress or anxiety. We often see them during the run-up to exam time in girls who have no previous history. But they can also follow physical pain - which might apply to Judy. Or even when the girls go on these silly diets." Sister Euphemia paused for a reaction but, detecting none, continued: "Students with epilepsy tell me they see figures moving within bright lights. Sometimes they hear voices. Not everyone thinks the experience is religious, but it can be confusing for someone who doesn't know what's going on. I can't claim to understand the science, but I believe it has something to do with a disturbance between the two parts of the brain which control the sense of self. When communication is lost between them, it's not uncommon to feel there's someone else present. As with any other frightening experience, people like to give that presence a name."

"I don't understand. If Judy's fine, why do you think she's had a fit?"

"She was seen falling to the ground. It's possible that she fainted."

"Oh my God!" Mrs Jones's hand shot up to her mouth. At the same time, she rose to her feet, taking several impatient steps. "And you didn't think of calling an ambulance! With *her* history!"

"She came round very nicely and was quite lucid - although she's clearly had a deeply troubling experience. Before anything else, I think we should rule out a medical explanation. I'd like you to keep Judy at home until she's been tested. Just to make sure."

"You're worried about the school's reputation!"

"It's for your own peace of mind, first and foremost. But yes, I *am* worried, Mrs Jones. It's…" She dismissed her original choice of word but, discounting others, was forced to return to it. "Unfortunate."

"Unfortunate?" Mrs Jones's expression was resentful, as if this were some challenge devised to test her parenting skills.

"Let me be frank. If any other fifteen-year-old girl made claims of this nature, we'd be able to contain it. They might be ridiculed but we could stamp that out. Girls can be so cruel. It's an unfortunate fact, but there you have it." She paused to draw breath. "But this worries me. The press have a prior interest. I've had to remove their photographers from outside the school premises more than once. Judy has an audience. There's an appetite for her story." Sister Euphemia watched as Mrs Jones's expression was transformed by a range of emotions, the least of which was panic. Her point had hit home: people were waiting for the next instalment. "I understand your concern for your daughter. You'll feel better once you've seen Judy. Talk it through with her. Maybe, once she's had the opportunity to reflect, things won't seem as certain. Perhaps you can help her understand that, if she persists with her story, there is protocol we have to follow. She'll lose control of the situation very quickly - and for a girl who's already been through so much."

Mrs Jones looked like someone who thought she had already seen things spiral out of control. "Her father will believe her."

"I'm aware of that. And I'm not saying it didn't happen. I'm just saying that it may be better to keep this under wraps. Here." The headmistress handed her a piece of paper she'd already written on. "My out-of-hours number. Should you ever need it."

Elaine knew that, in addition to believing Judy, Graham might want it to be true. What she had to do was unavoidable - she had to be the voice of reason. She couldn't let Judy down again. "She'll hate me," Elaine said with cold resignation, slipping the piece of paper inside her handbag.

"No, she won't. Not if it's handled correctly. Right now you have one very anxious young lady to deal with and, in my experience, the only way to deal with anxious young ladies is by remaining absolutely calm. So I'm asking you to put whatever you're feeling aside."

Elaine's sense of outrage flared. "With respect, Sister, I know how to be a mother."

"You're right." The headmistress bowed her head, appearing to concede the point. "I apologise."

Heels clicking efficiently, Elaine allowed herself to be guided along the putty-coloured corridor, its bulletin boards overflowing with endless lists of do's and don'ts, to the school nurse's office. She experienced the same nervousness as the occasion when she was led through the maze of sterile hospital corridors to see her daughter after surgery. On that occasion, warned that what she saw would not be pretty, she'd leaned against Graham for support. Now, Elaine knew that she was completely alone.

Judy was reclining on a couch. On seeing her, she opened

her eyes. "Mum!" she cried, throwing herself at Elaine, who hadn't anticipated her daughter's urgency. She released her handbag and circled Judy with familiar arms, stroked the back of her head. The discovery that her daughter was the same height as her came as a surprise: Elaine felt warm breath against her ear, heard a whisper.

"They wouldn't let me talk to anyone, but I know what I saw."

"Come along, darling." Elaine looked over her daughter's shoulder at the headmistress. "Let's get you home."

CHAPTER THIRTY

It was some time since Judy had been sent to bed and it felt like a punishment. Pushed towards the foot of the staircase, Judy translated the words, "You need rest," as 'Wait until your father gets home.'

She performed the small rituals of arriving home: replacing her nose stud; her regulation knickers; pulling on her jeans. She was attuned to tensions in the fabric of the house. The tap-tap-tapping of a solitary crow pacing the dormer roof above her bedroom, pausing to test the lead with his probing black tongue. From the kitchen, the angry clanking of metal as her mother tidied away cutlery and saucepans; hollow banging as drawers and cupboards were slammed shut. Blame was present in the sounds. Strange, how the noise of housework reflected her mother's moods. Sometimes, equally loud, it managed to sound joyful. A vivid clank followed by a whoosh, the central heating joined the debate, followed by the accusatory Chinese whispers of pipes and radiators. '*We know, we know, we know.*'

Judy had told a lie. It was not the first time. Simply the first time she'd been discovered, crumpled at the foot of the Station of the Cross. Returning to the convent grounds equipped with Mr Conway's Shepard Tone tape, she realised that she must have succeeded in inducing what others apparently chose to call a 'fit'.

Then Dad's voice. "I'm home!"

Oh, God! What had made her blurt out what she'd seen when even Miranda hadn't believed her? She had sworn that she wouldn't. Not until things were absolutely clear, and perhaps not even then.

False and out of place, Judy heard canned laughter from the radio, one shrill voice pitched high above the others: the suggestion of mounting hysteria.

"In here!" Words from below in the hallway, ominous and low: "We need to talk."

What had she unleashed? Already used to being a curiosity, Judy recalled the taunting looks that had followed her: pity, disbelief, enthralled that something so delicious should interrupt an otherwise dreary day.

"Do you mind if I catch the news? Reagan's dropped another clanger..."

"Oh, this is..." As the voices retreated, Judy strained to listen: "*better than the news.*"

Her heart pounding loudly enough to imitate approaching footsteps, Judy anticipated the rap of knuckles on her bedroom door. Instead, travelling up through plasterboard, underlay and carpet, odd words and phrases distinguished themselves above the muffled rise and fall of voices. "*Never here!*" "*For Christ's sake!*" "*Filled her head*" A disjointed argument spiralled, sounding curiously like Shepard Tone in its lack of a conclusion. There would be pacing going on. Hands on hips. Pointing fingers. Ancient frustrations were being aired.

"*You must remember!*"

"*Remind me!*"

Eyes becoming accustomed to the dark, Judy played a mental game of hangman, populating the gaps with what was not entirely guesswork.

"*Don't walk out of here, Graham. I'm your wife. It's -- you should be talk--- to."*

"W--- I need is spiritual guid----. For ---t, I need to ---- to Father Patrick."

There was an extended pause here. Judy held her breath, ears burning.

"You heard what ----- Euph--ia said. We ---- -- keep this to ourselves."

"-- --- really think he won't have h----? How often do you ----- the Virgin Mary makes an appearance -- Streatham?"

"One day, you'll come ---- ---- that church of yours, and I won't be here waiting."

"Don't --- that, Elaine. Judy needs you. I need you."

"I don't think I can -- ---- anymore."

And then the argument shifted from the kitchen to the hall, one voice high but volume-controlled, the other infuriatingly calm.

"I know how strong you are. Don't forget, I watched you give birth to our daughter. I watched you get Judy back on her feet. ---- ---- --. I ---- Father Patrick will be able to make sense of this."

"We should be talking to a doctor, not a priest!"

"I know whose advice I prefer to trust."

Still, the footsteps didn't come. A cold draught stole underneath the bedroom door. She pictured her mother standing in the hall, long after her father had taken the option of walking away. Judy felt abandoned. There had been many occasions when she'd stood by her mother's side to wave her daddy off; many evenings when she had waited for his return, hoping that he would be in the mood to dangle her over his shoulders; swing her round like a carousel. The delicious anticipation of his arrival and those few unguarded moments before he withdrew: the cough behind the newspaper; the upright figure at the dinner table saying,

'Elbows!' And now Judy would have to wait again.

Some time later, she became aware of movement on the landing. Pretending to be asleep, she heard a single sniff, the creak of the loose floorboard outside the door to the spare bedroom - the only room she had ever been banned from playing in. And then silence resumed.

It was an eternity later, after Judy had drifted into semi-consciousness, that she heard the hiss of her door being inched open, the pile of the carpet surrendering to advancing wood. She felt the dip of the mattress, the weight of a hand on her lower leg. Turning over, Judy spoke into the darkness. "Dad?"

"Shhhh." It was her mother's voice, the tone she used to calm nightmares. "I didn't mean to wake you."

Disappointment threatening to overwhelm her, Judy asked, "Isn't he home yet?"

"He had to go out." She heard her mother swallow. "How are you feeling?"

Judy propped herself up on her elbows, her eyes having adjusted to what little light there was. "I'm not ill."

Blinking, her mother reached out to brush hair from her forehead. "We're going to get you checked out all the same. Just to be on the safe side."

"Another hospital!" Judy's frown shrugged the hand away, and she allowed her head to fall back heavily onto the pillow.

"Judy." The voice was hesitant. "You've heard of epilepsy, haven't you?"

How could something she had caused to happen be the result of a medical condition? "Yes, but…"

Judy felt her mother's persistent hand coming to rest on her brow. "You collapsed. It's the first thing we need to rule out."

Judy had read how the children at Beauraing had thrown themselves to their knees. "I didn't fall!"

"People saw you, darling. You probably don't remember."

"I know what I saw." Judy remembered the lady quite clearly. She bore a striking resemblance to the statue in the courtyard at the convent, whose sculptor had been very perceptive.

"I know what you *thought* you saw, but we're going to talk it through with a doctor who'll be able to explain it better than I can. And in the meanwhile, you'll be staying at home with me." These last few words were spoken in a tight little voice.

Judy protested, "But I feel fine..."

"Sister Euphemia thinks it's for the best. And I agree. Maybe if you feel well enough we can do something together, just the two of us. Perhaps we could go shopping." The voice that said 'shopping' was borrowed from a different octave. "How does that sound?"

"She wants to get rid of me. She's trying to do to me what she did to Miranda."

"Shhhh. No one's suggesting you've done anything wrong, darling. First things first: we need to get you to the hospital."

"Don't you even want to hear what I saw?"

"I think it's best we talk about it when we're all together."

"What happened to 'You can tell me anything'?" Judy turned to face the wall. "Dad will listen: he'll believe me."

Elaine's voice was abrupt. "Yes, we all know your father's a saint." Another sniff and she appeared to relent. "But if I have to be the enemy to help you, Judy, that's what I'm going to do. You must understand that, whatever I do, it's because I love you."

She might have wavered at the sound of her mother's quavering voice, the sight of her brimming eyes, but Judy remembered that her mother hadn't expected her to walk again - and she'd been wrong.

CHAPTER THIRTY-ONE

A fifteen-year-old girl and her mother sat close together on uncomfortable chairs in a hospital waiting room, but they were worlds apart. Distracted, the girl pushed back the half-moons of her fingernails. She was confident the tests were a complete waste of time, yet being back in hospital, with all of its smells and noises, had unnerved her. The woman hid behind a copy of *Good Housekeeping*, occasionally clearing her throat. They were waiting for the third and final test of the day. 'The big one', as the nurse who had taken Judy's blood had put it, pressing a plaster into the inside crease of her arm. Eventually the specialist nurse they had been waiting for arrived. Pristine in starched uniform, she gave no indication of being remotely embarrassed to be running three quarters of an hour late. Large glasses lent her an owl-like appearance.

"Judy Jones?"

Blanching, Judy looked to her mother to save her, but she was busy trading glances with the nurse: concern in exchange for empathy.

"Judy." Her mother pushed her forwards and she knew that she was on her own, back in the cold custody of white-coated professionals.

"You might want to grab a coffee," the nurse was saying in

a pity-laced tone. "We'll be another hour or so."

Judy was led to a side-room containing a large white leather chair that wouldn't have looked out of place in a dentist's surgery. This is a test like any other, she told herself. The nurse covered the headrest with a strip of paper towel, then said, "Jump up there for me."

Judy sat awkwardly and squirmed her way backwards, demonstrating the inappropriateness of the nurse's language. She glanced about at what looked like office equipment - a monitor and a photocopier.

"You'd better make yourself comfortable, because I'm going to be asking you to sit very still. OK?" The nurse scanned the contents of the referral letter from Judy's GP and the form Judy's mother had completed, her expression giving little away, then rested the clipboard in her lap and smiled for the first time, thin-lipped. "Just so you understand what we can hope to achieve today, you should be aware that there's no conclusive test for epilepsy, but your medical history, together with the test results, will give us an indication of whether it is *likely* that you have epilepsy. You've only had a single seizure." Judy chose not to correct her. "Around five per cent of people suffer a seizure at some point in their lives, and it will just be a single event. Epilepsy is the tendency to have recurring seizures. Any questions so far?"

Judy smiled and shook her head.

The nurse took a sleeveless gown and swept it over Judy's top half, reaching around the back of her neck to fasten it with Velcro. "What we're going to do now is attach these flat metal discs called electrodes to your head."

The nurse held out a tangle of wiring and pulled a number of stems from the mess of it. Each head of metal had a black dot in it, as if it were an eye. Looking at this instrument of torture, Judy wondered momentarily if they were trying to frighten her into a retraction. Perhaps that was what her mother and the nurse had been talking about behind her back. She prepared herself, repeating well-rehearsed mantras. *Everything is as it should be.*

"We're going to use some of this sticky gel. How does that feel?"

Judy shivered. "Cold."

"It will warm up. The job of the electrodes is to pick up the electrical signals that your brain is producing, and the EEG machine records them all on a computer. Your brainwaves will look like wavy lines on a graph. Then we'll take a look at the results and see if anything unusual is going on."

Within twenty or so minutes - during which Judy might have been at the hairdresser's for all the meticulous attentions that were being paid to her, the deep sighs, the occasional feel of breath on her skin - the nurse had Judy hooked up to the machinery. If she could have seen herself, she would have thought she looked like an extra from *Star Trek*.

"I haven't got epilepsy," Judy told the nurse, who was studying her handiwork critically, making final adjustments.

The nurse, brisk and efficient, had a set of disbelief about her jaw. "Then you have nothing to worry about."

There was movement behind Judy and she tried to ready herself. *Nothing is ever as bad as you think it's going to be.* A line appeared on the monitor, etched in black like a barbed wire fence. She was unable to tell if the lack of pain was because her techniques were effective, or because the procedure wasn't supposed to hurt. Either way, she felt the tension leave her torso.

"OK, I want you to breathe deeply for me."

She took a single deep inhalation, as she would when her GP was examining her chest.

"Don't forget the out. Good. And keep going."

The lines became lighter with more severe ups and downs.

"And now I'm going to ask you to look at a flashing light."

CHAPTER THIRTY-TWO

As Elaine carried the coffee cups into the living room, she heard the singing: the kind of tuneless cacophony she associated with football terraces. "Since when have the local team adopted *Kum ba Yah* as their anthem?" But she became serious when she noticed that Graham was sitting unnaturally upright, his eyes glued to the television screen. Elaine could feel him deliberately not looking at her. His silence too, even as she put a drink in front of him, had something stubborn about it. A sigh of irritation later, she strode across the room with the intention of rapping on the glass, but her fist stilled when she saw them. *What the -?* A row of flickering candles laid out on the wall of their front garden. Several half-lit faces at a respectful distance. Hymn sheets. "I hope this is a joke." She pulled on the edge of the curtain sharply and turned to her husband.

"They're here for Judy," he said, matter of factly.

Elaine was aghast. That he should know and not say - not *do* - anything. Another thought pressed its way to the front of her mind. "You didn't!"

"You're right," Graham replied, disappointment shading his voice. "I didn't."

Looking at her husband, Elaine saw he was telling the truth. Who then? Sister Euphemia? "How long have they been out there?"

"The first couple were waiting at the end of the road. They seemed to recognise me."

You led them to our front door! "Then why are you just sitting there?"

"I thought if I ignored them, they would get bored and go away."

Ignoring his attempts to appease her, Elaine started for the phone, making a detour via her handbag to retrieve the piece of paper the headmistress had given her. While still reaching for the receiver but before her hand made contact, the phone rang. She pulled back and glanced uncertainly at Graham who was holding onto the doorframe. He nodded. *Go ahead.* Slowly, she brought the receiver to her ear. "Two-nine-eight-nine, hello."

'Someone's laughing, Lord. Kum ba yah.'

Instead of standing where she normally would, where her distorted outline might be seen from outside, Elaine flattened her back against the front door.

"Elaine? It's Irene from over the road."

Elaine could have laughed with relief. It was her opposite neighbour, elderly but quite robust, certainly more than capable of dishing out as good as she got. "Irene! How are you?"

"Do you need to ask? I've just been outside to have a word with your visitors. If they hadn't blocked my way, I'd be there giving you an ear-bashing in person."

"I can assure you, they've got nothing to do with us. In fact, I was just…"

"Oh, save it! They told me… well, I'm not even going to repeat what they told me, except that they used the phrase, 'Midnight Vigil'. I'm telling you now, if I hear a note out of them after eleven o'clock - a single note! - I will be on the phone to the police, the council, in fact everyone I can darn well think of. Get rid of them. I don't care how you do it, but get rid of them!"

There was a clunk, followed by a burr.

"That was Irene," Elaine said to Graham, sarcasm creeping into her voice.

"What did she want?"

"She was wondering if they take requests. *What do you think she wanted?*" Elaine unfolded the piece of paper.

"Who are you calling?" Graham asked, his voice suggesting that, whoever she chose, this wasn't the right approach.

'*Someone's crying, Lord, Kum ba yah, Someone's crying, Lord.*'

As the phone rang out, Elaine chewed on a nail. Sister Euphemia had barely announced herself before Elaine began, "Sister. It's Elaine Jones. We have company."

"Company?"

"Unwanted company," she said pointedly. Elaine would have liked to have accused, 'You promised,' but no such assurance had been given. However, what had been implied when she was asked to remove Judy from school was that there would be silence from both camps. "I thought you wanted to avoid publicity!"

"You think *I* -?"

"Who else?"

In the following pause, even above the sinister and intimidating voices, Elaine could hear Graham's breathing, the murmuring of the fridge. "All that *I've* done is to remove a few unwelcome visitors from our grounds."

"And you gave them our address?"

"I did not! Mrs Jones, I think you need to look a little closer to home for an explanation."

"My husband has assured me..." But Elaine's voice petered out as her eyes drifted up the stairs.

"You spoke to Judy? Explained the consequences?"

And again, as with all her dealings with the headmistress, Elaine felt that she was on the back foot. "Very clearly."

"And you're aware, I take it, that she's been visiting the convent grounds? After we agreed it would be best for everyone if she stayed away?"

"I -"

"This is what I was afraid of. We must all do whatever we need to do to prepare ourselves."

And with that warning ringing in her ears, Elaine couldn't help looking at her husband reproachfully. "Well. I hope you're happy! What does that rulebook of yours say about suitable punishments for shameless self-promotion? Because, right now, I'm not sure grounding Judy for a week is going to do the trick!"

CHAPTER THIRTY-THREE

The heavy oak door opened a fraction and Mrs Peel's face appeared, interrupting the two men with a sliver of an apology. "It's the Bishop, Father. Shall I put him through?"

If anything, Father Patrick was surprised the call had not come sooner. "Let's get it over with, shall we?" The priest held his hand over the receiver while he drew breath, and then said as confidently as circumstances permitted, "Bishop! How good of you to call."

"*Father Patrick, some rather disturbing rumours have reached me.*"

Pushing himself to standing, the priest turned towards the French windows, stretching the loops of telephone wire to full capacity. He was aware of the low rumble of his stomach. In his nervousness, he was inclined to lean on the humour that worked wonders in so many other situations. "On the bright side, numbers are up. We don't normally see congregations this size except at midnight Mass. Now, we have them standing in the aisles on a weekday morning."

"*I'd like your reassurance that you're taking my concerns seriously, Father Patrick. I want you to tell me you've got this situation under control. I don't want to hear any more reports that people have been breaking into the grounds of the convent.*"

And I want you to stop the local paper from publishing any more articles about this so-called Miracle Girl."

"How can I control what the papers choose to print? They're a law unto themselves!"

"Are you saying that the task is beyond you?"

"No, I -"

"Then you will find a way, Father Patrick. You will discover the source of their information and cut off the supply. Do I make myself clear?"

Humility was demanded: Father Patrick prayed for the imminent arrival of a bucketful. "Yes, Bishop."

Now was not the time to mention that, only the day before, he had been persuaded to be interviewed by Thames Television. If he hadn't complied, as the researcher had so eloquently pointed out, there would be nothing to counter the views expressed by that dreadful man, Alistair Fischer. Atheists were entitled to their opinions, but Fischer was without a modicum of respect, a shred of decency. And what's more, unlike the priest, he was used to performing in front of a camera.

"Get the parents on board," the Bishop was railing. *"On board, do you hear?"*

Graham's attempts at feigning disinterest suggested he, too, could hear, if not everything, then at least the Bishop's tone.

"Because, if you don't, Father, I will come down there and put an end to this thing myself."

Father Patrick wondered at his own culpability: how he had asked the sceptical girl who visited his church if she thought her near-death experience was religious. Seeing Judy's vulnerability, it had seemed like the obvious question. But what road had he set her on?

"Good. How many times is it now, Father?"

To little avail, Father Patrick lowered his voice, shading

both the receiver and his mouth with one hand. "Three, I believe."

"You believe? Haven't you made it your business to confirm the facts?"

It seemed the Bishop couldn't even let a figure of speech go uncorrected. "It was three."

"And how many people were there at the last?"

Fifty-seven was the reported number. Some of his own parishioners, a small core from St Leonards and some Hari Krishnas, would you believe? Quite an achievement, given that they'd all had to shimmy over the convent wall. "Approximately? Oh, thirty I'd say."

"And the girl's persisting with her story, is she?"

Through the window, Father Patrick watched the progress of a fly as it made its way onto a spider's web suspended between two rose bushes. "Oh yes, she's certainly very persistent. And *consistent*, I have to say."

"You've spoken to her yourself?"

"Absolutely." Judy's confessions had become more frequent. Those whispered compilations of inconsequential things that pricked at her conscience, such excruciating detail that Father Patrick suspected she wanted to maintain her state of grace. "There's no doubt in my mind that she's absolutely sincere."

"And the medical opinion?"

The spider was confident in his camouflage, biding his time. Even without knowing where its eyes were, the priest could tell it was watching. "Still waiting for the results, I believe." On an impulse, he opened the patio door and, the line refusing to stretch any further, removed the receiver from his ear so that he could break the threads of the web. The fly dangled from a silk trapeze, separated from its predator.

"...der the circumstances, I think it best that you tone down whatever celebrations you have in mind for the feast of the Assumption of Our Lady."

"But the children, Bishop. The procession is the highlight of their summer!"

"No highlights, Father, and no processions. If it means disappointing the children it can't be helped."

"Bishop." Father Patrick hesitated, a coldness invading his bones. "I'm worried that if I deny this thing altogether, people will say our religion is dead."

"Our line is that Catholicism is a complete religion, you know that: nothing to be added and nothing to be taken away."

Father Patrick found himself hanging on the end of a dead line. He had not imagined himself the spider. Turning to replace the receiver, avoiding Graham's inquisitive eyes, he took a deep breath and conjured a convivial tone from the depths of his humiliation. "Well, Graham, you've got me in all kinds of trouble again."

"Why is there this reluctance to believe, Father? You know the visions aren't just happening here." Graham reached in his jacket pocket and took out a small notebook, flicking through the pages to arrive at an entry. *The man kept a notebook, for goodness sake!* "Doesn't that say something to you? Look at Kibeho. And what about Medjugorje?" His pronunciation was hit and miss but his meaning was clear. Both venues were tempting, a world away from Father Patrick's little parish in Streatham.

"Well, the Church hasn't given them her seal of approval either. And is unlikely to, I might add. But the key difference is numbers. Visions are always taken more seriously when they're seen by several people. Judy is just one voice." He sighed. "She's a brave girl, I'll grant you that."

"She's not the only one. What about this Mrs de Menezes in Surbiton I've read about? I'm thinking of paying her a visit."

Father Patrick looked at the man and saw the father. He sat down heavily in his tired leather chair, hearing the small release of air as the seat tolerated his bulk. "Can I be honest with you, Graham? Mrs de Menezes is a laughing stock. Our Lady appears to her in a pine tree in her back garden and tells her all aborted babies should be proclaimed martyrs. I mean, seriously!"

"You may think it's a joke, but she's attracted a strong following. People need miracles more than you might think."

Don't I know it! Father Patrick nodded slowly in agreement. "And, as a priest, it's my job to protect them from every nutcase who claims to see the face of Jesus in their tealeaves."

Graham visibly bridled: "Judy's no nutcase. How can I tell her God spoke to me, then refuse to believe her? I have to stand by her."

The priest accepted his had been an unfortunate turn of phrase. "I'd expect no less. But could you possibly do it in a way that doesn't involve shouting from the rooftops?" Remembering the Bishop's instructions, Father Patrick pulled an embarrassed face. "And the papers, Graham. Could you please stop talking to them?"

"You make it sound as if I'm feeding them stories. Their reporters ask me to comment and I comment, that's all."

"You might try avoiding them."

"How? They're camped outside my front door!"

The priest knew that he was clutching at straws. "Then, perhaps it's the comments you're giving them that are the issue."

"So, if I understand you correctly, I'm to deny both my daughter *and* my faith?" Graham shook his head. *No.* "I answer their questions because I'm afraid what they might print if I don't."

Father Patrick nodded. What the man said made absolute sense. Perhaps he could remedy the damage with tomorrow's television interview. That would reach a wider audience than the local rag. "Fair play to you, Graham. Let's not the two of us fall out. You came to me for counsel, not a lecture."

"And you have your boss breathing down your neck."

"I do. I do. And, believe me, the Bishop's a pussycat compared with some of his lot." Father Patrick pushed what little was left of his hair from the front to the back of his head, his hand lingering on his crown. "Now, if you'll excuse me, I have a procession and a picnic to cancel, and then I'm going to start typing a sermon about false prophets."

As Graham stood to leave, Father Patrick picked up the telephone receiver, sighed, and replaced it in its cradle. "I'd never normally suggest this, but you might want to give Sunday a miss."

"We'll be there, Father," said Graham, pausing in front of the heavy door.

Father Patrick felt extraordinarily weary. Perhaps the task really was beyond him. "How will it look with Judy standing there? Think about it!"

"Believe me." Graham hesitated, his hand clasping the brass handle. "These days, I do little else."

CHAPTER THIRTY-FOUR

The lows were getting worse. The come-downs with their muddied thinking and migraines; the in-between days when all Judy wanted to do was hide under her duvet; the days when her mother kept such a close eye on her that she couldn't sneak out; the failed and foiled attempts. She was surprised when her anguish was mistaken for teenage mood-swings, her silences for sulkiness. Judy read that Edward Lear had called his lows 'The Morbids' and decided to borrow the term. She was comforted by the fact that hers was a temporary state of affairs. Reassuring herself that all of the elements were now lined up, Judy had no reason to believe that the task she was now sure she had been called to was beyond her. And yet, looking down from her bedroom window at the heads of people below, here to bolster her up with support, why did she feel completely alone? Why couldn't she feel the love they sang about?

CHAPTER THIRTY-FIVE

"**Y**ou must be used to an audience." The make-up girl had insisted on a little powder to take the shine off Father Patrick's nose. "You know, in your line of business."

Sitting in a director's chair outside a small van in the church car park, the priest closed his eyes and submitted to her attentions. "Not like this, I'm not." It was not unpleasant, the sensation of having powder daubed on his brow and cheeks.

"They're a doddle, these outside broadcasts. Ten minutes tops. Anyway, you're going to be great. I've got a sixth sense about these things."

"I wish I shared your confidence," he said, reminding himself to imagine he was playing to an audience of one: the Bishop.

"There!" Opening his eyes, he saw her smiling approvingly, a goddess admiring her own handiwork. "You're done."

And the reporter, too, had been equally pally - consulting him on the history of the church and its most interesting features - before the questions began. "Father, for those of us who don't have the benefit of your background, can you explain what an apparition is?"

"Well," Father Patrick tried - unsuccessfully - to brush his wind-ruffled hair back into place. He sought out the camera lens, as he'd been instructed. "It's a mystical experience. During an apparition, the visionary can see and hear Heavenly beings the same way that you and I can see and hear one another." He tried to focus but the presence of a camera crew was attracting attention. A few passers-by, that weasely journalist, those who were queuing at the hatch of the Veg Man's van, and a boy who, determined to get his face on telly, was larking about around the back of some gravestones.

"And for those of the Catholic faith, is it essential to believe in apparitions?"

Rather than let his hands drift to the top of his head, Father Patrick clasped them in front of him. "No, that's up to the conscience of the individual entirely. So long as the apparition contains nothing that contravenes faith and morals."

"Some would say it's extraordinary for a fifteen-year-old girl to claim that she sees visions of the Virgin Mary. What guidance have you given your parishioners about Judy Jones's visions?"

"To those who ask, I quote the words of Pope Urban VIII. *In cases like this, it is better to believe than not to believe, for, if you believe, and it is proven true, you will be happy that you have believed, because our Holy Mother asked it. If you believe, and it should be proven false, you will receive all the blessings as if it had been true, because you believed it to be true.*"

During his quote - his intention was to stick to the company line - several people from the queue moved to the railings and stood, gripping the bars.

"So, when will the Catholic Church be in a position to confirm whether Judy's visions are authentic?"

"Well." There was an awkward moment as Father Patrick realised the camera had panned in on him scratching the side of his nose. "The Church never gives her approval of an apparition without exhaustive investigation."

"And when are those investigations likely to be complete?"

"I should be very clear that there are no investigations underway - or planned for that matter."

"But Mr Jones has specifically told us that his daughter is undergoing tests."

"If Mr Jones says that's the case..." How much to say without knowing what Graham had volunteered? The priest felt the wind tug at the hair on top of his head. "My understanding is that those tests are of a medical nature."

"Are you saying that the Church has *no* intention of investigating Judy's claims at the present time?"

Father Patrick flinched involuntarily as the microphone was thrust closer still. "Would you expect the Criminal Prosecution Service to launch an investigation without sufficient evidence? Of course not. Neither will the Church."

"And what would be considered to be 'sufficient evidence'?"

"That's very difficult to say."

"But if you were -------?"

Somewhere nearby a workman's drill started up, drowning out the reporter's question. The priest put a finger in one ear and moved closer. "I'm sorry." In the periphery of his vision he saw a runner living up to his job title, sprinting towards the road.

The reporter raised his voice: "If pushed, what would you say?"

"Each case is individual."

"Then let me give you an example." The young man clicked his fingers and was handed a laminated sheet. He waited for the drilling to cut before reading out loud. "At Fatima, if I understand correctly, up to 100,000 people saw a large silvery-grey disc descend from the sky, flashing bright colours. Some feared for their lives. No movement or other phenomenon of the sun was registered by scientists at the time..."

Father Patrick blinked rapidly. "Yes, but there's been nothing like that here." What exactly was expected of the poor girl?

"Alright, let me ask you this. What would happen if resources were to be committed?"

"The Archbishop or Bishop of our locality would be granted the authority to form a committee, from whose evidence they would draw conclusions and pronounce a decree."

"Based on what, exactly?"

"There are four parts that the commission would look for: the moral certainty of the miraculous and exceptional occurrence beyond human explanation; the honesty, sincerity, mental soundness and moral conduct of the visionary..."

The potato struck Father Patrick a blow as if his head were a coconut shy. As he fell there were gasps from the spectators, a few of whom sprinted forwards.

Determined to clear his own name, the Veg Man held the boy down - it was one of his baking potatoes had done the damage. "The boy must have nicked it!" He was outraged, as if defending an accusation of arming local yobs.

Now off air, picking up the offending item, the reporter swung his arm. "Blimey, this thing's like a bowling ball!"

"Give it here," Father Patrick said, recovering from the humiliation and shock. "I'll have it for my tea. And let the lad go. The last thing we need is the police."

The make-up girl insisted on fussing over him until Mrs Peel could be located. Thames Television's cameras might have stopped rolling but the man by the gates with his zoom lens clearly couldn't resist the sight of a balding priest, spread-eagle on an overgrown path, being dabbed at by a pretty young girl.

After learning of his predicament, like the plumber who labels every other member of his profession a cowboy, Mrs Peel railed as she moulded a bag of frozen peas to his brow: "I don't know what on earth she thought she was doing, rolling a Diet Coke can across your forehead!"

Watching the broadcast as it aired, now holding a bag of frozen runner beans, Father Patrick saw the moment the nervous-looking reporter jumped back after the potato had struck, summarising his wince-inducing understanding of what Father Patrick had said, before the edit cut to the studio. Vincent Cox responded with flippancy before introducing 'eminent philosopher, Alistair Fischer.'

"Good evening, Vincent - do you mind if I call you Vincent?" Alistair had smiled charmingly - some might say sleazily - then launched into his own sermon. "Firstly, I think it would be useful if I make my position one hundred per cent clear. I have no doubt that Judy Jones is one of many victims of an outmoded belief system based predominantly on fear. With all we know in the twentieth century, I find the concept that there is no basis for morality without a God deeply insulting." He bared his too-white teeth to camera. "As I'm sure all right-minded people do."

Father Patrick couldn't recall when he had last felt genuine hatred, but watching the slick performance in the television studio - Fischer's well-cut suit, his carefully rehearsed words - the blackest of emotions flooded back. By contrast, filmed outside St Joseph's with the wind blowing a gale, his own stance looked awkward, his shirt - he now saw - in need of ironing, his words improvised. And the fact that he had been forced into this untenable situation did not help. Neither did Mrs Peel's well-intended words as she breezed through the room brandishing a can of furniture polish.

"You were heroic, Father."

Amateurish, thought the priest as he stared miserably at the television screen. "I doubt the Bishop will share your sentiments."

Pausing momentarily, even Mrs Peel seemed hypnotised by Alistair Fischer's Cliff-Richard charm.

"And here we have Father Patrick - clearly embarrassed to

find a member of his congregation making claims that support the very belief system he is peddling - saying, 'better to hedge your bets, so long as the apparitions are not *objectionable*.' It's rather like the arguments for the existence of God. Best be on the safe side, in case it turns out there's a hell. And I have to say, I find this brainwashing of the young particularly objectionable. Frankly, I worry for Judy Jones. That is the chief reason I was prepared to appear on your show tonight."

"The other being the launch of your new book!" Father Patrick addressed the set bitterly, breaking his housekeeper's reverie who, with cheeks colouring, sighed and moved on.

"I mean, *beyond human explanation*. Judy Jones is expected to provide proof - *proof!* The Church, whose priests and leaders have made careers out of demanding grown adults believe the improbable – who have never offered proof - is demanding a miracle in order to prove a miracle. And *mental soundness!* That phrase is enough to put the fear of - listen to me: I was almost going to say 'fear of God' - into you."

Vincent Cox indulged his guest by laughing.

"Oh come *on!*" To an observer it might have appeared that Father Patrick was appealing to an invisible referee.

"I ask you, where are the people who should be protecting this vulnerable youth? Her parents? Well, let me tell you: it's the father who first claimed his daughter has supernatural abilities. He's the one who's pushing her!"

Retrospectively, Father Patrick thought of all the things he might have said. *"So, what do you think of Alistair Fischer?" "To be honest, Scott - do you mind if I call you Scott? - I pity him. I think that anyone who can't bring himself to consider the possibility of God lacks curiosity and imagination. He pretends to be interested in the truth, to have conducted an academic study but, at the end of the day, he's only interested in lining his pockets. Deep down, he's a very angry man."*

But the truth was that he had never read any of Alistair

Fischer's books - didn't care one jot for *that man's* opinion. And, as he heard the telephone start its angry ringing in the hall, the priest reflected that he should have known that whatever he said would be manipulated to make him look a fool. But worse than that: not only would the Bishop be furious; he had publicly betrayed Judy's trust. After what he had said to Graham!

"Father?" Mrs Peel's expression as she interrupted was her habitual wince.

Clamping one hand over his mouth, Father Patrick raised his eyes to the ceiling and closed them momentarily. *Dear God in Heaven, give me strength.* "Yes, Mrs Peel, you may put the Bishop through."

"Oh, it's not the Bishop, Father. It's Sister Euphemia."

"Is it? Is it now?" He picked up the receiver. "Sister, what an unexpected pleasure! No, I'm not being at all sarcastic. I'm grand, thanks for your concern. Just a small bump to show for my foolish adventures. My own banner? I should be flattered. Father Potato Head, is it now? Lord, no, the Bishop won't be nearly so complimentary."

CHAPTER THIRTY-SIX

Elaine left the security chain in place. Reined in, the door jarred as she opened it. The blinding light that greeted her was quickly identified as photographers' flashbulbs.

"Mrs Jones!"

"Post!" a familiar voice announced.

She tightened the belt of her dressing gown and drew back the chain. "Morning, Charlie." Elaine's voice lacked enthusiasm, and she avoided eye contact. In his shorts, he had a boyish look about him, although she imagined, like her, he was well into his forties.

"They're all camped out front again, I see." The postman handed Elaine a pile of envelopes and delved into his pannier for the parcels, which he piled under her elevated chin. "*The End is Nigh*, I ask you!" He held up his hands in an impression of a ghoul that wouldn't scare small children at Halloween.

"Just one minute of your time!"

Elaine managed a pitiful smile: "I'm sorry you've had to battle your way through."

"All in a day's work."

"Hardly." She frowned as she saw the tops of large black letters on baggy white backgrounds above the garden wall. "Are those 'Relax' t-shirts?"

"No! These aren't your *Frankie Goes to Hollywood* fans. This is your different category of weirdo." The postman winced as though he regretted his choice of words, moving on quickly. "Your daughter's inspired a whole new clothing range. They say 'Repent'. You should demand shares! Might be a few quid in it."

Elaine sighed. "I wouldn't mind if it was a positive message. 'Rejoice', perhaps."

"See! There's no end of possibilities."

Jostling for a front row position at the gate, a newspaper reporter raised a territorial hand, shouting to make his presence felt. "Mrs Jones! Have you got anything to say about your daughter's visions?"

Not to be outdone, his rival was quick to join in: "Have you seen Our Lady of Streatham, Mrs Jones?"

Flash! Flash! Flash!

"Why can't you leave us alone! All of you! This is our home, not a bloody circus!" Shielding her eyes, Elaine called over the safety of Charlie's shoulder, and then smiled at him wryly. "They'll write a whole article about that. *Mother of Miracle Girl Swears.*"

The journalists appeared to be in an optimistic mood. "Mrs Jones! How do you feel about Judy's growing following?"

"Oh, I didn't realise you recognised the possibility that I might have *feelings!*" Elaine stepped forwards, the movement of her chin causing the parcels to grate like seismic plates. Having begun, she was unable to stem the flow: "Tell me, how would you feel if I camped outside your home, day and night? If the neighbours you'd been friends with for years turned on you. If you couldn't bring your post in without having your photo taken. If you couldn't pop out for a sodding pint of milk without being followed. See that?" She turned her head and nodded to a boarded pane in the bay window. "The other evening, we were sitting down watching television and a brick came flying through. A brick with a note wrapped round it."

Another journalist jostled for position. "What did it say, Mrs Jones?"

Lock up your daughter, was what it had said. "Mind your own bloody business. My point is that you would feel trapped! So, being honest, I wish you'd all fuck off! Yes, you heard me correctly! And, please, feel free to quote me on that." Elaine turned back towards the house and squeezed her eyes shut, allowing one to open to gauge Charlie's reaction.

"You certainly gave them their money's worth."

"Thank you," she said, her heart beating wildly. "I'm expecting a very flattering write-up."

"Trouble is, give them a performance and they'll demand an encore."

"Oh God, you're right!" Two choices presented themselves: laugh or cry. Elaine laughed at the whole horrific mess. "Graham's going to be furious."

"You bearing up?" Charlie asked, retrieving the scattering of small parcels she'd left in her wake and inserting them randomly into the pile.

"I'm still here, aren't I?"

Using her hip and the side of her bare foot, Elaine closed the door. She leaned back, mouthing her full repertoire of expletives, some of which she hadn't given an airing since her teens, and then composed herself. Entering the kitchen, she bent her knees and spilled the day's delivery onto the table, where Graham and Judy were seated behind a skyline of cereal packets, their faces the sun and the moon.

A spoonful of cornflakes poised, Graham asked, "Busy out there?"

"You could say that. But then it's perfectly normal to find a small delegation outside your garden gate at this time in the morning." She glared at Judy who hadn't denied she had encouraged their presence. Now, it seemed, advertising was no longer required. Word had spread like forest fire and, like forest fire, it seemed that nothing now would stop it. And Elaine, who hadn't turned to prayer, found herself resorting to half-remembered Sunday school lessons as a reference point: Mary locating the twelve-year-old Jesus in the temple after an agonising search: *Why hast thou thus dealt with us?*

"Are you alright, darling?"

"Of course. Why wouldn't I be?" Elaine rattled a brown paper cube before sending it spinning in her daughter's direction. "Another rosary. And here's another. And, oh look: there's actually a letter for me." Sarcasm evaporated as Elaine identified the blue franking on the envelope. Taking her seat, she licked her lips, finding them unusually dry. "It's from the hospital."

As Judy reached for her father's hand on the corner of the table, Elaine fought off a pang of jealousy. There was a time…

"Well?" After Graham's nod, she used the butter knife to cut a jagged line through the envelope and then scanned the letter, eyes zigzagging.

"Can I have a look? It *is* about me."

"Shhhh!" Refusing to be rushed, Elaine placed her index finger on the sheet and traced a horizontal line. "Urine sample: normal. Sugar levels: normal. No signs of infection. Blood tests: normal. EEG: clear."

"Remind me what that was." Graham put his redundant hand on top of Judy's.

"That's when they stuck those little pads all over my head."

"Well." He beamed. "It sounds like a clean bill of health."

Elaine exhaled slowly. Even though part of her was light-headed with relief, she had been relying on a finite and logical explanation.

"Anything else?" Graham raised his eyebrows.

Elaine felt the return of the involuntary twitching above her right eye as she digested the final paragraph. "It says here that, with many types of epilepsy, sufferers only have unusual electrical activity in their brains while having a seizure. Since the EEG only records brain activity at the time of the test, a clear outcome doesn't rule out the possibility that you may have epilepsy. No treatment recommended at the moment." She turned over the piece of paper, searching for that something she'd missed: nothing. "Come back if she has another seizure."

"They're just covering themselves." Graham squeezed Judy's hand in a congratulatory manner. "Well, it's back to school for you, young lady."

"Not so fast!" said Elaine, husband and daughter turning to her in astonished unison. "We have to talk about what this means."

Judy looked at her almost resentfully. "I thought you didn't want to talk about it."

"Now then." Graham activated his warning voice. "We've all been under a huge amount of pressure." Then he appealed. "It means that Judy is well."

"It means that our lives have changed!" Elaine said, hardly believing what she was hearing. "People have set up camp in the road. They're out there, frying bacon on their stoves. They're wearing *t-shirts*."

A crunching sound, movement on gravel at the side of the house, Elaine looked up to see the face of a woman looming at the kitchen window, just above the sink. "Jesus Christ!" Her hand flew to her chest.

"I'll handle this." Graham pushed back his chair and the sleeves of his v-neck pullover. He rapped sharply on the double-glazed panel of the kitchen door, raising his voice. "This is private property! Leave now or I'll call the police!"

Undeterred, the woman pointed eagerly at Judy. Elaine lip-read her question, "Is that her?" before she saw her walk towards the back of the house.

Elaine's face was marble, her mouth open, as her daughter disappeared into the hall, the t-shirt she had slept in skimming her scarred thighs. Of all the things she might complain about, it hardly seemed worthwhile mentioning that Judy was inadequately dressed to answer the door. A number of rosaries were looped around her daughter's wrist. She felt the touch of Graham's hand on her arm as Judy was haloed by a flash of bulbs.

"Is She here?" a voice shouted.

The press of bodies against the gate and the front wall reminded Elaine of the surge in front of the stage at the Led Zeppelin gig, arms grabbing like pincers, hysterical screaming. She wondered that rock stars didn't faint in terror at the sight of an audience.

She wondered at the sight of her daughter, apparently undaunted, walking towards the flashbulbs as if they were the sun's rays. "No. The Lady doesn't visit me here."

The more forward of the two journalists said, "Judy, I get the impression your mother doesn't share your belief. What would you like to say to her?"

The latch of the garden gate clicked open and those who had been pressing against it stumbled through onto the garden path. Elaine stepped back and, treading on the toe of someone behind her, instinctively apologised. Then, turning, she shrieked, *"Graham!"* The moon-faced woman was in their house! - here, in their hall - waving to the people outside as if this was all a lark.

"Get out of my *house!*" Elaine heard her voice rising. *"Get OUT!"*

The woman drew a map in the air, directing others to the side gate.

"This is for you." Judy was rewarding those on the path with sets of rosary beads, receiving murmurs of thanks in return. "She wants you to pray."

"*Graham!*" Elaine couldn't contain her violent shaking. "*Call the police!*"

"Listen to that authority," Graham whispered in awe, staring at his daughter as she steered people out of the gate, the crowd willing to step apart so that they could experience a front row view.

"This is madness!" Elaine said, still facing the moon-faced woman, who was bearing down on her, one arm reaching.

"*Go home now and pray with your families.*"

"Shhhh." Her husband appeared to be transfixed.

"Now, Graham! *Pick up the bloody phone!*" Elaine backed into him.

"It's alright. They're listening to reason."

Just as Elaine thought the moon-faced woman would touch her, she barged past, almost carrying Elaine in her wake. "Me! Me!" she was grabbing, one hand opening and closing like a claw.

Judy turned, smiled and looped a rosary on the woman's wrist. "I saved this one especially for you. Now, go home."

Watching, Elaine gulped back breaths of pure relief as, reluctantly at first, the crowd began to disperse, taking their folding chairs and fishing umbrellas with them, until only the hardcore, the homeless and the journalists were left.

"Got a few good shots. That was time well spent." A five pound note was peeled off a roll and thrust into the hand of a middle-aged man. "Thanks for the tip-off."

Elaine pulled herself inwards as her shoulder was crushed by Graham's arm. "I told you it would be alright," he was saying, and she found his confidence the hardest thing to accept.

"Are you mad? How is this alright? Any of it?" she protested, holding one hand across her body, the other securing it as if it were a small wounded thing in need of shelter. "I can't do this anymore. If they won't leave, we'll have to go. As far away from here as possible!"

Standing behind her, watching Judy's performance, Graham said, "How you remain unconvinced is beyond me. Look at her!"

Elaine looked. All she could do was look. Judy was out there, mixing with her people, touching their faces, smiling.

"We can't run away," Graham said. "This is our home."

CHAPTER THIRTY-SEVEN

Miranda hadn't heard from Judy for weeks. She responded to Mrs Jones's desperate telephone call by telling her she was grounded. Again.

"Please. Ask your mother. I'm sure she'll make an exception. I have to try and stop this. Judy won't listen to me, but she'll listen to you."

"I wouldn't be so sure."

"For months all we heard was Miranda this and Miranda that. I know you'll be able to get through to her."

Surprisingly, her request was met positively. She suspected her mother only agreed because she could detect reluctance.

It seemed every street corner had its sentry. Naturally, Amen Corner was the most heavily populated. A 'Personal Invitation to bear Witness' was thrust into her hand. She looked at it: handwritten and cheaply photocopied. She was only able to decline two more flyers on presentation of the first. It served one use, accepted in place of a password. The garden gate unlatched, Miranda chided herself for actually saying thank you and sounding grateful. After being ushered inside by Mrs Jones she found Judy in her bedroom, dressed in pyjamas in the middle of the afternoon. It reminded her of the moment the Wizard of Oz was revealed as an old man behind a curtain. Not a fake, but failing to live up to expectations.

From the recent headlines Miranda might have expected wings and a halo. Judy looked up at her with an expression of hope she would hate herself for dashing. Seeing the bags under Judy's eyes, the unhealthy pallor of her skin, Miranda said, "You look like shit," as she slumped down on the bed.

"Thanks."

"When's this going to stop?" She waved the flyer in front of Judy's eyes. "You can't possibly go ahead with it."

But Judy seemed remote as she shrugged. "It's not up to me."

There was a loose connection somewhere. Why hadn't Miranda noticed the moment her friend had lost the ability to distinguish between her own hype and reality? Had it happened after her suspension, or had something been lying dormant ever since the first headline had appeared, a gradual blurring of lines?

"Of course it's up to you! All you have to do is tell them that you were trying to prove a point." She moved to the window to look down on the heads of the Saturday afternoon gathering who should have been shopping or walking the dog or having a blue rinse or mending the sodding fence. "Which you've more than done, by the way."

But Judy was smiling listlessly.

"Judy, look at me! This is totally insane!"

"You think I *want* this?" It was not reproach but resignation Miranda heard. "It's not about me. It's about everybody who comes in hope of seeing Her. I can't let them down."

These sentences - this fervent voice - sounded like a poor imitation of the friend who had once defiantly stripped naked in the school changing rooms, and she had been proud to stand next to. "But it's a lie!" Miranda wondered for a moment if she actually knew Judy at all. Had ever known her.

Judy continued in her strange new voice, telling her how the memory of the vision was clear in her mind. Not like those childish memories she'd implanted and made real by repetition. She could recall every detail of the beautiful young woman dressed in white with a blue sash; her palms facing forwards, projecting light towards the earth like the rays of the sun; her feet bare, a yellow rose on each. To Miranda, whose blood pulsed in furious denial, it was a cliché that was being described. She wanted to cover her ears with her hands.

"If you don't believe me, come and see for yourself. What I feel is real. I'll prove it to you."

Miranda felt herself frowning. On the one hand, she envied anyone who believed there was a director in charge of planning and design, let alone that he would choose to communicate. But the universe was so much larger than ancient man believed. No. Now that explanations for lightning and plagues and failing crops were documented, God was surplus to requirements. As Jung said, once you know, there is no need to believe. "Feel or see?" she demanded.

"Are you trying to catch me out?" Judy asked, indignant for the first time, and at least it was a natural reaction. "You want me to compare it to ordinary sight? That's not what happens."

By this time it was as much as Miranda could do to shake her head and say, "You're mad, you know that?" The moment her words were out, she remembered that Jung had experienced his own visions, fearing that madness was the cause. Preferring the term 'active imaginations' he vowed never to let them disappear until they told him why they were there, recording everything in a private notebook. Despite respecting Jung's conclusion that there were things in his psyche which had effectively produced themselves, Miranda was less sympathetic to Judy. Go public, and you can't complain that your life is no longer your own. And there was no doubt that Judy had publicised the event herself. The handwriting on the flyer Miranda had been handed was unmistakable.

She left Judy in her bedroom understanding that discussion

was futile. Betrayed by the sound of her feet pounding down the staircase, she was apprehended at the front door by Mrs Jones.

"Did you talk to her? What did she say?"

Horse-like, Miranda snorted air through her nostrils. Words were inadequate. Backing out into the porch, her hands made stop signs.

Seeming to understand only too well, Mrs Jones covered her mouth momentarily and nodded. "She's not well." She made a grab for Miranda's shoulders. "The hospital missed something when they ran those tests, I know they did."

"Say goodbye for me." Miranda stopped, allowed herself to be mauled, aware of her own trembling.

"Don't stay away." Judy's Mum pleaded, and it was too, too much. "All her friends stay away. I'm sure that's part of the problem."

"Just how many friends do you think she has?" Having detached herself, Miranda took a few steps then hesitated at the garden gate, steeling herself to brave the gathering who, seeing anything that happened as reward for their patience, bore greedy witness to her tears, trying to translate them into something meaningful. "She's a freak!"

The crowd gathered in the grounds of the convent, Father Patrick and Sister Euphemia among them. The headmistress felt conspicuous in spite of the fading light.

"What do you think will be read into our attendance?" she asked.

The priest sighed. "Well, if it's Graham Jones we're talking about, I'm sure he hopes it's some sort of official recognition."

"Aren't you the least bit curious?"

"Huh!" Father Patrick's commentary consisted largely of things he would have preferred to be doing. The Sister wasn't surprised to learn that at about this time he would normally be enjoying a short after-dinner nap before meeting with the drama club, who were trying to bully him into giving them free use of the parish hall. Sister Euphemia (who found it difficult to relax) spent her evenings checking and re-checking schedules and statistics until her eyes refused to translate shapes into figures. But there was no question of choice. Her attendance was compulsory. The place where Judy Jones claimed the Lady had chosen to reveal herself was her home territory. Proving impossible to keep her followers out, the only other option had been to open the gates and invite them in. Erring on the side of caution, the headmistress had even arranged insurance.

Accustomed to estimating the numbers dotted among the pews like notes on sheet music, Father Patrick had been allocated the task of counting heads. One hand raised, he was scratching the back of his head in a frustrated gesture. "It's impossible! They're coming in from all angles. How many would you say, Sister?"

"A full assembly hall, at the very least."

"Imagine if she wasn't up against *Corrie*."

"Father, I hardly think everyone schedules their lives around soap operas."

"Oh, you'd be surprised, Sister, you'd be surprised. Ah, hello there, Mr McCrae. Good of you to come."

The man slapped the priest's back. "How's that bump on the head, Father?"

"See for yourself. It's come up like an egg."

Sister Euphemia warned, hardly moving her mouth, "The official line, Father, remember."

"I know, I know! It just came out." Father Patrick winced at her. "Tell me honestly: could you make head or tail of the essay the Bishop sent about malfunctions of the brain?"

The Sister smiled to herself, imagining Miranda referring to it as the *whole neuropsychology thing*. The headmistress possessed a near-photographic memory, but she had never read a scientific paper that explained away her certainty about the central truths of her faith. For her, the mystery - the unknowing - was what attracted her to religion. "It's fairly simple, as I understand it. According to Persinger, all apparitions can be attributed to the consequences of simultaneous biogenic stimulation of temporal lobe structures."

"You see, that's where your man lost me."

"What I gather is that the stimulation required to generate a deeply-felt experience can take a number of forms, one of which is epilepsy. The vision is effectively an electrical display. What the person thinks they're experiencing depends on their beliefs."

Father Patrick circulated one hand. "God, the paranormal, previous lives, et cetera, et cetera..."

"They're certainly possibilities, although apparently UFOs feature highly. If the visionary labels the experience 'religious', a good frame of mind might conjure up heavenly images, and conversely..."

"Him downstairs in his fiery furnace." Father Patrick rolled onto the balls of his feet and looked up at the sky. "I've always fancied seeing the Northern Lights myself. Just now, a remote corner of Iceland is looking particularly attractive." Jostled, and nodding away the apology once his dog collar was duly noted, Father Patrick enquired in what the head-mistress accepted was frustration, "Did you consider selling tickets, Sister?"

Still, she retorted, "Would you have me produce a souvenir range? No, Father, I did not!"

His brow lifted and settled like a roof tile during a gale. "I wasn't aware you'd branched out into sarcasm, Sister." He sounded hurt. "I'm not sure it becomes you."

"Forty years is too long to work with teenage girls. It must be rubbing off."

There was a growing restlessness all about them. It manifested in sudden surges and shouts.

"Yes, well. I'm claustrophobic and this is just about my limit." Sister Euphemia was conscious that Father Patrick was shuffling his feet like an impatient child. "I don't like the feel of this. How much longer can she keep us waiting, do you think?" Apparently, there were only so many positions that could help spread the weight of an overfed body.

"Are you talking about Our Lady or Judy Jones?"

"Ouch! You're on fighting form tonight, Sister."

But the headmistress was not on fighting form. She was horrified at what Mother Superior had asked of her, nauseous at the thought of having to carry out the task. What was the point when Persinger and his fellow academics had compiled enough data to give Joan of Arc cause for doubt? And the equipment she had been given to perform a scientific test for a miracle? A hat pin! "It's been sterilised," was the answer she received when she dared question its adequacy. *Sterilised!* Sister Euphemia had asked that the cup should pass from her lips, but protest was futile when faced with constant reminders of Christ's ultimate sacrifice. She wondered if Judy Jones had suffered her own anguish in the Garden of Gethsemane.

As dusk settled, bats flitted, silhouetted in the gaps between the sweet chestnuts, the aerial display drawing gasps from the otherwise sombre audience. Twenty or so feet behind the self-conscious pair, multitudes of midges captured like dust motes in halos of light made Miranda's skin crawl. She flicked at her disposable lighter to locate a raised bite on her arm and carefully scratched its circumference. Finding no relief, she turned to the child next to her who was studiously re-moulding the molten wax of a Price's household candle. Hoarded in some under-stairs cupboard for use during power cuts, no doubt. "Can I borrow that one moment?"

The boy, no older than eight, looked from candle to lighter and offered gamely, "Swapsies."

"Do I look like Maggie Philbin? On second thoughts, don't answer that."

Spilling hot wax onto the bite, Miranda replaced one form of physical discomfort with another. Waiting until the liquid solidified, she flexed her wrist to crack the surface. This gave her a child-like satisfaction, similar to painting her hand with Copydex and peeling back the 'skin'.

"Cool," the boy said in admiration. "Give us it back. I want a go."

She held the candle close to her chest. "Lighter first."

"What do you think we're going to see?" the lad asked.

Miranda shook her head slowly. "I don't know."

And she didn't. In the aftermath of her painful exchange with Judy, she'd felt the tug of that most useless of emotions: a guilt powerful enough to steer her Dr Martins in the direction of the iron gates. She had thought she might be turned away but, instead, there was no sign of recognition. Beneath her black beret, Miranda's dyed hair (the main cause of 'all that nonsense', according to her mother) was growing out to reveal auburn roots. Perhaps even her legendary performance in R.E. was forgotten. Now, overwhelmed by a sense of not-belonging, she wished somebody *would* demand to know what the hell she was doing there, offering an excuse for escape. Looking around her into faces that both registered hope and demanded that something – anything – should happen, Miranda reflected that perhaps Judy had been right: it was no longer about her. The thought turned her insides cold. Something bound this throng together. Faith – or if not faith itself, a *desire* for something to believe in that made faith redundant. But what if Judy couldn't deliver? Miranda had been in mosh pits when the atmosphere had switched from high spirits to plain nasty in an instant. She had once seen a crowd surfer dropped and trampled on. Would this pushing and shoving crowd turn into an angry mob?

Searching for something to cling to, her eyes met Sister Euphemia's. Miranda checked her breath, waiting for the nod of dismissal but instead the headmistress's mouth curled upwards into the slightest of smiles. Miranda had the distinct impression that Die Gut Schwester shared her discomfort.

A shout went up from the audience. Miranda stood on tip-toes; glancing through the gaps between heads and shoulders, beyond the raised candles. People were falling to the ground in a wave that surged from the front, leaving only those at the very back of the stalls – the sceptics and the journalists – standing. Judy had dropped to her knees, a position Miranda knew caused her pain. Her eyes were fixed on the holly bush by one of the Stations of the Cross: Jesus dying, watched by His mother and Mary Magdalene. Miranda wasn't close enough to see Judy in detail, but to her own left she was disturbed to see a young girl, eyes closed, the fingers of one hand holding a single rosary bead and her lips moving silently. The flame of her candle set her lower face aglow, as a buttercup casts its yellow reflection on the chin of a child.

A whisper of rapture rippled towards the back of the crowd and a wide-eyed woman turned to Miranda to hiss, "She's speaking!"

"Yes, of course we believe in you. What should I do?"

There was an unnatural silence, a collective holding of breath. Miranda felt the hairs on the back of her neck stand on end. Experiencing a moment's panic, she tried to seek out Sister Euphemia's gaze again. To her far left, isolated in an island, Sister Euphemia and Father Patrick were visible from their waists upwards, arms folded sternly across their chests. As if walking through shallows, knees lifted, the headmistress began to edge towards the blonde-haired figure who was the focus of attention.

Emerging, Sister Euphemia stepped forwards and knelt next to Judy, wincing as one of her knees found the sharp edge of a flint. Following her example, a couple of members of the front row walked forwards on their knees, halting to her left and Judy's right. The headmistress needed to act quickly.

Sister Euphemia took the sterilised hat pin from her sleeve, as she'd been instructed: *"Remember: you must remain objective."*

Father, forgive me. Tightening her mouth, she went to stick it into the fleshy part of the girl's left arm. Instantly, there was a noise like a gas cooker igniting, and her hand jerked away. Letting go of the pin, she looked down and saw the tail of an electrical arc. Judy began to sing, a loud and unwavering *Ave Maria*. Eyes trained on the girl's face, the Sister realised that she had suffered an electric shock. Later, when examining her own hand, she would find its white mark. No visible reaction, nothing reflected in the girl's expression but peace. She felt deep shame. Had there been some intervention to prevent her from sabotaging the event?

After the fourth verse, Judy spoke as if refuting something that was being alleged. "No. Everyone here believes in you."

There were murmurs of agreement, a single cry of "Amen" that prompted a response. Sister Euphemia found herself joining in. "Amen." Knowing the woman to her left had clearly heard her, she repeated it, louder this time and with greater authority, and it felt as if history was being written.

"Who?" Judy turned around and blinked. Concerned not to be labelled as the Judas in the crowd, people ducked from her all-knowing gaze. Then Judy moved her head to the right and Miranda's breath caught in her throat as, of all of the hundreds present, she seemed to have been singled out. The lady in front twisted her head a second time to hiss, "It's you!"

"No, it's someone behind me."

Another offered comfort: "She can't actually see who she's looking at. She always goes blind when Our Lady appears to her."

"Come forward." Judy issued an invitation. "Pray with me."

"Go on." Miranda was pawed at. "Don't be afraid."

"I told you. It's not me!"

Hands were now pushing her, forcing her to move. Miranda stepped between the kneeling figures, stumbling as she tried to avoid treading on fingers, afraid that the current might drag her under. All the while, people she didn't know and might have crossed the road to avoid wanted to touch her. This was not a performance she wished to be part of. She wasn't simply being asked to cover her friend's dignity with a damp yellow towel. Breaking free from the sea of clambering bodies Miranda shouldered her way towards the camouflage of shadows in the direction of the main gates. Seeing Mr Jones, his candlelit face wearing an expression of awe, she hung her head, heels lifting into a miserable jog. The minute she saw someone blocking her way, she changed direction. Close to the exit, she was straight-jacketed by someone's arms.

"Get off me!" she shouted, trying to shake herself free. "Get off!"

But it was Mrs Jones who replied, "Miranda, you're a good friend! I knew you'd come. What do you think?"

A sob rattled through her and Miranda shook her head. The honest answer? She had discovered someone special - someone with that rare blend of bravery and vulnerability - and now she was being forced to share. Miranda wanted her friend back, but she was gone, leaving headlines and candle-holding crowds in her wake. She wanted to walk away, walk and not stop. But she hesitated long enough to hug Mrs Jones, who, she was pretty damned sure, wanted her daughter back equally fiercely.

"It frightens me too." Mrs Jones spoke directly into her ear. "But I have to be here for her. I'd never forgive myself if anything happened and I wasn't."

There was an audible gasp. Conjoined, they turned in time

to see Judy fall sideways. Miranda felt her embrace discarded.

"Run and call an ambulance! It's happening."

But there was no need. Uniformed medics rushed forwards. Mrs Jones was navigating towards Sister Euphemia's voice of authority and beckoning hands, her frustrated voice demanding, "Let me *through!*" and "I'm her mother." There was nothing left for Miranda to do but watch. Even from the sidelines, having never seen someone fit, she was appalled by what little she could see of Judy's convulsions, a waterless butterfly stroke. Not only the fact of it, but the herd who displayed nothing but passivity. Was this the show they had really come to see? Did they want blood, with Judy as the sacrificial lamb? They weren't the violent mob Miranda had feared, but they were equally dangerous. The only other people who moved were the press photographers who, never laying claim to anything but self-promoting purpose, knew that the time for close-ups had arrived.

CHAPTER THIRTY-EIGHT

Elaine spent twenty-four hours in silent vigil by her daughter's hospital bed. Alternately holding Judy's hand or slouched in a chair, the only break she allowed herself was to stare out of the grimy window at the dappled grey sky. She tried to banish all thought, because thinking was torment. Elaine wanted the doctors to find out what was wrong with her daughter and to put it right. But why? So that Judy would be well? So that the terminally long year she had spent nursing her back to health - those angry days of recrimination - wouldn't have been for nothing? So that she could leave the house in the afternoons to go in search of strangers? But, whatever the reason - however horribly selfish - Elaine *did* want the doctors to find something wrong. She wanted a clear diagnosis followed by a cure. Nothing else was acceptable.

What kind of a mother did that make her? She examined her fingernails, longing for a file and a bottle of varnish so that she could occupy her hands with a simple, methodical task.

What kind of a wife did that make her? Elaine freed her feet of shoes and lifted them onto the chair, flexing her toes, nursing the depth of them. She saw Graham at twenty, as he had been when they first met. Then she imagined herself waking up and turning her head (her hair tousled attractively as it always was in her imagination, rather than the tangled mess of reality). But it wasn't Graham resting on the pillow beside her: it was the man with the grey eyes; the same man who had given her an avocado; bought her lunch; allowed her to escape for a couple of short hours. The scene wasn't one that had actually taken place, and yet it had crept into her mind so often it felt like a memory. He angled his head to kiss her forehead, whispering, "Good morning, sweetheart." And for a moment - just for a moment - she felt beautiful.

Elaine wanted release, but could only allow her shoulders to shake silently, one hand clasped firmly over her mouth. Looking beyond the grime and the grey, her heart cried out to the god of things that can never be: 'It wasn't the whole of something. It was so much more important than that.'

Elaine only accomplished the act of pulling herself together when an irony grabbed her: if the doctors discovered that Judy was seriously ill Graham would insist on taking her to Lourdes.

Graham knocked on the door of his boss's office and announced himself. "You wanted a word?"

"Sit down, Graham."

Graham sat, taking the visitor's chair. Usually apprehensive at being summonsed, today he had no reason to be nervous. There was a promise hanging in the balance that once the deal he had closed last week had been put to bed, they would 'talk'. He assumed this was that moment. Not the best of timing, with Judy in hospital, but Graham had never brought personal problems into work and wasn't going to start now.

"You know I've always been one of your biggest supporters."

He acknowledged Derek's blatant exaggeration with a humble nod, anticipating that his manager would try to take credit for his achievements in some small way.

"But, frankly, if your figures weren't so good this quarter, I wouldn't have a bloody leg to stand on."

Graham felt his stomach drop. He was thankful he had not been looking into Derek's eyes, that the man couldn't read his expression. He waited for clarification.

"When your family life begins to reflect badly on the firm we have a problem. And you have given H.R. a complete nightmare!"

"But -"

"This is hard for both of us, so let me finish. I think I have your back covered - just. But, if I were you, I'd keep my head down and thank my lucky stars I still had a job!"

Graham began to walk back to his desk, head reeling. He could have reminded his boss of the twenty years he had given to the company, but it might have been taken as a slight - given that the man had only been there for five of them. And, anyway, he suspected Derek would only have brought up the question of the extended leave he had granted after Judy's accident.

Distracted, Graham snapped at one of the secretaries (the one with the back-combed hair and the lace headband) who interrupted his private misery to ask a straightforward question, something to which he knew the answer. Consumed by guilt that demanded far more energy than the initial interruption, he used the last of his change in the vending machine and offered an apology in the shape of a coffee and a Twix.

"Alison?" Graham began nervously.

Displaying her false pink talons, she was curt with him. "It's Angela. Has been for the four years I've been working here."

"Well, that's another miserable start, isn't it?" Graham shook his head. "I shouldn't have taken my problems out on you and I'm sorry. Peace offering." He looked for a place to deposit the bounty on her desk, between the bulk of the

Olivetti typewriter and the pen tidy, its contents a daunting array of child-like colours.

"You didn't have to do that!" Angela reached up greedily to claim her prize.

"Oh, but I did." He returned to his desk followed by a stream of barely-stifled laughter, but Angela was not among those who mocked.

"It takes a big man to apologise," he heard her hiss in response to the sniggering. "Something you prize monkeys know nothing about!"

Stomach rumbling, Graham gazed at the framed photograph of his wife and daughter, reminding himself why he couldn't jack it all in. Elaine was pictured crouching low, Judy's arms thrown around her mother's neck, chin on shoulder, their heads close. He knew exactly where he'd been standing when he took the shot: on the dunes at Camber Sands. The photograph was only a fragment of the panorama of his memory. Graham could feel his feet sinking, warm sand trickling between his toes. They were so alike, his wife and daughter. He struggled to see anything of himself in Judy.

Despite his colleagues' laughter and his priest's misgivings, he would not deny his daughter. He would offer it up to his Maker - if only his infernal stomach would stop rumbling.

"Excuse me, Graham." Angela approached his desk, towering in sale shoes that looked slightly too small for her.

Graham had his fake smile prepared this time. "I still haven't answered your question, have I?"

"Oh, forget about that," she said. "I've only gone and made myself too many sarnies. And seeing as I've got a Twix..."

"Well." Graham felt untold happiness at the sight of neatly stacked triangles of anaemic bread. "That's really very kind of you." He hesitated, seeing that there were two halves in the Tupperware box.

Angela beamed. "Have them both."

In a café not far from home, browsing through the local paper - something he rarely did - a man's grey eyes were drawn to a familiar face. Elaine Jones, he said to himself: *So that's your name! And mine is David.* None of what he read made her any less wonderful in his mind. In fact, David thought her almost heroic. It was incredible how much one person could keep hidden, and not let it overflow as soon as there was the opportunity to sit and talk, or lie naked, entangled with another human being. This was the cause of her restlessness: what she had set aside and gone back to. Of course she hadn't been able to see him again.

"Tea." The bored-sounding waitress deposited a tired mug on the table with sufficient force to send a tidal wave onto the precious page. Moving it aside, he angled the paper stiffly at arm's length, encouraging the liquid to run onto the floor rather than soak into the photograph. Elaine, answering the front door, her white towelling robe now stained a light brown. They had spent two or three hours together at the most, and yet the tenderness David felt at the sight of her vulnerability was no less than the tenderness he had felt for his wife when, occasionally, she had appeared for breakfast looking slightly less than perfect.

"And here we are: full English."

"Ah, thank you. Are the eggs soft?" he enquired, without much in the way of hope.

The waitress had already produced an order pad from her straining breast pocket and was brandishing the pointed end of a pencil at her next customer. She glanced back at him over her shoulder. "Next you'll be wanting me to cut your toast into soldiers!"

The door opened, sweet wrappers pirouetting across the threshold. Three sturdy women wearing stout shoes and carrying placards with the words 'I'm a Believer' painted on them followed closely behind.

"Oh, no you don't! You can't bring those in here." The waitress was aiming her pencil point at the offending items.

"Well, we can't leave them outside." One of the women was almost as formidable as the waitress, who seemed to recognise she'd met her match.

Her expression said, *If you think you're getting free re-fills, you've got another thing coming.* "Over by the umbrella stand," she directed with a brisk nod. "And let's have the words facing the wall. Chef isn't a fan of the Monkees." Turning her back on the newcomers, she padded towards the kitchen, winking at a regular. "We don't want anyone thinking we serve nutters."

Reading the paper, Tommy Webber whistled softly through his front teeth. Local news had never been so local before: now he could reach out and touch it.

"You never really know who's living next door." His mother slapped past in her feathered mules, pointing to the hallway. "On the other side of *that* wall."

Tommy had spent hours fantasising about it. Not the daughter, but the mother. When Mrs J had stooped to ruffle his boyish hair, her blouse fell open to reveal delicate freckled skin and the lace of her bra. The first he'd ever seen, it had made him quite dizzy. On one of the endless summer days of early childhood he had sneaked through the loose fence panel, hoping for a glimpse of her underwear on the washing line. Instead, he found her attacking weeds with a blue metal trowel, the surprised smile that emerged from under the wide brim of her straw hat melting him faster than the Strawberry Mivi he was brandishing. Other than the hat, she wore only denim shorts and a bikini top: two triangles of candy-striped material shaped like catapults, linked together by a delicate rope; the whole contraption held in place by a bow (and not even a double knot at that). Fighting the urge to reach out and pull the end of one of the tails, Tommy imagined the loops shrinking, the material falling away. But even more than that unlikely prospect, he liked the idea that gardening was only a cover: Mrs J had been waiting for him - and he would find her waiting again.

Several years later, arriving home from Boy Scouts, Tommy had stood asphyxiated in the street, watching her silhouette stretch as she undressed behind the net curtains. He had seen most parts of her naked or nearly naked over the years, although never all at the same time, a jigsaw puzzle whose pieces he assembled nightly under the covers. But, of everything he'd seen, it was her bare feet that had made the greatest impression.

"Don't you like the grass to tickle you?" she'd asked.

"No," said the boy, who suffered nightmares about lines of ants taking a detour up his leg and under the hem of his shorts.

Judy, sniffing with hay fever in a spotted one-piece with a pink frill, had never been any competition for her mother. And now...

"Oh, come on!" Tommy's father erupted from behind the sports section of his broadsheet. "We've always got on with Graham and Elaine."

"*She's* alright, I grant you. But, ever since that accident, Judy's been out of control."

Here, Tommy felt the need to intervene. "She spent a year in bed, Mum! She's hardly running wild."

"Laid up she may have been. But I know who's in charge in that household." The table tipped slightly as his mother lent it her weight. The index finger of her right hand hovered in front of his face, as if itching to find a suitable surface to introduce itself to. "That's what happens when teenagers think they have the upper hand."

Sliding forwards in his seat, Tommy stuck his legs out under the table. "Fat chance of that happening here."

"Apologise to your mother!" Not a man whose newspapers ever went back into their original shape, Mr Webber folded his paper noisily. Tommy had barely opened his mouth before he continued: "Let's not go overboard. We're talking about a very specific set of circumstances here."

"Yes?" His wife's hands were on her hips, an unfortunate stance that exaggerated her ample width. "That very specific set of circumstances is sending the price of our house crashing." She removed one hand long enough to jab at the headlines in the local paper. "It's not just Elaine Jones who's 'Trapped in Her Own Home.'"

After a hopeful glance at his watch, Mr Webber tried to coerce the newspaper into his briefcase, the result similar to his attempts at persuading the cat into its basket for the previous week's outing to the vets. "I must be off."

"Well?" His wife's voice followed him into the hall, and she wasn't far behind. "What are we going to *do* about it?"

"It will all blow over." Opening the front door and, finding not one gormless face looming celestially over his hedge (whose sharp horizontal edge could be checked with a spirit-level), he felt cheerful enough to turn and plant a kiss on his wife's quilted cheek. "See? We're over the worst."

Stooping, he retrieved a handful of empty crisp packets that had blown onto his garden path from last night's candlelit vigil. *When the blighter responsible for* All Things Bright and Beautiful *composed his opus, did he have any idea how bloody irritating it would sound after forty-seven minutes non-stop?* Reaching over the giant daisies, Mr Webber set them free on the Jones's path, liberating the rebellious part of himself that hadn't been hen-pecked into submission. Seeing the younger of his two sons - the one who would benefit from National Service - glaring at him from the safety of the living room, he turned and gave a little click of his heels to show that he wasn't remotely embarrassed. And that was when he saw the graffiti on his car - THE TIME HAS COME! - his vision blurring with rage.

Sitting at her kitchen table, Paula, too, was reading the headlines.

"I knew something wasn't quite right," she said to her husband, taking no pleasure in the fact.

"Well, there you are then."

"And what's *that* supposed to mean?" She went to cuff him lightly, but he caught her hand and held it in both of his.

"It means that, in all the time I've known you, you've never been wrong about these things. And that, rather than satisfy yourself with that like most people would, you'll want to do something to help. I could try to warn you off but I doubt you'd pay the slightest bit of notice. And I wouldn't have you any other way."

"I'll have you know, you were one of those people once!" She pulled her hand away as he tried to kiss it.

"Well, there you are then."

Having walked into the offices of *The Daily Star* - a national! - as a struggling junior reporter from *The Streatham Comet*, Edwin Kay had just landed himself a very satisfactory offer for a position on the news desk.

"Remember!" His fiancée had kissed him that morning. "Don't ask, don't get."

Ask and ye shall receive, as his mother might have put it. Truth told, there had been no need to negotiate. When he set out what he could bring to the table, the job had been offered to him on a plate. "I'm impressed. Your hunch to go after the mother was spot on. Now that the competition has latched on, you've got to work out how to stay one step ahead. A bright lad like you won't have any trouble thinking of something.

You'll start immediately, of course."

Edwin paused at this: his contract demanded four weeks' notice.

"That's the deal. The story is ours."

"Absolutely."

Mine! Edwin picked up his pace, purposefully. And while everyone else was parked outside the convent gates waiting for a miracle, he made a decision. This was business. He couldn't afford a conscience. Not with his landlord increasing their rent.

Addressing the morning assembly, Sister Euphemia felt a lightness she hadn't experienced for years. "Let us take a moment to pray for all ex-pupils of this school. That they find their way in this often confusing world. That they achieve happiness and success in their chosen paths. And that they remain always true to themselves. Amen."

There was a feeble murmur. It would have to do.

"Do you know," the headmistress said. "Looking at you all, I'm reminded of one pupil in particular. I once asked this pupil of mine why she hadn't joined in with the Creed at school Mass. And do you know how she replied? She said, 'I join in. I just stop after the bit I'm comfortable with.' I thought that was quite marvellous. You see, here was a girl who was thinking about the nature of faith itself and what it means to believe in one God. This is our constant challenge. If you remain open to the many mysteries of the universe throughout your lives - even though you may not understand them - there's a good chance you won't stray too far.

"Last night I was here in the crowd with some of you. To bear witness." Sister Euphemia was aware that the murmurs being exchanged were louder than those lowly *amens*, and she raised her voice. "And I stand before you today to say that I don't have all the answers. But my one prayer is to remain open-minded. Because I think that if we close ourselves off from the possibility of a miracle happening here, in our lifetimes, it would be a denial of the love of our Lord Jesus Christ. Well, ladies. Here's Mrs Gleeson with a few announcements."

Instead of taking her seat centre stage, mouths gaped as Sister Euphemia marched out of the assembly hall and down the courtyard steps to the iron gates. Pulling them open wide, she secured the gates with a metal chain that, to the best of her knowledge, had never been used for the purpose designed. Then, stepping aside, she welcomed the waiting reporters: "Forgive me for keeping you waiting, but we're very proud of our tradition of starting each day with a prayer." She looked at them wickedly. "I assume you've already said yours?"

"Here, in the London suburb of Streatham, the latest teen sensation is not a pop star, but fifteen-year-old Judy Jones, who claims to see visions of Our Lady in the grounds of her convent school."

Having turned off the television, Father Patrick sat, head in hands. Breakfast news on the BBC: things were spiralling out of control. The priest had followed the Bishop's instructions but still the people came. His Rite of Christian Initiation classes were booked months in advance. There had been a surge of confirmations and weddings. The queues for confession demanded that Father Patrick rushed his regulars who tended to drag the whole thing out. He was tempted to say "Go away and sin no more" as soon as he heard the kneeler creak, but people didn't feel forgiven unless they worked up a sweat. The parish coffers overflowing, Judy Jones had achieved more in six weeks than he had managed in an equal number of years.

Father Patrick had always understood his focus to be bringing the good people of Streatham to a fuller understanding of Jesus. And yet here he was with strict instructions to 'stamp out fanatics'. It seemed that the Church wanted their Christians lukewarm. Father Patrick had experienced many personal doubts, but he had never before doubted what his message should be. Now, it appeared he was expected to destroy faith to save the Church.

The Bishop re-read the letter he had received from his superiors. '*Accordingly, there is to be no public activity in the churches, oratories and other properties of the Archdiocese of Southwark relating to the alleged apparitions and locutions.*'

In a foul mood, he picked up the phone, ready to have it out with Father Patrick - again. This time he would use words of no more than one syllable: get rid of the girl.

CHAPTER THIRTY-NINE

Elaine stared past the bulk of the man whose belt she'd been unbuckling and looked up at the cistern with its rusted chain, the expanse of dirty-yellow tiles, the damp unravelling of toilet paper. Hardly the venue for a romantic tryst! Remembering the waiter tapping the side of his nose - 'Aphrodisiac' - she imagined the men's laughter she could hear from the restaurant kitchen was at her expense. Pushed back against the cold wall, her breasts clinically manhandled, the words 'I don't want to be here' lapped the circuits of Elaine's brain until they reached screaming point, overflowing in a wild torrent.

A sharp laugh from her companion suggested he understood the statement to be spontaneous. "What?" He took a step back, leaving his cupped hands in place.

"I'm sorry." Elaine edged past the toilet paper dispenser, snagging her dress in its teeth. "This isn't what I wanted."

Laughter merged with disbelief, a suggestion of inappropriateness that chastised: "It's too late for that!" His belt hung loosely, his pastel pink shirt - mercifully - providing a tent for his erection.

"I don't think so." To her own ears, Elaine's voice sounded high-pitched and echoing. Too formal by far to use with someone whose buttocks she had been grabbing a minute earlier. She reached for the lock but, where it should have been, found his hand.

"I recognise you from your picture in the paper." His hoppy breath disturbed her hair. "I know where you live."

Stay calm, she told herself, although her need to escape was now urgent. "It's a lovely area. We've always liked it." Elaine might have been at a garden party, but for the fact that her dress was unbuttoned to its waist. Why hadn't she thought it through before she took the detour on her way to the chemists? But the truth was that she could think of nothing else. Sex - the hows, whos and wheres, as well as the mechanics of it - occupied most of her waking hours. It wasn't as if she found it satisfying or even plain comforting. Fumbles in restaurant toilets were not what she'd envisaged when she set out in search of escape. It had been impossible to replicate that original afternoon, no matter how hard she tried. And the risks, the risks she was taking! No longer crossing to the other side of town, no longer waiting for privacy. Once, in a local park - the shame of it.

"I can make life more difficult for you than it already is."

"I doubt that very much." Strange where you can find your strength, Elaine thought, contemplating what she had just said. Moving the man's hand aside as if it were simply part of the mechanism, she drew back the bolt. "Now, if you'll excuse me." Time for her curtain call. A man was using the urinals, his back to her, but there was no avoiding the fact that he would see her reflection in the mirrors. Trying to steady her shaking, Elaine spoke loudly enough to be heard from inside the cubicle, knowing that Mr B--- wouldn't dare emerge with a third person present. "They do an excellent avocado here." Quickly, she repaired the damage to her make-up and clothing as best she could - her dress would need a patch repair - and washed her hands. "If you haven't already ordered, you really should try one."

Christ, she was spectacular: the way she made a point of drying her hands thoroughly with two paper towels, one after the other; the way she applied a fresh coat of lipstick and pressed her lips together. Edwin Kay made a play of zipping himself up, feigning surprise at the sound of a female voice. Interesting that she hadn't gone through with it. He hoped she hadn't turned the corner. His research on the subject of sex addiction suggested that any efforts to control her compulsions would become less and less successful, that she would need to up the risk level. But, looking at the reflection of the man who was standing behind the cubicle door which was slightly ajar - the owner of the local department store, if he wasn't mistaken! - Edwin thought, *Everyone has their limits.*

Striding towards the door to the restaurant, Elaine's breath died in her throat as she encountered the man with the grey eyes coming in the opposite direction. Her own were unnaturally wide as she distilled all her efforts into not blinking. He hesitated, held one hand up as if hailing a taxi and opened his mouth, but exposed, ashamed, Elaine kept on walking.

David turned in time to see the door to the gents' toilets close on a younger man - possibly a student - who excused himself as he passed by in an awful hurry; then it was forcibly opened by a solid-looking man in his late middle age with shirt tails hanging out of his trousers.

"Bitch!" He shouted as the door to the restaurant closed, turning to David in disbelief. "I've just been robbed!"

"She took your wallet?" Any excuse to run after Elaine Jones would have done.

"Bloody prick-tease let me pay for lunch!"

He felt deeply wounded, just as he had when his wife left him. Sitting in the cubicle, it was some time before the floor tile David had been staring at came into focus. He remembered that he had not arrived alone: Tilly was waiting for him. And Tilly - just a flirtation, he had told himself - did not deserve to be kept waiting.

Brighter than he'd given her credit for, the girl had left. Apparently unprepared to let his flourish suffer because the table was empty, the waiter who was delivering their starters rotated the plates until the pattern was the right way up. David settled the bill, ignoring the langoustine and the barely-touched bottle of Chardonnay, and walked outside.

There she was, at the bus stop: a snagged yellow dress and laddered tights. Elaine Jones looked at him so mournfully that he felt compelled to walk towards her. She tipped her head from her seated position, letting it come to rest against his breast pocket, breathing a stream of words: "I'm sorry, I'm sorry, I'm sorry."

"You needn't apologise to me."

Inhaling sharply, Elaine removed her head. "I thought... never mind. I must have been mistaken." Her mouth stretched into a tortured smile, became shoulder height, and she began to move away.

"Hang on a minute!" David called out, watching her hair, her back, her shoes.

Elaine walked in a tight semicircle, coming face to face with him. "I always thought you'd come looking for me. In another supermarket."

"But you asked me not to."

"I hoped the temptation might prove too much."

"Elaine..."

She tucked stray hair behind her ear, and her voice became clipped. "So you know who I am? It seems everybody does these days - apart from me."

"Can we talk? Let me buy you a coffee."

"Far too dangerous." Again she was moving away, one raised hand pushing at the air as she shook her head.

"Elaine! I don't understand." David fell into step beside her. "Do you want me to follow you?"

She stopped short and sighed. "I'm not allowed what I want, that much is clear."

About to argue, he saw that here was a woman torn apart, the rope in an unending game of tug-of-war.

"I want to tell you this," Elaine said, her feet seemingly undecided whether to continue walking, her arms unsure whether to throw themselves about him, and so she appeared restless and clamped tightly shut all at once. "And then I really do have to go. It wasn't the whole of something. It felt like a beginning - could have *been* a beginning. You made me want to walk away. From everything. Do you understand what I'm saying?"

Close by, a mother was crouched on her haunches, shouting, *"No, Joshua, put that down!"* She prised her small son's fingers apart and removed what appeared to be a wooden stick from the centre of a lollipop - not so much to want in the grand scheme of things. The toddler, whose eyes were closed and mouth was wide open, surrendered his entire being to the act of expressing how unfair life was.

"Do you? But that option hasn't been open to me. Not for a long time. So I couldn't come looking for you. Instead I settled for... I'm not proud, but there it is." Elaine's hand located her mouth, as if to prevent it from saying any more. She succeeded in a subject change. "There's something that I must see through. Even though it can't end well. So you have to be a memory. Perhaps the only good memory in the middle of this mess." The words had stopped coming, and she appeared to have been released. "Do me one favour?"

"Anything."

"Kiss me. Just once: And then go."

David saw that she was very close to falling apart. Fighting the instinct to take her in his arms, he kissed her on her forehead, the precise place she pointed to, and walked away.

Realising that he had missed another opportunity to tell

Elaine Jones his name, he turned and shouted over the heads of dozens of people he was surprised had sprung up between them: "David! My name! It's David." But her heels carried on clicking.

Seeing that Mrs Jones was walking with her head down, one hand raised to her forehead - *Don't let her escape* - Edwin positioned himself on the pavement as if fielding a cricket ball. "Whoa there!" he said laughingly, catching her by the arms.

She looked at him beseechingly, the corners of her mouth twitching. "I'm so sorry. I wasn't... I'm not..." There had been a change in her. A red-eyed middle-aged woman in a torn dress, she had lost her magnificent bravado.

"Are you alright?" He frowned. "Stupid question: obviously you're not."

She seemed incapable of answering, except to clench her jaw and shake her head. There was something very vulnerable about her, something that made him remind himself, *the job is the story, and the story is mine.*

"I'll tell you what. How about a cup of tea? I think I just passed a café." Still holding on to one of her arms, half afraid she might escape, Edwin glanced over his shoulder.

"Brandy," she gasped.

He was surprised how quickly she'd leapt at his offer. "Brandy it is. Let's find a pub."

"Not a pub, no. Somewhere private. Your place." Rather than escape, she was standing uncomfortably close to him.

"*My* place?" he laughed, taken aback. After rejecting a man who might have been old enough to be her father, was it possible...? But there was no mistaking her meaning: Mrs Jones was toying with the end of his tie, pretending to tighten the knot as she succeeded in pulling his head towards hers.

He swallowed, trying to extract himself. "Let's just sit down and talk." Edwin wondered for the first time how he would feel if someone was watching him, perhaps misinterpreting what they were seeing, exaggerating it for the sake of a good story.

"Oh, I think we can do much better than that..."

"I'm about to get married. Mrs Jones!"

"Elaine! Call me El-" She stopped, eyes wide with panic. "You know my name?"

"I'm a journalist. Do you understand? A journalist."

The enormity of Elaine's predicament seemed to strike her: "You've been following me? Of course you have. For how long?"

"Since I recognised you in the Co-op."

"Brandy," she said, blanching, and he steered her into the nearest pub, making sure she was safely seated in an out-of-the-way corner before he ordered.

"Is your mother feeling unwell?" the barman asked, nodding towards Mrs Jones.

"What?" Edwin twisted his head to look at her. "Yes. A little."

He was afraid that, even after he had folded her hand around the stem of the glass, watched her drink, she appeared to be in shock. "I felt it. All along. But nothing's been printed..."

"Not so far. The paper I used to work for wasn't interested in that angle. But I've just taken a job at a national -"

"Please, please, please." She shook her head. "I don't think I could cope... You can't..." He felt her desperation, so strong that shame didn't enter into it. She kept talking, telling him other things, private things, things he would have rather not known.

"Stop! You don't need to do this."

"But I do. Don't you see? I can tell you any number of

things you can print. Anything but this. What do you want to know? Drugs?"

Perhaps it was the barman's mention of his mother; perhaps it was the disgust Edwin felt at himself for following a couple into the toilets in the hope of listening to them have sex; perhaps it was because he knew from his research that Elaine Jones was in need of help. "To be honest, I don't think I'm cut out for this. It feels... wrong, taking advantage of people's problems. Here." He delved inside his jacket; pressed what he found there into her hands. "Take my notebook."

She turned her face to him, open-mouthed. He had rarely seen a look of such gratitude.

"Take it," Edwin insisted. "Before I change my mind. It's everything I have on you: dates, times, places."

Without daring to look at its contents, she held the small spiral-bound book in her lap. "What will you do?"

"I don't know. Tell them I can't deliver, I suppose."

"But you'll lose your job!"

Edwin shrugged, understanding his own predicament. He imagined responding to his fiancée's disappointment by asking what kind of a man she wanted to marry, and feared her response. "If I'm lucky I might get my old job back. They'll probably put me on the sports desk. What will you do, that's the real question? Just because *I* don't write the story doesn't mean it *won't* be written."

"There were others?"

"Not so far, but I had to hand in an outline story at my interview. That's what got me the job. They'll probably use it."

"I see. Then, I'll go home, I suppose. Face up to my responsibilities."

As Elaine elbowed her way through the gathering of God-botherers, intent on bearing witness to all manner of things that didn't concern them, she was asked, "Mind if I come in and use your toilet?"

With her head down, she replied, "Yes, I do mind, actually."

"I was only asking, wasn't I?"

She had to pull on the straps of her handbag to dislodge it from where it had become trapped between two bodies. "I also mind that you're asking."

The hand that fumbled for the front door key was shaking.

"Thank Goodness!" Graham greeted Elaine in the hallway. "I was starting to worry."

"No need." She settled her bag on the telephone table, somehow allowing an escape route for a lipstick and the tube of Extra Strong Mints she had bought to mask the smell of alcohol. "I just got a bit held up."

"Did you collect Judy's prescription?"

"Damn!" Bending one leg at the knee, her eyes on the door, it might have been tempting to leave the house again but for what was waiting for her outside.

"I thought that's why you went out."

She posted the stray items into the dark recess of her bag with a violence she knew she should disguise. "You know, running around after you two isn't the only thing I have to do with my time!"

"I thought... never mind." Graham was saying.

"You thought what?" Her mouth tight, Elaine faced her husband whose eyebrows twitched, his reluctance obvious. "Well, come on! Something's on your mind."

"Later."

"Later there will be dinner and then you'll be at your church meeting, no doubt."

"It's just that - and I'm not meaning to criticise, love - but what with Judy only just home from hospital, and you so anxious to secure a medical diagnosis, I thought her prescription would have been top of your list." His expression undertook a metamorphosis, emerging as joy. "I see... I get it: you're not convinced Judy needs to take the medication!"

"No, Graham, I am! Really I am!" Elaine was infuriated

that her husband always looked for the good in her. "We both saw her collapse."

All that Elaine wanted to do was to lie down in a dark room, covering her shame with a duvet. The twitching above her right eye had returned, the persistent knocker who wanted to be let out. Despite the comic opera her life had become, Elaine realised he had abandoned his post the minute she left the house.

"There are other explanations. People who experience visions often suffer what appear to be convulsions. I've read about it…"

"And people who suffer from epilepsy often think they see things. You're not the only one who's done his homework!"

"I can see you're upset, but just supposing Judy takes the medicine and keeps on having visions. Will you believe her then?"

"I can't deal in ifs. I can only deal with what's happening right now. And I'm not even very sure about that."

"I love you," Graham mumbled, leaving Elaine staggered. She was unreasonable and *this* was his response? Stranded, the words were not accompanied by a kiss or a hug. The declaration, once issued, weighed heavily; a responsibility rather than a gift. Elaine couldn't find it in herself to respond with words. Instead, she watched her reflection in the hall mirror - a person she barely recognised - pat her chest next to her heart, something she couldn't remember doing since the early days when they had both felt too full to speak.

Graham endorsed her gesture with an expression resembling relief. "Nothing else is very clear to me, so I have to cling to that. If *we're* confused, I can't imagine how poor Judy is feeling. But I don't worry for her in the same way you do, because I know that she's at least half you." And then he went and ruined it, as far as Elaine was concerned, by adding, "The rest, I leave in God's hands."

"Shepherd's Pie?" Elaine asked, an image of efficiency as she blindly pressed past her husband to loop her apron over her head and free her trapped hair.

"Excellent: must be Tuesday." Graham was so close behind her she could hear him salivating. "Oh, Elaine. Look at that."

"What now?" Elaine glanced up at the kitchen window nervously, expecting to see another t-shirt with a face above it.

"You've snagged your lovely yellow dress."

If it was to be said at all, it needed to be now. "Graham, sit down. There's something I have to show you."

From her room, Judy listened to the house breathe. It was so quiet that she wondered if she was alone. Dinner time had come and gone without the usual summons to lay the table. It didn't matter: she wasn't hungry. This was the night when Judy planned to ask The Lady the questions: Who was She? Why had She come? What was Her message? It was what everyone wanted to know, Father Patrick perhaps the most insistent. Dressing for cold weather she came across the black fingerless gloves Miranda had lent her. After putting them on she fingered the cigarette burn in the centre of one of the palms, marvelling, not at all the lazy hours they had spent putting the world to rights, but at the impression of the holes in Christ's hands.

CHAPTER FORTY

This time, Judy didn't get as far as the convent before experiencing that sense of déjà vu. The air around her seemed to be moving in waves. Not yet! Not here! She willed it to stop. *Stop!* But her eyesight was already blurring, even though instinct told her the scene in front of her was in perfect focus. She experienced nausea, the sensation of time slowing down and then rapid acceleration, a ride at Alton Towers but with none of the adrenalin rush. Sounds were distorted, like the single by OMD Judy had bought, finding that the hole had been punched off-centre. The singing of the group of followers who trailed behind at a respectful distance faded in and out, in and out, the single drum beat marking time. Then there was nothing but a trembling white light.

"Why now?" Graham demanded of his wife. "Is it because of the threat that I'd hear it from another source? Perhaps read about it?"

"No!" Elaine protested fiercely, then, staring at a fixed point on the floor, appeared to concede. "Yes *and* no. It had to be over, and saying it out loud was the only way I could be sure."

"If it was as simple as that, why wait this long?" He pressed down on the notebook she had pushed across the table, as if distancing herself from its contents. Graham could barely believe that his still small voice of calm had been lying. What it told him had seemed so real: all of the evenings when his dinner had arrived on the table at six o'clock sharp; all the Monday mornings when he opened his wardrobe to find five freshly-ironed shirts smelling of cut grass, collars starched, creases crisp. And it wasn't just one man. Wasn't that *worse* somehow? If he had understood correctly, it wasn't even about the men. They were so incidental Elaine hadn't given them names or numbers, although apparently they were all here, if he cared to look under his hand.

"I've tried to stop, I really have... I hoped I could, I don't know... spare you."

"So you *weren't* going to tell me?" Having seen Elaine flinch as he raised his voice, as though she thought he might strike her, he shook his head. "I wish to God you hadn't told me."

He tried to construct order around his thoughts, his next wish a hopeless one: that she hadn't done it in the first place.

Graham's reaction to the first ring of the doorbell was *ignore it*. Had there been hints? The engagement ring left by the side of the sink. The dancing partners. *Look at me, Graham. Tell me what you see.* What other cherished moments would she have him re-examine?

A second ring: Elaine stood.

"Where are you going?"

"Nowhere," she said, turning out the kitchen light, her response to Trick or Treaters and unwelcome guests. "Oh God, have you seen the time?" she whispered, swiping at her eyes only, he knew, when she thought she was out of his line of vision.

Since his conversion, Graham had become conscious of

how often his wife used God's name in the place of swearing. "Would you mind not…" Unable to help himself, he growled, one hand raised and trembling.

"Sorry." She spoke awkwardly - as well she might, raising something as trite as mealtimes after the poison gas she had released directly into the heart of their home! Elaine made no excuses. He almost wished she would. Then he could rail: *Oh no! You don't get to blame this on me!*

"It's just that Judy hasn't eaten." She leant on the table, resumed her seated position, opposite but angled away from him.

Should he open the notebook and read? Would he be shocked at the numbers? She'd had no shortage of opportunities. Would he recognise names or be left to wonder? Somehow Graham realised that if he didn't destroy the book - tear the pages from their bindings and set light to them - it would always have the power to torture him. He would creep from his bed in the middle of the night to devour it one page at a time; retrace - perhaps re-live - his wife's footsteps as he walked the streets of his hometown.

His response was deliberately flat. "She'll be asleep by now."

There was urgent tapping and the sound of the letterbox being lifted. *"Mrs Jones? Mr Jones?"*

"I'll go," Graham insisted, but the heaviness he felt only enabled him to rise slowly, wiping his palms on his thighs, lifting one foot and then the other to straighten his trouser legs.

"It's the police."

He heard Elaine's breath shudder. "I thought I recognised the voice," she said.

"I bet one of Judy's fans has redecorated another car. I can't afford to pay for everybody's to be re-sprayed."

Aware she was shadowing him, he opened the front door.

"You're home!" the policewoman said, obviously relieved.

"You've caught us at a bad moment," Graham apologised. "We thought it was someone fooling around again."

"For once, I'm sorry it's not. Judy's had another collapse."

"No!" he protested, his wife's voice an echo of his own. In denial, at least, they were united.

They both reached for their coats, stepping aside after a collision of hands. A politeness that felt unnatural after twenty years of marriage.

Elaine's immediate reaction had been to add another layer to her husband's refusal to believe, but with evidence to the contrary, she feared it made her look like a worse mother. She should know exactly where her daughter was.

"I'll take you straight to her." Efficiency contradicted the fact that the policewoman appeared to be only a couple of years older than Judy. But she'd proven herself capable, responding to Elaine's calls of distress when she found Judy's followers pressed up against the living room window while Graham was out, and when journalists accosted her in the street, blocking access to her home because she refused to answer their questions.

In the back of the car, Elaine's hand jumped involuntarily at her husband's touch. The smallest gesture, he had breached the faux-leather divide to link the little finger of his right hand with hers. Welling with gratitude, she tightened her finger around his before he could withdraw it. An attempt to raise her eyes fell short of target, but it was close enough to see the nods Graham was dispensing: *yes, Judy's safe now; yes, we're still both her parents.* But not necessarily, *yes, you're still my wife.* Her eyes fell to their hands, two links in a chain and, in the abstract interior of light and shadow, the white skin stretched tightly over knuckles was highlighted. Again, Elaine experienced the sensation that her hand was alien to her. Next to Graham's it was small and frail, a frightened animal in need of his protection.

"They picked Judy up on Wellfield." The officer twisted her head towards them. "She's taken quite a tumble."

In search for her voice, Elaine coughed, the hand that was not linked to her husband's lingering above her mouth where it toyed with the soft fleshy groove.

"She wasn't in the convent grounds?" Graham was asking.

"Still making her way there, as I understand it. It was a good thing she wasn't on her own."

Judy was unable to leave the house alone these days. Even her walk to school had become a public procession, complete with banner bearers, candles and a solitary drummer. Up until now, Elaine hadn't thought of it as a comfort. Although Judy took it all in her stride, Elaine found it sinister, the only religious processions in her experience being those top-hatted and veiled events trailing slowly behind the hearse at funerals. When Elaine spoke, it was to confess: "I honestly thought Judy was in bed." She was making an evening of it: why stop there?

The driver grinned into the rear-view mirror. "My kids are still at the age where I'm happy if I can get three solid meals into them every day. I'm not looking forward to teenagers who creep out the minute your back's turned."

Oh, for a return to something so ordinary!

Glaring headlights blurred past, distorted by raindrops that clung to the side windows and windscreen beyond the reach of the wipers. Elaine hoped to block out the close-ups that appeared with every blink, projected onto the insides of her eyelids: the unfamiliar contours and elongated lobes of an ear; growth of fine hair above a pin-striped collar; her own hands greedily struggling with the buckle of a leather belt. She was already unbuckling her seatbelt as they pulled into the hospital car park, as if she could slam the door, trapping the images inside the vehicle.

"Hang on. Let's get you closer to the entrance," the driver said.

"Here is fine," Elaine replied, poised to break into a run as soon as her feet found tarmac.

"We've sedated Judy," Dr Singh informed them. (They hadn't dealt with him before, but he had the same white coat, the same kindly-but-firm manner.) "When she came round, she was extremely distressed and disorientated."

"Have you been given her history?" Graham asked.

"Quite a file we're building up." The doctor tapped his clipboard with the end of his biro. "Has she started taking the Epilin we prescribed?"

Glancing towards his wife, Graham saw Elaine's fingers splayed on the surface of her handbag as if, caught in a searchlight, they had frozen in an unnatural position. "Not yet."

Dr Singh's sigh escaped the camouflage of his professional smile. "The list of side-effects is daunting, I admit. Many patients - and their parents, I might add - read them and panic. And it's early days: it might not have got into her system yet, but - please - it's important we make a start. As soon as Judy comes round would be best. Are we agreed?"

Graham saw no option but to nod.

"Good. I'll nip down to the pharmacy in a moment. So -" He looked from one of them to the other "- who's taking the nightshift?"

"We'll both stay." Elaine edged out into traffic. Although Graham had hoped for time alone with his thoughts he decided not to contradict her.

"By all means." Dr Singh pulled back the curtain and showed them their daughter. Graham took stock, the sight of Judy in a hospital bed becoming more familiar but no less shocking. *I'm warning you, she won't be pretty.* He saw sheets and stitches and gauze. Dr Singh populated the silence, making it possible to exhale. "The cuts on her face are superficial: they should heal quite nicely. She might be left with scarring on her lip. And she's lost three of her front teeth. She'll need some dental work."

To Graham, Dr Singh might have been explaining how to go about polishing out scratches on a second-hand car: the art of making something less than perfect presentable. *A good wax, and a professional valet will have that looking like new.* And Graham's trust in the medical profession was only marginally greater than his trust of car salesmen. "So what's next?" he asked, feeling a ripple of annoyance that his wife was already claiming the chair nearest Judy's head, her hands finding purpose smoothing brow, hair and bedclothes.

"We let her sleep it off for a couple of days; monitor her for concussion."

"And then?"

The doctor moved his head from side to side. "We'll run some more tests: rule out what we can; focus on what we're left with."

"Is it always so... experimental?"

"Really, it's quite logical," Dr Singh continued in his calm voice. "We make no assumptions. When we've worked out what we're dealing with, we treat it."

"And what will you be testing for, exactly?"

"We'll try to work out what's going on in Judy's brain: if there's an underlying cause for the recent activity."

"Anything in particular?" Finding that he was staring at a rebellious hair growing from a mole between the doctor's brows, Graham frowned in concentration and folded his arms across his chest.

"Seizures can be a symptom of brain injury. Judy's suffered a recent trauma. Although she didn't appear to have an injury to her head, we might find scarring. Sometimes the cause is infection. And we want to eliminate the possibility of a tumour."

Balking at the sound of the word, Graham repeated, "A tumour?"

"A brain tumour. It's one of the first things we hope to rule out."

He hadn't - and still wouldn't - allow himself to consider such possibilities. But Elaine - how would she take this information? "And if you don't find anything specific?"

Dr Singh nodded. "We may well conclude that the cause is genetic, or due to a chemical imbalance. As is the case for seventy per cent of sufferers, I might add."

Graham lowered his voice. "I presume you take into account what triggers the attacks?"

"We most certainly do. Sleep deprivation, food allergies, toxins such as alcohol and smoking and, the one that most people are familiar with, strobe lighting."

As Graham opened his mouth to enquire about other strong sources of light - those his daughter described with such clarity - Dr Singh took him by the arm. "But these are all just triggers, Mr Jones. Even if we suppose Judy's claims are true, there would still be an underlying cause."

Accepting the futility of his questions, Graham wondered if Elaine's instinct to simply offer comfort was right. He turned his attention to Judy lying in the metal-framed bed, her head lolling to one side, mouth open. "How long before she comes round?"

"It's a light sedation to allow her some natural sleep. If she's into her usual pattern, you could be waiting some time."

"We're not going anywhere," Graham said. *We're.* He had used the plural automatically. *What God has joined together, let not man separate.* But *men?* Blinking the thought away, he tried to focus all his energy on his daughter and pray. But even as he prayed, Graham couldn't prevent his mind from wandering. In prayer, he couldn't give way to anger, although Graham felt it dishonest not to acknowledge it, lurking outside the gate like Judy's followers. For now, a deep hurt descended. It was as though he had filled his pockets with bronze weights from the kitchen scales, symbolic of something hanging in the balance. The Elaine he knew was no Jezebel. Unless everything he held dear was a lie - something he wasn't prepared to accept - at some point he would have to ask himself a few unpalatable questions: *have I neglected my marriage? Failed my wife?* But a part of him rose up defiantly: *what have I done that a dozen other men in my position wouldn't have done, and* not *have their wives cheat? What could I have done differently?* This life he had taken for granted, shored up with a solid-looking home, insured against all eventualities including accidental damage, filled with the best of British goods, regimented with routine and rules, was suddenly fragile. He knew he had to make a conscious decision to forgive, hoping this would kick-start the process, like faith, and love before it. They needed to talk about Judy; how best to help her. And for that to happen, he had to make it possible for his wife to look him in the eye again.

He summoned all his internal resources. "You must be tired," he said.

"Exhausted." A moment passed before Elaine turned her head slightly and made a reciprocal enquiry. "You?"

"I've never needed my sleep like you do." One hand flapped reluctantly against his chest, like the side gate when it was left untethered. "Why don't you try and get some rest?"

It pained Elaine to be in close proximity of someone so obviously in agony and be incapable of offering comfort, knowing herself to be its cause. She did not mistake Graham's offer of a makeshift pillow for forgiveness, but she did see it as a measure of the man she had married.

She settled against his chest gently, as if tending to a bruise, one hand supporting the weight of her head. Her eyes hurt even when she closed them, the skin surrounding them so taut it took time to settle, and she thought that she would never sleep again. But whatever else Graham said, Elaine heard as the murmur of deep-sea vibrations through the rise and fall of his chest.

She dozed sporadically, dreaming in snapshots.

Back in her parents' house, quickly dressing, while Graham, still hopping into his trousers, made his sack-race escape down the garden path.

Slick, underwater movement. Bodies taut: coil-sprung. "That's what they call the cobra position in yoga," she'd told his chest as his head curved away from her. A bead of sweat dripped from Graham's forehead onto hers. Closed-eye grinning followed happy collapse. She projected a jet-stream of cool air over his shoulder and down into the v-shaped hollow of his back.

Judy was crying. Would not stop, no matter how long Elaine shushed and patted.

She was floating. A foetus in her mother's womb, listening to the world from the inside. It sounded very similar to Graham talking as she lay with one ear to his chest.

Judy woke, not cursing with the strength of several demons, although she had an indistinct memory. Someone who may or may not have been her. The only thing that was clear was the knowledge that something had altered; could never return to the way it was before. Her swollen tongue - she had bitten it - was resting against the grooves of the roof of her mouth. Where it usually would have encountered resistance, there was jagged gum tasting of iron. Before opening her eyes, Judy knew how to reply if asked if she knew where she was: in hospital. The sterile smell; harsh fluorescent lighting that penetrated her lids; constant pacing of rubber soles, something felt rather than heard. Judy had passed out this time: there was an undeniable chasm in her memory with no way of crossing to measure its width.

The view through flickering eyelashes revealed her parents, together for the first time she could remember in recent months - other than when seated round the dinner table. Using her father's chest as a pillow, her mother's mouth had fallen open leaving a dark stain on his shirt.

"Mum's dabbled." To her own ears, Judy's voice sounded different, and she put this down to the lack of some of those... what were they called? Those little white bones in your mouth.

"Hey, soldier, you're awake!" Her father smiled, shifting his head awkwardly to see her better without disturbing the sleeper. "What's that you're saying?"

"Mum." Judy nodded. "She's dabbled on you."

Her father looked. "I think you mean 'dribbled'. That's nothing compared to what you've done to me over the years." How long had she been asleep? He appeared older somehow. Properly middle-aged. "How are you feeling? They say you took quite a fall."

"My head..." Judy put two fingers in her mouth to confirm what the movement of her tongue had already told her: a gap.

"I'm not sure how the tooth fairy operates these days." Tooths: *that was what they were called*. "She's probably had to stop off at the bank. Don't worry, we'll get you some new gnashers. You'll be able to compare notes with Grandpa."

"They won't be like his, will they?" Judy asked, imagining her mouth collapsed, like Grandpa's when he forgot to wear his dentures. Her mother's father had famously insisted on having all of his natural teeth extracted on receipt of his call-up papers. He had no fear of enemy bullets but he'd be damned if he was going to let a foreign dentist lay a finger on him.

"You won't be able to take them out. They fix them into your gums. On posts."

Judy couldn't picture what her father meant. The only post she could think of was the concrete one outside the convent gates. "I hate the dentist's," she said.

"And this from the girl who sticks needles through her nose."

"Once!"

In the space that followed, to please her father, Judy pretended to reach out and snatch an air-born kiss he had blown from the palm of his hand, slapping it into place on her cheek.

Then, timidly, she asked, "Did anyone else see Her, Dad?" She hoped her meaning would be clear: although she was no longer in control, this hadn't been a simple fit, something doctors could cure.

Her father stiffened. "No, darling."

Judy turned her head slightly. Her body felt weak, as it had done in those days after her plaster casts had been sawn off. It was coming back to her; why this time had been different. "She said it was the last time She would visit." It was over, then, her ordeal - but also the greatest peace she'd known.

"I thought that because you didn't get as far as the convent…"

Judy nodded and, with her father watching, a single tear rolled down her cheek, heavy and unrestrained. An emptiness opened up inside her. She was a hollow shell once more. "She won't be coming back. Not to me, anyway."

"Well, Father Patrick will be relieved. He's had the Bishop breathing down his neck ever since we joined the congregation at St Joseph's."

"I'm serious." Judy's saliva was stretchy, like the cheese used for pizza topping.

"Sorry, darling. Just attempting to cheer you up." He paused. "Did She have anything else to say?"

"Can you write it down? In case I forget."

While her father found a biro and abandoned his search

for paper in favour of skin, Judy concentrated, trying to remember the precise words. Her lids were so, so heavy. Sinking, they narrowed her view. There wasn't long before sleep would demand her company again, but she fought it. "We'll be given one last chance. There will be a warning. A bright light will appear. But if people don't repent, planes will start to fall out of the sky, all over the world. And, in England, millions of trees will be torn up by the roots in a single night."

"Trees? Are you sure?"

"That's what She said."

"But millions? I mean, even with Dutch Elm disease..."

"Don't get obsessed with the trees, Dad! People are going to die. And it's going to take years to recover. But we can still stop it if we're truly sorry. If we stop using God's name to justify the evil men do."

Her father was nodding as he wrote on his palm. "And did you manage to ask for a sign, like Father Patrick suggested?"

"I was going to... but..." Judy failed to control the trembling of her lips. "I've let everyone down."

"You haven't let anyone down, Judy. I never want to hear you say that, understand me?"

Elaine had been awake since the news that this was to be the last time Mary would appear to her daughter. Excluded from the exchange, she tried to work out in her own mind what it meant. Would her daughter's fits stop? Perhaps people only thought they were experiencing visions until they took medication. Maybe the Epilin would stop the visions but not the fits: instead of thinking someone was watching over her, Judy would feel completely alone. Elaine wished they could have seen the same doctor as before so she didn't have to start from the beginning every time she wanted to ask a simple question... if only there were simple questions.

Beyond, lurked thoughts of Graham and questions that

seemed equally difficult to answer. Earlier that same evening
- a lifetime ago - Graham had said their love for each other
was the only thing he was sure of, and she had brushed his
words aside. Did he still love her? How could he possibly,
when she so disgusted herself? What would she do without
the safe anchorage he provided?

And now there was talk of bright lights and falling planes
and uprooted trees (she shared her husband's mystified reaction to news of the fate of millions of trees, as if plane crashes
were somehow less violent), and it sounded like madness! But
Elaine had to open her eyes and face the insanity, because this
was what her life had become. This was her family: there were
things only she could make right. Elaine had thought they
had already hit rock bottom and had been floundering there,
but perhaps, if this was it, there was some slim hope that they
could begin the gradual ascent.

"Judy," she said, lifting her head, patting Graham's chest by
way of thanks, quite distinct and unconnected from the rest
of him. About to comment on how pale her daughter was,
Elaine felt the gloop of wet cotton. "Oh, look at that," she said,
wiping saliva from her cheek. Her daughter grimaced, a brave
attempt to smile in spite of her tears, revealing the new gap.
Elaine made a silent appeal to Graham: *For Judy's sake, please.*
"Look at the three of us. What a mess we all are!"

Separated from his daughter, Graham was forced to sit
forwards and lean his elbows on his knees. Elaine was right:
what an awful mess. How could they get back to the way they
had been before he had become an obsessive father? How to
steer his daughter back towards ordinary teenage issues like
boyfriends and smoking. How to repair his relationship with
his wife. How to convince his boss that he could put private
matters aside and deliver. And to still leave space for God.

But first, he was forced to acknowledge that there was

something he needed to do. He dispensed the pills into the palm of his hand and walked to his daughter's bedside, where he picked up the tumbler of water.

"Dr Singh said you were to take these as soon as you came round."

"What are they?" she asked.

Hoping she was too tired to resist, he held the tumbler to her lips. "Medicine. To help you feel better."

CHAPTER FORTY-ONE

laine's first reaction when Graham announced she had a visitor was panic. Perhaps it was the journalist, come to tell her he hadn't been able to get his old job back and that he would be forced to publish. Weeks had passed and there had been nothing, but she knew how they held onto human interest stories - the equivalent of Victorian freak shows - going to print when news was slow. Roll up, roll up! Come and see the mermaid girl, the bearded lady, the Miracle Girl's mother. Who else could it be? In the past - now viewed with a sense of nostalgia Elaine never suspected herself capable of - visitors had been neighbours requiring small favours; parents of Judy's school friends. She rarely heard from her sister these days. Liz seemed embarrassed when she telephoned: once a lifeline, phone calls were now stilted, and it was just easier not to.

None of those. Instead it was Judy's headmistress.

"Sister Euphemia," Elaine looked up from her ironing, embarrassed by her slovenly appearance. "This is... unexpected."

"An unexpected pleasure is what she means," Graham prompted, rushing about and putting things that seemed quite unnecessary into his pockets. "I'm afraid I'm just on my way over to my mother's, but I'm sure my wife will take good care of you."

Surprised to find her forehead kissed - they had been treading so carefully around each other - Elaine felt a tug of something under her skin before it struck her: she was being abandoned. What had Graham been thinking of, showing the headmistress into the breakfast room? But his mind was elsewhere. His mother was ill and intent on ignoring her doctor's advice - a ploy, Elaine suspected, to have her only son visit.

Sister Euphemia had brought flowers. "Picked in the convent grounds. I have no idea what they are, I'm afraid. But I thought Judy might like something to let her know we're all thinking of her."

"I'll find a vase." Elaine was glad of the distraction, unable to behave naturally with the headmistress's presence crowding the space. "Can I offer you some tea?"

"No. Thank you." Sister Euphemia appeared to increase in height but, really, Elaine saw, she was only rocking onto the balls of her feet. "I just wondered when we can expect Judy back at school."

En route to the table, Elaine froze. "You want her back?"

"Of course." Sister Euphemia's expression suggested dismay at any suggestion to the contrary.

"Frankly... I must say, I'm a little surprised. We thought there might be somewhere she'd fit in better. Given the circumstances."

"I'd advise against moving her, so close to the exams. But you know what's best." Sister Euphemia's voice, suggesting quite the reverse, softened. "We'd really be very sorry to lose Judy."

Elaine saw that this was true - at least as far as the headmistress was concerned. She also acknowledged the sense in what was proposed, but this didn't prevent her from bristling with resistance when the Sister added, "We look after our own."

"Since when has...?" She realised how foolish her

unfinished question was. Everyone had staked their claim in Judy. Elaine's own (which, by rights, should be the larger part) was diminishing. "You understand that she has to stick to a strict regime? We're still getting used to it ourselves."

"We've coped with far worse, I can assure you."

"There are side-effects."

"Just let me know what she needs."

"And how do you think Judy will be welcomed back to school by the other girls? You said yourself how cruel they can be."

"I really don't think there's any danger of bullying. I think that, if anything, they'd be very protective of her."

Elaine had hoped that perhaps, removed from so much religious influence, Judy might become distracted by more usual teenage preoccupations but, during her extended absence, she had displayed little interest in new clothes and none in boys. "We'll have to ask her how she feels."

"Good." The headmistress nodded as if everything had been decided and, again, Elaine felt angered by Sister Euphemia's assumption that she knew Judy's wishes, all the time knowing that the convent - the grounds at least - still held a very strong draw.

CHAPTER FORTY-TWO

Paula needn't have fretted that she wouldn't be able to find Elaine's address. She knew it as the 'posh' neighbourhood, a haven of grass verges and Edwardian semis. Only two streets from home, it wasn't a frequently-trodden route - no need to venture into the maze of side roads with the High Street a stone's throw away. It wasn't a route Paula thought she would be taking again in a hurry.

The Jones's street was defined by the number of For Sale signs that had sprung up, as if they were the season's must-have garden accessory. This was a road unloved, the reason all too obvious. Nobody wanted to live there, but no one could afford to leave. Paula sensed a demarcation between those who appeared to have been invited to this strange, unseasonal street-party-cum-travellers'-site and those who had not. Some of the original cast of residents had hoisted felt-covered card tables into front gardens, displaying pyra-mids of canned drinks marked 'not for individual sale' and a bizarre array of trinkets comprised, chiefly, of unwanted gifts and undervalued heirlooms, to which they added teetering piles of dog-eared paperbacks. They heaved themselves out of sagging deckchairs at the approach of a potential customer, toothy grins turning upside down as Paula inclined her head towards the Pyrex dish she was carrying in lieu of an apology.

She negotiated an orderly queue that had formed outside one semi, where a handmade sign pointing to a side gate offered use of the outside toilet for five pence (extra for toilet paper), or a bucket of water for twenty pence. A small child, sent to patrol the queue with an empty jam jar, was struggling to keep track of the handfuls of pennies thrust in her direction. Paula was forced onto the verge, its muddied grass trodden thin, finding herself apologising to a sleeping bag whose quilted edge she'd failed to circumnavigate.

Aware of being observed by those who had retreated behind defence-lines of glass and folded arms, Paula nodded in a manner she hoped was indicative of her peaceful mission. She was stared straight through. Some homeowners had adopted a less subtle approach, taping handwritten signs saying 'No Camping Outside This House' and 'Leave Our Street Alone' onto the inside of bay windows. She sensed hostile eyes at upper windows and, imagining herself in the sights of an air rifle, hurried forwards, head down.

There was no shortage of anoraked individuals to direct Paula to number 42. Tellingly, estate agents' signs were lashed to the gateposts on either side. One woman in an olive green all-weather poncho appeared to have appointed herself official gatekeeper.

"I'm a friend," Paula announced, willing the act of saying this out loud to make it true.

"Do you actually know her?" the gatekeeper gasped, dispensing with her demand for a toll. Inside the garden gate, Paula was distracted by the rose bushes. She hated to see plants so neglected: dried heads swaying precariously on brittle stalks. But with extras from the *Thriller* video patrolling your doorstep, you'd hardly be inclined to venture out for a spot of deadheading. She glanced over her shoulder to see an elderly lady placing tea lights on the brick wall as if this were an everyday activity, her ivory smile the perfect advert for denture cream. *What am I doing here?* Oh, don't be daft, she gave herself a strict talking to. With fresh resolve, Paula turned back to the front door, puffing out her cheeks. Elaine came to you and, straight off, you knew something was wrong.

Raising the Pyrex dish to the level of the doorbell, she extended an index finger and made contact. There was a two-toned ring from deep within, so disconnected it seemed unlikely anything she had done would have created it. Paula stepped back so that whoever answered the door would be able to see her through its brass spy hole, the splintered wood suggesting this was a recent addition. There was the sound of Marley's chains.

"Who is it?" a man asked, peering out through the narrow gap.

"Friend of Elaine's," Paula said, trying to sound confident in her new capacity.

There was more rattling and the door was pulled inwards, catching on a rectangle of carpet that was protecting identical flooring underneath. "She could do with one."

"I come bearing chicken soup." Paula held up the proof, as if to verify what she said before passing through Customs. "Well, it's curry actually, but the thought's the same. I'm Paula."

"Graham." The man stepped aside, glancing quickly at those loitering outside, who had now edged closer. "Come in, come in. Let's get the door shut." She noted how he bolted it. "And then I can take that from you."

Paula followed as if entering a show home she had no intention of buying - a huge amount of space for three people - taking in the thin stripe of the wallpaper below the dado rail and the plain wallpaper above. Oh, and they had one of those plant stands on the little landing halfway up the stairs. What were they all about? "What a lovely house!" she enthused.

"All down to Elaine. Speaking of whom…" Graham

announced on entering the kitchen.

Paula smiled down at the withered woman sitting at the kitchen table among toppling piles of correspondence, then glanced at Graham for reassurance that this was not someone he had found camped outside and taken pity on. But Elaine's eyes flickered with recognition, not so much at the sight of her face, she felt, as at the sight of her cardigan - the same cardigan, Paula now realised, that she had slipped around Elaine's shoulders on the night the wall came down. It always had been the ideal thing when you were feeling under the weather, or wanted to curl up in an armchair and read a magazine.

"A visitor. And she's brought some rather wonderful smelling curry."

Beside his wife, Graham had lifted the lid from the Pyrex and was inhaling, eyes half-closed in pleasure. Paula detected he was trying to encourage Elaine, who certainly looked in need of a square meal.

"Secret recipe." Paula's mouth watered as the aromatic concoction of cumin, ginger and garam masala reached her.

"Grab a seat." He put the lid back on the dish as if everything were perfectly normal, so Paula pulled back one of the hand-painted chairs, thinking, I'll play along if you like.

"Let me put the kettle on, then I'll make myself scarce so you two can catch up. Have you come far today, Paula?"

"Only down the road."

"Then I can't think why we haven't… Or perhaps we have?"

Paula put one hand on Elaine's arm. "Your wife and I met the night of your daughter's accident. My husband" - she couldn't help betraying a little pride - "was one of the men who helped move all those bricks."

With tears pooling in her eyes, Elaine bit her lip and nodded.

"Then we owe you more than a cup of tea!" Graham looked

behind him from both directions, arms flailing, as if unsure of his surroundings. "But I'm not sure we've got anything stronger in the house."

"Tea's fine. Really."

"Come here." He approached Paula, open-armed.

Not knowing what else to do, she allowed herself to be hugged. "Oh!" she laughed, turning her head so that the side of her face was cushioned by his bulk.

"Thank you a thousand times."

Paula's response was muffled by Graham's jumper. "Anybody would have done the same."

"I suppose there must be others, mustn't there?" The awkwardness of the embrace was short-lived, Graham stepping backwards to enquire, "Have you met Judy?"

"No, I..."

Her protests unheard, he already had his hand on the doorframe, his head angled in the direction of his daughter's bedroom. "Judy!"

"*What?*"

Graham smiled an apology before projecting his voice again. "Could you spare us a few moments? There's someone here you need to meet."

There was an awkward delay while Judy thumped slowly downstairs, a small child's descent, bringing both feet together before lowering her right foot onto the next step. Paula's view revealed a face set with pain and determination. She smiled at her hosts, embarrassed about the effort that was being taken on her account.

Beckoning excitedly, Graham stepped into the hallway to pull Judy over the threshold. "Come along, slowcoach! This is Paula. You have her and her husband to thank for the fact that you're still with us."

Paula's first impression was that the girl seemed fairly ordinary, but for the fact she was minus her front teeth.

Wearing headphones around her neck, large cartoon-character slippers and - was that a nose piercing? - she certainly didn't look as if she belonged with the crowd outside. Judy's eyes met hers then, blinking, they trailed to her mother's, who smiled through damp lashes, nodding encouragement.

"Thank you. They said I was lucky you were there."

Paula pitied Judy's self-consciousness at being exhibited, the fact that it was in her own home making it no less of an ordeal. "We call it 'The Night the Wall Came Down'. I don't expect you remember too much about it."

The girl's jaw dropped and she looked at her mother's tears afresh. "Nothing." Despite brave appearances, a brief flicker of torment behind Judy's eyes spoke to Paula of half-remembered moments. Not nothing. Perhaps not even next to nothing. "One minute, I was walking down the road, the next..."

Beside her, Elaine appeared to have been ambushed by a breath as it rushed inwards, rattling her chest and shoulders. It struck Paula that Elaine might have been superstitious that talking about the accident could somehow alter its outcome. And Graham, who spoke to the reporters with such conviction, hadn't seen what they'd seen. "Well, if you ever want to fill in the gaps..." Afraid she might be speaking out of turn (she didn't know these people, for goodness' sake, and who'd want to remember being buried alive?), Paula hastened to add, "I can't tell you how happy we were to hear you're back on your feet. And look at you: typical teenager!"

"Have you seen my blue sweatshirt, Mum?" Judy's brow wrinkled, as if keen to prove Paula's point. This was a girl torn between thoughts of escape and wanting to ask more.

Elaine pushed back her hair and it fell forwards in exactly the same position. "I expect it's in the washing basket."

"I haven't worn it for over a week!"

"I've been busy," Elaine countered. "Dealing with your mail, mostly."

Paula blinked. Despite the circus outside, this was a normal home. Still the need for answering mail and sticking the laundry on. Still the everyday squabbles.

"Well." Graham steered his daughter by the shoulders. "Let's give them some privacy." He took the position of the back of a pantomime horse, lowering his mouth to Judy's ear, but not his voice. "You don't have to leave it to your mother. Even *I* can work the washing machine." After exiting, he returned for a brief encore. "Don't run off without saying goodbye. I haven't finished with you yet, Paula." Then he pulled the door until it was almost closed, leaving a carefully calculated gap.

After his daughter had loped upstairs to her bedroom, Graham stood with his back against the wall in the hallway. Closing his eyes he crumpled internally, his lungs heaving like the bellows of an accordion being compressed by an unseen player. He had taken to eavesdropping on his wife. It pained him to do it, but he felt it was necessary until they were back on track. He waited for his breathing to settle and then edged towards the door until he had a clear view through the gap.

Paula had turned to Elaine and was laughing: "You look as if that's come as a surprise to you - about the washing machine, I mean."

"It's not that - although Graham wouldn't have a clue about separating the colours."

Graham opened his mouth in silent protest and then closed it as he acknowledged he hadn't realised he was supposed to.

"Safer not to let them near it, I find!"

"It's just that Judy's so different with other people. I can't tell how she's going to be from one minute to the next." There was gratitude in his wife's expression as she said, "I expect she was overwhelmed by meeting you."

"She seemed fine to me. As I say: normal teenager. But it wasn't her I came to see." Paula paused, as if embarrassed to continue, but then appeared to have a change of heart. "I read what that horrible man wrote in the papers: I was worried about you, love." Graham detected a flicker of fear in Elaine's eyes. "And now I've seen it with my own eyes I can understand why you feel trapped."

He saw her breathe again. "I know I should try harder, but sometimes I just can't keep my mouth shut."

"We're the mothers. They expect us to cope. There's no manual for this sort of thing."

What about the fathers? thought Graham from his sentry post. *We don't get a look in!*

Elaine met Paula's gaze. "Judy's epileptic." She appeared keen to dispense facts.

"Oh?"

"She has fits. And sometimes, when she's fitting, she thinks she sees things. For someone who's had one close shave, it's not surprising she's got a bit of an obsession with the afterlife."

Graham sighed, one hand at his forehead: *Oh, love, you want it to be simple. But it isn't, it isn't.*

"I found it difficult to accept at first. It seems unfair, one girl having to go through so much. But it's easier not to fight the diagnosis. The only way I can help Judy is by making sure she gets the right treatment."

"I see." Paula blinked. "It's a shame the newspapers don't think to mention that. It might discourage that sorry lot who have set up camp."

"That wouldn't be much of a story, would it?" Elaine's bitter laugh turned into a sigh. "You know, it's funny. I used to think my life was dull. I longed for something to happen and now... what I wouldn't give to be anonymous!"

As Graham saw his wife give way to tears, only he knew what she would be thinking. That she didn't deserve pity, let alone kindness. Not when it was from someone who barely knew her, who had done so much already, and now brought chicken curry.

"Oh, come here!" Having pulled her chair closer, Paula offered Elaine a shoulder and wrapped her in both arms. "That husband of yours was hugging the wrong person, wasn't he?"

Stranded in the hall, Graham vibrated: I *needed that hug. Me!* He recognised in Paula a woman who could hug with no agenda other than comfort. With his wife, there was the risk that he would be pushed away because his unintentional erection was a barrier between him and a simple act of intimacy, causing her to protest, "No, Graham. We're not ready yet. I want you to be sure you've forgiven me first," when the real issue was that Elaine wasn't ready to allow herself to be forgiven. But you can't say these things, not when you love someone; when you want to put their pain before your own. At this thought, Graham felt repulsed by what he was doing: listening in on an innocent conversation. He staggered the few steps into the living room and crash-landed on the two-seater. "Dear God," he began, tuning out of the muffled conversation beyond the wall. "Teach me to trust my wife again."

"Come on, love." Paula was steadying the head that was resting on her shoulder with one hand. "Let it all out."

"I can't." Elaine trembled.

"You can," Paula cooed. "I won't tell a soul."

Gradually, Elaine's shoulders stilled. "You saw how Judy was. It's the side-effects. She never complains, but she's become so sluggish and morose since she started taking the drugs. She's constantly tired; just stares at the television without taking anything in."

"What does your husband say?"

"We don't talk about it." Elaine sniffed and excused herself. "Graham thinks it's his job to stay upbeat, so he injects enthusiasm into every sentence. It's exhausting, watching him act as if nothing's wrong." Elaine lifted her head from Paula's shoulder and sat back, clasping her arms around herself in a desperate embrace. "After Judy's accident, we didn't talk about her scars. It wasn't Graham's fault: he had no idea how bad they were. Judy wanted to keep them hidden and I..." Paula watched as Elaine began to rock back and forth, back and forth, as if her limbs were ropes and her body a small boat trying to break free from its mooring. "I thought she deserved that much privacy when everything else had been taken away from her. As you say, there's no manual... but now, we seem to be repeating that mistake. I want Judy to be well. I want her to be happy. And this seems to be what we have to accept: another unmentionable compromise."

Noting the husband was excluded when it came to wishes, Paula dismissed it as a turn of phrase, nothing more. "If you can't talk to your husband, could you talk to the doctors? Ask them if this is a normal reaction? There might be something they can suggest."

Elaine nodded, eyes downcast.

"Good girl," Paula found herself saying.

"It's just, I thought we'd hit... I thought it might stop. But they're never going to leave us alone." As Elaine sat back, Paula followed her eyes to the piles of envelopes: Basildon Bond; watermarked; plain brown; small and pink; airmail with blue and red flagged margins. Strewn among the breakfast debris, slotted into the toast rack, weighed down by a pot of lime jelly marmalade.

"I wondered what this lot was."

"Letters for Judy. Each envelope is from some desperate soul. It sounds insane, but I feel responsible for them."

"You reply to them all?"

"Hah!" A small cry escaped Elaine. "I wouldn't know what to say! They break my heart. People on death's door, or whose children are seriously ill. They're sending Judy money, asking her to pray for them. And these are just today's."

In dismay, Paula saw each envelope take on the personality

of someone with a terrible burden to bear, limping and bandaged, crying out in agony. There were not enough hugs to go round.

"I mean," Elaine continued. "What would you do in my place? Would you rip up the cheques and let them think they're being ignored? Or would you take the money, because then at least they might think their prayers will be answered? Or should I forward it to a charity that might actually be able to help them?"

Paula looked at a Sheffield postmark and the smudged ink of the address that looked as though it had been left out in the rain. "But you read all of them, do you?"

"As many as I can. Judy hasn't got time. She's revising for her O-Levels. I think if she can just get them under her belt, then we can think about going… oh, I don't know. Somewhere they don't know us."

"What about your home?"

"My home is wherever my family is."

"I don't know how you cope," Paula said with sincere admiration at this show of courage.

"Very, very badly. If you want the truth, I had been plotting my escape." Elaine's attempt at joking revealed what she'd intended to hide. Paula came very close to seeing how she had tried crawling through an adult-sized hole in a fence, but had found parts of herself on the other side that had frightened her. Things she hadn't thought herself capable of, like a soldier returning from war determining never to speak of the unspeakable.

"But not anymore." Paula looked at her sternly, a call to duty.

"No. I'm past that now."

"Mind if I…?" Paula nodded in the direction of an unfolded letter written on a humble sheet of paper ripped from a pad, the remnants of punched holes resembling a chain of decapitated paper men.

"Help yourself."

Paula encountered the mother of a girl with a rare bone disease and whose options had run out. And to think this was just one of many! She rubbed her eyes, realising that the tears that had smudged the ink might have been Elaine's. It was impossible to remain detached. "What about that lot out the front?"

Elaine sat, head in hands, pressing fingertips to her closed eyelids. "What about them?"

"They can at least make themselves useful." Paula stood, the scraping of her chair making Elaine jolt to attention, and picked up a pile of letters. "Coming?"

As if on automatic pilot, Elaine picked up another pile and followed her into the daylight, blinking and mole-like.

"Right you lot: gather round!" Paula leaned over the gate at the end of the path, holding a handful of envelopes as if they were the first prize in a raffle. "These people need your help. Write to them. Let them know you're praying for them, but make sure you come back for the next batch."

There were surprisingly few protests. Many hangers-on seemed happy to have been given a task, as if they had been expecting instructions. People filtered away, heads huddled, comparing the hands they had been dealt as they would holiday snaps.

The post distributed, Paula turned back in the direction of the house. "That's that lot sorted. Now what we need is a bucket and something to make a sign with."

"What for?"

"So you can leave the letters outside. Unless you want to risk facing the zombies every day."

Watching the slow retreat, Elaine laughed. "They do look a bit like…" Then, released, she laughed louder. "You're a bad influence!"

In the kitchen, Elaine took paper and a laundry marker from a drawer and put them on the table, and returned to rummage under the sink. "I know we have a bucket that doesn't look as if it's been used for wallpaper paste. Here we are."

"What'll we call it?" Paula drummed her fingers on the table, and then clamped the pen between her teeth to remove the lid. She wrote the words 'Judy's Prayer Network' in a confident scrawl and spat the lid out. "That should do it. Sellotape." She thrust out a hand.

The label stuck on the bucket, Paula weighed it down with a few sizable stones from the edge of the path and placed it on the gatepost. Then, retracing her steps, she gave herself the satisfaction of snapping a few flower heads, their powdery centres disintegrating. Paula passed Elaine coming in the opposite direction, her hands rattling with small plastic boxes.

"May as well let them have the rosary beads so they make a good job of it."

"Worry beads, my mother called them. Now, let's get that washing on."

From his seat in the living room, Graham heard the lilt of Paula's voice, issuing commands. *Powder! Conditioner!* He supposed he should be happy to hear the house coming back to life, but he couldn't help feeling excluded. He would only ever be the father: second best.

CHAPTER FORTY-THREE

Judy inhaled sharply at the unfamiliar sound of women's laughter. Remembering nothing of the last few moments, she found that she was perched on the end of her bed, staring vacantly. Sister's Euphemia's flowers were there on the dressing table, the water turned a sickly-sweet smelling brackish green, faded crepe-paper petals beginning to drop. The cassette she had been listening to had finished, but the defibrillating jolt had failed to shock her back to life.

Was this what the doctor called a *petit mal*, or was she as much of a daydreamer as her teachers accused? The new drugs left her constantly drowsy, and it was an effort to focus on revision. Every time she lay on her bed with an open text book, she would wake with the skin of her face indented from the raised wavy lines of her bedcover - resembling the wavy lines of her brain patterns - another hour closer to the exam. Checking her watch and referring to the timetable she'd drawn up, Judy saw that she should be doing biology revision: The Life Cycle of a Tapeworm. What was God thinking of, relying on a pig eating excrement and humans eating pigs before the worm could reproduce? It was just about the most repulsive thing she'd ever heard of. Living things lurking in her guts were the new stuff of nightmares. This was the reason people became vegetarians.

"It's certainly one of the reasons Jews don't eat pork," her father agreed, after she'd taken the opportunity to recite her exam answer over last week's Sunday roast.

Mum had glared at him, snapping a piece of crackling in two. "Pack it in, the pair of you. It's fine as long as the meat's not pink."

Judy put her knife and fork together on her plate. "I don't feel hungry anymore."

The crash vibrated down through the ceiling.

"Judy!" Elaine heard Graham yell from his position on the sofa, as he might have done when their eight-year-old daughter had used their bed as a trampoline, every bounce making the light-fitting dance.

Elaine reached for her utensils' drawer and extracted a wooden spoon. "Oh my God, oh my God." She exhaled slowly, counting, just as her mother had taught her to count the seconds between thunder and lightning. She felt Paula's alarmed eyes trained on her face, waiting for instructions; guessed she would be wondering why no one was moving.

Then the more subdued thumping started.

She ran, finding her husband taking the stairs two at a time.

"Spoon!" Elaine cried, and he reached down over the banisters to grab it. Turning back to the telephone table, she saw Paula, receiver to ear, index finger tracing the semicircle of the first nine.

"Go!" Paula mouthed.

"Number 42," Elaine said before following Graham upstairs.

"Watch out for the broken glass!" Her husband's voice was amplified with concern, his back hunched over their pulsating daughter who had fallen in the confined space between bed and dressing table. Hesitating at the threshold, Elaine looked down, seeing shards swimming in the spillage, flowers in various states of decay floating on top of the whole mess. Sidestepping, she flung herself bodily onto Judy's bed, her first view her daughter's dressing table: an overturned pot of nail varnish teetering with thoughts of escape; blood on one corner; downward-sliding bloody handprints on the front of one of the white drawers.

Graham glanced at her, the whites of his eyes wild, like those of a horse being reined back - although it was Judy he was trying to rein in. She propped herself up on elbows and looked down. Elaine saw the inverted pyramid stamped on her daughter's forehead. The negative of the corner of the dressing table disappeared as it filled with blood.

Judy was on her side now, grinding the wooden spoon between her teeth, the bowl pushing further towards her mouth as her face rocked and rocked. Her pallor was blue-tinged, but for the overflow of blood from her head-wound.

"Hail Mary, full of grace," Graham was saying through teeth gritted with the effort of trying to anchor their daughter. His eyes closed, sweat beading on his brow.

I wanted there to be something wrong with Judy and now there is. Elaine's lips began to move in time with her husband's. And then, because it silenced unwelcome thoughts, she prayed out loud. Not because she believed the words (except that they were about being a mother, something she used to think she was good at), but because Judy did. Elaine reached down and peeled matted hair from the side of her daughter's face, uncovering an ear. *Blessed is the fruit of thy womb.* She wanted furiously to believe there was someone watching over them, but desire alone did not make it true. Words conjured a longing for the time when belief had been simple and attainable: God, Father Christmas, the tooth fairy. All once central players in her life. The prayer kept the terrible gargling-sound that rose from her daughter's throat at bay.

She was aware of the flickering of Judy's feet, ridiculous in oversized slippers, thrashing about as if Graham was trying to drown her in shallow water. Elaine wanted to reach out and remove the slippers, but dared not take her eyes from Judy's bloodied and contorted face, as if the act of looking alone could make the fit come to an end.

The noise stopped and Graham - who Elaine had thought was entranced in prayer - gripped Judy under her arms, dragging her body over the glass shards to an open space by the door. It no longer mattered that cotton was slashed, that skin was cut: priorities had changed. Elaine had been praying for the fit to be over, and now it was. How was it that her prayers were so powerful when she didn't believe there was anyone to hear them? "No!" she heard herself cry out. "*No!*"

Graham rolled Judy onto her back and tilted her chin upwards - violent movements. He carved her a new mouth by scooping out the contents of the old, his fingers coming out gloopy.

"Cloth!" he ordered, extending one grasping hand.

Elaine pulled Judy's t-shirt from under her pillow and put it in his impatient claw. Graham wiped foamy vomit from one side of his daughter's face and, clamping her nostrils shut, covered Judy's mouth with his own. He breathed twice, pausing long enough to say 'one banana.' Then, spitting something aside, he linked his hands together and began the compressions, his breathing becoming heavier and heavier.

Helpless in the way of one who can only watch, Elaine recited the *Hail Mary*, over and over, until words no longer had any meaning - not even about the role of mothers. *Pray-for-rus-sinners-now-an-dat-the-hour-of-our-death-amen.* Until the ambulance men came, like adjudicators of a nightmarish examination, and told them it was time to stop what they were doing.

CHAPTER FORTY-FOUR

Elaine remembered where she was when JFK was assassinated. When Martin Luther King was gunned down. When Elvis died an undignified death. When Lennon was shot. She hadn't imagined for one moment that she would be there when her daughter stopped breathing. She refused to acknowledge the fact of it. Denied it access. There was still urgency in the paramedics' movements. An expectation that they could do something, do something. *Do something! Judy, Judy, Judy, Judy!*

Dr Singh lowered his stethoscope, blinking. He didn't need to look at the name on the chart to know who the girl was: he identified her by her nose stud, the gap in her teeth. This was the part of the job he would never get used to, his only comfort being that he thought it was something you *should* never get used to. But it was something that had to be done; done now and with dignity.

"I don't understand." Elaine straightened her back, looking up at Dr Singh from under the tent of grey blanket that had been placed around their shoulders, as if it might contain them. Graham, her silent mirror image, moved as she moved.

"Sudden Unexplained Death in Epilepsy. I'm afraid

we don't understand why it happens. Judy simply stopped breathing."

"Why weren't we warned?" Elaine shook her head. "If we'd been told…"

"*Mummy fix it!*"

"It's very rare. And it wouldn't have made a blind bit of difference. Your husband did everything right. There was nothing more you could have done." As Dr Singh reached for one of Elaine's shoulders, she shrugged his "Either of you" aside.

"*No darling, there are some things Mummy can't fix.*"

Beside her, Graham was staring and blinking. Occasionally he moved one hand from his mouth to his chin and back again. Suddenly he placed both hands above his knees and launched himself to standing. His section of tent deflated, draping itself on his vacant chair. He walked down the off-white corridor, where the walls were almost indistinguishable from the floor, as a still grey sea is from a cloud-heavy sky. Elaine watched Graham pause under a neon sign for the chapel. Momentarily, he rested his forehead on the door frame before, stiff-armed, he pushed the double doors inwards with the flats of both hands.

Elaine stood, pulling Graham's portion of blanket towards her so that she was at its centre, covered from shoulders to knees. Her feet not yet prepared to obey, she extended her neck slightly as if this might help her to see around the corner, into the chapel.

"*No, not good enough! I am not Abraham: Judy was never part of the bargain.*"

She heard her husband's distant shouts. The clash of metal. The pounding. Oh, my poor darling, she thought, you can't bargain with God. Didn't you read *The Heart of the Matter*? It doesn't end well. Or was it that you believed your faith was stronger. That it could carry us all in its wake? Well, it carried us - we had no choice - and brought us back here. Full circle.

There was sudden movement as two uniformed men came running from the far end of the corridor, elbows pumping. Reaching for a reference point, her mind travelled from Graham Greene to *Star Wars*. The men were fast but, now that her feet understood the need for urgency, Elaine was faster. She placed herself in front of the double doors, her back to the chapel.

"Step aside, Madam," one of the security guards demanded, his voice controlled but firm.

"You'll have to wait. My husband is praying." Just one woman facing two men.

"*A pregnant daughter, I could have dealt with! A daughter on drugs, I could have dealt with!*"

Frowning, the man moved his head to peer through the glass panel in the door. "It's not like any prayer I've ever heard."

"*A paralysed daughter, I could have dealt with!*"

"I'm going to have to ask you again. Step -"

"Our daughter is dead." The act of saying the words was a release. Having admitted it, Elaine's eyes pooled. "He has things that he needs to say."

"I'm afraid he'll have to say them elsewhere."

"He can't." Elaine was amazed by her own calm. "This is where it all started."

The shouting continued. Like a boxer hitting a punchbag, Graham punctuated each sentence with blows and kicks. Elaine found a strange poetry in it, something that wouldn't have seemed out of place at The Wholly Communion. Perhaps nothing happens by chance, she thought. We walk through life picking up armour, not knowing when it will come in useful.

"He's going to do himself an injury."

Standing squaw-like in her blanket, while her husband, usually so controlled, let his Maker know the depth of his fury,

Elaine couldn't help pitying the younger of the two security guards, who couldn't possibly understand pain of this nature. "He can't do anything that will make him feel worse than he already does. Who knows? It might even help."

The men glanced at one another, each apparently expecting his partner to make a decision.

"We'll pay for the damage," Elaine said, her face a mask. It would be a good use of the cheques, one she refused to feel guilty about.

Dr Singh arrived behind the security guards. He looked past her, through the glass panel of the chapel door and then nodded at her. His eyes communicated to Elaine that he had seen grief take many forms: theirs were two of them. "I say we let this run its course. He'll burn himself out before long. I'll take full responsibility."

"Thank you, Doctor," Elaine said.

The doctor took his place beside her, his hands clasped behind his back, respecting her dignity with his silence.

CHAPTER FORTY-FIVE

In the weeks and months that followed, Paula came every day, a friend disguised in the clothes of a cleaning lady. Uninvited but never turned away, she moved silently through the house; being of use; doing the things that needed to be done; cooking meals that went untouched and were scraped into the depths of the pedal bin; all without criticism or complaint.

The letters arrived in greater numbers than ever. Paula read as many she could because no one else had the energy, and she understood that they must be read. Most, she had to admit, she placed in the bucket on the brick pillar at the end of the path. The letters of condolence, she bundled together with elastic bands for a time when Elaine and Graham were ready. Some, addressed only to Elaine, troubled Paula. One from a man called Edwin, saying he was glad that he had spared her pain when he had been able to, sorry that she had not been spared this. One from a man called David who wrote that she wouldn't be familiar with his name, but hoped she would remember him. She wasn't sure what to do with them, so she put them to one side, safely out of the way. Then, there were those who wrote that Judy was a saint. Frankly, that was diffi-cult to believe of a girl who wore Garfield slippers and didn't know how to put the washing machine on. But they were saying the same thing about that foul-mouthed Irishman who was always in need of a shave, and met with world leaders wearing jeans and slippers. Saint Bob, they called him - and that was *after* he used the F-word on telly.

Father Patrick came every week to visit Graham, armed with words of conviction that God had taken Judy because of His great love for her. The priest blessed Graham, who sat mutely, bent forwards from the waist, elbows resting on his knees, palms flattened together and pointing downwards at an angle. He administered the Eucharist. He sat in silence, telling himself that silence between two men was companionable; that it was enough just to be there. But Father Patrick had the impression that Graham didn't move far between his visits. The man had turned inwards, and he wasn't sure if it was God or his own demons he found. Father Patrick punctuated the silence by suggesting, "Maybe you should think about going back to work. You never know, you might find it a comfort."

When Graham responded with a pitying nod, Father Patrick observed that Graham was beginning to look like a man you wouldn't want in your employ.

In exasperation, he ventured into the kitchen to consult the cleaning woman who occasionally brought a tea tray into the living room. "Do you know what's going on?"

"It's not my job to ask," she said, although he noted she was more than capable of secretarial duties. How they could afford a woman like that he didn't know.

He encountered Mrs Jones in the hall, like an apparition.

"How goes the spiritual guidance?" she asked.

"Your husband needs more than spiritual guidance. Has he seen a doctor?"

"Graham isn't ill."

"There are things that can be done for depression."

"Graham's not depressed: he's sad," she said. "It's natural to feel this way when you lose a child."

"But, Mrs Jones, there are new drugs. If he could feel better …"

"I know you mean well, but no thank you!" She herded him towards the front door. "We don't need that sort of help here."

"Elaine, don't shut me out," Father Patrick appealed, the fact that the door was about to be closed in his face the least of his concerns. "Graham needs the comfort of his faith at a time like this."

"You think it's a comfort that the God he believes in would do this? I'd prefer he lost his faith!"

The priest walked away knowing that Graham would need it now more than ever. Because, without faith, none of his suffering would be worthwhile.

The crowds still came, loitering on the grass verge outside the house. Elaine no longer felt threatened because they were there for Judy, and some of them looked as lost as she felt. In their own way, the reporters - Edwin sometimes standing among them - were helping to keep her daughter's memory alive. Occasionally, she turned to face his camera when she opened the door to Charlie, who silently hauled the sack containing the day's post over the threshold, seeming unsure where to look. Her house a refuge, Elaine was no longer its prisoner. The crowds were her sentry guards keeping the world at bay.

Some of the For Sale signs came down in sympathy, but the sign next door changed to Sold.

Answering a ring at the front door - only because she had been passing - Elaine found Tommy turning to face her, shocked, as if caught in the act of escape.

"Mrs J!" he said, without flicking back his hair (an excuse, she presumed, to avoid eye contact).

It pained her to see him standing there, only a year older than Judy and very much alive. But Tommy had made the effort when people she'd thought of as friends stayed away, and Elaine knew she had to find it in herself to do the same. "Tommy, how are you?"

"I came to say goodbye." He shuffled his feet. "We're off first thing tomorrow."

"So soon!" She eyed the Sold sign as if it, too, was capable of betrayal. "Are your parents planning to come by?"

"They're still busy packing." Tommy looked down at his left trainer where the rubber was peeling away around one of the toes. He stood on it with the sole of his other shoe, letting it snap back into place.

"Then I'll drop round later."

Tommy winced, "They'll probably be at it all night," and Elaine saw how it was. The Webbers - her neighbours of eighteen years - were planning to drive off behind the removal van without so much as a backward glance.

"Perhaps you could say goodbye from me." She looked at Tommy - it would be for the last time - preparing to say something to the effect that, of all the children in the road, he had been her favourite. Shaking her head Elaine said, "Let's do this properly. Meet me round the back?"

Standing in the garden, arms wrapped around herself, Elaine saw the black sphere fly over the fence, causing a momentary eclipse, so it felt as if it might be the moon she was reaching for when she crossed the lawn and bent down. The ball felt cool to the touch, the softness of the leather moulding her hands into a natural curve. Elaine recognised it immediately: Tommy's first leather football, the one that completed the evolution. He had been so proud of it, counting out loud as he practised keepy-uppies for hours at a time. She held it against her stomach like the swell of a pregnant belly.

She heard the scrape of the loose fence panel being pushed aside and Tommy's face appeared in the triangular gap. "Can

I have my ball back, Mrs J?"

"I'm busy," Elaine answered, straight-faced. "You'll have to come and get it."

Tommy performed an undignified head-first manoeuvre, compressing his shoulders inwards, spiralling onto his backside and then edging out.

As he struggled to his feet, brushing clods of earth from his jeans, Elaine asked, "Do you remember the day when…?"

Looking at Mrs J - towering over her - wanting to be accepted as an equal, Tommy realised he had never even used her first name. He would have liked to tell her - even if it was only jokingly - that she was the first woman he ever loved. Perhaps it would be enough if she understood that he remembered everything. That he wouldn't forget she'd been kind to him when he had most needed it. Aware that there was more behind each word than was being said, Tommy interrupted: "Of course I do."

"Yes," Mrs J said, smiling and looking down at her bare feet. She seemed surprised to find she was still holding the football, and held it out to him.

Tommy left his hands in the pockets of his jeans. "Keep it," he nodded.

Elaine now understood the real value of things. She knew that Tommy was entrusting the best of his childhood to her. He wanted to ensure that an important part of him stayed behind in the road where he had lived for the whole of his life. It wasn't only her who had to face a future she hadn't made plans for. If Tommy felt that change was being forced on him, he didn't complain. Elaine accepted: "Thank you. It's a wonderful gift." Still, she offered it to him. "Throw it. Wherever it lands, that's where it will live."

Tommy launched the ball into the air and headed it into the darkness at the bottom of the garden. The rustle suggested that she would discover it in some bush or other when she was weeding. "So," Elaine sighed. "What's next for you?"

He shrugged, toying with his hair. "Dunno."

"It's best like that." Elaine put her hand to the place where her voice was catching. "Take each day as it comes."

Sister Euphemia came to the front door once, compelled to bring the strange gift of Judy's form register from the year she had joined the convent. It listed her name, etched in Tippex, with those of her classmates, Miranda Potipher's standing out proudly among them. The headmistress didn't know exactly what her gift meant, but she had an idea it might hold significance for a mother, intent on collating evidence of her daughter's too-short passage. The headmistress wasn't allowed to own things, but she couldn't deny their attraction. You didn't stop longing for colour when you accepted a uniform of grey. Her index finger a pen, Mrs Jones had caressed each contour of her daughter's name.

"It seems funny to see 'Judith Jones'. She was always my Judy."

"Like the Beatles' song? No, sorry! That's Jude isn't it?"

"Yes!" Mrs Jones touched her hand. "Like the song!"

Sister Euphemia hoped this response meant that Judy's mother realised she was not a robot.

The headmistress came at other times too, leaving evidence that she was thinking of the family, clippings from the holly bush in the grounds of the convent. She left them in the plastic bucket on the gatepost, where other people seemed to deposit offerings. Always, she was surprised at the sight of the silent vigil outside the house, day or night. The candles that were left burning on the bare brick of the garden wall, held in place with pools of molten wax, their sides plastered with white volcanic eruptions and frozen waterfalls.

Miranda came, but got no further than the gate. She stood, staring across the unbreachable chasm of black and white tiles towards the front door. Wondering whether she would be welcome and, if so, what she could possibly say. She took the sprigs of holly from the bucket placed on top of the gatepost. She hung a set of black rosary beads around her neck, pushing the cross down under her hooded sweatshirt. It was an exchange: the Joneses had buried Judy wearing her headphones, forgetting that they had been borrowed. Miranda didn't mind. It was good that something of hers had gone into the ground with Judy. If nothing else, they would always have that connection.

Once, Sister Euphemia and Miranda met by the gatepost. They stood shoulder to shoulder. Instead of placing her sprig of holly in the bucket, Sister Euphemia handed it directly to Miranda, who sought out a place between the spikes of the leaves.

"Not exactly an olive branch, is it?"

"No." The Sister smiled. "Not exactly." The triangle of lines between her eyebrows twitched as she tried - and failed - to think of something meaningful to say. "How were your O-Level results?"

"Alright, I guess."

She risked another sideways glance. Miranda wore a beret angled over her auburn hair, which had been cut into a jaw-length bob. Her earrings, if they remained, were hidden. Her glassy green eyes, no longer outlined clumsily, shone with intelligence. She looked younger if anything, softer. But only a fool would have mistaken Miranda for someone who was hard. Used, sometimes. Loyal, brave, true: always. "Happy with your grades?" she asked.

Miranda nodded, clearly irritated at the presumption that Sister Euphemia knew she had passed, and passed well.

"I expect you want to say, 'No thanks to you.' And I wouldn't blame you. But with a mind like yours, you can be anything you want to be."

The girl turned on her: "You see, I just don't get that! How is it any help when I have no idea *what* I want?"

The headmistress laughed, the sound surprising her as much as it appeared to surprise Miranda. Outside the school gates, Sister Euphemia was more inclined to admit she didn't know everything. "You have an extraordinary gift, Miranda. Your honesty gives other people permission to be honest in return. And, before you ask, the answer's 'No'. In my experience very few people say what they think. So I take it back. You've reminded me what it was like to be your age, and, whilst I see your enormous potential, I won't insult you by saying that everything will turn out fine. Not when we're standing outside Judy's house. But I will say this: even when you think you know where you're destined, there's an inclination to fight it."

Miranda, whose expression had moved from annoyance to something nearing shock, restricted herself to a mere question. "Did you always know you'd become a nun?"

"Part of me did. I ignored it for as long as possible."

"But then, you've never had to worry about whether you'd ever get a job... be able to afford a house. Or if you'd ever... I dunno... meet someone."

Sister Euphemia dropped her head to expel another involuntary sound. "That was part of the trouble. I had a fiancée, you know. He was rather insulted to learn I would rather enter a convent than marry him."

"That's got to dent your ego."

"I think he would have preferred to hear there was someone else." Sister Euphemia paused before confessing. "I didn't want to be a teacher either."

"So why did you?"

"You've heard about the Lord finding work for idle hands?" Sister Euphemia hesitated. "Actually, it was my Mother

Superior. She said I couldn't use the convent as somewhere to hide from the world."

"Is that what you were doing?"

"I didn't think so." Sister Euphemia shivered. "But it's a frightening place out here, isn't it?"

They were silent for a while, the headmistress realising in the act of breathing that perhaps it wasn't the world she had been frightened of: it was herself. Of her potential to be... someone. And of sex in particular. Of this cavernous yearning she'd felt. Still felt sometimes, in the rare moments she allowed herself to be still. Associating it with the temptation she'd been taught to fear, she remembered wanting to remove herself from the source of the yearning. She had undergone a second metamorphosis - a reversal - and emerged as someone plain and unattractive. And still it was not enough. As ash dropped from Miranda's cupped palm, Sister Euphemia encountered an idea as if she'd been hit by a car. There could have been another way: *motherhood*. Imagine this girl - this intelligent and remarkable creature - was your daughter. That would be something you could be truly proud of. Something seemed to be trying to escape from her throat, physically shaking her. How could she begin to say that she was sorry for something she'd been the architect of? Wanting to hear the girl's voice again, Sister Euphemia inclined her head towards Miranda's hand. "How do you manage the smoking when you're at home all of the time?"

"It's hardly *all* the time. I get let out for good behaviour occasionally."

The headmistress breathed. "I've never tried a cigarette. Not even once."

"Want to?" Miranda flicked the carton open and offered it to her.

It was hardly the forbidden fruit. Still, she was nervous. "Will you light one for me?"

Miranda held the ends of the two cigarettes together and sucked air in, then she offered the end that had been in her mouth to the Sister, who took it in her shaking hand, put it between her lips and inhaled. The smoke remained in the cavern of her mouth where she felt she could keep it under control, but releasing it brought calm. She inhaled again and blew smoke out at an upwards angle through a small hole at the side of her mouth. "When Judy came to the convent I thought she needed taking down a few notches: our Miracle Girl."

Miranda felt awkward to be hearing this confession. She wasn't used to how honesty sounded when it took on another voice.

"You were there that evening. What did you think?" Sister Euphemia asked.

Avoiding the need for a direct answer, she contemplated her Dr Martins. "I let Judy down. I didn't realise she was so ill."

"Nobody could have known that."

"She tried to explain it to me. But I was distracted. It was just before… you know."

The Sister filled the gap. "The whole disciplinary thing?"

Miranda recognised the expression was an attempt at self-deprecation rather than a dig. "I thought she was making it up. But now I think it was real - at least, it was to her. She said she'd prove it to me and then she looked right at me, you know?" Miranda turned her eyes away, blinking. "Judy picked me out of the crowd without even knowing she was doing it."

Beside her Sister Euphemia nodded, then her hand appeared to take on a life of its own as it jerked her wristwatch into view. "It's late. I should go." She paused. "It was good to see you, Miranda. I mean that."

Miranda was surprised to see that Die Gut Schwester was not making a throwaway remark. "Don't tell me you miss me?

I was a complete pain in the arse as a student." She laughed. "And now I've said 'arse' to a nun!"

"Twice. But, seriously, I'd rather you than all of those yes-men. You knew how to keep me on my toes." Sister Euphemia stood with her hands clasped in front of her. "Well."

She had taken Miranda by surprise and now this was all she had to say: "Well?"

The headmistress sighed. "I suppose you deserve more of an explanation but I don't have one. Except that it's my job. It's what I have to do. Underneath, I'm almost human." She paused. "I like your hair, by the way. Black never suited you. When you dress in grey every day of the week, you appreciate a little colour."

Miranda watched Sister Euphemia walk away, wondering whether to run after her and say that she was going her way. The mention of her hair had been a cheap parting-shot. Miranda's ginger was still a source of embarrassment. She had come *this* close to liking the woman before she was reminded that the whole human act was smoke and mirrors. What with the mention of a boyfriend and everything, Miranda had forgotten to ask Die Gut Schwester if she believed in Judy's visions. Perhaps the answer was there in her hand.

Miranda put the sprig of holly in the plastic bucket and let it find its own level after it conducted a slow circle of the rim, obeying the law of gravity.

At night Graham and Elaine turned to each other, sometimes violently, sometimes tenderly, with only the comfort of the other in mind. Without words, they navigated altered land-scapes and sensed the other's need for urgency or for stillness. Graham, who had never found it easy to say that he loved his wife, distilled the words into the touch of his lips. The hand he placed on the side of his wife's face said *Forgive me* and, when he moved it to cup the crown of her head, *I only ever wanted to protect her.* When they lay on their backs staring at the ceiling and he angled his head so that it touched hers, reaching across his chest with his far hand to curve its four fingers round her shoulder, he was asking *Do you miss her as much as I do?*

Elaine thought her husband's fingers resting on the skin of her shoulder looked almost child-like, and was moved in the same way that the ruined statue at Luxor - the small pair of feet resting on the larger pair - had moved her, although she couldn't say why it affected her so.

There was little sleep for either of them, but there was surrender at the end of each day, and there was darkness.

It was in the darkness that Graham sensed that the sex itself frightened Elaine. He understood now that it had become an addiction. That it was exactly as she had said: the men were unimportant. She had thought she was taking control over her life - because Elaine was someone who needed to be in control - but sex had taken control of her. Graham realised that it was this fear rather than him she had been pushing away. In moments of passion, Elaine sometimes became a stranger - even to herself - and it took her a while to retrace her steps.

It was in the darkness that Elaine discovered Graham sometimes just wanted closeness, but hadn't known how to ask for it, and she allowed herself to mother him, pulling his head to her breast.

In the contrast of daylight they would pass on the staircase, politely moving aside, almost surprised to find another person in the house. They sat opposite each other at the breakfast room table, the teapot between them, the newspaper untouched. Never at the dining room table, because that would have been too painful. There, confronted by two empty placemats, Elaine would have torn herself apart, wondering why she had allowed herself to be obsessed with what might have been when her daughter had been sitting there beside her, present and wonderful and real.

Once - just after the funeral - Elaine attended Mass at St Joseph's. Hoping for answers, she was completely bewildered by what she saw and heard. Only one phrase made an impression on her: *Do this in memory of me.* Later, washing up, she was wondering what it was she should do in memory of Judy when she saw rainbows in the soapsuds. Remembering her stubborn insistence that Judy rinsed them away, Elaine stacked the foam-coated plates in the rack, rainbows clinging, intact.

Graham staked claim to the living room, sitting for hours on end with the blank television screen in front of him. Elaine imagined that, if she turned it on in an attempt to give him the appearance of activity, he would jump up and say, "I was watching that." In fact, his mind was active, perhaps more so than it had ever been. Rummaging through the photograph albums of his mind. Fixing all of those pictures in place with photo corners. Labelling each one with a place and a date: pushing his daughter on the baby swings, her nappy-padded bottom crammed tightly into the space; the caravanning holiday on the Norfolk coast when he had dipped Judy's toes in the sea and she had shrieked at the cold, Elaine rushing to confiscate her.

The time when Judy found what she thought was the biggest shell ever. She was so surprised it turned out to be a tortoise that she fell over backwards with it still in her hands, and it had peed all over her, the colour of milk.

Getting dressed all on her own, insisting on putting both legs into the same trouser leg, then hopping around the room: "Look at me! I'm all boingy, like Tigger."

Boingy. It was an excellent word.

Saturday morning outings with his pint-sized daughter when they had done nothing more (or less) exciting than ride upstairs on a double decker. Distracted by his omnipotent view from the front window, Graham would find the seat beside him vacant, Judy having attached herself to someone more responsive.

"We're going to my aunty's house later, only she's not my real aunty. Do you think it's lying if you call someone something they're not? Oh look, an airyplane! What do you think keeps it up in the sky?"

"Judy!" Graham would zigzag up the aisle to retrieve her, bouncing off pillars and passengers' shoulders with repeated apologies. "You shouldn't be bothering this nice lady."

"Oh, she's not bothering me." He would be beamed up at, too-perfect dentures bared, the face that surrounded them appearing in danger of decay. "We've been having a lovely chat."

Judy would embarrass him as she hesitated at the top of the staircase, saying loudly, "Sorry I wasn't allowed to talk to you. I thought you were really nice."

Elaine often found herself in her daughter's bedroom, sitting at the foot of the single bed. It was difficult at first, the memory of the final day so raw, so violent. Even the act of wiping away the bloody handprint, picking glass shards from the carpet pile, restoring order to the dressing table, had seemed like a betrayal of Judy's final act: her death. She was compensated by the discovery of secrets. The book Judy had been halfway through when she died: *One Flew Over the Cuckoo's Nest*, the story of one man's struggle against madness. Had Judy thought herself similarly afflicted? The last single that she'd played, still on the turntable: *Here Comes the Rain Again* by the Eurythmics, painful in its stringed beauty. The last album she had listened to on her Walkman: *A Day at the Races* by Queen, which seemed a strange departure from her usual taste. Things that reminded Elaine that her daughter had been ordinary, even though extraordinary things had happened to her. She asked herself if Judy had known time was running out, but why, then, would she have hoarded Waterman ink cartridges in a shoebox? Why would she have stuck used chewing gum on the wooden slats underneath her bed, knowing that Elaine would eventually find it?

She discovered a photograph of the three of them together outside Hampton Court Palace in the hidden drawer of Judy's bedside table. There were surprisingly few photographs of them as a family because Graham was usually behind the viewfinder. Elaine had once asked Judy if she knew where the photograph was and had received an, "I don't know which one you're talking about." Finding a spare frame, Elaine placed it carefully on her daughter's bedside table next to the brick, the sight of which she'd once found so distressing. For every time that Elaine had felt redundant as a mother, she now imagined her daughter looking at the photograph last thing at night and then closing the drawer. "It's OK," Elaine said out loud, "I would have let you keep it."

One day, Graham walked into his daughter's room to find his wife dancing, her back to him, records strewn across the floor, escaping from their paper sleeves. It was a strange trance-like dance. Elaine moved her lower body very little, but wove her hands in symmetrical shapes above her head. When her head swung in his direction, Graham saw that her eyes were closed, but she must have sensed his presence. As she opened them he backed away pulling the door behind him.

"Come in," Elaine beckoned, "Come in." She went to him and, facing him, held his hands. Moving them into an upright position, she placed the flats of her palms against his. Their bodies not quite touching, Elaine circled her arms like a swimmer, leaving him to do the back crawl. The music was urgent but ethereal, the man's voice strangled. It wasn't a good voice, technically speaking - although it was clearly in tune. Graham took his hands away and let them drop.

"It's OK," Elaine said. "I'll go." Then she hesitated. "Or we could just lie down here together."

Graham sat on the edge of his daughter's bed, kicked off his shoes and lay on his side with his knees bent.

He heard Elaine draw the curtains and put the record back to the beginning before the mattress dipped, and she slotted herself behind him. An arm circling his waist, he felt the touch of her fingers grazing his hand before they settled and closed.

Graham shuddered as he heard a drum beat like the rattle of the 17.50.

He heard instruments he couldn't identify.

A voice, choked like his, told him to remember things from his past that he had forgotten, and things that sounded so true they might have actually happened, and things that had yet to happen. It was as if time no longer operated in a straight line, and that he was at the centre of a spiral. It was something that Graham had sensed for some time but had been unable to articulate, and so he had simply stopped speaking.

He heard the longing, and it was his longing.

He heard regret, and it was his regret.

He was disturbed to be reminded of Judy's prophecy: of trees falling down.

"What's the song called?"

Graham felt his wife's body tense. "It's *Just One Kiss* by The Cure."

"*Just One Kiss.*" He repeated.

"By The Cure." Elaine pressed her lips to the skin behind his ear, and he felt as if their touch might be life-giving. "Please say something else. I've missed talking to you, Graham. I've missed hearing your voice. Tell me one of your stories."

"What stories?"

"Your stories! You had three."

"I don't remember."

"You used to tell them to everyone we met."

"Please tell me they were interesting!"

She pressed her forehead to his back, as if she were hiding. "Put it this way, people never came to dinner more than twice."

He couldn't think of anything to say, except: "The music: I think I like it."

"Does it remind you of Judy?"

Graham was surprised to hear their daughter's name sounding peaceful once more. He had heard it used in anger, in frustration and, most recently, repeated in Elaine's plaintiff cries.

"No. It reminds me of me. Can you put it back to the beginning again when it finishes?"

Graham didn't speak again for several days, but he lay listening to more of Judy's records to see if he could find anything else about himself that he had forgotten. Or had yet to discover. And he realised that he still had much to learn.

CHAPTER FORTY-SIX

When Elaine discovered that her daughter had turned her eyes to the sky the year before she suddenly stopped breathing, she, too, turned her focus upwards. Not because she was looking for evidence of a prophecy coming true. But because, somewhere in the midst of people chasing progress in the name of science, was her daughter.

Judy had followed the maiden voyage of the Space Shuttle *Discovery*. Rather than noting down the facts and figures that would have interested Graham, she had recorded the human quota. The original mission that had been planned for 25 June 1984 was aborted after a series of technical hitches. Judy had put her confident curved tick in the margin of the exercise book as if to confirm that this decision had averted disaster. Elaine was quite sure that her daughter hadn't possessed special powers. Forever losing things, Judy had acquired five hairbrushes. It was only the act of buying a new one that caused the others to reveal themselves - usually when Graham sat on one, yelling, "How many of these things can one girl need?" Elaine read how on 30 August 1984, after a stomach-churning last-minute delay when a private aircraft flew too close to the launch pad, *Discovery* made its ascent with a six-person crew: Henry W. Hartsfield Jr., Michael L. Coats, another Judith (this one with the surname Resnik), Richard M. Mullane, Steven

A. Hawley and Charles D. Walker. Who were these people with initials in the place of middle names, that they would risk everything to carry a cargo of three communication satellites? Two people per satellite: since when were satellites more important than people?

There followed a series of firsts. On 5 October 1984, a man called Marc Garneau becomes the first Canadian in space, aboard the shuttle *Challenger*. And on 11 October 1984, Kathryn D. Sullivan became the first woman to perform a space walk. These things had passed Elaine by, but she remembered - so clearly - her daughter's first steps after three months of standing, unwilling to let go of the furniture.

"She's just finding her balance." Graham had laughed at her impatience.

Judy's look of shock turned to pleasure as she moved under her own steam, zombie arms stuck out fast in front of her, equalled only by her determination to walk again after her accident. The papers had been right in calling her daughter The Miracle Girl. Every child is a miracle.

The last entry that Judy had made was on 4 December 1984. Hezbollah terrorists - claiming to be acting on behalf of God - hijacked a Kuwait Airlines plane, murdering four passengers. Judy's writing was spiked with anger. She had underlined the word, 'claiming'. There were no names, no initials: just the number four. Like Judy's life, the entry looked as if it had been interrupted.

After that, Elaine kept watch on her daughter's behalf.

On 15 June 1985 Elaine read how, the day before, TWA Flight 847 had been hijacked by Hezbollah. They beat a passenger called Robert Stethem until he was barely recognisable, then they killed him, dumping his body on the tarmac. Elaine waited for announcements on the news. It was two weeks before she was confident the others held ransom wouldn't suffer the same fate.

On 24 June 1985 Elaine and Graham watched *The Six O'clock News* together, holding hands as they learned that a Boeing 747 had exploded over the Atlantic Ocean just south of Ireland.

"With no evidence of survivors, all 329 people on board are feared dead."

It was those who survived the explosion only to drown that Elaine's heart went out to. She had some idea of what it felt like to think you were saved, only to find it was a brief respite. Elaine spent an evening on the phone to her sister, Liz, trying to convince her to cancel her holiday to Florida.

"Statistically speaking," Liz had argued, "Nick says now's the safest time to fly. And Boeings are the most reliable planes in the air."

"You're right," Elaine said, worried about the power of her own thoughts. "Go back to your packing. You must think I'm an idiot."

"No!" Liz insisted. "After everything... well, it's not surprising, is it? Besides, we've saved up for over a year. I'm going on this holiday if it kills me." There was a pause, before she added, "Oh, look, I'm sorry..."

"No, it's fine. Really." This is what it had come down to: constant fear of treading on toes.

But as the story unravelled and it became apparent that the explosion was caused by a bomb, Elaine couldn't relax until she knew that Liz was safely home. Her sister didn't think to call: Elaine heard it from her parents.

On 2 August, it happened again. A plane travelling from Florida (Elaine's breath had caught in her throat) to Los Angeles crashed while coming in to land, killing 135 people. The miracle was that there were any survivors at all. It was declared an Act of God - as opposed to one carried out on his behalf. The plane flew into a thunderstorm and was caught up in something the reporter called a microburst. Whatever that was, the speed of the plane increased as it came in to land, and then, as the captain tried to slow the craft down, it suffered a sudden loss of power. His voice was recorded saying, "Hang on to the son of a bitch!" as he struggled to regain control. Elaine thought of Graham's attempts to breathe and pummel life back into their daughter, as she stood by and said, *Now and at the hour of our death, Amen,* not knowing - how could she? - that Judy's hour had arrived. Delta Flight 191 struck the ground north of the runway, bouncing back into the air. It came down again on State Highway 114, striking a Toyota Celica (Why the obsession with the vehicle? What did it matter?) and killing William Hodge Mayberry. He could have been going a few miles faster per hour, or a few miles slower, and he would have been fine. If only Elaine hadn't sent Judy out for stamps. If only Judy hadn't stopped to make a phone call. Debbie had told Elaine at the funeral that they had been speaking when the wall collapsed. "About what?" Elaine had asked. "Nothing much," came the reply. A stupid, unnecessary phone call! They had tried to keep the ceremony private, but Judy had become public property. Elaine had wandered among the lingering crowds, dumbfounded by their numbers, saying, "Thank you for coming," and trying to mean it; looking for a boy with a gashed head, a boy in school uniform, a boy in a foil blanket, a boy shaking and pointing, the ends of his fingers stained yellow. But it was a tall young man in uniform who sought her out.

"Edwin," she said. "You came. And you're an ambulance man, now?"

"Only a driver. I was never going to make it as a journalist. Too soft by far." Elaine had been going to say *thank you, thank you so much.* But he continued, "And I've become a Christian."

"If a Christian is someone who puts others first, I think you already were. Excuse me if I don't stay and…"

When the plane struck a lamp post, the fuel tank ignited.

Skidding into the airfield, it exploded. There were survivors in the back of the plane - the smoking section - which broke free.

"Poor devils," Paula said as she stubbed out a cigarette of her own. (Elaine tolerated Paula's habit, a small price to pay for friendship that seemed to know no bounds.)

And the planes kept on falling out of the sky.

Those fragile things, they kept on falling.

If you were planning to wreak vengeance on an ungrateful world, planes were an obvious target. The results spectacular: you were guaranteed prime time coverage.

Graham broke his silence to ask, "Do you think we should talk to the press?"

"The press?"

"To tell people what Judy said about this being our last chance?"

"I think we need to let Judy rest in peace. Let her rest, Graham."

On 12 August 1985, Japan Airlines Flight 123 (another Boeing 747) crashed into Mount Ogura killing 520 passengers, the world's worst air disaster. Elaine wept, wondering if she'd been wrong. If there was any chance - however slim - that they could have prevented this, shouldn't they have taken it? Before take-off, the plane had been refuelled, the captain changed. Eleven minutes into the flight, Tokyo received a distress call. Permission to return to the airport was granted, but the Boeing couldn't be made to turn. It had lost a large section of its tailpiece. The cause: an inadequate repair some years earlier. If at all possible this, somehow, made it worse. Rather than a direct Act of God, or people claiming to be his instruments, it was a failure of man. The survival of four people was hailed a miracle. Elaine knew about the dangers of this firsthand: being labelled a miracle is too much to live up to.

By December 1986, the apparent folly - this arrogance of man - in trying to make further inroads into the heavens meant that Elaine failed to appreciate the accomplishment of Richard Rutan and Jeana Yeager, who circled the globe in an experimental plane without refuelling. Tommy's balsa wood planes had sailed over her garden fence, nose-diving into her rosebushes. Once, a small rubber figure had waited three days for rescue, suspended from his plastic parachute by string caught up on a thorn. Tommy had talked about being "behind enemy lines." Elaine had never really understood which side of the fence Tommy's enemies lived on, although she sensed undercurrents in the Webber household. You live next door to another family long enough, it's polite to pretend you don't overhear their muffled (and not so muffled) arguments.

In early 1987, Judy's light - the promised sign - came in the form of a supernova, something Elaine had previously thought of as being dreamt up by scriptwriters for *Star Trek*. A man called Shelton saw a supernova in a large Magellanic Cloud, the first that had been visible to the naked eye for 383 years. It turned out to be a nearby galaxy, all of which had improbable-sounding names, as if from the imagination of Douglas Adams: The Sagittarius Dwarf; The Canis Major Dwarf Galaxy. This brought Graham out of his armchair temporarily, as he stood silently, expectantly, in the back garden gazing at the speckled indigo sky.

The grass felt damp as it flattened under Elaine's bare feet when she ventured outside to take him a mug of hot chocolate, wearing only a thin nightdress and her new 'granny' cardigan. "Anything, or is there too much cloud?"

He shook his head.

She strained her neck looking upwards, wondering if there was a star up there, a new star, brighter than all the rest, but saw only the red blinking of an aeroplane. She shivered, the looking and not finding more than she could bear.

"Well, if you don't think the world's about to end, I'm going to bed." She stood on tiptoe to kiss her husband's cheek, then loitered, holding onto Graham's elbow. "What do you think it would look like if this really was it? Would there be a huge firework display: rockets and Catherine Wheels and starbursts?"

So many answers she'd been given since Judy died were complete nonsense that she preferred it when Graham simply pulled her to his chest and kissed her forehead.

Father Patrick did not seem to be inspired by the activities in the night sky when Elaine explained why her husband hadn't got out of bed the next day for the priest's eleven o'clock visit. "Graham stood outside until gone four. He thinks it was the sign Judy talked about."

"I didn't think you believed in signs," he replied.

"No." She presented him with a mug of coffee. "That's your line of business, Father."

"I've enough trouble as it is."

Elaine sat and listened, sympathetic but disinterested, as Father Patrick told her about several members of his parish whose anger was directed at him personally after the Pope's condemnation of artificial insemination. They had seen developments in fertility treatments as a cause for hope, and didn't see how it conflicted with their beliefs.

"But if I - their parish priest - can't sanction it, they will have to reconsider matters. Reconsider matters! I suppose I should be flattered they think I've that much sway in the Vatican."

CHAPTER FORTY-SEVEN

"Earlier today, apparently, a woman rang the BBC and said there was a hurricane on the way. Well, if you're watching: don't worry, there isn't."

Graham and Elaine were in bed, Graham behind his wife, one arm resting comfortably in the dip of her waist. When the bed began to shake, Graham thought she was kicking - as she sometimes did - on the edge of sleep. He hoped she wouldn't kick herself awake.

"Graham?" She rocked back against him, nudging him in the ribs. "Stop those earthquake impressions, will you?"

As he rolled onto his back Elaine turned with him, installing herself in the warm niche under his arm. "The bed's still moving." They lay quietly vibrating, listening to the roof tiles lift and settle, lift and settle; fearful that, with the next gust, the tiles wouldn't settle.

Graham squinted at the luminous hands of the alarm clock. It was three thirty. He swung his legs over the edge of the bed and reached for the lamp, pushing the switch one way and then the other. He tried again. "Power's out."

As he moved towards the bedroom door, he heard the rustle of sheets and Elaine's urgent voice: "Where are you going?"

He pointed towards the bathroom, stifling a yawn. His

feet shuffled on the lino. As Graham pissed, he listened to the fierceness of the gale. Trundling metallic sounds, what he thought must be dustbins rolling about. The side gate next door: bang-bang-bang.

"It sounds so angry," his wife called out. "Is it any wonder the Greeks named their gods after the four winds?"

He flushed and washed his hands.

"It's just as well we're not on the east coast. Michael Fish said they'd have it worst." As he approached, Elaine lifted the covers to make way for him. Graham climbed back into bed, his skin several degrees cooler. "Poor old Norfolk -"

They both froze at the sound of a terrifying splintering followed by more crashing. There was no need to look out of the back window to know that the apple tree had fallen on the greenhouse.

Trees! Thousands of them!

Elaine gathered the duvet around her. "That's it. I'm going to sleep on the sofa."

When Graham didn't follow quickly enough for her liking, she retraced her steps and beckoned impatiently, "Coming?" then left her arm outstretched until he positioned himself inside its curve.

Downstairs, Graham opened the back door. The resistance of the handle in his hand told of the force of the storm. If he let go, he felt he might be lifted clean off his feet. But there was warmth in the air that brushed his face, and when he licked his lips they tasted of salt. The closest Graham had come to setting foot outside for some time - he couldn't remember how long it was exactly - and every cell of his being felt energised. The wind had travelled a long way to get to them, and it would blow all the way to the Midlands before the night was through. The streetlights out, the sky was as dark as night skies Graham could remember as a boy, and there were stars dotted among the clouds. Only his neighbour's security light above the garage remained, powered, no doubt, by the emergency generator he had often boasted about. His attention was drawn to movement just above ground level. Plastic pots raced the length and breadth of the garden, and glass shards and timber window frames danced. In the periphery of his vision a loose fence panel flapped one final time then broke free. Graham wasn't afraid of the chaos - the awesome energy - although the world was noisier than he remembered before his retreat. There were police sirens and car alarms, a chorus of dogs barking in unison. Graham felt that Judy was very close by.

Behind him, Elaine was tugging at his elbow, cutting swathes through the darkness with the beam from a torch; pulling the door shut and locking it. "Come away from there, Graham. I want you to help me move the sofa away from the window in case the glass goes."

Graham turned towards her, his face glowing. He wondered that she lacked his curiosity. Circling the walls of the room, the torchlight crossed his face and then returned to it. His eyes protested.

"What are you smiling at?" she demanded.

Graham tapped his chest near his heart three times. And he saw the glint of Elaine's eyes as she said with mock-impatience, "I love you, too. Now get a move on!"

Already, by this time, Shanklin Pier had been reduced to driftwood. Already the side wall of a Dorset block of flats had collapsed, opening the building up like a dolls' house. Already a roof had been torn clean off an old people's home, leaving residents gaping at the planetarium above them - a curiously unscheduled entertainment - until someone came clapping their hands to break the spell, telling them it was time to get up.

On the Hampshire coast (where hurricanes hardly ever happen), a cargo ship stuck fast, driven onto the sand. Small boats ripped from their moorings were dropped onto pebbled beaches. A Cypriot bulk carrier sank somewhere just off the coast at Dover. The Home Office detention ship, *The Earl William*, carrying a cargo of terrified Tamil refugees, ran aground at Harwich.

A stone minaret came crashing through the roof of Brighton's Royal Pavilion, damaging a priceless carpet. In the town of Hastings, a chimney stack collapsed inwards, pulling three storeys of a hotel after it. An elderly couple plunged through two floors: the man died; his wife's fall was cushioned by a mattress. One guest was left staring into the abyss through a splintered hole in the floorboards, suspended from a door handle that he prayed would hold. Fifty people lost their homes when a caravan park near Folkestone was wrecked. Lorries were tossed about like matchbox toys.

None of these things should have happened in the south of England, where the weather was predictably dreary and damp, and sometimes there was a little fog. Where betting shops offering odds for a dry Wimbledon fortnight rarely had to pay out. Unsettled weather is what the nation dressed for, no pin-striped city businessman complete without his black umbrella, no child without a pair of red wellingtons. Leave the storms to the Highlands, the tornadoes to the Americas. They have a whole season dedicated to them, Hurricane Floyd just one in a long line.

It takes coincidences to create conditions in England capable of laying waste to over fifteen million trees. Warm air drifting eastwards (a father's love for his daughter makes him fearful), unnaturally warm air surrounds the Bay of Biscay (a mother says, "Take what you need from my purse"), a cold front moves from Iceland in the direction of Iberia (a girl swings her hips and enters a telephone box). It was a once in every two hundred years occurrence. The insurance giants would claim it was another Act of God. Graham Jones was one of those who believed they were right.

And still the wind blew furiously. Chartwell, former home of Sir Winston Churchill, had its trees pulverised, trunks reduced to matchsticks. At Kew, the botanical gardens lost its most magnificent specimens. The trees, too, were merciless. One crushed a fire engine - a moving target responding to an emergency in Dorset - killing two of the crew who had thought their helmets would protect them. The trees fell on buildings. On power lines. On telephone lines. They blocked roads, these mighty oaks, horse chestnuts, sycamores. Severed branches gouged trenches out of carefully tended lawns. Tree-lined roads became giant domino sets. Parks that had previously promised hours of tree-climbing and the shelter of boyish dens would disappoint for decades to come. As the strength went out of the storm, trees that had balanced at precarious angles simply lay down and died.

In Streatham, ignoring the preservation order, the Great Storm toyed unpityingly with the branches of the tallest plane tree in London. No one knew quite how old Streatham's tree was, but its arguments of 'I was here first' had pushed even its most ardent admirers to their limits.

When the wall was re-built, the semicircular section constructed to accommodate the trunk left room for growth, as you would when buying school uniform for a child. Apparently, still thinking of itself as a teenager, the tree had rebelled by entering a new growing phase.

Paula woke to the sound of snapping coming from directly underneath her. Instinct unsettled her. She had always been nervous about living in the shadow of something so large, ever since the insurance people had refused to cover the house for subsidence. The tree ate up daylight. The front garden refused to be the showpiece imagined when she'd dreamt of owning her first home. The garden gate needed re-painting twice a year and she noticed how the wood rotted. (Next time she would insist on metal.) After the wall came down on top of Judy Jones, Paula had been plagued by a single thought: it could have been us.

Beside her in bed, John was snoring. She grabbed his shoulders and shook life into him. "Wake up! It's about to go."

"What's about to go?" He appeared oblivious to the sound of the wind, but they both felt the darkness shift.

"Downstairs! Under the table!"

Paula's feet were rapid fire on the staircase. Bang, bang, bang, bang, bang! "*Now* you're ordering me about!"

"Don't argue, woman! It's what we did during the Blitz."

With barely the space for two adults, they crouched; their view, the kitchen cupboards. Waiting, waiting for the crash that didn't come. John insisted neither of them moved, even though Paula had cramp and felt her bladder might burst. Slowly, the anger went out of the wind. It stopped pelting their home with metal and wood. Paula located a button that she'd lost the previous week and pocketed it. Realising that there might be a tomorrow, she began to compile a list of things that needed doing. It was just after six o'clock when a ring at the front door set them free.

"Go!" Paula shooed her husband away. "I'm right behind you."

They found Elaine and Graham standing on the doorstep in their dressing gowns. Elaine stepped forwards and threw herself at the two of them. "We've been so worried. We thought…"

It was only too obvious what they had thought. Paula watched as her husband walked the short length of garden path, both hands on top of his head. He was faced with a view of the roots protruding from the rubble of the wall. They had to be over four metres high! Beneath, spanning the width of the road was a hole, as large as any bomb crater they had played in as children. Looters were already collecting bricks to complete unfinished building projects, skirting the edge of the crater as if it was the slightest inconvenience. Tipping forwards into it was John's white van, its bumper ripped away like a torn nail. One hand clamped over his mouth, Paula imagined he was assessing the trade-off as if estimating for a plastering job, judging it more than fair.

Graham, who had followed closely behind, clapped one hand on John's shoulder and shook his head. As John turned open-mouthed, Paula watched Graham hug him, full-bodied and forcefully. Having fallen victim to one of Graham's hugs before, Paula nodded at her husband's bewildered face, suggesting that he might find it in himself to reciprocate. Paula had some idea of what Graham would be thinking: this was the man who had pulled his daughter from the rubble. But even Elaine, who knew him better than anyone, might not have translated Graham's hug as it was meant. That, without John, Graham would never have known how strong Judy was. How determined. How good. If Judy had been killed by the wall, Graham would have cherished the memories of her teetering about on her chubby cowboy legs, but he would never have glimpsed what she was capable of. Now, he thought, he could allow himself to re-live her last three years and try to see them as a gift.

John's flailing arms located Graham's shoulders and slapped them. Satisfied, Paula said, "Seeing as you're here, let's have some breakfast. I think this calls for tea. Graham…" She held out one arm to him protectively, as if he were a small caged animal who had been accidentally set loose.

The fact that there was no electricity would have phased less practical people, but Paula remembered they had a camping stove in the shed and John soon had a billy-can on the go.

"I can't comprehend it." He interrupted what he was doing - still dressed only in pyjamas - to retrace a path to the front gate and stare at the tree roots and the crater. "I can't seem to get my head around it."

Graham, it seemed, felt comfortable enough in Paula's small kitchen with her husband - who was not really a stranger, although they had never actually met - to shake his head and say, "I know."

No one but Graham, who sensed his daughter's work, could understand why the tree fell in the opposite direction. It had always leaned towards the street. Rightfully, the laws of gravity dictated it should have fallen straight onto the terrace of houses, Paula and John's in the middle. In the weeks to come, officials in hard hats would shake their flummoxed heads and say it must have taken a gust of wind stronger than those officially recorded to blow it the other way.

Graham saw his wife looking up at him and felt pressure on his thigh as she squeezed it. Only after securing his nod did she turn to Paula. "You'll come and stay, won't you? While all this mess is sorted out."

An open-mouthed reaction suggested Paula was about to say that they couldn't.

"You practically live at our house anyway." Taking Paula's hand, Elaine said, "Let me look after you for a change."

And Paula agreed, because there was no shortage of space and she knew that dealing with other people's problems was sometimes a blessing. Besides, she thought, John might be able to do wonders for Graham. Already, the silent man had spoken.

Somewhere in the midst of the devastation, a Sussex woman cried out as her waters broke. The roads blocked, her husband ran to the local village where he came across a social worker using his CB radio to check on elderly neighbours. They were able to locate a competent midwife, who put one end of a toilet roll tube to her ear and the other end to the mother's belly and measured the heartbeat of the unborn child.

"Right, then," she smiled, rolling up her sleeves. "I think

we'd better get this show on the road."

By the time that the ambulance arrived she had it nicely under control. The boy was born on a copy of *The Independent* and weighed on the Post Office scales.

The father looked at his wife and tiny son through eyes filled with wonder and thought: *this is what life is about; here are the two people I will work for and protect with every means in my power.* As a new life began, he discovered something he had never thought himself capable of: a father's love.

ACKNOWLEDGMENTS

There are things in this book that are true and things that are invented. There are other things that have been reported as fact, but the jury remains out.

Not intended to be a discussion on faith, it simply asks the question: what would happen to an ordinary family if their daughter reported that she was seeing visions?

THE VISIONS

Graham refers to a number of reported visions in conversation with Father Patrick.

Between 1981 and 1982, Our Lady is said to have appeared to a number of teenagers in a college in Kibeho, south-western Rwanda. The most dramatic of the visions occurred on 19 August 1982, lasting over eight hours. The children saw rivers of blood and suffered extreme reactions including tremors and comas. Locals regard the visions as the foretelling of the Rwandan genocide of 1994, during which some of the visionaries were killed and the college became a place of slaughter. Controversy continued when the Catholic Bishop who approved public devotion to the apparitions was accused, and then acquitted, of involvement in the genocide.

Our Lady of Medugorje is said to have appeared to six Herzegovinian Croat children since June 1981. (Reported daily sightings have continued for thirty years for three of those involved.) The site, not officially recognised by the Catholic Church, is visited by thousands of pilgrims each year. On 4 June 2008 Pope Benedict XVI publically blessed a statue of Our Lady of Medugorje in St Peter's Square and on 17 March 2010 it was announced that a committee had been formed to investigate the matter.

Although gaining a following of devotees from fifty countries, reports of Our Lady of Surbiton appearing daily to Mrs de Menezes have been flatly rejected by the Vatican as fraud. The Congregation for the Doctrine of the Faith was unconvinced by the content of the messages said to have been conveyed to Mrs de Menezes, and has refused her appeals for formal recognition by the Pope.

MEDICAL CONDITION

Sudden Unexplained Death in Epilepsy is the name given to the cause of death when no other cause is apparent. Approximately 500 people die from SUDEP in the UK each year. Exactly why it happens is not known, although it is thought that death may occur when the part of the brain that controls breathing is affected during a fit. For more information please visit www.epilepsy.org.uk

JUDY'S PROPHECIES

Details of the plane crashes and 'firsts' recounted after Elaine turned her eyes to the skies were traced from news reports and have not been embellished.

The Great Storm occurred on the 13 October 1987. All of the events reported (including the birth) happened, except, that is, for Judy's miracle: the fall of the great London plane tree. The tree described in the novel is imagined. The great London plane tree in Carshalton, in whose shadow I live, was - and still is - the tallest of the London plane trees.

MUSICAL REFERENCES

Music was what made sense of my teenage years. The eighties, written off by some as the decade that taste forgot, was my decade, and it was magical. When I listened to some of my favourite music from the era to achieve the correct mindset, it somehow crept into the storyline.

'Souvenir' was a 1981 single by OMD, taken from their album, *Architecture and Morality*.

'Oblivious' was a 1983 single by Aztec Camera taken from the album, *High Land, Hard Rain*.

'Nightporter' (Elaine's Waltz) was a 1982 single released by Japan.

Tommy sings 'Reel Around the Fountain' by The Smiths.

'Just One Kiss' appears on the b-side of the 1982 single 'Let's Go To Bed' by The Cure.

'Relax' was the debut single by Frankie Goes to Hollywood, released in late 1983 and reaching number one in January 1984. Frankie Goes to Hollywood appeared on Top of the Pops before Mike Read refused to play it and the BBC banned it. A trend in t-shirts followed. I have always found it embarrassing to dance to 'Relax' in public.

'Here Comes the Rain Again' was a 1984 single by The Eurhythmics, taken from the album, *Touch*.

'A Day at the Races' is a 1976 album by Queen.

THUNDEROUS APPLAUSE

To Lara who taught me new words such as 'boingy' and reminded me of the correct application of old ones, such as *disgusting!* To Amy, who thinks it's hilarious to get dressed with both legs in one trouser leg. To Sarah Hurley, the real heroine of the story of 'Mummy Fix It!' (although the original subject was a worm). To the poor fool who attempted to teach me to ski by making me chant, 'my name is Jane and I can ski' and 'F*** the mountain.' To The Literary Consultancy Service, Kath Golding, Anna South, Debi Alper and Helen Enefer for editorial advice. To Rod Osborne for putting up with constant harassment about my website. To Anne, my memory-keeper, to Louise for reining me in, and to Amanda Osborne and Sarah Marshall who keep on reading whatever I write. But it is for Matt, to whom this book is dedicated, I stamp my feet the loudest.

ABOUT THE AUTHOR

Jane Davis is the author of six novels. Her debut, Half-truths and White Lies, won the Daily Mail First Novel Award and was described by Joanne Harris as 'A story of secrets, lies, grief and, ultimately, redemption, charmingly handled by this very promising new writer.' She was hailed by The Bookseller as 'One to Watch.' Jane's favourite description of fiction is that it is 'made-up truth'.

She lives in Carshalton, Surrey, with her Formula 1 obsessed, star-gazing, beer-brewing partner, surrounded by growing piles of paperbacks, CDs and general chaos.

For further information, to sign up for pre-launch specials and notifications about future projects, or for suggested questions for book clubs visit www.jane-davis.co.uk.

A personal request from Jane: "Your opinion really matters to authors and to readers who are wondering which book to pick next. If you love a book, please tell your friends and post a review."

OTHER TITLES
BY THE AUTHOR

Half-truths & White Lies

I Stopped Time

A Funeral for an Owl

An Unchoreographed Life

An Unknown Woman